TRIXIE

Dear Paul,

Well here it is —
not the final-final here
pass (you'll see a typo here
and there) but it's all there
It! I'm pleased with results to
and so glad that you kept saying
I should shift the focus from
Caliban to Sycorax. I've really
enjoyed all the research —
as well as the story.

Stay Well,

Love
Libby 10/7/2020

TRIXIE:

THE CHILDHOOD OF SYCORAX, WITCH OF ALGIERS

Libby Colman

Windy Mountain Press

Trixie: The Childhood of Sycorax, Witch of Algiers" is a work of fiction. Two of its main characters, the witch Sycorax and the demi-demon Caliban (as well as several minor characters mentioned in the text) are re-imaginings from the story told by William Shakespeare in his well-known play, *The Tempest.* Some characters and many of the geo-political events in the story are loosely based on more or less accurate histories written within two centuries of the events. All of the characters in this story have been shaped by the author's imagination. Any resemblance to modern people, living or dead, are coincidental.

Dedication

For Joni Lee Fritz, the best sister ever.

Prospero.   Hast thou forgot

The foul witch Sycorax, who with age and envy

Was grown into a hoop? hast thou forgot her?

Ariel.   No sir.

Prospero.   Thou hast. Where was she born? speak; tell me.

Ariel.   Sir, in Argier.

Prospero.   [...] This damn'd witch Sycorax,

For mischiefs manifold, and sorceries terrible

To enter human hearing, from Argier,

Thou know'st, was banish'd: for one thing she did

They would not take her life...

(*The Tempest:* I, ii, 250-267[i])

Acknowledgments

I'm fortunate to have an abundance of generous friends who also happen to be astute readers. Chief among them is my sister, Joni Fritz, who read draft after draft of *Trixie*, always with alert attention as though it were her first reading while noting details so that she could express approval or disapproval of changes.

Bill Broder and Jackie Kudler have been involved in my efforts to bring to life the world of Caliban and Sycorax since 1972, when I taught *The Tempest* at North Bay School in Sausalito, CA. Bill is a sophisticated reader, great cliché-detector, and a gracious human being; without his advice I would not have enhanced *Trixie* with painful but necessary re-writing. Jackie has been a sensitive supporter since I first conceived of this project. I owe her most for tactfully suggesting that perhaps I could do with fewer battle scenes. I've done my best to comply but, as they say, all the faults that remain are my own.

Other readers have not been aware of the project for as long as Bill and Jackie but deserve special thanks:

Ingrid Cole, who has earned my love and gratitude over many decades, especially in the role of co-grandmother to our beloved Max. She proved to be a careful and intelligent reader. Max himself was a great help in my early struggles; we had long conversations over Chinese dumplings discussing the pros and cons of authorial commentary in footnotes.

Rohana McLaughlin has been a steady friend for decades and can always be counted on to consult with (and calm) an agitated author.

Rupam Colman, mother of my grandsons Jacob and Romi, revealed her incredibly astute and detailed mind when she parsed a chapter with me.

My colleague Lynn Loar's clarity of thinking and wise advice were especially useful when I became sloppy with punctuation.

Ari Colman's enthusiasm for Carthaginian history and Tannit worship was a great pleasure to encounter and useful in directing me toward some good background reading about the Punic Wars. Ari's wife, Elizabeth Proehl Colman, deserves special thanks for saving me from including a truly dreadful illustration.

Shoshana and Josh Hecht shared enthusiastic feedback after a joint reading of the manuscript.

George Crossman helped me with the professional eye of a true proofreader. That he also took pleasure from the project encouraged me immensely.

My husband Paul R. Kaufman read my first draft twenty-five years ago. At that time, I was focused on Caliban's experience alone on the island. I am eternally grateful for his suggestion that I should consider writing about Caliban's mother, the witch, rather than on the abandoned 'monster.' As a consequence, I have become immersed in the fascinating history of 16th Century Algiers and have come up with the device of Caliban as narrator.

All the children who participated in the annual North Bay School Play over the years from 1972 to 1980 live forever in my memory, especially the ones who first brought to life the characters of *The Tempest* while I read an hour-long summary of the play. A seven-year-old Ariel, a twelve-year-old Trinculo, a fourteen-year-old female Prospero, a Caliban who grew up to be a professional actor; they were and are my inspiration!

Author's Preface

Many years ago, I taught Shakespeare's play, *The Tempest*, to elementary school children. They loved everything about it, especially Caliban, a half-human, half-demon "monster" who had been born to a witch named Sycorax. The kids appreciated Caliban's rebellious spirit and his vigorous intelligence. His first speech in the play reveals what he thinks of his master, Prospero:

> *As wicked dew as e'er my mother brushed*
> *With raven's feather from unwholesome fen*
> *Drop on you both! A southwest blow on ye*
> *And blister you all o'er!*
>
> I, ii, 321-324

Caliban cursed with the best of Shakespeare's characters, often in elegant blank verse. He wanted to call up a "southwest blow" to get revenge on his cruel master. Unfortunately, his curse was ineffectual. Prospero had clever spirits in his service, as he revealed when he responded to Caliban's curse:

> *For this, be sure, tonight thou shalt have cramps,*
> *Side stitches that shall pen thy breath up. Urchins*
> *Shall, for that vast of night that they may work,*
> *All exercise on thee; thou shalt be pinched*
> *As thick as honeycomb, each pinch more stinging*
> *Than bees that made 'em.*
>
> I, ii, 325-330

It seems the duke was as spiteful and vindictive as his slave. I began to wonder about the childhood of Caliban and how he might have been influenced by his mother, whom Prospero called a witch from "Argiers" who had been impregnated by a demon named Setebos and was exiled to a deserted island, condemned to give birth alone. She eventually died, leaving Caliban as the only (semi) human on the island. He grew up to be wild and uncivilized but also possessed of a deep sense of justice. Was Shakespeare revealing something astute about human nature or just relating a fairy tale? Were there others, perhaps non-human, who helped raise him?

This was the beginning of my musings about Sycorax. Maybe she, like her son, was deeper and wiser than Prospero appreciated, and deserving of compassion for all she suffered.

Finding a historical context

Shakespeare's play is a fantastical romance that could take place in any time or place. Some scholars point out that his description of the tempest and the island were influenced by letters written about storms and shipwrecks on the Caribbean island of Bermuda[ii]. While accepting this literary influence, I prefer to place the island in the Mediterranean Sea, a location that could be reached by Sycorax, setting out from Algiers, Prospero, set adrift near Milan, and the wedding party, traveling home to Naples from Tunis. I also prefer a time close to Shakespeare's own, though a classic or mythic past would suit the story very well.

I read histories of Algiers looking for an historical event of the 16th Century that could provide a starting point for the story of Caliban's mother, something that would explain Prospero's remark: "but for one thing she did, they would not take her life." (I, ii, 266-267) What historical event could be that one thing? It did not take long to find what I was looking for.

In 1541, the Holy Roman Emperor and King of Spain, Charles V, led a major expedition to destroy the city of Algiers. He assembled a fleet of at least 500 ships and 25,000 troops from all over Europe which sailed to the Bay of Algiers, dropped anchor near the city, and spent four days preparing for the siege. Charles establish his command post atop a promontory on the Plains of Mettajia, east of the city walls, while his men dug trenches and created placements for siege engines and artillery.

The very day the assault was to begin, a mighty tempest arose. The European land troops were mired in mud and unable to keep their powder dry. Christian ships were blown onto the beach, crashed on rocks, and floundered at sea. When the storm had wiped out most of the fleet and immobilized the land troops, the Algerines and their allies attacked the crippled invaders. The defeat of the armada was devastating. So many Christian prisoners were taken in Algiers that it was said in the marketplace that a slave was worth less than the price of an onion[iii].

Why not have Sycorax, Witch of Algiers, call forth this storm? It would make an elegant counterpoint to the tempest raised by Prospero at the beginning of Shakespeare's play. With this in mind, I set the story in the period between 1492, when the Christians defeated the last Muslim-controlled region of the Iberian Peninsula, and 1615, a few years after *The Tempest* was first performed in London. I decided that if Sycorax were born in 1505, she would be 36 at the time of the Siege of Algiers, old enough to have a reputation as a wise woman and sorceress with a specialty in controlling weather. From there I created the back-story that you will find in *Trixie: The Childhood of Sycorax, Witch of Algiers.*

My biggest surprise in reading about 16th Century North Africa was the extraordinary mobility of the people. They traveled for work, for pleasure, for pilgrimage, for edification, and for self-preservation. They went by land and by sea. They crossed un-mapped deserts and oceans, sometimes to escape persecution, sometimes because they had been carried off as slaves, and sometimes to seek new sources of gold or new markets for their goods. The historical figures had lives more exotic than any fiction: the brothers, Arouj and Khizir (a.k.a. Khier ed Din) Barbarossa, Khizr's protégé Hadim Hasan Agha, and my personal favorite, Hasan al-Wazzan, better known as Leo Africanus. Learning about their era has enriched my life beyond measure. I include "Appendix B: Historical Characters" to help readers with their sometimes-confusing names and "Appendix A: Fictional Characters" to identify the characters invented by me as well as those created by Shakespeare and re-envisioned by me.

I imagined that Sycorax's ancestors were shaped by many centuries of invasions, cultural exchanges, migrations, and inter-marriages, so I made her father, Musa Ibrahim, a Moor born and raised in Granada, and her mother, Tazrut Azulay, a Berber of a Kabyle tribe raised in a mountain village southeast of Algiers. While the two came from separate continents, both carried the legacy of people who had been in North Africa for centuries, blending the influence of invaders from the Near East (Phoenicians and Arabs) and Europe (Romans, Greeks, and Vandals) as well as traders from every significant port on the Mediterranean. If they could have sent their DNA to *Ancestry.com*, they could have found roots in sub-Saharan Africa, coastal North African, Europe, and the Levant, but the primary source for both would be found in the mountains of Kabylia, in the legacy of pre-Muslim villagers.

The two branches of the family tree split from the ancestral trunk when Musa's forefathers left to invade the Iberian Peninsula in the Eighth Century, while Tazrut's remained in North Africa, settling finally in the (imaginary) village of Jadizi. They were united after the Christian kingdoms that became Spain fought their way back to re-conquer the Iberian Peninsula. The last Muslim region to fall was Granada, in January 1492.

In 1495, when my tale begins, Sycorax's father Musa fled from Granada to Algiers. At that time, the city was an insignificant remnant of a metropolis that had once been part of the Roman Empire and was surrounded by a region known as Barbaria to Europeans. Spain as we know it did not yet exist, though the married monarchs, King Ferdinand of Aragon and Queen Isabella of Castile and Leon, ruled together over all the Iberian Peninsula except that which belonged to Portugal.

By 1518, the year of the final chapter of *Trixie* (excepting Caliban's Epilogue which he 'wrote' in 1615), Sycorax was 13 years old. Algiers was establishing itself as an infamous slave market on the Coast of Barbary. Its surrounding territory was increasingly dominated by Sultan Arouj Barbarossa and, after his death, by his brother Khizr, who was beginning to forge a tentative alliance with the Ottoman Empire.

Surrendering to 'poetic license'

The contemporary historical writings about this period in North Africa are typically unreliable propaganda pieces. They are also bewildering to the uninformed because of their multitude of languages and alphabets. Take a simple detail like the name of the coastal city currently called "Bejaia" on English language maps. A 2020 *Wikipedia.com* article calls it "Bejaia" but lists six other names as well: the Arabic spelling, an alternate English spelling ("Bijayah"), two Berber versions ("Bgayet" and "Beyeth"), and two former names ("Bougie" and "Bugia"). In Turkish it is "Bicaye." For this story, I have chosen "Bougie" for no better reason than I like it best (and because it gave me the opportunity to refer to Arouj as the "Bougie Man.")

That brings me to the proper names. The historical figure often referred to as Arouj Barbarossa was born on the island of Myteline (formerly Lesbos) to a Muslim father and a Christian mother. You will find his given name variously spelled 'Oruc, Aroudj, Arouj, or Aruj. It is well known that he was a sea captain, but he was also referred to as a privateer, a pirate, or a corsair, depending on the point of view of the writer. His men and the Muslims he rescued from Granada were devoted to him and called him 'Baba Arouj,' Father Arouj. Christians, who considered him to be a bloody pirate rather than a heroic corsair, called him 'Barbarossa,' either because he had a red ("rossa") beard ("barb") or because that was what they heard when his men referred to him as "Baba Arouj."

These linguistic details can get in the way of storytelling. I tried to choose a name and a spelling for each particular place or character and stick with it, but I selected them from various traditions. For example, I decided to refer to the point of land at the north end of the Bay of Tunis by its modern European name, Point Farina, but the spit of land east of the Lake of Tunis by its Arabic name, Halq al-Wad. That choice was relatively painless. More challenging was the decision to stop referring to the firearms used by the soldiers as "arquebuses" and start calling them muskets. Technically, I believe, they were arquebuses. As exotic and delicious as the word might be, it is unfamiliar to a modern English-speaking audience and often awkward in sentences, particularly in the plural. Besides, I didn't want to commit myself to historical accuracy, which would be impossible for me to achieve. Little was written down and much was lost or destroyed. Must I really be precise about the detailed military and political behaviors of the people who fled from Bougie in 1509 (or was it 1510; even calendar years get distorted in translation)? I chose to exercise an author's right to "poetic license."

Imagining the young Sycorax as "Trixie"

As the title suggests, *Trixie: The Childhood of Sycorax, Witch of Algiers* covers the period during which the main character, Sycorax, discovered that she had special powers. The nickname "Trixie" is sometimes used for girls named Beatrix. That is not why I chose it, but I embrace the connotation. In Latin, Beatrice means "she who brings happiness." Prospero referred to Sycorax's "sorceries terrible," but to her own family, she might once have been a playful and beloved little girl who went on to become a healer, a leader, a warrior and, perhaps, even a trickster.

Once I started writing the story, it told itself. I hope to write two more books for *The Sycorax Trilogy*, one, *Sycorax: Sorceress of Algiers*, covering the years between 1518 and 1541, and the other, *Caliban's Mother*, recounting her time on the island from 1541 to her death in 1556.

Libby Colman
Estes Park, CO 2020

Table of Contents

CALIBAN'S PROLOGUE

Caliban's Prologue

Here in Milan I am called Prospero's Moor or, more derisively, Prospero's Monster. Few know that my true name is Caliban, Son of Sycorax.

My mother was a Sorceress from Algiers who had been seven months pregnant with me when she was exiled by her countrymen for witchcraft. She would have been executed but, as my master Prospero put it, "For one thing she did they would not take her life."[iv] She told me a different story, that she was spared because her loyal followers would have rioted if the authorities had tried to execute her. Instead they carried her off to our island, where she gave birth to me and died before I had reached manhood.

My father, Setebos, was a demon (or "djinni" in my mother's tongue) who wanted nothing to do with me, for I turned out to be more like the mortals than like the djinn. I grew up among the wild birds and beasts of my island, along with assorted nymphs, satyrs, elves, goblins, and wood sprites, who more or less accepted me as one of their own, at least until Prospero and his daughter Miranda arrived. But that is a story for another day.

Prospero brought me to Milan fifty years ago. Once here, he encouraged me to read all the books in his library. I was most interested in those about the Maghreb (which he called the "Barbary Coast"). I always hoped there would be some mention of my mother in the histories, for she was a powerful sorceress with strong connections in high places, but her name must have been suppressed by her enemies. I could find no references to her.

Now that I am old, I feel compelled to share what I can of my mother's story, though I never met any of her relatives or any other human who ever knew her. It turns on the moment of the great tempest — no, not the one raised by Prospero with the help of his servant, Ariel (which I hear has been made famous in a play by the English bard, William Shakespeare), but that greater storm raised by my mother with the help of her djinni (or god, as Prospero called him) Setebos.

In 1541, the storm she conjured determined the balance of power between two great powers struggling for control of the Mediterranean: The Holy Roman Empire in the West and the Ottoman Empire in the East. Because of her, Algiers remained Muslim and allied with Suleiman the Magnificent instead of falling in defeat to the Christian Emperor Charles V. Because of her, Islam continued to thrive throughout the Maghreb. Sycorax was the kahina of her people, a heroine and sorceress, a woman warrior who led the mountain tribes into battle to preserve their way of life.

Prospero knew nothing about her. He believed the libels told by Ariel, who bore a terrible (though justified) grudge against her. I tried to enlighten him, but he preferred his trickster spirit, Ariel, over me. Ariel seems to have gained access to the ear of Shakespeare as well, perhaps when he was sent by our master to fetch more "dew" from the stills of the "Bermudas," the nickname for a rather disreputable neighborhood of London, I believe.[v] I have not seen the play, but I have read a pirated version in Italian, and many who have visited the island kingdom have quoted long passages for me. It bemuses me to think that I have been so defamed in a place where I have never been, but then the same was done to both the Barbarossas throughout the Christian world, so I should not complain.

Contrary to reputation, my mother was neither terribly old nor particularly ugly when she died. I can testify to this because I remember her well. Yes, her hair was wild and gray. Her body was tall and scrawny, her fingers long and bony, and her feet, well, they were like those of a peasant, not like the soft, white appendages of our delicate Miranda; and true, she did hunch over her stick when she walked, but it was an exaggeration to say that her back curved into a hoop. As for the unspeakable acts Prospero claimed she had performed, I do believe she was responsible for some deaths. Perhaps many. And she used her sorcery to take revenge on certain parties she resented, like her own father. But the people who speak ill of her would consign anyone who consorted with a djinni to the fire. Prospero exaggerated when he said that she had done only one good thing. If Hadim Hasan Agha, who was the Regent of Algiers in her lifetime, were alive to testify, he would tell glorious tales about the many lives that she saved.

And then there are the things Shakespeare had to say about me. I did tell Prospero that he taught me language and that, "my profit on it is I learned to curse."[vi] Of course, I meant only that he had taught me HIS language. I spoke Arabic with my mother and communicated effectively with all the spirits and beasts of the island in various verbal and gestural ways. Until Prospero arrived, I had never heard a European tongue and furthermore had never met anyone I wanted to curse.

Nevertheless, I gather that the poet understood the sensitive side of my nature, for I hear that he placed in my mouth poetry far more felicitous than I could have spoken on my own. He knew that I grew up hearing the music of the spheres, the songs of passing whales, the chirps of friendly dolphins, and the subtle language of the trees, though I was young and too impatient to attend much to their discourse. Goats and sheep were another matter. I absorbed their language with my mother's milk, as they say, for I was nursed by a nanny goat. I understood her long before I could decipher my natural mother's speech.

Sycorax scolded me because I was not interested in learning to control things. I've always tended more toward philosophy than Magic or Sorcery, except when I was young and very angry at Prospero's treatment of me. Once, I led a failed rebellion against him. Foolishly, I chose two drunken servants as my co-conspirators. Back then I would have done anything to have the power to overwhelm him, even kill him, to regain my freedom.

Like my mother before him, Prospero ultimately discovered the impotence of his 'rough magic.' That's why he cast his books into the sea. I did not want to read them anyway. I already knew more than they could possibly reveal about how to communicate with spirits, and I had seen what happened to mortals who presumed to dabble in things that civilized people call 'the dark arts.'

You may notice that I have said little of Setebos. He was not a significant factor in my mother's childhood, which is the period I write about in this volume, but when the time comes, I will put down all that I have learned and all that I remember about him. It may or may not be true. As Homer once said, "it is a wise son who knows his own father."

I can only imagine what life was really like in those days more than a century ago. I was not yet born for most of this story and not old enough to understand the rest until later, so you, dear reader, will find that most of what follows is an imagining rather than a memoir. Please accept my apologies for my small offering. It is the best that I can do.

I have struggled all my adult life to get people to appreciate that I am a rather pragmatic person, much more human than my greenish complexion and fish-like eyes would suggest. My mother was the opposite. She looked like a regular girl and was called Trixie because she was playful and clever, not because they suspected she could perform magic tricks. Only two people knew how unusual she truly was: her father, Musa, who thought she was born evil, and her Auntie Titrit, who suspected that she had used sympathetic magic on her father when she only three years old. They were probably both right; they were the two who understood her best, though one hated her and the other loved her.

I will begin my story of Sycorax's childhood by describing her dawning awareness of her special powers and her concern about the possible dangers of exercising them. I will also tell you about her family history and the complicated politics of the times in which she lived. Her childhood holds the seeds of all she was to become later.

Caliban
Milan, 1615

PART ONE: TRIXIE'S GIFTS EMERGE.
JUNE 1512

1. In the Shadow of the Peñón

Trixie stood on the roof-top terrace gazing over the Bay of Algiers. Reflections from torches lighting the Spanish fortress on the rocky island danced toward her in sparkling rows. The highway of stars that crossed the sky shimmered back along the surface of the sea. All around her, flights of bats cast fast-moving shadows, allusive and never quite material.

When an owl flew by on silent wings, she yearned to follow it, to fly out over the Mediterranean as she had once before, when the Spanish fleet arrived in Algiers two years earlier, but she pulled herself back. She remembered that she had promised her Auntie Titrit that she would never do it again, because it could be dangerous; she could even die. Tempting as it was to flap quietly over the fort to observe the soldiers up close, she decided to be wise, 'and even obedient,' she thought.

She watched the owl turn and glide softly to a landing on the low wall near her. It adjusted its feathers, rotated its head left, then right, blinked calmly, and stared straight at her.

"You're telling me not to do it, aren't you," the girl whispered to the bird. The owl closed both eyes briefly and stared openly again, the faint light of the full moon reflecting softly in her eyes.

'Must I be patient?' She so wanted to see if she could do it: transform again, perhaps into a frivolous bat, or a solemn owl like the one who watched her now.

Her companion closed one eye in a distinct signal. For Trixie it was as though she heard the words in Auntie Titrit's voice, 'Yes; I am telling you not to. Patience is the way it's done.'

'You're right,' she answered. 'I must learn to wait. I will try. She clasped her hands together in front of her chest and bowed with a reverence she had never felt before. 'Thank you.'

In the two years since the Spanish garrison moved into the fort on the rock they called the Peñón, Trixie had grown into a precocious seven-year old who was learning as much as she could about the world around her. Her mother, Tazrut, wasn't much help. She spent most of her time in her darkened room and rarely noticed what the children were doing. If only her little brother Faisel had her curious and adventurous temperament, she wouldn't be so bored at home.

That's why Trixie sneaked up the stairs and climbed over the terrace wall to her Aunt Nouri and Uncle Itzak's house next door. They took her seriously and tried to explain things to her, and their son Beni was her loyal companion and mischief-maker, always ready to tag along wherever she went. Nouri's ancient slave, Fatima, was supposed to watch over the children, but they could count on her nodding off to sleep, leaving them free to go where they wished. Trixie was determined to run off with her young shadow whenever she could.

When Trixie saw that her mother's slave, Emilia, was busy dealing with one of Faisel's tantrums, and Tazrut was napping, she slipped up the stairs, across the terrace, and over the wall separated her roof from Beni's. Her timing was perfect. As she'd hoped, old Fatima was dozing against a pile of cushions, and Nouri had wandered off to attend to the mysteries of household business. This was their chance. She gestured for Beni to follow her as quietly as possible.

She led him up to his terrace and helped him climb over the wall to her house (though she always thought of it as Baba Musa's house, not hers or her mother's), then down two narrow flights of stairs to the kitchen. She peeked around the door. The scullery boy was preparing vegetables for the evening meal. When he went into the pantry, she tiptoed into the kitchen, pulled over a stool and climbed up on a counter to reach the cupboard where the cook kept his best serving bowls. She grabbed three of various sizes, tucked a collection of long-stemmed wooden spoons under her arm, and ran back through the door. She giggled at the startled look on Beni's face and led him through another door to a small garden near the wall that separated their lower floor from the back alley. There she collapsed in a patch of basil, overcome by laughter.

"What are we going to do with these," asked Beni, still looking anxious and confused.

"Play soldier, of course," said Trixie with all the condescension a seven-year-old girl could muster. "Put this on your head," she ordered.

"Wow; great!" His fear of getting caught turned into excitement and, with the bowl upside down on his head, he felt like a Spanish soldier. "Oh, for pantaloons," he declared.

"Don't worry, you have a sword," said Trixie handing him the longest of the wooden spoons.

"How do I look," he asked.

"Like this," she said, plopping a larger bowl on her own head, her thick hair and scarf helping it fit.

"Let's fight…" they clacked their swords and laughed, trampling recently planted cumin as they dueled. They didn't even notice Emilia coming around the corner, dragging Faisel behind her.

"So, there you are."

Trixie could tell from her voice that they were in trouble. In an attempt to distract Emilia, she turned her attention to her brother.

"Come on, Faisel. We have a pot just for you, and a really big wooden spoon. You can pretend it's a musket."

"Just look at you two, stealing the cook's good bowls and stamping on his garden. He'll be furious, and I'm the one he'll blame. Shame on you. What if he complains to Musa? Then it will be your mother who will suffer. But no time for that.

"I've been sent to look for you. Grandfather Samir is back from his trip to Nahla, and he wants the whole family to come over for tea. He's sure to have sweets for you, not that you deserve them, running around like disreputable servant children and causing us all endless trouble and concern. Trixie, you're old enough to have more sense."

"Oh, fine lady," the mischievous girl replied in an accent she imagined would suit a Spanish soldier. "Won't you come home with me and be my wife?"

"Don't you mock me, sassy child. Those soldiers bring hope to people like me, forced to live here among heathens for all these years and put up with mocking remarks from ungrateful children."

Trixie grew suddenly still. "Emilia, you're crying."

"No, I'm not," she answered, though obviously she was. A soft tear rolled slowly down one of her cheeks.

"I'm sorry, Emilia. I never thought about it that way. You had another family before you came here, didn't you?"

"Of course, silly goose. What do you think, that I rose from the sea on an opalescent shell, like the ancient goddess?"

"I never thought about it at all. You have always been here in this house."

"Well, once upon a time I was a young woman in Naples, lady-in-waiting for a gentlewoman who was traveling to Spain to marry a nobleman."

"Did pirates capture you on the high seas? Did they fire cannons and climb aboard? Did they? Tell us, please tell us," pleaded Beni with what Trixie thought was insensitive enthusiasm.

"Not quite that dramatic. We had stopped for water on a big island. I still remember the beautiful beach. It was warm and sunny, but the ground seemed to heave beneath my feet. It was like the way I had felt on the ship at first. I was almost seasick on dry land. Our galley was anchored in the narrow bay when your Uncle Itzak and his crew rowed around the point. They easily commandeered our galley, killed the few sailors left on board, and freed the slaves who had been chained to the rowing benches. The captain, on shore with the rest of us, pulled his sword but quickly realized that if he didn't surrender, he and all his men could be killed or stranded on the beach until another Christian ship happened by, and the odds were just as good that the next ship would be Muslim. He asked me to remove my petticoat, which he draped over the end of an oar and waved in the air for the corsairs to see. He knew he would be treated well, for he was a nobleman and could bring a big ransom."

"And did your lady marry one of the pirates," asked Beni? "Not my Baba Itzak, of course, because he would never marry anyone but my Ummi, but one of the others."

"Oh, no. They knew from her clothing that she could fetch a good price from her family back home. Truth be told, she was rather homely, not anyone a sultan would want as his concubine."

"I know what happened to you," said Trixie, as she realized how it must have been. "Uncle Itzak thought that you would be a good companion for my mother, so he brought you here to us."

"That is exactly right. He gave me to Musa, who is not a bad master, but still, I yearn for my village near Naples, or even for the awful villa where I served my first mistress. It is hard to live in a land where few speak the words of home."

"Maybe you can teach me, so I can talk with you."

"Well, you just might. My tongue is very much like Spanish, and I hear Nouri practicing that with you."

"Yes, and Auntie Titrit speaks Kabylian with me whenever she is here, but don't tell Baba Musa. He thinks Arabic is enough for me."

"Your father; I almost forgot. They are waiting for us next door. Grandfather Samir will have tales to tell."

"And I bet he has honied treats for us, too," squealed Beni.

"Of course, silly, when does Grandfather Samir ever come back from Nahla without treats for us? Let's go," answered Trixie.

2. Samir's Tale: 1512

The grown-ups had already gathered in Itzak's courtyard to celebrate the return of Beni's Grandfather Samir from a trip to his ancestral village near the city of Bougie. The delicacies were even better than usual. Samir's cook, Ahmed, who had moved with Samir to Algiers when Bougie had fallen to the Spanish three years before, had rolled out his specialty to celebrate Samir's safe return: paper thin pastry dough steeped in sweet Nahla honey and topped with crumbled pistachio nuts imported from the Levant.

Samir had big news to report. Trixie wasn't interested in the stories of elderly relatives she had never met or adult cousins who cared for nothing but bees and business. She wanted to hear about what had happened to Bougie since the Spanish had captured it, driven off the sultan, and slaughtered most of the citizens. Samir had barely escaped to Nahla with his life; he had delayed his departure packing the books and scrolls from his shop and sending them ahead in a donkey caravan. She grew impatient when Samir did not say a word about the occupation. Her Auntie Titrit had told her he was in touch with the sultan in exile and thought that he had regular agents informing him of plans to re-take the city, but he talked as though he was only interested in family gossip.

Then the children were sent off with the slaves. She was sure it was so that Samir could share his darker news.

Sometimes they treated her like a big girl, but when the men were around, they sent her off as though she was still a baby. Didn't they think she wanted to learn about Bougie and other places far away? Didn't they understand that she could be as quiet and well-behaved as any grown-up? They must know by now that she could keep a secret, even from Beni. Why, she was old enough to read from the Koran, and she was starting to memorize the Spanish alphabet.

She certainly wasn't going to hang around in the family rooms and listen to Emilia and old Fatima argue over the advantages of a wealthy young wife having a wet nurse rather than breast feeding. She recognized the gleam in Fatima's eye when she said it was best for a wife to return her body to the exclusive use of her husband as soon as possible. Emilia disagreed; if SHE had a baby, she said, she would keep it at her breast for as long as she could.

"Yes," replied Fatima, "that's because you are a slave and just want to own something. But if you had a man who gave you gifts and kept you safe, you'd soon change your mind."

Trixie wasn't interested; she couldn't imagine being a slave or a mother any more than she could imagine being a beekeeper or a merchant. A corsair like her Uncle Itzak, or a man of the world like Samir; they were the grown-ups she admired.

As soon as she could, she abandoned the boys and baby Ali with the slaves and sneaked back to hear what the adults were talking about. She concealed herself behind a low wall abutting a vine-covered trellis, eager to get a peek at her father Musa, if she could be sure he wouldn't notice her. 'He is more like a raven than a human,' she thought. She took a quick look around a column to see. He sat with hunched shoulders, moving his head quickly this way and that, pointing his beady eyes and large nose at one person and then another, as though calculating whether to attack or flee. Yes, a raven.

Itzak, on the other hand, sat on his cushion like a friendly fox, bushy-tailed and alert, but also relaxed. Nouri stood near her husband like an elegant egret, confident in her own stillness, head held high and watching from behind her light veil. Samir looked like a large gray cat, aware of everything while seeming to pay no attention. And Tazrut, Sycorax's own poor mother, well, she seemed most like a pet donkey, sweet but sad, standing silently in her head scarf, which fell to either side of her face like drooping ears. That's how she always was, no matter how hard Trixie tried to cheer her up.

Trixie was about to sneak back to the inner rooms when she heard Itzak ask Samir about the recent failed attempt to re-take Bougie from the Spanish.

"Are you wondering whether Sultan Abdelaziz really did come down from his refuge in the mountains and chase out the oppressive Spaniards?"

"Yes, we heard about that and also that he had invited Sultan Arouj to come up from Djerba with a dozen ships and many cannon to help him lay siege to his own city and its two strong forts. When you didn't return as soon as we expected, we worried that you might have decided to go to Bougie to help," answered Itzak.

"I didn't go there, but I have brought you the latest news. My agents galloped to Nahla as soon as it happened, and I came directly here."

Trixie ducked back behind her wall. She wanted to learn more about Baba Arouj, the best-known corsair in the world. Emilia called him 'the notorious Barbarossa,' and said prayers of thanks that she had been captured by Itzak Reis, not 'that infamous spawn of the devil Arouj.' Trixie settled down to listen to Samir's tale.

"It? What," demanded Itzak. "Is it over?"

"Can't you tell," said Musa, speaking up for the first time. "The battle must be over. I told you it would end like this. Imagine, that fool Abdelaziz asking Arouj for help. The city was lost because the pirates were undisciplined rabble," sneered Musa.

"Not at all," said Samir. "The renegades and Turks conducted themselves like professional soldiers, from all I have heard. Until the last moment, that is."

"You mean they lost courage in the end," Musa remarked, still sure he was right. "They probably fled in fear."

"They were as brave as any men could be, willing to die for their sultan."

"And yet?"

This was getting good. Her father sounded ready to mock whatever he heard. She wished she could become a chameleon so she could safely creep closer without being seen. Or even better, a spider. Then she could climb up a tree and see everything. But she knew she shouldn't do it. She'd been good for two whole years. She repressed the thought of transformation with an almost audible sigh.

"After days and days of firing, they finally opened a breach," said Samir, "and Arouj led the charge, storming through the gaping hole blown in the wall. But Allah works in mysterious ways."

"Surely Arouj wasn't killed," gasped Tazrut.

Trixie couldn't bear it; she had to creep closer. She stretched out her arm, tentatively, to pull herself forward on her stomach and, behold, her limb was strangely articulated and covered in dark hair. Indeed, she could feel eight separate appendages. It had been so easy. She had wished herself a spider and now she was one. Auntie Titrit wouldn't like it, but it wasn't her fault. She didn't do it on purpose. It was like second nature to her, and it certainly didn't feel dangerous. Now everything around her seemed huge, so she knew she was small and inconspicuous. She crawled slowly along the crack where the wall met the tile floor as though it were the most natural thing in the world to be an arachnid barely two inches long. When she reached a tree, she crawled up its trunk to get a better view.

Samir continued with his tale. "As I heard it, Arouj clambered up the pile of debris and paused at the top, sword in hand, while gesturing with his left arm for his men to follow. As he stood before them all, arm extended, blood suddenly gushed forth, and they saw him collapse on the rubble. A shot had struck near his elbow. They no longer cared about the Sultan of Bougie or the fort in front of them. Their Baba Arouj was wounded but alive. They thought only of getting him to Tunis, where they could find the best doctors in the world."

As Samir talked, Trixie felt as though a powerful force had just ripped her own shaggy left-front arm in half. She looked at it in disbelief. It was still there, but bent and useless. Itzak's voice reached her through the shock and pain.

"Why didn't his brother Khizr take charge of the men and continue the assault," asked Itzak, as though that was what any younger brother would do if his elder were injured in battle. He would abandon Musa on the field and lead the remnants to victory.

"Khizr was the one who rushed in to tie the tourniquet around the arm to stop the blood from spurting. Then Mustafa Agha, Arouj's gigantic bodyguard, lifted him in his arms, for all the world like a sleeping baby. Remember, they were still under heavy fire. Two dozen brave men fought off the onslaught of the Christians while Mustafa carried the stricken hero to his flagship."

Trixie lay still, panting in excitement and pain, but listening carefully.

"Then Khizr ordered his men onto their ships and headed back to Tunis. I have heard that on his way, Khizr captured a Genoese galleon filled with great riches. That might have been some consolation for Arouj, but not for Abdelaziz, who had lost his city."

"They are pirates still," commented Musa. "It may be remarkable that these outcasts, these criminals, could have organized themselves to serve as a military force, but they are not to be trusted. They are the scum of the earth, and a sultan asks them to help him. What is this world coming to?"

"To an age in which a town can't be safe without cannons," Samir commented ironically. "But I think it is remarkable that his men valued the life of their leader over victory and plunder.

18

They not only call him 'Baba,' but they seem to serve him with filial devotion."

"Do they think he will recover?"

Trixie tried to focus on Itzak's question, but she was shocked and confused. Why did she feel this man's injury in her own arm? What was he to her that his pain became her own?

"No one knows," she heard Samir say, responding to Itzak. "Apparently he is still alive. His thousands of followers still consider him to be their leader."

"You don't seriously think Arouj will rise to fight again?" Musa asked contemptuously.

"I have spent time with him," answered Itzak for Samir. "He seemed almost superhuman to me then, and he's grown stronger since."

"If he does return, it will be like a bad dream, a monster come from the dead to haunt us all," remarked Musa.

As her father said this, Trixie shuddered. Suddenly she knew what would happen. The one-armed man would survive. One day he would come to Algiers, bringing death and destruction with him.

Strange as it might seem, she was sure this bloody scene of battle in Bougie was connected to her, even though she was only a little girl who lived far away. She wished she would never hear of Arouj again, and yet she knew she would. Like her father, she feared he could come to Algiers and destroy them all. She felt compelled to listen to more.

"Arouj might have been the best bet for Bougie," Samir was saying. "A privateer always puts self-interest first, so you know where he stands. He adapts to the modern world by forging alliances that suit his moment and help him survive. I hope he or, if he doesn't recover, Khizr, will join forces with Abdelaziz again. They could yet drive off the Christians and return Bougie to its rightful ruler."

"Don't count on help from Turks," commented Musa. "They are not to be trusted."

"Arouj has no affiliation with the Ottomans," Samir responded. "He chose the wrong brother when he turned to Prince Korkut for patronage in his early days as a corsair. Now that Korkut's brother Selim is Sultan, Arouj would not trust any overtures from Constantinople. He knows the sultan considers any friend of Korkut to be his enemy."

"We have learned to live with the Spanish here in Algiers," insisted Musa. "They stay in their fort and rarely come to the city, because we pay our tribute regularly. The garrison and Emir Salem are keeping us safe from the dangerous tribes that surround us. What is the difference between one distant ruler and another? You are foolish to look for a better solution."

"Have you forgotten why we left Granada?" Itzak asked, staring at his brother as if he could not imagine such a thing.

"That was different," said Musa. "They wanted our land. Here the invaders only want the rocky island in our bay. They won't try to destroy us unless we give them trouble."

"You ought to listen to your brother," Samir cautioned Musa. "The Ottomans have no one like Cardinal Ximenes. They will not target you because you are Muslim. The Spanish are far more dangerous for us."

The conversation was turning to matters that Trixie didn't understand, and she was getting weak from the pain in her left arm. Titrit had told her that one of the risks of transformation was getting stuck in the wrong body. That must not happen. She crept painfully away in the shadows. When she was safely on the other side of the doorway, she wished herself back in the family quarters and found herself there, intact but with a throbbing pain below the elbow in her left arm.

This time she understood she must be careful, but she was irresistibly drawn to the man whose injury she had felt. Arouj Reis, Baba Arouj, Barbarossa, whatever he was called, he was the red-bearded pirate captain whose men loved him as their father. She felt as though she had stood with him on the pile of rubble, framed by the gap in the wall, gesturing to his followers, then dropping amid the stones and mortar, writhing and spouting blood. Suddenly terrified by the memory, she ran to find Beni.

The boy was pouting over her absence, but she told him, "Just wait. I'll tell you a story that you'll never forget."

His eyes grew wider and wider as she repeated everything that she had heard about the assault on Bougie, but she left out her real feelings. Instead, she told it as a swash-buckling fantasy fit for a young boy, an adventure that had happened far away or in a dream, though to her it was as though she had been there. In her tale, the corsair was a hero, fighting to drive off the Christians and win back the city. He was the man who sacrificed his arm in a brave attempt to allow Beni and his family to move back to their native city. Khizr became the clever sidekick, risking all by creating a diversion so the hero could be carried off to safety.

Beni was excited by her story. "Let's fight the Christians, Trixie. Let me be Baba Arouj, and you can be Khizr and save me."

'Save you,' she thought. 'If we have a battle here, we will need someone to save us all.'

Part Two: Family Origians
Granada and Kabylia

3. The Ibrahims, Granada

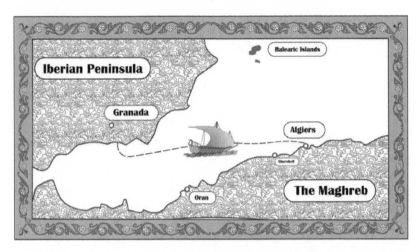

Loud knocking startled fourteen-year-old Itzak Ibrahim awake. He was the first family member to reach the door and opened it to find a scruffy sea captain and three sailors standing before him. He was so amazed he could think of nothing to say.

"Are you looking for passage to the Maghreb?" The captain seemed impatient and eager for a clear answer. "We've run into a bit of trouble, but we leave immediately for Algiers and have room for two more if you can pull your weight at an oar."

Itzak's heart soared; this was his dream. A corsair come in the dead of night to carry him off to a new home. Glamor. Adventure. He glanced around looking for his seventeen-year-old brother, Musa, hoping he would share the excitement, but instead saw the older boy standing in his night clothes, still half asleep, looking pale and staring down at his palms in confusion.

'Ah,' thought Itzak, 'Afraid of blisters. He never liked to get his hands dirty.' Musa kept the records for the family and enthusiastically encouraged his father to acquire additional lands but studiously avoided livestock and, especially, barns. Itzak wondered if Musa could wield a sword even to save his life. 'Fear might drive him past cowardice,' he thought, 'But maybe I'd be better off without him.'

Before he could answer the captain with an enthusiastic "count me in," Itzak's father Abdul arrived, still adjusting his night clothes. The elder Ibrahim looked at the stranger on his doorstep and demanded, "Who are you, and what are you doing at my door in the middle of the night?

"I'm Muhmed Reis, formerly in the service of the great Kemal Reis on a mission for Sultan Bayezid, but now a corsair operating out of Algiers. There's no time to waste. My agent in your village says your whole family plans to leave Granada. I only have room for two, but I hear that your strong sons might want to leave immediately. If so, our needs match: I have lost two of my men, and you need to get your boys to safety."

"My dear sir," answered Abdul Ibrahim. "As you already seem to know, we are making arrangements for the whole family to re-locate to Fez. All our contacts assure us that is the very best place to go. We will book our journey when we are ready, not before."

"You must be crazy," replied Muhmed. "I'm offering free passage."

Itzak hid his smile when he heard the disrespectful tone this rough captain used toward his father. "Don't you know things are heating up? Rebellion is in the air. The authorities see every young man as a possible agitator or an outright rebel. You may think you are safe, so far from the city, but your boys are in danger."

"I understand it is urgent that we leave soon," answered Abdul. "To Oran or Bougie, perhaps, if Fez cannot be arranged. But Algiers? Really, you can't expect me to send my sons off to an insignificant place where we have no connections."

By then Musa had stepped out of the shadows. Itzak watched Muhmed appraise him.

"I can see by the look of your fine son here that he is destined for great things," said the Reis with a light sarcasm that delighted Itzak. He looked over at his brother, who was tall and attractive but with a jutting chin that always seemed defensive. Somehow, Musa never quite looked trustworthy, even to Itzak.

"I don't blame you for wanting better for him. But it is time to be realistic. He can hardly further your family fortunes if he stays here. He may decide to turn away from our religion to find favor with the Christians. They may start confiscating the property of Muslims just like they did the Jews. My advice to you is to send your sons with us tonight. Then, when and if the rest of you leave, the boys will be waiting in Algiers for word to join you."

Itzak was delighted when Abdul reluctantly agreed with Muhmed Reis. Secret departures could not always be carefully orchestrated. Even the organized ships carrying affluent Moors from Granada had a bad reputation; many disappeared along the way. Passengers who wrote they had safely landed in Oran too often failed to arrive in Fez. Perhaps, Abdul decided, he should seize this opportunity to send his sons to a safer place.

"Get your things," he told Musa and Itzak. "Just a few clothes for the journey. I'll ready a packet of valuables to help establish you in your new land. We will bring you to Fez soon after we get there."

Itzak trotted behind Musa down the familiar path from their family villa to an inlet near the village. 'Surely Musa can go faster, even in the dark,' he thought. 'I knew this would happen; he's afraid. A chance like this, and I bet all he can think of is how he will miss his mommy. And she told him to look after me. Oh, the irony.' He was tempted to push past his brother in the dark and quicken his pace.

As though sensing his irritation, the sailor behind him urged gruffly, "hurry up."

'It's not my fault, it's my dumb brother,' Itzak wanted to shout but thought better of it. This was no time to complain or make excuses.

Itzak recognized two of the three sailors. They had been fishermen in the village but had disappeared a year before. Like so many young men, they had fled after Granada had been occupied by the Christian armies of King Ferdinand and Queen Isabella. He had never seen the captain before. Muhmed Reis, from Algiers, he'd said. He told them he had come to pick up two families who were paying him for passage to Algiers. As they ran down the path, the corsair running next to him described what had happed.

When they had pulled into the inlet, the ship was discovered by a pair of Christian watchmen making their rounds. Fortunately, Muhmed's men spoke the local dialect. The soldiers almost believed their story of springing a leak, coming into the cove to spend the night, and planning to make repairs in the morning, but they seemed suspicious.

When they had the chance, three corsairs slipped their daggers from their belts and came up behind the watchmen. One slit the throat of the first before he could defend himself. The movement and noise alerted the second, who pulled out his dagger, spun around and stabbed one of his attackers in the gut just as the third corsair thrust his long blade into his back. In short, three men died: two Christians and one Muslim. The crew hastily hid the corpses in the underbrush. Some stayed behind to guard the light ship, others went to rendezvous with the contracted families, and Muhmed took three companions to the home of the agent who kept track of Muslims trying to flee. There they were told of the two strong Ibrahim boys and decided to seek them out.

'Too bad they didn't have room for all of us,' Itzak thought. 'But the family will be safe for a bit longer. The Christians can't be the monsters our Imam makes them out to be.' Even as he thought it, he didn't believe it. He'd heard rumors of terrible abuses, including confiscation of property, torture, and forced conversions. In his heart, he knew the worst could happen, even to a respectable family like his.

Itzak and Musa arrived at the inlet with their escort to find a dozen sailors and two large families from the village pacing nervously on the beach. They had been awake and waiting with their luggage when the sailors came to fetch them. Now Muhmed gathered together the able-bodied men and assessed the group. He counted twenty-eight who could row, including himself. The father of one of the families was a skilled carpenter; the other was a blacksmith. Both were robust themselves and had strong sons.

The ship had ten oars on each side, so seven oarsmen would rest, and one keep watch from the high stern deck at all times. They should be out of sight of land before the sun rose. With luck, they'd pick up a following breeze to fill the lateen sail and speed them on their way.

Itzak scrambled aboard Muhmed's ship and stowed his bag beneath the bench that would be his for most of the long haul across the sea. He was grateful for the experienced mariners who showed him how to establish an easy rhythm, leaning forward with straightened arms, then pulling back and drawing the oar handle all the way to his chest, then pushing it forward again, repeating the cycle time and time again, in perfect unison with his nineteen fellows. Only by submerging himself in this fluid communion could he keep going, hour after hour, one with his oar, one with his ship, and one with his shipmates.

Over the hours, he had time to reflect on what he had done. It had seemed so exciting, but now it was dreary and exhausting. He began to doubt his impulse to leave home, but as the sky lightened in the east, the sailors began a rhythmic chant, faintly at first, then more boldly. He soon caught on, for it had little melody and fewer words. When his voice joined the others, it seemed as though they moved across the waves inside a vessel propelled by pure energy rather than by their aching muscles and bloody palms.

When the sun rose high above the horizon, he felt they were suspended on gently heaving open water. The sail hung limply around the mast, but the men rowed vigorously, heading ever south and east. For a time, the warmth on Itzak's back eased his efforts, but as the sun rose higher, it also grew hotter. He learned to unwind his turban and dip it in the sea as he saw the seasoned corsairs do.

As his shift ended, he went beneath the deck for his break. Curled up in the shade with his head on his bag, he heard the water rush more quickly under the hull as though the movement of the vessel had picked up speed. The wind filled the sails, and they moved swiftly across regular waves, carried by the steady force pouched in the canvas triangle that stretched from the mast to the bowsprit.

At midday, he ate some bread and cheese from his pack and returned to his place on the bench. Even Musa did not complain at the labor, for they were all eager to reach the African shore. 'Any shore might do,' Itzak thought.

He was still at his oar when the sun set in their wake, disappearing first behind the poop deck so he could not watch it slide below the horizon. As the sky grew dark and the stars appeared, Itzak felt he movee through an infinite dome of sparkling lights that slowly traveled to the west while he and his companions rowed steadily to the east. For the first time in his life, he understood why some navigators thought the earth was round. The sky appeared to him as the inside of a great sphere that rotated slowly above him. The stars that disappeared in the west were sure to reappear in due time in the east, part of an elegant celestial dance which went on its intricate round whether mortals attended to it or not.

For the next two days and nights, every few hours the captain would tell Itzak to take a break. If it was night, he would lie propped against baggage on top of the deck, too excited to sleep. During the day, he sought out the shade below deck but still rarely slept. Yes, all his muscles ached, but here he was, far from home, starting the adventure of his life.

Well before dawn on the fifth day, he returned to his oar and rowed on, suspended between sea and sky, until his next break. Even by starlight he could see a mist spreading along the horizon. Gradually, dark mountains loomed above the layer of fog, growing closer and closer as they moved south, accompanied by the creak of the oars and the splash of waves against their hull.

Soon the mountains were parallel to the ship rather than in front of it. Itzak was back at the oars as they rowed toward a rugged bluff so close it seemed to rise to the sky. Jagged rocks loomed out of the sea on their starboard side. The ship rounded a wild headland where the winds were so chaotic the crew lowered the sails.

They reached a sheltered bay and unfurled the sheets, so the rowing was easier. The cliffs and mountains were now to the west as they traveled south in what seemed to be a great bay shaped like a giant horseshoe. In the growing light he made out a small river with sandy beaches spread out on each side of its mouth. The dark shadows of tall palms stood above the sand like protective djinn watching the ship's passage.

When Itzak looked over his right shoulder, he saw calm water spread out to a distant shore encircled by the shadow of mountains behind which the sky announced the imminent appearance of the sun. The world around him changed from glowing red to orange and then pink.

"The Bay of Algiers," said the sailor from the bench behind him. "We're almost home. That is Cape Matifou, and the mountain is Djurdjura. In the winter, you will see snow on its crest. Now look to starboard: the walls of Algiers."

Itzak twisted to see over his left shoulder while still pulling automatically on his oar. The walls ran all the way down to the shore where the water lapped against the foot of the nearest tower. White houses stacked one upon the other on the east-facing slope behind ancient fortifications. Looking up, he saw sun-gilded houses high on the hill while the shadow of the night slid lower and lower until the entire city was in sunlight, like a great white dove nesting within protective walls of stone.

They rowed up to the large tower at the northernmost corner of the walls, near the mouth of a river that ran down the steep hill into the sea. They tied up to a metal ring on the narrow dock near the gate.

When he dis-embarked, he almost swooned to the ground, which seemed to heave beneath his feet more violently than he ever felt at sea. His friend from the next oar laughed and told him to lean against the wall outside the gate before trying to go farther. It was good advice; within a few minutes he had his land legs back and walked through the gate into the city. The streets were filthy, and the neighborhood smelled of fish and decay.

Many buildings were uninhabited and looked as though they had been for generations. No wonder the reis had been eager to recruit new men.

"As you can see, you won't have any trouble finding a place to live," commented Muhmed cheerfully. "Go along with the other boys. Take your brother. Choose a good place for yourselves, for we are bringing home catches like you every day, more men than Algiers has seen for generations. By the time your beard grows, there will be many talented fellows vying for the finer houses up the hill. You've been landowners in Granada, but my advice is that you take to the sea if you want to make a name for yourself in Algiers. The land on the plains is fertile, but there are Arabs and Berbers aplenty tilling them and grazing their cattle on the pastures. The way of the future is trade. You will find merchants from Venice, Genoa, Milan, even Constantinople living here much of the year. They take away more goods to sell in their home cities than they bring here to us, but just wait. If you are adventurous, you will find living and afford a trinket or two from the lands across the sea."

Itzak embraced his new life in Algiers. He was equal to any other ambitious young man willing to work hard and take risks. He enjoyed his freedom from parents, his escape from his religious studies, and his sense that he was again safe in a Muslim land, as he had been as a child, before the armies of Aragon and Castile had conquered Granada.

While his brother steadily developed a respectable business as a merchant, Itzak engaged in the darker economy of the Maghreb. He became a corsair who brought others from Granada to Algiers when he was not raiding and plundering Christian ships. He soon became a master of navigation and shipbuilding.

He hadn't thought about the life and death part of his new career until the first time he was attacked by Portuguese pirates who hoped to seize his ship and its load of refugees from Granada to sell them as slaves in a colony on the West Coast of Africa. Fortunately, his crew and passengers were well armed and had the zeal of men fighting for their lives, while their assailants were only hoping for a good profit. It had been a bloody struggle, and one he'd rather not think about, but he knew that it was for survival, his own and that of his people.

He and Musa lived in daily expectation of hearing from their family. They were sure that a messenger would arrive from an address in Fez and a purse filled with gold to pay for their journey, but no such messenger ever arrived. They sent letters themselves, but never heard back. They inquired of others arriving from Granada, but no one had news for them.

It took three years to raise the money. As soon as they could afford it, the Ibrahim brothers invested in a shallow-draft galliot with six oars on each side and a lateen sail. It could make headway even in a becalmed sea and was small enough to navigate narrow inlets or be pulled ashore on any strand yet large enough to carry the crew (including themselves), their family of five, and as many possessions as they could fit in the hold. They sent word ahead so their parents and siblings could prepare for a sudden departure, but they did not receive any confirmation. They decided to go immediately.

Itzak hired his savior and mentor, Muhmed Reis, for the venture. Together they selected a crew that could pass as fishermen from their old village and set out for the cove near the villa in their new galliot.

They had a brisk breeze from the northeast and arrived fresh and eager. They pulled into the inlet below their family home, left their boat with four of their crew and headed up the path they had fled down years earlier.

The change was immediately apparent. The path was overgrown, the orchards untended. Fearing the worst, they quickened their pace. When they came to the house, they saw it was intact but strangely silent. Entering, they saw the furniture was undisturbed but dusty. An old retainer and his family tentatively entered from one of the outbuildings. The old man wept on seeing the two strong young men, recognizing them as the sons of his former employer.

"You've arrived at last," he said. "I was the only one here to receive your message. Your family left for Fez a year ago. They packed the goods they valued most and put me in charge of the property. They promised to send an agent to handle the sale once they were comfortably established in their new home. I never heard from them again. I don't know if their ship sailed, or if they arrived safely in Fez. If you want to know more, you will have to seek elsewhere for news of them."

4. The Azulays, Kabylia, 1499

In 1499, Titrit Azulay was a plain but determined child, just past thirteen years-old, living in the village of Jadizi, high in the mountains southwest of Algiers. The first time she saw Musa Ibrahim, the man who was to marry her sister and father her niece, was at a fair in her hometown of Jadizi. She knew that he and his brother, Itzak, were merchants from Algiers looking for hand-woven cloth and tribal pottery to take back for sale. Others like them had come before, and she had a deep distrust of them all. Every time she saw the creations of her people carried off by strangers, she felt as though a part of her own body went with them.

In Titrit's opinion, Musa was the worst of a despicable group. She imagined him hovering like a tentative raven near a coveted object, calculating opportunities and risks, scheming to snatch up baubles. He was different from the village men she knew, especially the ones who competed in the camel races that were a regular side show at a fair. They knew how to achieve the fusion between man and beast that won a race. Musa was a man of the city whose spirit was disconnected from the essential nature of things, whether they were beasts or people or rugs. He evaluated everything he saw by its value in currency or exchange.

Her older sister Tazrut seemed to have a different impression. 'Typical,' thought Titrit when she noticed Tazrut flirting with Musa.

Tazrut was a sensitive dreamer. She often wore flowers in her hair or brought a wounded bunny into the house to heal. Her skin, like Titrit's, was the color of oiled walnut shells, and her hair curled thickly around her face, barely contained by bright scarves and looping chains of brass. She proudly wore the tattoo of their tribe on her chin but did not follow her mother in service of the Goddess.

Their mother Mayam was the kahina of the village, so they held a place of high status in the community, but in Titrit's opinion, Tazrut lacked the common sense to follow in Mayam's footsteps. She did not have the temperament to be either a wise woman or a priestess, much less a leader of her people in battle if such a thing were to be needed.

All the other girls giggled together and glanced flirtatiously at Musa Ibrahim, but Tazrut went a step farther. She stared boldly at the young merchant from Algiers, turned away, then cast a coy look over her shoulder in his direction. Was that a wink? Titrit was appalled that her sister could be so bold with such an unsuitable man.

"Why were you flirting with him?" Titrit demanded after the fair, poking her big sister in the ribs. "He is not a free man. He lives inside high walls and is confined by the burdens of his station. He is out of touch with the spirits and probably believes Allah is the only god and controls all of creation. Can't you tell?"

Tazrut looked at her with irritation. "What do you know about such things," she said, dismissively.

Titrit understood more than Tazrut suspected. She knew that a man and a woman were like warp and woof. Together they created the colorful fabric of their community. Women held the greater power in the clan because their bodily rhythms were in synchrony with the cycles of the moon, waxing and waning in eternal creation, being, and dissolution. Men plodded on in their daily tasks, providing strength and support in the service of the community, less sensitive to the ways in which all things were inter-connected.

Musa existed entirely outside this tight weave. Titrit knew he did not understand why the village women dedicated their work to the Goddess. He just wanted them to produce goods that he could buy and sell abroad.

When Titrit spoke with her mother, Mayam, about Tazrut's infatuation with Musa, the conversation did not go as she expected.

"You must realize that I can see at least as well as you, Titrit," Mayam pointed out.

"Aren't you going to forbid her looking at him that way?"

"And if I did? She would run away and break off all ties with us. I have prayed to the Goddess, and she has shown me the dangers of that path. It has happened in other families. There is no safe way forward. Our best chance is to accept the alliance if one is offered and hope that the tribe might someday benefit from it."

"Tazrut's not to be sold or traded for the good of the village," Titrit cried. "She isn't a carpet."

"It's no use complaining. Look clearly at your sister, and you'll see that what is happening is beyond our power to change. I have communed with the Goddess. It is meant to be."

Later that day Titrit approached Tazrut. "Do you realize that Mayam might marry you off to Musa Ibrahim," she asked, just to see what her sister would say.

"Oh, Titrit, really? No, she hasn't said anything to me about it. But if only she would..."

"What can you possibly see in that man? And the prospect of moving to Algiers. Ugh."

"Algiers; I dream of it. The white city gleaming on the hill above the sea. It is rumored to have colorful gardens and elegant mosques. The casbah has the largest and most ornate buildings this side of fabled Tlemcen. Imagine what life would be like in such a place."

Titrit did imagine, and now she understood. For Tazrut, the fantasy of moving to Algiers was her dream of a place outside her current confines. She believed she would emerge like a larva from a cocoon, pause a few moments to soak in the sun, then unfurl her wings in a world of wonder and delight. She would flap languorously from blossom to blossom, sucking nectar amid the serene beauty of a well-tended garden.

"Please, Tazrut, don't go. It won't turn out the way you think."

"Just leave me alone. Don't you understand? Mayam can't protect us. Nobody can. I remember much more about our brother Izil than you do. He was lost when you were barely old enough to speak. He was her own child, and she couldn't save him. She watched helplessly while he suffered from a fever. We bathed him. Young as I was, I helped take precious water in the heat of summer and pour it over his limbs. It turned to steam as it touched his skin, and he died anyway. He was cremated and his ashes buried with the other children near the altar of the Goddess.

"Why does it have to be so? Our mother says that it is part of the great cycle, that birth and death are the same, that we are like the moon. We go through phases, wax and wax, shine brightly down on the world, and then wane and wane until we pass on and join the stars in the far distance. Well, I don't want to be cold like the moon, cold like our little brother after his fever passed and he lay still and dead. I want to LIVE. I can't do that here. I shall run away to a land ruled by the sun, not the moon. Even if Mayam didn't bless the marriage, I would run away with Musa."

Tazrut had her way. The wedding was celebrated in traditional village style. The bride sat patiently for hours while Mayam and Titrit created permanent tattoos on her cheeks to commemorate the day. They decorated her elaborate headdress with strings of beads and jewels until it dwarfed her face.

Musa was irritable and impatient through all of it. Titrit was sure that if it had been his choice, he would have simply taken the girl and left. But he sat as still as he could through the ceremony and even the feast, though he had no idea what they were saying, since it was all in their dialect. Neither did he understand that the new room added to the house was for them, and the post in the center of that room represented Tazrut, the central support of the family. He would have laughed aloud at that; a woman, the central post of a family? Nonsense.

The newlyweds spent their first night in the new room, but to everyone's surprise, the next morning Musa ordered his slave to pack up his little donkey caravan, told Tazrut to prepare for the journey, and took her with him back to Algiers. There she stayed, among strangers, without mother or sister or cousin beside her.

For months, Titrit watched her mother sitting under the olive tree at the shrine of the Goddess, but when she returned home each evening, Mayam said that she still did not 'know' any more about her daughter. After two years of hearing nothing, she had 'seen' that her Tazrut was pregnant and that a baby girl would be born in March, but that was all. No family event had ever been so obscured from her.

Then, a full moon later than Mayam's 'seeing' had led her to expect, a messenger arrived from the city to announce that a child had been born. She was a girl, and they had named her Sycorax.

"Sycorax," Mayam spat back. "What kind of name is that? Some wicked djinni must have whispered it in her father's ear for him to pass on to Tazrut. It sounds more like the hissing of a snake or the violent blow of a fist then a name for a child."

"You're the one who told me what to expect when she married Musa Ibrahim," Titrit reminder her. "She gave him all the rights men demand when they live by the laws of Allah."

The messenger assured them that it was true; Tazrut's husband, Musa, had whispered all the traditional Islamic prayers into the new mother's right ear, including the baby's name. When she was seven days old, he would slaughter a lamb in her honor and distribute the flesh among the poor. Thus, the messenger assured them, the child belonged to Musa and his people, not to Mayam or the village.

"Furthermore," he said, "my master will not receive any visits from his wife's relatives until the forty days of childbirth have passed, when he presumes it will be safe for her to be around infidels such as her family from Jadizi."

Then he climbed on his donkey and headed down the mountain back to Algiers.

"How could this be?" Mayam moaned the question over and over again after he left. "Why didn't I know? I lost a daughter and a granddaughter in one blow, and I didn't expect it."

"You did see it coming," Titrit reminded her. "You said it was the will of the Goddess that Tazrut marry Musa Ibrahim."

"You have as little compassion as your sister," Mayam declared. "The Goddess told me she would go to the city, but not that she would refuse to let us be with her, even for the birth of her child."

"It was a risk we could not prevent," Titrit reminded her.

Mayam responded in an oracular voice that Titrit had never heard before.

> *"I shall not go inside the walls of Algiers again as long as her husband lives, but when the prescribed time of childbirth is up, you will visit your sister and her baby in my place. You will tell him-whose-name-I-shall-not-speak never to ascend the path to our village again, for if he does, a chasm will open beneath his feet and he will fall into the fires of hell."*

The two women stood in silence for a few moments. Then Mayam spoke in her normal voice. "Tell him that you will visit as often as you wish, and that you will help your sister raise her daughter."

"How can I do that? Musa won't allow it."

"He will not be able to prevent your visits. I can assert that much influence over him, even from this distance, as long as I have the help of the Goddess. Your destiny, Titrit, is to watch over them. You shall forsake other choices. Look upon no man, except for momentary pleasure. Think not of having a child yourself, unless you are prepared to leave it here with me. You must watch out for your sister, and if evil befalls Tazrut, tutor Sycorax in the ways of revenge so that his own child shall turn against him and plague him all his days. My consolation is that Sycorax will be ours in good time. Tazrut could move to the ends of the earth, even across the sea, and still the baby would be ours. It is preordained."

"But how could she give birth with neither friend nor relative in attendance?"

"It is the saddest thing a woman can endure, but she chose it. Now we must do our best with what is foretold: that her daughter shall become our new kahina, a priestess and a warrior. Like Dihya Kahina, so many generations ago, she shall save her people, but she will not lose her life in the struggled. Instead, she will be accused of sorcery and demonic possession by her rivals. That is all that I can 'see.' I do not know how her life will end, but we must do our best to prepare her for her destiny."

5. Titrit In Algiers

Titrit felt like just another bundle piled on top of her favorite donkey, Sisi, as she rode toward Algiers to see Tazrut and her two-month-old baby, Sycorax. She had never been away from Jadizi before, except to go to monthly fairs in neighboring villages. Now she must face her brother-in-law while helping her sister and newborn niece. Meanwhile, she was plodding slowly behind her mother's companion, Meddur, leading two heavily laden donkeys roped behind him, and the trip seemed to be taking forever.

As the sky lightened to translucent gray and the sun gilded the tops of the highest mountains, they reached a village where Meddur's friends, Misdak and Fareed, joined them. They were mounted on ponies, and each led a donkey piled high with bundles of goods to sell at the souk in Algiers.

The little caravan wound along a rugged road that went in and out of deep ravines and across steep hillsides, always downward. By full daylight, they had descending through twists and turns almost to the plains. Each time they emerged from a gorge and rounded the bulge of the next ridge, Titrit could glimpse the Bay of Algiers with the tallest coastal mountain, Djurdjura, far away and, north of that, Point Matifou. Sometimes she could see the white buildings of Algiers glowing in the morning sun. Beyond them, craggy hills plunged down to the sea and rocky islands rose from the water not far offshore.

Before mid-morning, they reached the East-West caravan road which ambled through foothills and across the fertile Plain of Mettajia, past Arab villages surrounded by neat orchards and fields of cultivated grain. They followed it west, the coastal mountains rising to their left and the Bay of Algiers lying off in the distance to their right.

Riding toward the Bab Azzoun, the main gate in the eastern walls of the city, they passed a Bedouin encampment where robed children played in the dust and hobbled camels moved their jaws from side to side, munching on sparse fodder. As they approached the city, tents and shacks clustered more and more closely together until they seemed almost atop each other. Here nomadic and semi-nomadic peoples came down from the mountains to stay for a season or a lifetime.

The group stopped to rest and water their animals outside the Bab Azzoun. As Titrit rested in the shade of a wall, munching on dates, she could see the guards inspecting some travelers while they waved others on through. She asked Meddur, "will they make us pay?"

"They could," he answered, "if we were strangers. But this one knows us. You'll see."

When they got back on their animals and moved forward, they were waved through without question. She was relieved, but Meddur just shrugged. "He does not bother regular vendors. It's a different matter for large caravans. Their cost of entry will depend on the mood of the guard and the value of the property they carry."

'What a confusing way to live,' thought Titrit.

The world inside the gate amazed her even more. So many people, and they all seemed to know exactly where they were going. Women covered in knee-length haiks, with only their eyes showing above white veils and full-length skirts, traveled in pairs and small groups. Kabyle tribesmen in baggy pantaloons, long shirts, and colorful vests, dark-skinned sub-

Saharans in bright prints and elaborate headdresses, and Arab men in hooded burnous, walked purposefully through the network of streets. Shops overflowed with goods. Donkeys moved slowly through the crowds with kitchen wares exposed in open baskets on their backs and dangling from ropes in tempting display while their peddlers sang out praise for the goods. Titrit was glad that she rode on Sisi; she could not imagine pushing her way through so many people on foot.

In only a few blocks, she and Meddur said goodbye to Misdak and Fareed and turned up a side street toward the casbah. Their way took them along narrow passages paved with stone steps which climbed irregularly upward between high walls. Even Meddur, who knew the city well, became unsure of the way. He asked directions for the Morisco Quarter. Once they heard the people around them speaking Arabic with heavy inflections of Granada, they asked for the house of the Ibrahim brothers. Everyone seemed to know the name and pointed out the way.

The house was on a narrow street with two-story, white-washed buildings on both sides. Its door was recessed into the wall, two well-worn steps up from the roadway, and made from heavy boards held together by substantial brass studs. When Titrit slid down from Sisi's back and took her small bundle from atop the stack of skins piled on the beast's rump, the building seemed to tower above her and lean ominously over the street.

Meddur dismounted, stood beside her, and raised the door's heavy knocker to summon those within. "I'll leave now," he said. "I'm not quick to anger, but I would not want to test what I might feel at the sight of that man, your brother-in-law. I know you will not let your tongue be ruled by wrath. Mayam has asked the Goddess to protect you. Musa will have no choice but to let you in." With that he climbed back onto his pony and, adding Sisi to the line with the other two donkeys, quickly headed back down the street.

Titrit stood alone staring up the building in front of her. Only two narrow windows, high up and covered with iron bars, broke the facade.

Meddur was out of sight and still no one had come. Finally, Titrit knocked herself but still got no response. She knocked again, more boldly this time. Where was Tazrut? Why didn't she run to the door and throw it open? What if Musa decided not to let her visit?

Titrit knocked a third time, and in the silence that followed, wished she had asked Meddur to stay until was let in. What would she do if no one came? She turned away, about to leave, when the heavy door swung open, revealing a giant Nubian who stared sternly down at her. 'She even keeps slaves,' Titrit thought. 'Can she have changed so much?'

"I am Titrit, come to see my sister, Tazrut," she said with more assurance than she felt. "She is expecting me. Take me to her."

Titrit seemed to have struck an acceptable note, for the large man showed the slightest flicker of an amused smile as he stepped aside. She didn't mind if he patronized her, as long as he let her see her sister. As she entered the front courtyard, he raised his hand and gestured with a flourish. A small woman peeked out from the shadows and then turned to disappear through an archway. Within minutes, Tazrut appeared in that very place, looking hesitant and a little confused as she stepped into the sunlight. At first Titrit didn't recognize her. It had been two years. She looked like some anonymous city woman. Where were the fine embroidered clothes they had worked on for months before the wedding? Where were the earrings that had been handed down from her grandmother? Where was the village girl Titrit had come to visit?

"Tazrut," she cried, suppressing her shock as she ran toward her. Then they were in each other's arms, hugging and sobbing. She seemed familiar for that moment, but as soon as she stepped back and looked at her sister, Titrit again saw how much had changed and how pale she had grown. She feared Tazrut would fade from her, from the clan, from all that they had known, from life itself, as though her inner light was dimming. Would there be a time when only a shadow remained?

Tazrut led her to the family quarters where they were greeted by a round young woman with yellow hair holding a plump, dark-skinned two-month-old she took to be her niece, Sycorax. Much as she wanted to get a good look at the baby, Titrit turned first toward Tazrut.

"How are you, my sister?"

Tazrut smiled a little wanly but claimed that she was very well. "And just look at my pretty Sycorax," she said.

The baby was indeed pretty as well as vigorous and alert as she snuggled securely in the arms of her slave.

"This is Emilia," Tazrut told her. "She was on a ship Itzak captured a few months ago. He gave her to us. Emilia takes care of the child, so I am free to enjoy my position as wife, and my status as mother, even if I only have a girl so far. Musa says next time it will be a boy. Then he will give me all I could possibly wish for."

"May I hold her?"

Emilia stepped forward and gently passed Sycorax to Titrit, who looked deep into the infant's eyes. Titrit felt a tingle in her spine, as though she had connected with a primal energy that seemed new and at the same time familiar. 'We are one,' she thought, not knowing whether she meant herself and the infant or all humans and the entire universe.

Was it only a moment or several minutes later when her sister touched her on her arm?

"What do you think?" Tazrut was eager for her sister's praise.

"She's perfect," Titrit replied. What she felt was more than that. While she held the baby, everything seemed perfect, not just this infant. She did not want to look away from those compelling eyes to engage with Tazrut again, yet she knew she must talk with her sister.

She had many questions. "Who received the baby? Who else was with you? Did her birth go smoothly?" They rushed out all at once. She hoped to hear that Tazrut had been loved and supported in such an important moment of her life.

"I had the services of Halima, a Kabyle midwife," Tazrut told her. "Musa says she is the best in Algiers and comes to the homes of all the most prominent citizens. She knew what to do. I'm sure she was as helpful as Mayam could have been if she had been there, though I missed you terribly. I tried to think of the baby and how good our life will be, here in Algiers. Halima swaddled her tightly and handed her to Emilia."

Titrit looked over at the slave, who blushed and said, "I had never seen a child born before, and I was frightened, but when I looked into her eyes, I loved her. I took her to Tazrut. At first, we were afraid to tell the master that Tazrut had a girl. He had bragged for months about a son. But then Tazrut looked into her eyes, and I saw the two became one as surely as they had been when Sycorax was in the womb."

"It's true, Titrit. I no longer cared whether my baby was a boy or a girl, whether Musa embraced her or rejected her. I knew she was mine and that I would do all that I could for her."

Emilia excused herself so that the sisters could catch up with each other. Titrit was surprised when she took the baby with her.

"Musa worries about my safety," Tazrut said. "He says I shouldn't dress in my village clothes. No more embroidered blouses, no more colorful vests. I always wear my haik when I go out, and as you see, even at home I try to dress like a proper Muslim. And you really must know that he would never approve of you appearing uncovered in public. He seemed comfortable enough when he came to our village, but down here he wants things done his way."

"You mean I must cover my face when I come here?"

"Oh yes, he would insist."

"If I must, I will do it for you, Tazrut, but I think it is a silly rule."

"It is very important, if you want to visit me. Musa won't let me go up to Jadizi anymore. He doesn't think our people really understand about Allah; don't we have altars to The Goddess and Garzul? Don't we wear tattoos with pride rather than shame? It wouldn't be proper for his wife to spend time with such people."

"How do you feel about that, Tazrut?" Titrit couldn't resist asking, though she knew she would make her sister uncomfortable.

"Musa understands these things so much better than I do," she answered. "He is my husband; he knows what is best for me," Tazrut assured her.

Titrit nodded and tried to smile. Her slight distrust of Musa grew into cold anger. This was what Meddur had meant when he said she would need her mother's prayers to help her control her feelings. If she said what she really thought, she would just frighten and confuse Tazrut, and they would grow further apart. She resolved to visit as frequently as she could, but not tell Mayam how much had changed in her elder daughter's life.

The next time she went to Algiers, Titrit stopped outside the Bab Azzoun, slipped off her donkey, took a long, white haik out of her bag and slid it over her clothes and face. She was surprised to realize she actually felt safer when she was covered. She had forced herself to ignore the stares and occasional insults that she received when she passed through the city streets in her village clothes.

Over the following months, Eli, the Nubian, became almost friendly, and the small, wiry housekeeper greeted her graciously. When the master was not at home, all his people welcomed her warmly; when he was in the house, all but Emilia remained stern and reserved, which suggested that Musa did not trust Titrit any more than she trusted him. Truth told, she rarely saw him, and was glad of it. She couldn't help wondering about his younger brother, Itzak. How did he fit into her sister's life? She never mentioned him.

6. Trixie's First Year

Musa had not found the baby attractive when she was first born. In fact, he was appalled. She had been red-faced and skinny, with hair like the fuzz on a baby hedgehog and did nothing but wail. If she had been a boy, things might have been different.

In the early weeks he spent a few pleasant moments sitting in the courtyard enjoying a breeze off the sea with the family. He was especially happy at the end of the day, when his bachelor brother Itzak would come back from the shipyard full of good will and telling stories in the robust humor of the men in their employ. His life seemed in perfect balance, and he believed his future would be just as he wanted. Then things began to change.

During the pregnancy, Musa had dreamed strange things about the purity of his wife and the nature of the creature who was growing in her belly. He could never quite remember them when he awoke, so he sought out Sidi Abdullah, a marabout who spent long days and nights fasting and praying in the mountains west of Algiers. Musa wanted the holy man's opinion. Maybe his wife wasn't really carrying the son that he so much wanted. Maybe it was a fantastical djinni that was blowing up her belly and would disappear when it was time to be born. He had heard of such things, of women who grew round over the months only to give birth to nothing but air. He had heard of Mayam's curse and what might be in store for him.

Sidi Abdullah had a solution. He wrote a prayer in ancient Arabic on a scrap of paper and blessed it in a ceremony that included incense, chanting, and a generous donation to his congregation. "Keep this with you, say your prayers according to the Koran, and come to visit me when you are worried," the holy man told him. "No curse from a witch of Kabylia can be as powerful as my blessing."

Thus reassured, Musa had returned to his family and his dreams had been less disturbing for a while, but when they came back, he visited the sidi again and again.

Then the baby turned out to be a girl. Musa wasn't sure whether that was from Mayam's curse or just bad luck. Perhaps Sidi Abdullah wasn't as powerful as he claimed. But the holy man convinced him that he had a fertility potion guaranteed to bring him a boy next time. He should try to impregnate Tazrut as soon as possible.

This turned out not to be as easy as Musa had expected, even with the help of Abdullah's elixer. For the first weeks after the birth, he had to honor the prohibitions imposed by religious law, but when the wet nurse started suckling the baby, Tazrut's breasts dried up, and Sidi Abdullah told him, "you can resume the husband's duty of giving pleasure and satisfaction to your wife."

Unfortunately, he found that this concept of duty did not engender desire. He went back to the sidi.

"Since the baby arrived, I have had no desire for my wife. I fear that Mayam's curse is upon me," he said.

The sidi had a suggestion. "Sometimes an evil spirit enters the home with a newborn child. Perhaps that is the case with you. Has your wife properly purified herself since the birth?"

"The midwife says that she has."

"Try a further purification." The holy man gave him instructions for cleansing the entire house. He guaranteed that would rid them of any annoying djinn who might have entered with the baby. This, of course, entailed many trips to the mountain to purchase herbs and incense to burn in rooms and doorways, and elaborate prayers to say upon entering his wife's bedchamber.

Nevertheless, as the nights grew longer, Musa found himself almost afraid to go to his wife. Sometimes her body simulated welcome, but he suspected she used oils and preparatory ministrations from Emilia to make herself minimally receptive to his love making. His worry deepened. Could his wife secretly be interested in someone else? If it was not a djinni, perhaps it was a human rival.

Little by little, suspicion crept over him. Even after six months, Tazrut did not seem to be the beauty he remembered. He had expected to see her body grow fat during the pregnancy. That was for the good of the child. But now he thought it hadn't been a good investment. What had gone wrong? Surely, he deserved a son. He had been eager to resume trying, but when he didn't immediately succeed, new problems emerged.

He went to Tazrut's bedchamber and, as far as he knew, did all the things a man needed to do to conceive a sturdy boy to fill out his family, but months passed. She had resumed her regular bleeding and was not yet with child. He was sure it was her fault. Her body was no longer lithe and young; during the pregnancy, her breasts had expanded like udder on nanny goats that hadn't been milked. After the baby was born, they deflated until they were so flabby her nipples drooped toward the floor. She was so dry it hurt to enter her.

He learned never to look at her when she was naked, but even with his eyes closed she was not the same. She seemed worn-out and limp, like a rag doll that been had been dropped by a careless child. In order to perform his husbandly duties, Musa closed his eyes and thought of how Tazrut had been on their wedding night, or he fantasized about Emilia and the things he could do with her, for she was his possession too. And there were always more women he could buy--or even marry.

As the baby grew old enough to respond readily to human faces and giggle when tickled on her tummy, the wet nurse sometimes brought her to join the family as they gathered by the fountain in the evening. Musa watched the others play with her and receive big smiles, but he could hardly bring himself to touch her. She was an alien, with wild dark hair that could not be normal for a five-month old, he thought, and an intelligent gaze that made him feel judged when he held her stiffly on his knee. His brother Itzak seemed to have a natural way with her, as he did with horses, camels, and even dogs. Back in Granada as a boy, Itzak had hiked into the hills to visit the shepherd on long summer days and sometimes spent the night wrapped only in his cloak, eating nothing but humble stew prepared over an open fire. In those days, too, the family would listen with delight to the stories of his adventures and admire him more than his big brother.

"You have an inquisitive daughter," Itzak said as he propped Sycorax on his knee and let her fumble for the hilt of the dagger he kept tucked in his cummerbund. "A habit of every good corsair," he had once told his brother with a laugh.

When Musa watched Itzak with his wife, he felt a strange tension in his chest. Didn't Itzak notice the ravages that childbirth had brought upon her? And wasn't she more animated in his presence, almost like her old self? Not even the infant roused her as much as Itzak did. She had betrayed her mother by marrying him and moving to Algiers; would she now betray him with his own brother.

Itzak knew that Musa's 'holy man' Abdullah was a fake, especially when it came to scholarship or study of the Koran, but he also knew that many Algerines found his advice and his interpretation of the law attractive. They even welcomed him into their harems as a healer, especially for infertility. What he did with the women there no one knew for sure, but Itzak suspected the worst. Nevertheless, he hoped his brother would find inspiration and comfort in following the sidi. Unfortunately, things only seemed to get worse.

Musa's sarcastic cruelty turned to jokes about Tazrut's beauty and Itzak's supposed envy, until life became intolerable for Itzak. The confines of a small, crowded ship at sea seemed spacious compared to the constraints and criticisms he experienced at home. He took more and more trips to Andalusia and brought back more refugees than ever before until Muhmed Reis called him aside.

"You need a diversion, my boy," his mentor told him. "We are working hard here in your shipyard, but we would all benefit from learning what is happening in other ports. Have you thought of traveling to Tunis? It is the most cosmopolitan and powerful city in the Maghreb. I have heard that Arouj Reis, the corsair that Christians call Barbarossa, is tearing down the galleys and carracks he has captured and using the lumber to build swift but roomy vessels to serve their needs. You could learn a great deal about shipbuilding on a trip to their yard at the Halq al-Wad, the outer port of Tunis."

"Yes, I think you are right; a trip is just what I need. I'll go to see the infamous corsair in his own lair. Would you come with me? I've never been on the seas that far to the east."

"When do we leave?"

Itzak laughed. "As soon as storm season is past."

"Done," said Muhmed.

In the early months after her niece was born, Titrit brought baby Sycorax a snuggly doll made from sheep rovings shaped and decorated with yarn. Emilia told her that this simple, soft object had become the baby's special comfort. "She won't go to sleep without it. She drifts off rubbing it against her cheek while I whisper in her ear."

When Sycorax started to sit up and hold things in her hands, Titrit brought her a thick-bottomed pottery cup, glazed and fired in the village kiln, just the right size for a child to hold and sip from before she was ready to be weaned. She was already crawling around the room and pulling herself up to cruise the length of the divan.

Titrit was delighted to see Sycorax take her first steps and toddle about the courtyard soon after her first birthday. The child was fascinated with sticks, which she picked up and proudly carried to her mother as a great treasure, hoping for a smile in return. She collected wet stones from below the fountain and watched them glitter in the sun but lost interest when they dried and turned dull. She could stare at the dragonflies almost endlessly. When songbirds came to bathe, she ran up to them and was disappointed when they flew away.

Meddur carved a complete set of dolls for her: mother, father, girl and boy, which Titrit dressed in the style of the village. She took one with her on each monthly visit. They were such a success that, after the entire family had been delivered, Meddur carved a charming animal each month thereafter. Titrit called them by their Kabyle names so the little girl would become familiar with her mother's tongue. Sycorax collected a small menagerie and carried on imaginary conversations with the animals, but her speech was not yet clear enough for anyone to understand her babbling. "It's like she has a secret world with them," Emilia joked to Tazrut.

Titrit noticed that Musa's mood had grown darker. He complained about the way the Baldi, the ruling Berber families of the city, discriminated against him because he was a newcomer, not their kind of Muslim. He felt he wasn't respected by the Genoese or the Venetians because he was not a Christian. He found fault with everyone and insisted that it was because they found fault with him. Titrit assumed that he spoke disparagingly of her as well. He had nothing good to say about anyone.

One afternoon in April, as Titrit was preparing to depart for Jadizi after a three day stay, Emilia came to her in private. "Itzak says he must speak with you. He will be waiting at the Bab Azzoun. When he sees you on Sisi, he will proceed up the road. When he turns into a Bedouin tent, follow him."

Titrit wondered what it would be about. She had not seen him in months. She sensed that he avoided the family; could he be moving out? She hoped not. Tazrut needed someone with more authority than Emilia to protect her from Musa's temperamental complaints.

As soon as Titrit passed out the gate, she saw Itzak leaning against a tree and staring down at the river as it rushed below the city walls. He casually straightened and mounted his horse. She had no trouble following him east for about half a mile along the caravan trail. Then he left the road, dismounted outside a Bedouin tent, tied his horse to a post, and went in. She waited until he was out of sight before she got down from Sisi. She tied the donkey beside Itzak's horse and ducked inside the tent.

Titrit was briefly overwhelmed by darkness and the smell of felted camel hair, wool, and goatskins blended with cardamom, pepper, and cumin. The air inside was so hot and still that she could hardly breathe, but as her eyes adapted, so her nose accepted the heavy scents which were all familiar, but much more concentrated than she was used to. Soon she made out Itzak, standing next to a support pole. He greeted her and thanked her for coming.

"I am grateful for this chance to talk with you about our mutual concerns," she answered. "I hope you asked to meet because you are as worried about Sycorax and Tazrut as I am."

"Yes, because of Musa. He is greatly changed."

"I sense that. Tell me what you know."

Itzak summarized as best he could, trying to put into words the feelings he had about how Musa blamed him and, even more, Tazrut for imagined slights.

"Sycorax too, I think."

"So, you have seen that. It confirms my worst fear. I think he has strange notions about her. He even suggested that she may be possessed by a djinn. He pretends to be joking, but I can see that he is serious."

"That is my fear as well," said Titrit. "What can we do?"

"Perhaps with me out of the household, his crazy notions will disappear. You can come together as a normal family and be happy. I have decided that the only thing I can do is to leave."

"Where will you go and how long will you be gone?"

"I will go to Tunis and Halq al-Wad to study shipbuilding with the infamous Arouj Reis and his brothers. I expect it to take at least two weeks to get there. My plan is to leave as soon as the weather is good and stay for the summer. I'll return just before storm season in the fall."

"I hope that is long enough for Musa to be convinced that there is nothing illicit going on between you and his wife. And even more, I hope that it is long enough for you to become free of the dark shadow cast by your brother. His thoughts are not those of a healthy man."

"We agree. My only concern is for the wellbeing of Tazrut and her daughter. If you were not here, I wouldn't be able to leave. I know the confidence that your entire village has in you. I place my family in your hands. Do what you can to protect them."

"Your trust in me is humbling. I will try, but it is in the hands of the Goddess," she said, raising her hands in a worshipful gesture. To her surprise, he took them in his own hands and clasped them to his heart.

"I am forever in your debt," he said.

"And I in yours," she responded. Both knew that it was a deeper and truer pact than either had ever made before.

7. Itzak in Bougie

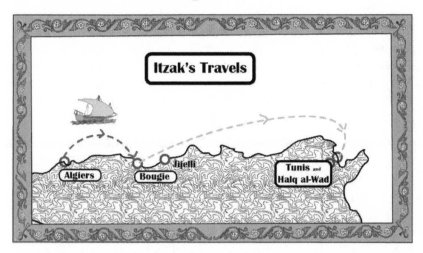

Itzak's Travels

Algiers   Bougie   Jijelli   Tunis and Halq al-Wad

Itzak stood on the deck of his ship as the crew rowed him past the galleys anchored in Bougie's bay. He had been a seaman for eleven years and visited many ports on the coast of Spain, the Balearic Islands, and the Maghreb, but he had never seen one as beautiful as this. Like Algiers, Bougie was an ancient city fortified by the Romans, built on a steep hill against the backdrop of tall mountains, and blessed with a protected harbor and sandy beaches, but it seemed ten times finer in every regard than the place he called home. Its walls were taller and thicker, its hill larger and steeper, its mountains grander, its port in a more convenient bay, and its beaches lovelier. Add to that its easy access to tall trees, perfect for masts and boards, that grew in profusion on the mountain slopes, and its reputation for intellectuals, scholars, physicians, and international merchants, and he wondered if he would ever choose to leave.

On their second day in Bougie, Muhmed suggested that they change their plans and spend a week or two here, studying the ships in the yards and learning what they could before moving on to Halq al-Wad. "The men are tired after five days of almost constant rowing. If we are lucky, the winds will help us more on the next stage of our journey. My old bones could use a rest, and I have fond memories of Bougie from the days I spent here with Kemal Reis."

Itzak readily agreed. He knew he could leave Muhmed to acquire knowledge in the shipyards while he went off to haunt the intellectual cafes and shops of the city. His education had been interrupted when he fled from his childhood home, and he had never been exposed to learning in a secular environment.

In Bougie, Itzak found what he was looking for among men whose gatherings honored knowledge and erudition. He discovered that he hungered for their company. Their conversations were as exciting to him now, a man in his prime, as the life of a corsair had seemed to him in his teens. The weeks stretched into months. He decided to postpone his trip to Halq al-Wad and started to think seriously of making Bougie his permanent home.

His favorite refuge was little more than a narrow alcove along a street in the book-seller's section of the old walled city. Side by side with respectable Islamic religious texts, the tiny establishment carried the latest romances in many vernaculars, including Spanish, French and Italian. Here he rubbed shoulders with erudite Christians and Jews as well as Muslims. Within the confines of these walls, the multi-lingual conversations were about the new mathematics and the relative merits of two translations of a classic text, not about how to take revenge on Spain or how to build a better rudder.

As the shop keeper, Samir Mazigh, got to know him, Samir brought out his specialty: illuminated manuscripts on fine vellum. Itzak was excited by Samir's eclectic offerings, his liberal attitude towards literature, and his openness to all faiths.

Each time Itzak ascended the two worn steps into the little shop, exchanged bows and salaams with Samir and sat with him over a cup of mint tea, he felt as though he had stepped onto a magic carpet and discovered a verdant oasis, a realm free from the corruption and dangers of his life. He no longer smelled the stench of galley bilges filled with the excrement of shackled slaves nor feared the risk of death on a venture to rescue Moriscos from the Andalusian coast. When he was in this shop, he could open the pages of a quarto or unroll a scroll and live in a primeval garden untouched by violence or betrayal. Even his hatred of the Spanish faded from his awareness.

One afternoon, when he was enjoying an exquisite illumination in an old Christian manuscript that depicted the snake enticing Eve with the apple, he looked up and saw a beautiful woman standing before the window reading a quarto. She appeared as a dark silhouette backlit by sunlight, which created the image of a golden halo around her head. Her scarf draped luxuriously over her shoulders, and her face was unveiled. He watched as she turned the page of her book and tilted her head ever so slightly, scanning the text from left to right and back again. He had been surprised that she could read at all but now realized her book was not even in Arabic. If he was not mistaken, it was a chivalrous romance, probably in Spanish.

He stood, rapt, until she replaced the volume on its shelf and disappeared behind the carpet covering the doorway to the private quarters. Itzak knew that he would not leave Bougie until he had learned more about this extraordinary woman— either to marry her or to return, desolate and alone, to Algiers.

Itzak discovered that everyone he asked knew Samir. He was from a prosperous and respectable family descended from Arabs and Berbers who had inter-married over the centuries and carried the blood of ancient Phoenician traders, Carthaginian elites, and early Greek and Roman settlers as well. They were learned but not above mercantile interests. This shop was only a small part of his total holdings, which included lands in an agricultural village as well as a palatial home in the heights of the city.

Nouri was rumored to be literate in Latin and Spanish as well as Arabic, though it was said by some that she only understood a minimum of the dialect in her family's Kabyle village, Nahla. Her father's brothers still produced world-famous beeswax candles in on their ancestral land, less than a day's ride away. She was a city girl, proper enough to wear the veil when she went out, but at home in her father's shop, she sometimes neglected to cover her face. The family drew criticism from strict Muslims in Bougie for allowing painted images on the pages they offered for sale, but living among Christians and Jews as well as Muslims, the Mazighs had developed a relaxed attitude towards beliefs that suppressed common sense or personal freedom.

It was better—and worse—than he had dreamed. Her father was as rich as she was beautiful, but she was not just literate. Rumor had it that she was a true intellectual, erudite and opinionated, and he hadn't read a book since he left Granada. How could he be worthy of her?

Only by going to Samir's bookshop near the souk and asking him to recommend books for an ambitious young man whose education had been disrupted by war.

Itzak soon learned that he enjoyed discussing politics, culture, and history with Samir. Ibn Khaldoun was the older man's favorite, so Itzak bought a copy of his masterpiece, *The Muqaddimah*, which he studied diligently. From then on, the two often discussed Khaldoun's philosophy, especially as it related to political realities.

"Khaldoun says that it is the larger supply of labor that leads to the inhabitants enjoying the more favorable conditions which lead to obtaining more luxuries," Itzak said one day as they were enjoying a hookah in a back room of the shop. "Since I arrived in Algiers ten years ago, the population has been steadily growing. If we get to be as large as Bougie, will we become as civilized as you?"

Samir laughed. "You might, if you work hard and have a good way to make a living. But don't forget the other factor."

"Which is..." Itzak prodded.

"Peace and security, which are necessary to sustain large populations. These are best achieved by royal authority and large dynastic power. Ibn Khaldoun makes it clear that only those who share in a group feeling can establish and protect a dynasty. That is what we have here, under our Sultan Abdelaziz and his family connections with the Sultan of Tunis. How can you achieve that in Algiers? You have the Baldi, but they have no one family in power over the others."

"You are suggesting that when a city like Algiers grows larger and more diverse, it will become even more difficult to govern? As I recall, ibn Khaldoun has written that lands with many tribes rarely establish a secure dynasty because each group is loyal only to its own people. They want to assert their own collective power rather than work for the good of all."

"Yes, Algiers is a good case in point," Samir concurred. "You used to pay tribute to Tlemcen and now you pay to Bougie, but neither will be able to defend you if you are attacked by a large force, such as Spain."

"You are right; the Baldi don't even regulate transactions among our immigrant Moors, the old families, the local Arab tribes, and the Kabyle villagers. We don't share a feeling of being one, and yet we live together peacefully. How do you explain that?"

"What if one group gets out of balance and takes an unfair share of the luxuries of others? Or if an outside power forces peace upon you by repressing your interests and carrying off all your goods to its own land, whether to Tlemcen or Bougie in the Maghreb, or worse, Constantinople or Seville across the sea?"

"That is what happened to us when we were Moors in Spain," said Itzak. "The Christians chased us out of our homes in the north, and decade by decade, century by century, we fled farther and farther south until only Granada was left. Our Sultan betrayed us by forming an alliance with the Christian King and Queen. My greatest fear is that those same Christians will pursue us across the sea. For the moment they are busy bringing gold and gems from the New World and think little of us, but sooner or later they will remember that we still pray to Allah and notice that we live in a rich and fertile land. Then they will come after us."

"Are you preparing for the day that a Spanish armada appears in the Bay of Algiers?"

"It is something I think of from time to time. I came here on my way to Halq al-Wad to study shipbuilding under Arouj Reis, but I also want to get to know him as a sea captain. I would rather have him as an ally than as an enemy."

As they were talking, Nouri entered from behind the curtain in the back of the shop.

"You both look so serious," she teased.

"Ah, yes," answered Samir. "My young friend wants to go to Halq al-Wad to learn about privateering from Arouj Reis."

"Oh Baba," she said to her father, "All you are interested in is the business of things. I suspect Itzak wants to meet Arouj because he is one of the most exciting and exotic men in the Maghreb. You talk of him as though he were all about account books and competition, but some people make him sound like a character out of a Spanish romance, a figure of daring and adventure."

"I haven't heard that part of his story," said Itzak. "What has he done that is so amazing?"

"Surely you know that he was captured by the Knights of Saint John and chained to the oar of a galley. Few survive that."

"I had not heard. How did he get free?"

"His loyal brothers ransomed him. Originally there were four of them. One died in the assault during which Arouj was captured, but two others, Khizr and Isaac, were able to buy Arouj's freedom. They are still his loyal lieutenants." Itzak enjoyed watching Nouri become more animated as she spoke. With every word he grew increasingly sure that this was the woman for him.

Samir responded gently. "My dear, you see it as a romantic adventure. Just to keep up my reputation as a hard-nosed pragmatist, I will point out that Arouj also learned how to be a better pirate from the Knights. They taught him that captives can be more valuable than candles or fine olive oil. A corsair is like an alchemist; he turns his property into gold with the simple demand of a ransom. If that incantation does not work, he can sell his prisoners to be used in whatever capacity they can fill: a concubine for a sultan; a scribe; a craftsman. Only those who have no other use will be chained to the oars and worked to death."

"There is truth in what your father says, but we corsairs from Algiers do not rely on slaves to row our ships, and I suspect that Arouj does not either. We need every man on board to be loyal and willing to fight to the death as well as to row through the night. There is no room on our agile ships for untrustworthy slaves."

"It sounds as though you are serious about meeting Arouj," said Samir. "I can give you a letter of introduction to the Sultan of Tunis. I have never met Arouj Reis, and I understand that the corsairs trust no one, but I do have some associates among his men. I will write letters of introduction to them as well as to the Sultan, who will also put in a good word for you."

Itzak shifted uncomfortably in his seat. It was time for him to let them know of his change in plans. "I have decided to delay my trip for a few months, but your letters will be welcome when I do go," he said. "I have written to my brother that I am learning a great deal here and plan to postpone my departure for Halk al-Wad until next spring."

He watched carefully to see how they responded to his news and was gratified to see that father and daughter glanced quickly at each other and shared a warm smile. It was as he had hoped.

Itzak lost little time pursuing his intentions with Nouri and her family. They easily reached an understanding over the months of winter. He would take his trip to Halq al-Wad in the spring. When he returned, he would marry Nouri. He wrote to Musa to tell him of his plans: to finish his studies of shipbuilding the following summer and return to Bougie to marry Nouri in the fall of 1507. His return to Algiers was indefinitely suspended.

8. Trixi Emerges

Sycorax was a lively and curious toddler when she was with people, but she learned to be patient around birds and insects. She sat so still at the edge of the fountain that dragonflies perched on her head or hovered in front of her face as though in conversation with her. She loved to go up to the rooftop terrace to visit the roosting doves who fluffed their feathers and preened at her approach. She also played imaginary games with her collection of carved animals her Grandmother Mayam sent down to her from her mountain village. By the time she was two, everyone could understand her when she spoke, except when she was playing her 'little games' as her mother, Tazrut, called them, when she carried on in a secret language no one else could understand. "She has some tricky ways about her," Emilia said of her, and that's how "Trixie" became her nickname.

One day, Trixie's Auntie Titrit from Jadizi brought moist clay wrapped in damp leaves as a special gift. The little girl enjoyed kneading it with her pudgy fingers. She learned to roll it into balls and then elongate them and call them snakes. Titrit taught her to shape smaller balls into legs, and so her first lizard was born and named "Izzy" after her Uncle Itzak, who had gone away. Soon her menagerie grew to include lizards, spiders, and snakes.

Not long afterward, Titrit asked Tazrut if she could take Trixie down to the stable to meet Sisi. Trixie had known nothing about this part of the house. She held her auntie's hand on one side and ran her other hand against the cool stone wall as she moved down, one foot to the lower step, then the other foot to join it, repeating the process as she descended into a world she had not known existed. Even the sounds and smells changed as the stepped farther from the main house and closer to the stable. When they reached a landing, Titrit stooped down and swept Trixie into her arms. "I'll carry you the rest of the way," she said. "We are getting close, and I want you to be able to see Sisi eye to eye."

The heavy odor of sweat and urine and dung surrounded them. At the bottom, Titrit placed her candle on a shelf and pushed open a door that swung into a large, dimly lit space filled with the breathing and munching of beasts and the sharp odor of fresh straw. Titrit's candle supplemented light coming through two tall, narrow windows on the far side of the room, and soon Trixie could make out stalls lining the side walls with a broad aisle between. Most were empty, but the heavy heads of donkeys leaned out of three of them. While all three looked up with interest, only one nodded her head, snorted, and whinnied gently.

"Yes, Sisi," Titrit said to the donkey. "We've come to see you, but we are not going for a journey yet. I just want you to meet Trixie."

The beast seemed to smile as she stretched her muzzle out to be touched. Without hesitation, Trixie responded and scratched Sisi on her forehead and behind her ears.

"I thought you two would get along," said Titrit. She opened the stall and led Sisi into the open space, put Trixie on her back and walked with them in a small circle to the delight of all three.

After her first adventure with Sisi, Trixie tried to create a donkey out of clay, but she didn't have the skill. When she couldn't get just the shape she wanted, she gave the partly formed creature to Titrit and said, "You do it."

Titrit didn't get it quite right either. Trixie became insistent. "Like this," she said, demonstrating the exact angle of the ears or muzzle or legs through hand gestures and her own body posture. After a great deal of practice, Titrit managed to shape clay into a figure that satisfied Trixie, who declared it was a donkey named Sisi, though to the others it seemed little more than a blob of clay with four fat snake-legs and droopy ears. Sisi became a favorite toy, nevertheless.

Trixie took great pleasure in the hummingbirds by the fountain, but she grew frustrated and petulant when she could not capture their shapes in clay either. Neither Titrit nor Emilia could manage a form that satisfied her. She had better luck with dragonflies.

"Your daughter is remarkable," Titrit told Tazrut. "She knows the essence of each animal. She may carry the gifts of her grandmother Mayam."

"Allah spare her from that fate," responded Tazrut, turning away. "I don't want my daughter to be a warrior or a priestess either one. Let her just be a happy little girl."

Titrit took the clay animals up to Jadizi and fired them in the kiln, then brought them back to Trixie, who spent hours playing with them and their wooden fellows as though they were all alive.

At first Musa felt some relief with Itzak away, but it didn't last. He was restless, feeling abandoned by his brother and alone with only his wife, who was of no use to him anymore. He tried to curry favor with the Baldi by attending their governing meetings, but he had no affinity with them. They did not appreciate his strict interpretations of the Koran and his Andalusian manners. He felt that they, like his own father, favored Itzak over him. Even his sessions with Sidi Abdullah and his followers felt flat.

Nevertheless, business was going reasonably well. He took regular trips to the villages in the mountains (except Jadizi; his assistant went there for him) and sold blankets and pottery to Venetian and Genoese merchants. He owned a medium-sized merchant ship and hoped to buy another as he developed contacts in the cities along the coast of Italy, but still he was wracked with anxiety. What if his agents were not able to sell his wares, or his ship should sink? His whole life could collapse. He trusted no one and felt that no one trusted him.

In October a donkey caravan from Bougie arrived with a letter from Itzak. Musa learned that his brother had decided to spend the winter in Bougie instead of going on to Halq al-Wad. He would continue his journey in the spring. He also wrote that he had struck up a friendship with a bookseller named Samir Mazigh whose family made beeswax candles in a local village. They were talking about going into business together. The candles were of high quality, he said, especially valued in Genoa. Musa should look for additional markets.

Musa wrote back immediately:

> "I look at the accounts and I see disaster. Without the income from your raids and without the workers you bring back from Andalusia, our family economy is doomed. The Genoese and Venetians dominate trade and look down on Moors like us. They think we are only good as craftsmen. We will never be able to take the candle market away from them. Come home, we need you here."

He was furious; Itzak must come home. He'd always thought him irresponsible, but this seemed the worst thing he had ever done.

After six weeks with no response to his letter, Musa started to inquire of every ship and caravan that stopped at Algiers, did they have a letter for Musa Ibrahim from Itzak Reis? The answer was always no. His mood grew colder and darker as autumn turned to winter. He trusted his brother less and less. As the winter solstice passed and the days became longer, he became obsessed with the possibility that his brother might be dead. His anger turned to despair then back to anger again.

In June, a carrier with a donkey caravan from the east delivered a letter for Musa. He knew immediately that it was from his brother.

"Ah, so you have traveled all the way from Tunis, have you," he asked the messenger

"Not I," replied the man. "I and all my packets come from Bougie. Itzak Reis handed this one to me himself, some weeks ago. A very fine man, your brother. He insisted I deliver it directly to your hand, so here I am."

"Still in Bougie? Has he fallen ill?"

"To the contrary. You may be assured that he appears to be in excellent health."

"That is a relief. Here is a bit for your troubles. You'll pardon me, but I am anxious to read what he has to say."

Musa closed the door to his private study and opened the letter. *"My dear brother,"* it began:

> *I was saddened to hear that you did not immediately understand what a very good business we could establish with my associate, Samir Mazigh, in Bougie. Perhaps you will reconsider your decision when you learn that he will become my father-in-law in the fall. By the time you receive this letter, I will be on my way to Halq al-Wad and Tunis. I will be returning to Bougie to marry Samir's exquisite daughter, Nouri. No praise can begin to convey her merits or her beauty. This is as good a match as our family could possibly hope for. We shall prosper and flourish.*
>
> *My plan is to pass next winter in Bougie with my new family. I will bring my wife to Algiers the following spring, but my ultimate plan is to return to Bougie and make my life there with her family. The possibilities for trade are enormous for us all.*
>
> *Please convey my affection and best wishes to all the members of your household, most particularly your dear wife Tazrut and her daughter Sycorax.*
>
>

Your loving brother,
Itzak

As Musa was finishing reading Itzak's letter, Eli knocked softly at the door to his room to ask, "Sir, should I bring fresh ink and parchment for you? I know you'll want to be responding to your brother's letter..."

Musa rose from his desk and picked up an oil lamp that sat next to the open letter. He threw it at Eli's head with all his might. As it bounced off the door jam and sprayed oil across the tile floor, he started to yell at the slave, the only object he could find for his rage. Eli ducked and ran for cover, but the tirade had only begun.

When Titrit first heard the shouts, they sounded far away. Her little niece, Sycorax, was playing on the carpet with a pottery lizard she had named Izzy. Titrit always smiled at the name, for it reminded her of Musa's brother Itzak who was now away in Bougie. She imagined that Itzak, like the toy animals, hovered in Trixie's mind between real and imagined worlds. But the noise in the corridor had terrified Tazrut and Emilia. In a moment she knew why: Musa burst into the room, clearly furious and blaming Tazrut--for what was unclear.

He took two great strides toward his wife, his scolding finger forward as though she had done something terribly wrong, when his foot landed on Trixie's lizard, which broke with a loud crack.

Trixie cried out when she saw her beloved toy smashed into jagged pieces of pottery. Musa looked down.

"Who left this underfoot," he yelled, interrupting his own tirade. "Pick up those pieces before they are ground into the carpet. Tazrut, make that child shut up. Emilia, get her out of here. This horrid girl will drive us all mad."

Sycorax knotted her brow and glared at him so intensely that her pupils turned into big, pitch-black circles surrounded by a thin rim of dark blue. She clenched her mouth in a fearless expression that was more contemptuous than vengeful.

"Don't you stare at me like that, you wicked creature," screamed Musa. "Were you born with the evil eye, like your grandmother?"

Titrit saw that Trixie was not intimidated by her father. If anything, she was angry and indignant. What if she did the unthinkable--yell back? Titrit tried to WILL her niece to be quiet. A little girl simply could not reprimand her own father.

Titrit was relieved to see Sycorax lower her eyes. The danger seemed past. Emilia took her from the room, as Tazrut tried to assuage Musa's rage.

"I'm so sorry, my dearest," she crooned. "The child can be so irritating."

"You are as bad as she is," he raged. "You're witches like your mother, both of you."

"But what have we done? What is it?"

Titrit had to admire her sister's ability to stay calm in the face of Musa's anger, but she seemed only to make it worse. Fortunately, Emilia returned with information from Eli about what had caused Musa's rage. Once they understood it was about the news from Itzak, Tazrut and Emilia knew how to calm him.

"Oh, my dearest," Tazrut said in her most soothing voice, "how upsetting that your beloved brother will not be returning. It must be sad for you, but we all know that you are the master of the house, and that you will make sure that things run smoothly, even without Itzak. You are our rock!"

"Everything will be all right. You'll see," Emilia kept repeating.

Titrit watched in amazement. She had never seen anything like it.

The next morning, as Titrit was on her way to the stable to find Sisi, she glimpsed Musa painfully limping along the colonnade on the other side of the courtyard. She went back to Tazrut's room and asked her what was wrong with her husband.

"Nothing, as far as I know," Tazrut answered. "Why?"

"He's limping. It couldn't be from stepping on Trixie's lizard, could it?"

Tazrut answered that she had not seen Musa since the previous day, when Titrit noticed Trixie sitting on a cushion at the foot of her mother's bed. A sly smile playing across the girl's face. Then Titrit saw the father doll from Meddur resting on her lap, its leg strangely twisted.

When Trixie noticed Titrit was looking at her, she tucked the doll under her shift. Could that have been a look of guilt, wondered Titrit, or perhaps satisfaction. Then Trixie looked straight into Titrit's eyes and said innocently, "Why do you have to go, Auntie? Can't you stay with us longer?"

For just an instant, Titrit thought that Trixie was trying to distract her from something, but the thought disappeared from her mind before she even realized it was there.

"Oh, sweetie, I'd love to," she answered, "but I have to get back to Jadizi."

"Why, Auntie? Where is Jadizi?"

"Would you like me to show you? We could go up to the terrace and I can point out the way."

"What a lovely idea," said Tazrut. "It's time for her to start learning more about her grandmother."

'Yes,' thought Titrit. 'That's just what I had in mind, now that Musa brought it up.'

The sky was clear when they stepped into the sunlight on the terrace. In front of them lay the Bay of Algiers. Straight across the water, to the east, they could see Point Matifou and the beaches that lined the rim of the coastal plains. The mountains loomed up behind the plains both across the way in the east and as far as they could see toward the south, until the buildings on the hill above them blocked their view.

"The mountain of Jadizi look very much like the ones you see over there," Titrit said, pointing to the southeast. "When I leave here, I will ride through the streets of Algiers to the Bab Azzoun, then follow the caravan trail, the road that you can see over there, until I turn to climb up the mountains that we cannot see from here."

"How long does it take you," Trixie asked.

"About four hours, because I'm riding on Sisi."

"And is it true that my grandmother lives there?"

"Your Grandmother Mayam. She is my mother and your mother's mother."

"Did she really send a djinni to disturb Baba's peace?"

"Of course not. You are not possessed, and Mayam would have nothing to do with evil djinn anyway. Musa was just upset."

"Is my Uncle Itzak in Jadizi too?"

"No, he has gone much farther away. He is in Bougie, to the east, past those mountains." She pointed to Point Matifou and the hills beyond.

"Will he come back?"

"I think so, though I can't be sure."

"I think he will. He'll come with his wife, and they'll live next door and have lots of children for me to play with."

Titrit stared at her, wondering how she could sound so sure, but then Trixie interrupted her thoughts with another question. "Will I ever meet my Grandmother Mayam?"

"Yes, I am sure of that. Some day you will come to Jadizi and learn all about our ways. Your grandmother is the most powerful person in our village."

"How can that be? Isn't she a woman?"

"In Jadizi, women are in charge. We even have a goddess, along with other gods."

"Not Allah?"

"We have Allah too. Down here, people only have one god, and that is important to remember, even if you don't understand it."

"Ummi told me that Musa was happy when I tried to say, '*la Ileana Illa Allah*,' even though he was mad that I didn't say it very well.'"

"It is very good for you to find ways to make your father happy. I think he tries very hard to be a good father and a good husband."

"I think he should try harder."

Titrit decided not to respond to that. She'd never heard anything quite like it from so young a child.

On her way down the hall to the stable, Titrit overheard the house slaves gossiping about Musa's limp. They heard he had injured his foot when he stepped on his daughter's toy. Titrit thought that strange, because last night it hadn't seemed to bother him at all, yet this morning he could hardly walk. She thought again of her niece's face when she was sitting at the foot of her mother's bed. What had she hidden under her shift? Could the little girl have done something?

Titrit dismissed the idea; her niece was only two-and-a-half years old. Surely, she couldn't curse anyone yet, and even if she could, she wouldn't direct it at her own father, would she?

9. Itzak with Arouj Reis

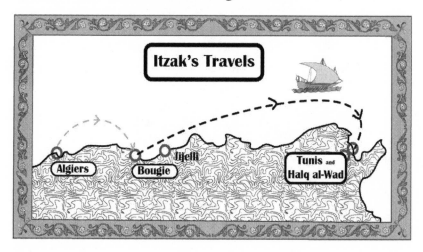

After twelve days and nights of steady progress, Itzak and his crew rounded Cape Farina and headed south into the Gulf of Tunis. A following breeze filled their sail, so the men relaxed and enjoyed a pleasant journey past the sandy beaches and occasional bluffs along the coast. When they saw the ancient ruins on the hills near the run-down village of Carthage, they knew that they would soon arrive at Halq al-Wad, where they would establish their contact with Arouj before proceeding on to Tunis to visit the court of Sultan Muhammad.

They rowed along the narrow sand spit of Halk al-Wadi until they reached the passage known as "the gullet," the throat through which all ships must pass to reach the lagoon referred to as the Lake of Tunis. It was carefully guarded by Sultan Mohammad's soldiers at the custom house, who would be reinforced by Arouj and his men should any trouble arise.

Itzak was told to tie up at a dock inside the narrow passage, the Goleta, or "throat," to the Lake of Tunis before returning for a full inspection. They found a temporary berth at a busy marina where mariners from all around the Mediterranean spoke all the languages they had ever heard and some they never dreamed of. Arabic was the lingua franca, but Itzak recognized Turkish, Spanish, Italian, and Portuguese as well. Even the special rhythms and accents of Arabic from Granada and Spanish from Aragon caught his ear.

As Muhmed was arranging for their ship's berth and inquiring about their own accommodations, Itzak saw a robust captain walking briskly along the quay surrounded by a half dozen men who seemed to follow every gesture and word. His red beard made it clear he must be Arouj Reis, called Barbarossa by Christians.

Following some ten or fifteen paces behind came a somewhat shorter and slimmer man walking with a teenage boy. Feature for feature, the second man did not resemble Arouj, but he shared with him a distinct way of carrying his shoulders, high and with a lilt at each step. Both men walked with their toes turned out slightly, which conveyed grounded deliberation. Itzak could imagine either of them on the deck of a ship absorbing the rolls and surges of the sea, and both radiated authoritative confidence.

As they drew closer, their differences became more apparent. Arouj wore an open expression and moved with unusual physical grace. Khizr, assuming it was he, knotted his generous brows above his bulbous nose in an expression of intense concentration and seemed so distracted by his own thoughts that he might have bumped into things if his young companion had not tugged at his elbow from time to time to alert him to obstacles. The most distinct difference between the two was the color of their beards. Khizr's was auburn, not red.

Arouj stepped up to the newcomers, introduced himself, and asked where they were from. As the elder, Muhmed Reis responded first, that they had come from Algiers.

"Certainly, there was a time when you came from farther east, Constantinople, perhaps," suggested Arouj.

Muhmed laughed and replied, "You have a good ear. I left as a youth as a member of Kemal Reis's crew when you were still a young boy getting in trouble in Myteline. Sultan Bayezid sent us to explore the western reaches of our sea."

"Then you know a thing or two about the Straights of Gibraltar, I'd guess," said Arouj.

"And beyond," answered Muhmed. "I sailed on the great sea as far as the islands and down the coast where the Portuguese are now so active. But that was long ago. Now I work with my young friend here, Itzak Reis, a corsair like yourself, though of much more modest means."

Itzak stepped forward and greeted Arouj. "We have spent the winter in Bougie," Itzak informed him. "I have brought letters of introduction to Sultan Muhammad and to some of your associates from Samir Mazigh of Nahla." He thought Arouj gave him a more serious evaluation when he heard Samir's name.

"Have you come on business of your own or as an agent of Samir Mazigh?"

"A bit of both, I suppose. I left Algiers in search of adventure and knowledge. My plan was to learn as much as I could about the adaptations you and your men have made in shipbuilding to suit the trade of corsair in the Mediterranean. But after my time in Bougie, I determined to return there and marry the beautiful daughter of none other than the sultan's friend, Samir."

Arouj guffawed loudly. "Hear that, brother Khizr. This young fellow is planning to marry and settle down already. Have you ever heard such a thing?"

"The marrying part I can understand, but I have not yet had any urge to settle down. Perhaps you and I have not spent enough time in Bougie to get the infection. We have much more to explore before we can think of such a thing.

"Itzak Reis, I hope you will tell us all you can about Algiers: the situation of its port, its weather, its governance, and the nature of its immediate neighbors as well as those farther to its west: Shershell, Tenez, and Oran in particular. We are currently tied to the service of Sultan Muhammad of Tunis, but our adventures are likely to carry us farther and farther west."

"We shall have time enough to pick each other's brains," declared Arouj. "But first our visitors must pay their respects to the Customs House. Hasan, can you see to it that things are done in a timely way? Then show them to the best hostel on the spit. We will welcome you at the shipyard in the morning."

The next day, Itzak inspected the shipyard and admired the clever ways that the Turks overcame their lack of wood on this narrow sand spit. They took the lumber from galleys they had captured at sea and re-built them as smaller, slimmer galliots well-suited to the conditions of the Mediterranean, particularly when operating out of a region with shallow, sandy beaches such as Halq al-Wad.

Back at the hostel, Itzak was approached by a gruff captain who introduced himself as Kara Hasan. "I hear you have arrived here from Bougie. I am leaving tomorrow for that very port and would like to hear what I can of the conditions, and any advice you might have about how to make fruitful contacts among their corsair community."

"I am happy to give you contacts," replied Itzak, especially if you deliver a personal letter from me to my future father-in-law, Samir Mazigh."

"It is a bargain," replied Kara Hasan.

The two men supped together and exchanged information about the current condition of the coast between Halk al-Wadi and Algiers. Itzak's companion hoped to travel to Algiers and beyond.

Itzak excused himself early and stayed up late writing to Nouri so that he could send his letter to her with the corsair.

> *My dearest,*
> *We learned a lot on our first day with Arouj Reis. How fondly I remember the time you teased your father by saying that Arouj was as exciting as a hero from a Spanish romance. He is without doubt the most charismatic man I have ever met. He is strict but deeply respected by his men. They call him Baba Arouj, but they seem to look upon him more as a god than a father.*
>
> *It is important to note that he is reported to be cruel when roused. Nevertheless, I am happy to write that he rarely uses*

slaves at sea. He wants every man at oar to be a trusted fighter.
That is one reason he prefers the smaller galliots over larger war
ships. Lean and mean could be his motto. I suspect it is utility,
not compassion, that dictates his choice.

By reputation, his brother Khizr is second only to Arouj in
courage and intelligence. The men say that he is more
calculating but less cruel. I will spend most of my time with
him, soaking up his knowledge of shipbuilding and naval
strategy. He's very serious but also companionable. I have not
yet met the third brother, Isaac. He has a reputation for
administration more than action, though the men talk of him as
a leader whom they would gladly follow into battle.

Tell your father that I will have much to report when we
meet again. I shall remain here a week, then go to Tunis, where
Sultan Muhammad has promised to treat us as distinguished
visitors. Samir is apparently well-known as an intimate of
Sultan Abdelaziz and therefore welcome in the court. I had no
idea that I was marrying into such a distinguished family.

I will be home before the weather turns in the fall, my
beloved.

Your almost-husband and eternal beloved, Itzak

The city of Tunis lay on the west side of the Lake of Tunis, making it as secure a city twelve miles across the water west of Halq al-Wad. It could only be reached from the sea by passing through the narrow opening called the gullet under the watchful eye of the fortified Customs House. Tunis was as secure from a naval assault as any city on the coast of North Africa. Nevertheless, it must have been a comfort to Sultan Muhammad ibn al-Hasan to have over a thousand fighting men led by Arouj Reis guarding his outer gate.

Itzak and Muhmed were rowed by a handful of their crew across the Lake to the capital to be received at the court. A pair of Christian soldiers from the sultan's elite guard stood at attention as they disembarked outside the Sea Gate and led them to the palace, a grand building set on the crest of the highest hill within the walls of the city, which would have been thought little more than a mound in either Bougie or Algiers. The building itself had little wood but was decorated with exquisite mosaics on the floor and elaborately sculpted and painted plaster on the walls.

They were received in the great hall of the palace. The Sultan, dressed in sumptuous, brocaded silk that could not hide his paunch, sat on a raised platform. He wore a huge, be-jeweled turban that helped to dwarf his conspicuous bulk. A dozen personal attendants flanked his throne, and elaborately dressed officials stood in rows nodding whenever he spoke. Itzak was struck by his remote smile. His eyelids seemed to droop, and his speech was sometimes slurred, suggesting that the ruler might, as rumored, be under the influence of the hashish for which the city was known.

The ceremonies were tedious, but Itzak noticed that the sultan asked rather pointedly if he had brought any message from his relative, Sultan Abdelaziz of Bougie. Itzak had to admit that he had not yet met the sultan. Muhammad showed some surprise at that and then seemed to lose interest in the meeting and soon dismissed him.

Itzak was unsettled by the encounter. It seemed overly elaborate for his status. He wondered if there was something he didn't know about Samir.

They stayed in rooms on the grounds of the palace that night, but he and Muhmed were happy to return to Halq al-Wad in the morning. They spent another week with Arouj and the corsairs, then headed back to Bougie.

Nouri was sure that Itzak would live up to his promise to arrive back in Bougie the first week of September. She missed him while he was away but felt that he was contributing to the future of their life together, forging alliances with the Barbarossas, meeting the Sultan of Tunis, and soon he would be introduced to Abdelaziz, the Sultan of Bougie, who insisted that Itzak should be presented at his court as soon as he returned from Halq al-Wad.

On the day of his arrival, Nouri dressed decorously, choosing a long tunic of fine silk covered by a veil that, combined with her head scarf, hid everything but her eyes, which were carefully outlined in henna. Her old nanny, Fatima, advised her that this was the way to be most alluring to her beloved.

She waited with Samir and most of the neighborhood at the bookshop in the souk. Word of his arrival had preceded him. He seemed surprised and touched by the warm reception. He was being formal with her, and yet it seemed he looked toward her frequently. She wondered if he could tell that she blushed every time he caught her glance.

When the greetings were over and the neighbors returned to their shops, she saw Samir pull Itzak aside. She knew what it was; two letters had arrived from Algiers. One was clearly from his brother. The other was sealed by a scribe from the marketplace. It could be from anyone. She watched carefully as he looked at the inscriptions and thrust them inside his shirt. He seemed worried, but not deeply distressed. He and Samir exchanged a few words, and then he came over to speak with her.

"Do you fear bad news from home," she asked.

"Nothing that could interrupt my plans here in Bougie. I have written my brother of my intentions and described the benefits to us all. I am sure he will bless our union."

She lowered her eyes in relief and felt her father's arm around her in a warm embrace. He, too, wanted this marriage to go forward.

They arranged for Itzak to share the evening meal with them at their formal residence in the hills and left him to refresh himself in the comfortable quarters behind the shop, which had been turned over to him until the marriage took place.

That evening, Nouri was grateful that Samir did not pry into Itzak's personal affairs. Eventually, her fiancé brought up the issue himself.

"As you know, I have received two letters from Algiers. One was from my brother." Nouri held her breath. She knew that Musa was older and therefore head of the family. He could order Itzak not to marry.

"He is concerned about the impact of my absence on our business ventures. He does not yet appreciate how much we will all benefit from this alliance. I have promised him that we shall marry and spend the winter in Bougie, then come to Algiers for a visit in the spring. I know that when he meets Nouri and hears the details, he will be eager to embrace our plans.

"The second letter is from Titrit, my brother's sister-in-law, who tells me in confidence that Tazrut is not well. That saddens me, but there seems nothing I can do until next spring. In short, I shall write to them both and send my deepest concern, but also share my happiness and ask for their blessings."

Nouri could see that her father was as relieved as she; they both were eager to bring Itzak Ibrahim into their family.

After the wedding, Nouri found she was invited into the harems of the elite of Bougie, women who had never wanted to see her before because of her liberal ways and her intellectual ideas. Now they welcomed her as though she had always been one of them. They asked her to tea and took her arm as they strolled through the gracious gardens of their palaces.

Samir gave the couple a modest palace as a wedding present. It was situated on a point high above the sea. From the west terrace, they overlooked the ancient walls of the Roman ruins far below. This became their favorite spot for watching the sun go down. There was an equally charming terrace on the east, from which they could see the sun rise over the mountains that loomed behind them. There was always a sheltered spot when the wind was strong or a cool place to pick up a breeze off the sea when the day was warm. There were no fewer than three courtyards, each more elegant than the last. Her own quarters were grander than those her own mother had occupied. Her old nanny, Fatima, lived with them. She had been her mother's nanny as well and had been present the day she was born and the day she died. This wise old slave had helped Nouri celebrate every important event of her life and now enhanced the satisfaction of her marriage, for Fatima brought an old woman's blessing, carrying the combined power of mother and grandmother.

Nouri had loved Itzak the first time she saw him. It was no accident that she stood in her father's shop that day, without a veil, showing off her literacy. When he left to study with Arouj, she had suffered a loneliness that reminded her of the days when she was a little girl and her mother died. Now that he was back, they were as one. It seemed to her their marriage was sweeter because of the absence she had experienced. She was eager to face the adventure of the sea voyage to meet the family of whom she had heard so much. She wondered if she should fear Musa, though she believed in her heart that she would heal any rift that might exist between the brothers. She felt ready for whatever life might hold, as long as she had her Itzak.

10. A 'Visit' to Algiers

When Titrit came to Algiers in the weeks before the anticipated arrival of Itzak and his bride, Tazrut talked with her about nothing but the imminent arrival of her brother in-law with his new bride.

"Do you think I'll like her? She is supposed to know how to read. I'm afraid I'm not very good with intellectuals."

"Don't worry, Tazrut. Itzak wouldn't marry anyone who isn't generous and kind."

"Did I tell you that Musa is buying the house around the corner, the one whose terraces connect to our own? You only have to step over one low wall to go from our terrace to theirs."

"Isn't this just a visit?"

"Musa hopes to convince them not to go back. You know how mad he has been at Itzak, but that's because he misses him so badly. Musa pretends to be in charge, but he really counts on his brother for a lot of things."

"How do you feel about having another woman practically part of your own household?"

"I don't know. It depends on how we get along. Emilia thinks it will be good for me. I grew up with so many people around in the village, and now I spend most of my time alone or with the house slaves. If they stay and have children, that will be really good for Sycorax. I haven't been able to give her a brother yet, and she is getting spoiled."

Titrit could feel that things were going well as soon as she arrived for her first visit after the arrival of Itzak and Nouri.

"Just wait until you meet her," Tazrut gushed. "She is generous and lovely. Not intimidating at all. She just seems to understand things. Let's go to visit them, and you'll see."

They could easily have climbed over the wall that separated one terrace from the other, but Tazrut was certain that Musa would want them to be decorous, so they dressed formally, went out to the street and around the corner to the front door of Itzak's house. The host himself came to the door.

As soon as she saw Itzak, Titrit was relieved. He still projected the solid presence she remembered from before, but there was something new as well, a relaxed and mature confidence. She was pleased to find that he saw a change in her as well.

"I still think of you as the awkward young girl at the fair, that very first day I saw you and your beautiful sister. And now, here you are, for all the world like a woman of Algiers. Tazrut tells me that you have become a respected wise woman in Jadizi, like your mother."

"You make me blush," she said frankly. "It is true that I have become my mother's apprentice, but I am a long way from earning a status of leadership in my clan. Mayam has no peer. I may be a moderately accomplished herbalist; at least I have learned to tell one plant from another and have an interest in the medicinal effects of potions made from them, but I am still learning."

"You are as modest as you are wise," laughed Itzak. "But I should not tease you. Come, make yourselves comfortable in the courtyard," he said while making a hand gesture that sent the houseboy to fetch the women of the household.

They stood alone for those few minutes, and she knew that he, too, was remembering their last meeting and their pact to be partners in protecting Tazrut and Trixie from Musa's rages. She was glad to have her ally here in Algiers.

At her first sight of Nouri coming through the archway into the dappled shade, Titrit felt as though a heavy burden had been lifted from her. She could see that, while they were different from each other in many ways, both Tazrut and Nouri were sensitive young women trying to make a good life in a strange city. They would become good friends. Nouri would keep an eye on Tazrut and understand what a strain she was under, living with such a controlling husband.

Fatima entered with Nouri. Her face was marked by dark tattoos of symmetrical lines that seemed to deepen her wrinkles. She wrapped herself in a scarf long enough to cover her body with length left to use to over her head and even to pull across her mouth when she wanted to hide her embarrassment at her missing teeth. Titrit was glad to see that Tazrut would have a true elder here in Algiers. She hoped earnestly that Musa could convince Itzak to change his mind and settle in Algiers.

The next afternoon, Nouri and Fatima came to tea at Tazrut's house. Trixie begged Titrit to play her tambourine so she could dance. Trixie ran to fetch Titrit's bag, and within minutes the courtyard rang with laughter and song. Trixie stomped her little feet and twitched her hips in rhythm to Titrit's beat, and Fatima raised her voice in a quavering soprano that conjured memories of nights around the campfires in mountain villages. Even Tazrut laughed, for she remembered the old song well and soon joined in. Even Emilia was so moved that she turned in slow circles and snapped her fingers, her full bosom jiggling with each snap. Fatima seemed to get the most pleasure of them all; her almost-toothless smile grew wider and wider as she nodded her head, shook her shoulders, and waved her arms while perched on a pile of cushions.

After a while, the music and dancing subsided into the quiet voices of the women gossiping accompanied by young Sycorax's gentle babbling with her imaginary friends, the bright melodies of birds who sang above the basso continuo of the falling water, and the scuffle of dry leaves as lizards dashed from one hiding place to another.

'This,' thought Titrit, 'is what I wish for my sister.' She was reminded of a story she had heard about the Garden of Eden, and she hoped they would never be turned out of this blissful place. She imagined that the little girl could become a link between their separate pasts and lead them toward a shared future filled with many children, much laughter and great prosperity. But Titrit knew that there was a snake never far from sight in this Eden.

She sensed that Musa no longer worried about a possible sexual liaison between Itzak and Tazrut, although he seemed jealous of Itzak's associations in Bougie and, particularly, of the grace and sophistication of his wife. She noticed his sullen glance, which reflected a wish to destroy anything that evoked envy and included anyone who was blessed and contented, even his own brother. 'But,' she thought, 'there is good reason for him to be jealous. Itzak is his superior in every way. And Musa will never be happy until he controls everyone around him.'

In the fall, Itzak was provisioning a ship for the return voyage to Bougie with Nouri and Fatima. Both had proven themselves to be good sailors on the way over, but he wanted to make the trip back as comfortable as possible. Their problem was Musa. He was insisting that they stay.

"I bought the house for you; this is where you belong. The business needs you. Why should you want to go back to Bougie?"

Itzak tried every argument he could think of. "Nouri is homesick. She misses the only life she has ever known. She yearns for her father and her home on the hillside."

"She has a home on a hillside here. This is your family; she is yours. Let her father come here if it is so important for them to be together."

"But we need their family business. You have not yet met Samir. He has wealth and connections beyond anything we have ever known."

"So, we're not good enough for you, is that it?"

"I want to have homes in BOTH cities. Algiers is dear to me. I imagine helping turn her into the jewel of the Maghreb, a port to rival Bougie and Oran."

It was no use. Musa wanted to have his way, and he was the older brother. At first Itzak thought Nouri would be able to persuade him, but he was only irritated by her insistence. If she had been anyone else, he would have been infuriated.

Itzak also noticed that Nouri seemed pale and listless. 'Perhaps because she's homesick,' he thought, though she never complained. He knew how close she had always been to her father, and how much their community of regulars at the book shop had meant to her. Then one day in early September, she swooned and would have fallen, had he not been standing right next to her. He laid her down on a divan and ran to get Fatima.

When the old nanny heard Itzak's description of what had happened, she laughed. "I think we have little to worry about," she said. "I can guess what is wrong without even seeing her. You go back and wipe her brow with a damp cloth and tell her I'll be along as soon as my old legs can carry me."

Itzak looked at her in confusion, and she laughed again. "Men," she declared. "Have you not thought about what happens to women after they have been married for a year?"

Then it dawned on him. Could it be? A baby? He might become a father; he never dreamed of such a thing.

Itzak postponed his return to Bougie to accommodate the pregnancy and lying-in. They would go back in October, after their child turned six months old.

When Musa heard the change in plans, he felt his prayers had been answered. Itzak would stay in Algiers. The Ibrahims would thrive as a family and as a business, as in the old days in Granada. Now all he needed was for his wife to bring forth a son, and life would be just as he wanted. Unfortunately, Tazrut showed no signs of pregnancy.

Musa went at least monthly to see his marabout, Sidi Abdullah, and bought all the fragrant herbs and sweet elixirs recommended to him, but to no avail. 'Nouri will give Itzak a son, and I will be left with nothing but a daughter. He is my younger brother and has always had all the luck. A beautiful wife, a well-connected father-in-law, and now, I'm sure, a healthy son. But they owe everything to me. They live in the house I bought for them and work in the business I built for them. They are Ibrahims, but they act like ungrateful strangers.' His mind went briefly to other subjects, but it always came back to this. Tazrut's failure was making his life miserable.

He wanted his brother to live near him because he liked the idea of being the head of a big family. A son would carry on the name, but it should be HIS son, not his brother's. Whenever he had that thought, his mind flared white, as though he had stared at the sun, and then he couldn't think.

When Itzak and Nouri moved in next door, Trixie sensed that family life was growing more complicated. She watched the grown-ups very carefully. Itzak and Musa were said to be brothers, but they seemed so different from each other. She felt she could always trust Itzak, but Musa, never. When he looked at her, he tightened the muscles around his eyes and bared his teeth; his lips turned up at their corners but were tight, not relaxed or happy. To her it looked like a grimace, a mockery of a loving smile. Even when he tried to be nice, she could feel his anger.

She thought his bad mood had something to do with the baby inside Nouri, but she wasn't sure. Sometimes she saw him glare sidelong at Uncle Itzak with a smile just like the one he turned toward her. Musa pretended to be happy about Itzak's good fortune in expecting a baby, but Trixie knew better. Even confident, self-assured Nouri was uncomfortable around him.

Musa overflowed with envy and every look seemed to threatened destruction of things he hated. Nouri was so uncomfortable around him she had asked Titrit for a talisman against the evil eye, and Trixie was glad to see that she kept it with her all the time.

In April, Titrit came down to attend Nouri in childbirth. Fatima and the midwife, Halima, were there as well. In the early hours, Trixie came along with her mother and Emilia to be with the laboring woman, but at her usual bedtime, she was sent home with Emilia.

The next morning, she ran to find the slave. "Let's go to see what's happening," she suggested. Emilia was happy to comply. They learned, early as it was, that Nouri's son had been named Benjamin, Beni for short. He had been born after only six hours of effective labor. Titrit had been asked to say the blessings of the Goddess over him, then Itzak made sure that they followed all Muslim customs. Trixie understood that he and Nouri wanted every possible deity to look with approval on their son. Only Musa was unhappy. He asked them to call upon Sidi Abdullah to bless the occasion and was silently furious when they didn't.

On the seventh day, Itzak held a great feast to celebrate the birth of his son. Everyone Trixie had ever seen was there, not only family, but also neighbors, colleagues of Itzak, and even slaves and servants from both households. Musa's irritable cook took charge of the arrangements and glared at Trixie every time he got a glimpse of her, so she hid behind a door frame to watch everything. A fat lamb sizzled on a grill set over a fire bed near the kitchen garden. Serving boys ran back and forth on errands between the two houses. A stream of guests came to share in the feast. Beggars she'd seen crouched with outstretched hands in alleyways, barefooted women carrying babies with half-naked older children clinging to their skirts, the one-armed man who brought fresh fish to the kitchen every morning, these and many more came for the feast and praised Itzak for his bounty.

Amid it all, Musa acted as though it was his event, not Itzak's. He bragged about the size of the lamb and the quality of the beverages that were served, as though he had been responsible for it all. He joked about the delight Itzak and Nouri took in their son, saying, "You would think that no one had ever had a baby born into his family before." The people around him always laughed, but Trixie heard him say it often. Each time, new people laughed, but she knew it was not really funny, though she could not quite tell what was wrong with it.

11. The Enemy of Your Enemy

Itzak walked along the soft, white sand that curved in front of him toward the northwest. The calm blue sea sparkled as the lowering sun tipped each little wavelet in gold. Behind him, the handsome walls of ancient stone embraced Algiers. Beautiful as it was, he yearned for Bougie, the sophisticated world where he would live in the gracious palace that Samir had provided and spend long evenings in intellectual conversations with his wife, father-in-law, and friends, who would even include the sultan. Musa was finally convinced that the family would benefit from operating out of two prosperous cities. The Mazigh clan would bring them important connections to the great ports of Europe: Genoa, Naples, Venice, and even Rome as well as across the Maghreb.

He had come down to the shore to supervise construction of a galliot with eighteen oars on each side. He should have been proud and excited at the sight, but all he could think about was his Beni and the blessings that seemed to fall effortlessly upon him this year. Then he heard a commotion near the sea wall. Some men who had hauled out a ship for repairs pointed north. Looking that way, he saw a small shape coming toward them: a boat with oarsmen pulling so hard they left a wake behind them on the darkening surface of the sea. Soon he could make out that it was one of his own. The sail was up, but the scant breeze barely created a bulge in its canvas. A sturdy man stood in the prow. Muhmed Reis, he was sure, waving his arms. Itzak joined the others running towards the water's edge to help. The old man started to talk before the keel scraped the sand.

"Oran is under attack," he declared. "He's finally done it. Cardinal Ximenes is said to have come himself to urge the men on. We always knew he'd try to use Mers al-Kebir as a base for capturing Oran."

"Ximenes." Itzak spat out the name.

Muhmed jumped stiffly ashore and moved as quickly as he could to meet Itzak on the beach. "They say it's bad," he gasped as he reached Itzak's side.

"Of course, it's bad if it's Ximenes. First, he convinced Isabella to expel all the Jews. After she died, he did all he could to force Muslims to convert. Now he's been made the Grand Inquisitor and is bringing his crusade to the Maghreb!"

"Another ship is said to fly the flag of Pedro Navarro."

"Ah, Ferdinand's man. A great engineer. Perhaps they will be in Oran for a while, fortifying the town. What next, do you imagine?"

"No one knows. More news should be arriving, but for now we only know that Oran is under attack, but Ximenes has always wanted to carry the *Reconquista* all the way to the Sahara."

By the third day after the news first arrived from Oran, ships filled with refugees were arriving regularly. It was as Itzak had feared. Oran had fallen and its citizens were fleeing the rampaging soldiers. Rape, murder, and mayhem were the order of the day. Thousands had been slaughtered, more thousands captured and enslaved. He heard lurid descriptions of Cardinal Ximenez riding a mule among his troops. So great was the zeal, the 73-year-old crusader had come across the sea to be present for the assault. He seemed determined to destroy all traces of Islam. When the city was defeated, he created a great bonfire of books and manuscripts in the main square and announced that all the mosques would be converted into churches.

Throughout June and July, refugees arrived by sea and by land, all with tales of horror. Most of the old families had fled inland to the south, to Tlemcen. Thousands of recent immigrants, Muslims and Jews from Andalusia, had gone southwest to Fez or east along the coast to Shershell. Those who journeyed on from Shershell arrived in Algiers with stories of death and destruction all too familiar to Itzak and Musa from their youth.

There was gossip. Ximenes and Navarro had a falling-out. Ximenes readied his fleet and headed back to Castille, leaving Navarro in charge of Oran.

After weeks, news arrived that Navarro's share of the armada had departed from Oran as well, leaving a well-equipped garrison behind. Corsairs in small, swift boats set out to track the course of the Spanish; the flagship of Commander Pedro de Navarro was seen heading back toward Aragon.

In July Itzak received a letter from Samir telling him not to return to Bougie.

> *Although I hear that the armada has returned to Spain, there are rumors that Oran is just the beginning. There are political tensions between the crusader mentality of Ximenez from Castile and the conquering instincts of Navarro from Aragon. Reliable sources write that King Ferdinand is intent on sending Navarro back to the Maghreb to wipe out more 'dens of pirates,' as he calls our ports. My best estimate is that Tunis will be safe, but others, especially Bougie, might be targeted. The question is, 'what will they do next?'*

"Sultan Abdelaziz should send us help from Bougie," declared Musa after Itzak read the letter to him. "That is why we pay him tribute."

"I agree with you," answered Itzak. "He should, but will he? We are small and insignificant. Bougie has to defend itself. If the worst happens, we might have only these old walls and our hatred of the Spanish to defend us. Every immigrant from

Andalusia shall fight to the death, though I'm not so sure of the Baldi or of any of the tribes who live within a day's ride of us."

"You're dreaming, brother. Our walls are neither as high nor as strong as those of Oran, and yet theirs fell. The Sultan of Tlemcen was supposed to help them, and yet they fell. It may be time to recognize the supremacy of Spain. Did you learn nothing from seeing what happened to Granada?"

"Only that we've fled for the last time," retorted Itzak. "My ship is already provisioned for a trip to Bougie. Instead of returning with my family, I'll leave Nouri and Beni with you and go to Bougie to beg for military help."

"Are you mad? The armada might be traveling here even now. What if they sail into our bay while you are gone on your fool's errand? Think of me. Because of your folly in asking for help, they will seek me out and kill me. Let someone else go. Send Muhmed Reis. Think of your family."

"I am thinking of my family. Remember, Algiers is insignificant to Spain. We offer no immediate threat and have no great treasures to seize, no libraries to burn. They are more likely to attack Bougie than Algiers. I'll take a crew of sixteen. Muhmed's lookouts will give you advanced notice. If any ships come this way, send the women and children to Jadizi, where they'll be safe. We need to contact Sultan Abdelaziz or find another protector."

"You sound determined to go."

"It's our best chance. I must see my father-in-law, Samir. He is well-connected. We are more likely to get help if we have him on our side. I'm sure that the Baldi will agree."

Until the moment Itzak came to her and told her that he was going to travel to Bougie to ask for help in defending Algiers, Nouri had loved everything about being a woman, because her father had raised her as a learned and competent person. Her mind made her a friend and companion to her husband. Her body had performed well in the womanly functions, from pregnancy through birth and breastfeeding, so she felt she had the best of both worlds. She was used to being admired and had seldom yearned for something she couldn't have.

Until now.

Was it too much to ask? She just wanted to go home with Itzak, to see her father and learn what the Spanish might do. She wasn't afraid of being attacked on the sea. She wasn't even afraid of the war that could come. She had always been fortunate, and she had every expectation that she would continue to be so.

"Take me with you," she demanded when she heard Itzak's plan. She was excited at the prospect of a great adventure out of some Spanish romance.

"Samir would never forgive me if I did. It is too dangerous for a mother and child," answered Itzak.

"We could leave Beni here with Fatima. Tazrut would be like a mother to him, and we would be back within two months."

"He is still suckling. You said you would never rely on a wet-nurse. You can't just wean him over night. Ask Fatima; she'll tell you."

She knew both arguments were true; her father would never forgive Itzak if he endangered her at sea during these times, and Fatima would say that it would be bad for a child to be weaned abruptly.

These were the constraints of femininity that she had heard other women complain about. She could admit that he was right, but that didn't keep her from wishing that she had as much freedom as Titrit to make her own decisions.

"Musa will keep us safe here," she told Itzak, pretending she believed it. She knew her brother-in-law might be as much a problem as a help, but she must learn to play the role of good wife and assure her husband that she would be all right. Itzak was the best person for the job. He would return with an army to keep Algiers safe, and he'd bring Samir with him.

"You will be our hero," she said bravely. "It is too risky for the baby. I will stay in Algiers and pray for the best."

Late in the afternoon on the second day of his sea trip to Bougie, Itzak saw a lone galleon approaching from the east. When it came close, he recognized Kara Hasan, the Turkish privateer who had carried his letter to Nouri from Halq al-Wad. Itzak hailed the ship and pulled close to exchange information.

"We were anchored at Bougie when the armada came into sight," Kara Hasan told them. "I'd guess they had two or three dozen ships, all armed. I recognized the flag of Navarro flying on the largest. We did not wait around to see what would happen. That was two days ago. As far as we know, the fort and the city are still under attack, but I don't see how Sultan Abdelaziz and his fighters can hold out."

"My wife's family is there," Itzak told him. "I would have been there myself if we had not postponed our return until my new son was old enough to travel."

"If they value their lives, your relatives will have left by now," replied the rugged captain. "Search for them elsewhere, that's my advice."

"Well taken, my friend. That is what I shall do. Where are you headed?"

"Shershell. I've parted ways with Arouj Reis; struck out on my own, if you will."

Itzak had heard that unprincipled Turkish privateers were moving into ports farther and farther to the west. Would Kara Hasan prove to be an ally or a threat? Itzak did not trust him, but he might need the help of just this kind of desperado. "Will you be stopping in Algiers on your way?" he asked.

"If it is safe."

"It should be, with the armada engaged at Bougie. If you do stop there, look up Muhmed Reis and give him a message for my wife. Tell him that I will go directly to Nahla, and if Samir is not there, I will go on to Bougie."

He thought for a moment, then added, "If you are not in too much of a hurry to get to Shershell, you might stay in Algiers a while. We could use extra fighting men if the fleet does come to us." He realized he had taken a dangerous step, inviting a devil like Kara Hasan into the bosom of his community, but it was a necessary risk.

"If I fled Bougie before an assault, why should I wait for one in Algiers," Hasan laughed. "What a dreamer. But I will deliver your message and collect as much information as I can. Before I decide to fight, I make sure it is a battle I can win."

"Spoken like a true captain. I expect no more and no less. Go in peace. Unlike you, we Andalusians can no longer choose to flee. They seem to seek us out to destroy our entire way of life."

Kara Hasan laughed more raucously. "That, dear sir, is the price you pay for settling down. The only way I could stay in one place would be if I were the sultan, wielding absolute authority over others. No, this ship is my realm and shall take me wherever I choose to go, and my men with me."

Itzak said his goodbyes sincerely, reminding himself of the old adage, "the enemy of my enemy is my friend." One never knew when the two might meet again.

As night fell, Itzak and his men pulled into a small cove for cover. The next morning, they travelled on toward the east. They soon encountered the first boats filled with refugees. Some were small feluccas loaded down with entire extended families. A few were large merchant ships carrying prosperous citizens who could pay their way to a safe port. Some hailed them to ask why they were heading east.

"Avoid Bougie at all costs," they warned.

Each successive group told stories worse than the ones before. Sultan Abdelaziz had fled to the mountains. The Christian cannons breached the walls in just two days. The commander, Pedro de Navarro, who had once been a pirate himself, released his soldiers to sack the city. There was no respite from their vicious assault on citizens. All those who could, fled. "Turn back," was the universal advice.

Itzak asked each boat if any aboard were familiar with Samir's ancestral village, Nahla. One captain knew the area well and gave specific instructions. They were told to find a small estuary and row inland as far as they could, then follow the course of the brackish stream through the marsh and up the gradually narrowing valley at its head through the coastal mountains until they reached the village.

They easily recognized the estuary from the instructions and concealed their boat when the creek grew too marshy to navigate. They found a worn path that led them along relatively solid ground across the wetlands to the hills, where the land rose steeply to a verdant plateau and then to heavily forested mountains. On a second plateau, they came upon the outskirts of Nahla. The way was lined with fruit trees; each house had its own vegetable garden, growing more than enough to feed even a large family.

Itzak knew he was in the right place when he saw the bees swarming around the artfully planted flowers that surrounded each mud-brick house. This was Samir's land of honey, where busy bees sweetened the diet and provided the raw material for their candles. The beauty of the landscape would have pleased Itzak if he hadn't known about the rape and murder going on just a few dozen miles away. He had come here to learn about that horror, and yet he could see no sight and hear no sound of its reality in this peaceful village.

Samir had arrived the evening before. He and his entire extended family were safe at their ancestral property, which Itzak found easily.

"Come to Algiers," he told his father-in-law. "You could set up your business there and start a new life near your grandson. It's not Bougie, but more people are moving there all the time, mostly ambitious young men who want a bright future for themselves and their sons. Some imams are establishing mosques with schools for the young boys, so we might yet be able to raise another scholar in the family. Your book business would flourish, and you would be with family."

"I'm not ready to abandon Bougie," replied the old man. "I believe our ancient rivalries will be forgotten in the service of a greater good. After the fleet departs, we can raise an army in support of Sultan Abdelaziz. If they only leave a few hundred Spanish soldiers behind as a garrison, in time we will be able to defeat them."

"Yes, a few hundred Spanish in a strong fortress, with armor, muskets and cannons, who can fire at will upon foot soldiers and cavalry armed with nothing but bows and arrows, swords and spears. Your brave army, no matter how many tribes joined in the struggle, would not stand a chance. Not without artillery and gunpowder, and not without the ability to attack from both land and sea."

"As you say, not without those things. But just suppose those things were available, at a price."

Itzak stared at Samir. "You cannot mean you would seek help from Arouj Reis and his band. That price would be too high."

"Too high for my home? For my pride? For my people? Didn't you go to Halq al-Wad to see the ships of the Turks in the harbor and observe their construction? Didn't you inspect their modern fleet and their fighting men and discuss the finer points of ship design with them? You said their skills were superior to any you had seen before."

"Take it from me, Father Samir, there are times when one must make a calculated exit. I have done it. We have our lives. You have escaped with most of your stock. In Algiers, there is no fort guarding the harbor, no garrison enforcing a tariff on ships that pass in or out. Flee the Christians and avoid making any bargains with that devil Arouj. He is brilliant, but he is dangerous."

"My dear boy, we seem to have reversed roles. You are giving the cautious advice of an old man. I, the elder, am more inclined to take risks. But nothing is decided. I am only yearning for my lost property. Our people are still unsettled refugees. We must wait until our sultan establishes a court in exile, until we know how many tribes support him. My guess is that he will have many allies committed to purging the Spaniards from Bougie. If he decides to fight, I'm with him. If not, it's bees for me. I'll stay right here and join my family in their traditional practice of creating light from beeswax. If I can, I will also resume my trade in illuminated manuscripts. Life will go on, one way or another. Now that I have a new grandson, it is even more important that I work toward a stable society in the Maghreb, grander than anything even Khaldoun imagined."

"Promise me that you will remember what I have said," answered Itzak. "There is another home for you in Algiers. Your business could flourish there. I am sure Musa would welcome your candles, and you and I could establish a book shop near the souk."

"I promise you that I shall visit you at the time of the full moon following the first storms of the season. By then I shall have a better picture of events both here and there," said Samir. "But enough of this talk."

He changed his voice and inhaled deeply, lowering his eyelids slowly, then opening them briskly and, looking directly at Itzak, said, "I have managed to save almost all our books and scrolls, carrying them here on the backs of donkeys. Among them is a treat that I want you to take back for Nouri--the latest chivalric romance from Seville. It is called *Las Sergas de Esplandin*, about a black queen who ruled a society of women. It was written as a compliment to Queen Isabella, a warrior and a wife, but since she died, it has become just a popular extravagance. It will remind Nouri of the tales she heard from her grandmother about Dihya Kahina, the priestess queen who fought against the Arab invaders so long ago. Just ask Fatima; she will tell you. We need another leader like that, one who can unite the tribes.

"The tide may turn again. Someday all of us may feel like a single tribe, our Arab brothers and sisters united with us as well. After all, the same moon looks down on all of us, and now we do have a common enemy."

Itzak found inspiration and hope in Samir's vision, but he did not think it would come to pass. Men like his brother Musa would never want a government that gave equal rights to Berbers, Arabs, Moors, and Kabyles, much less Christians, Jews, or women. If Musa and his Sidi Abdullah had their way, they would burn books and smash statues as the Christians did in Oran after the Spanish victory. The legends of the Arabs and the Kabyles would be replaced by strict teachings from the Koran. Not Itzak's dream, nor Samir's either.

He and those of his crew who had accompanied him to Nahla spent the night in Samir's family compound and hiked back to their boat the next morning. The short trip down the estuary was uneventful, but as soon as they rowed out of its mouth, they saw ships, small and large, dotting the sea almost in a line close to shore. It was sobering to be among them. Itzak knew full well that he and his family might become refugees too, if the Christians chose to land at Algiers. The only good in it was that many of these ships contained men who could swell the ranks of fighters prepared to defy the Spanish. He would encourage them to settle in Algiers.

✦

As the fall progressed, Samir increasingly felt that he could be of more use in Algiers than in the small town of Nahla. His agents reported to him from all the ports and cities of the Maghreb and told him that Algiers was growing rapidly, with the families brought from Spain by the corsairs as well as refugees who fled from Oran and Bougie. Many of the new settlers were skilled craftsmen. Some were expert at making guns while others knew how to manufacture gunpowder. Long-abandoned houses were being repaired and rebuilt. New schools and mosques were springing up. He decided to join his daughter and her family in the city he believed could be the New Bougie.

In mid-November, he arrived in Algiers with a caravan of donkeys, as planned, after the full moon following the first rain of the season. He toured the city with Itzak, ostensibly to examine storage areas for the candles and discuss the possibility that Samir open a shop for his books and manuscripts in Algiers. They were serious about going into business together, but their more important goal was to inspect the city's defenses. The walls were old, but slaves were hard at work reinforcing its ancient façade. Samir was skeptical.

"Let us hope that King Ferdinand does not send Navarro here. I saw what his cannon did to the walls of our fort at Bougie. I doubt Algiers could withstand even two days of heavy fire. Algiers would have no chance. And with Sultan Abdelaziz in exile, there is no army that can come to protect us."

12. Trixie Tries to Help

Trixie squatted behind a screen in her mother's room, absorbed in the movements of a large, black beetle as it struggled to climb from the flat tile floor onto a pillow. 'How does it keep track of all those legs,' she wondered. 'Why don't they move together? Does each have a mind of its own? How do they all know where they are going?'

She tried to imagine what it would be like to be inside a body like that, to have a dark, shiny shell, and legs that could bend in so many places. Things would look so big; a pillow would loom up like a mountain where you could climb into unknown realms, away from everything.

Tazrut's retching had gone on so long that it seemed to tear at Trixie's own innards. Her only comfort was to concentrate on the beetle. Emilia had carried off a bowl, dumped its scant contents and returned with a damp cloth. Now she was wiping Tazrut's brow while whispering comforting words in her ear.

Trixie looked up from the beetle. All she wanted to do was comfort her mother, if only she knew how. She had tried telling stories and sharing her favorite toys, but neither could distract Tazrut from her misery.

On her hands and knees, Trixie peeked around the screen, calling on all her courage, so she could be wise and brave and help her mother. She tensed her muscles, about to get up to climb into the bed next to Tazrut, when Musa appeared at the door. Trixie froze.

"How is she doing, Emilia?"

"She is resting now; I have just fetched this water for her."

"Give it to me; I will care for her now. You must have other things to do."

"Yes, master." Emilia bowed and left.

Musa moved towards Tazrut's bed. A tabletop concealed most of him from Trixie, though she could see his slippers and knew he was sitting on the edge of the bed. She suspected he did not know that she was there.

"What is wrong with you?" Was that kindness in his voice? She knew from experience that his gentle tone would not last.

"All you have to do is eat and sleep and let our son grow strong inside your body. Is that too much for you?"

She heard her mother's suppressed sobs and flinched, waiting for Musa's contempt to explode.

"Why can't you be fat and jolly, like Emilia? Why can't you just eat and sleep like a normal woman?"

Trixie knew what was coming as well as she could anticipate the next part of a fairy tale that she had heard many times.

"If you give me another girl, I will send you back to your village and take a new wife, and it won't be a mountain peasant, I promise you that. A proper Muslim, that's what I want."

She heard her mother's voice, hoarse from retching, barely a whisper. "I can't control whether it will be a son or daughter..."

"Control? You cannot even keep your food down. Eat, I tell you, eat. You risk the life of my son. Why are you doing this to me? It's Mayam's curse, isn't it? Oh yes, you don't think I know about it, but I have my ways. News from the village reaches me, even down here in Algiers."

Another whimper from the bed. Trixie couldn't quite make it out, but it didn't matter. Nothing Tazrut could say would satisfy Musa when he was like this.

"Your mother hexed you to punish me. That jealous witch doesn't want you to give me a son."

Trixie shriveled inside every time he said this. It couldn't be true. Her Grandmother Mayam would not utter a curse that might cause Tazrut to suffer such agony. No mother could do that, could she?

Tazrut's whimpers turned to moans as she thrashed helplessly on the bed. Trixie felt Musa's words thud like rocks striking an injured bunny. If only she could drag herself and her mother to some place of shelter, she thought, but there was nowhere to hide. She could only be grateful that she was concealed, at least for the moment.

"Look at you. Can you do nothing but cry? I don't deserve this," he shouted, then stomped from the room.

Trixie crept from her hiding place and went to her mother's side. Now she knew what to do. Tazrut needed kindness. Placing her little hand on her mother's brow and soothing back her damp hair, she said, "It will be all right, mother. I am here. I know you are trying your best. You will feel better soon, and our baby will be strong inside of you. It is a boy, I'm sure it is. And when he is born, Baba will give you many gifts and forget that he ever felt cursed. Don't worry, mother. Auntie Titrit will come down from the village soon to take care of you."

She felt Tazrut relax as she spoke.

"How do you know these things, Sycorax?"

"I just know. Drink a little water. I'm going to fetch Emilia and tell her that you are ready to eat something. Then I am going to go to my bed and think about Grandmother Mayam in her village far away. She will hear me."

"Silly girl, it wouldn't work even if you could do it. She wouldn't do anything for me even if she knew. No wonder we call you Trixie. But you are so sweet. I know you love me, and for your sake I will drink this water. And for your sake I will try to eat the food that Emilia brings."

"That's right, mother. For my sake and for my brother's. We need you so much, and we honor you, for you created us and will sustain us. Titrit told me how a woman brings forth new life. She said that I will see your belly grow round like the moon until it reaches its fulfillment in creation. 'We are here on the earth for this little life, and we will go back to the sky when our time is up,' she said. 'It's all a great cycle,' she told me. Like I will grow up. And I wonder: will you grow down? Is that what the cycle means?"

"Oh, Trixie, my beloved. You are so wise and yet so simple. That is almost exactly what it means. Now go tell Emilia that I am ready to eat."

⚓

Early the next morning, in Jadizi, Titrit returned home from helping a robust young woman give birth to a second son. She was surprised to see Mayam sitting in front of the dying fire and staring deeply into the coals. Titrit quietly moved across the room and sat next to her.

"You must go down to Algiers. Things are not well with your sister," Mayam said.

"Is Tazrut ill?"

"She will be if we do not intervene. She is expecting a second child next spring and cannot eat or drink."

"How do you know this?"

"As I was sitting here tonight, I felt my granddaughter Sycorax's presence as close to me as you are now. She told me about her mother."

"But she is only four years old. Did you reach out to her?"

"No, I suspected nothing."

"A second child; it might be a blessing. I know Musa wants a son above all else."

"So much so," answered Mayam, "that Tazrut grows sick with anxiety. I saw her condition as I stared into the fire. When she starts to vomit, she cannot stop. When she goes to bed, she cannot sleep. When she should eat, she has no appetite. That man is making her sick, and she will die if we do nothing. I can take care of your responsibilities here. You sleep now. I will prepare a bag of elixirs and herbs for her, and an amulet I have blessed. You will have your work cut out for you down there; it is hard to protect a wife against the curses of a man who does not recognize the damage he does to others."

"That's Musa," replied Titrit. "What a fool he is to underestimate the gift of a daughter and to fail to cherish his loving wife."

"He will pay," muttered Mayam. "Someday and in some way, he will pay."

"Thank goodness his brother Itzak has returned. He and Nouriare an even greater comfort for Tazrut."

"Yes," agreed Mayam. "Itzak always was more trustworthy than Musa. He will always be our ally."

Tazrut was startled to see Titrit arrive. "Sycorax said you were coming, but I thought it was just a wish she believed she could make come true."

Titrit nodded without commenting. She already had suspicions about Sycorax and her 'tricks,' but she knew that Tazrut wouldn't want to hear them. She wanted her daughter to be 'normal,' not a seer like Mayam.

Meanwhile Trixie was tugging impatiently at Titrit's pantaloons in the expectation of a treat. Titrit knelt down next to the bag she had dropped to the floor and from it withdrew a ball of dough soaked with honey. "Here you are, Trixie. Now find Emilia. I have another bag, with clay for molding. She will help you with it while I talk alone with your mother."

"About secrets?"

"You curious little thing. Perhaps not secrets, but private things. You must respect the right of others to keep some thoughts to themselves or to only share them with others whom they carefully choose."

"Oh, yes, I understand that. Mother is going to give me a baby brother, and for the longest time she chose not to tell me, though she did tell Father and Emilia, and Emilia told Fatima who, of course, told Nouri."

Titrit's eyes narrowed as she looked at the little girl. "Are you saying that you knew about it before anybody told you?"

"No one had to tell me. I just knew. I wanted a playmate, and Ummi wanted Musa to love her, so it seemed like a good idea."

Titrit relaxed; maybe she was just a regular little girl after all. "It's always nice when something you wish for comes true," she commented.

"Yes," replied Trixie. "I wished it very hard and sent my wishes to Musa, but he doesn't like me, so I was afraid it wouldn't work. But, you see, it did."

Titrit laughed. "If only it were that simple, my dear. Well, you run off so Tazrut and I can talk. There are many things that grown-ups must plan before a baby comes."

"I know. I want to learn all those things. I'm not old enough yet, but even a little girl can help in some way, just by loving, I think."

"Darling Trixie, you are just right. That will be your job, to love your mother. It is what she will need most of all."

"Yes. Father is not very good at it. I will do the best I can for all of us."

As Trixie ran off to find Emilia, Titrit and Tazrut stared quietly at each other. What was there to say? This was not an ordinary child. Some moments she was wise beyond her years and other times she believed in the magic of her own thoughts, just like any little girl. And yet there was something strangely convincing about her knowledge of the pregnancy, and Mayam said she had heard Trixie speak, "as if she were sitting as close to me then as you are now." She would have to keep a close eye on her little niece. For now, she must focus on Tazrut.

"Does Musa know you're here?" Titrit could feel the fear in her sister's voice as she asked. They both remembered how he had forbidden her to visit until after Sycorax was born.

"Don't worry," she said. "He will tolerate my presence. Mayam will make sure of that. He believes I am the only one who can keep his son alive in your womb. Itzak will help us convince him that it is so."

"His son? Are you sure that it's a boy?"

"Yes, and so is Mayam."

"Sycorax said so too..." Tazrut's voice trailed off, not wanting to think about the implications of her daughter's comment, if she really had the knowledge.

"For extra protection, Mayam sent down this amulet, which she blessed while praying at the shrine of the Goddess." Titrit held out a pendant shaped like a simple cross, but with its top arm curved into a loop, almost like a handle. A chain passed through the loop so the sacred object could be worn on a chain. "Keep it with you at all times so that your baby will be safe."

Tazrut eagerly reached for the holy object. Reassured by her sister's gift, Tazrut stopped vomiting, and the pregnancy progressed smoothly over the following months.

13. Trixie Takes Flight

Over the winter, Tazrut's nausea passed and Trixie saw she was more robust. Life seemed to return to normal for the family, but the little girl remained vigilant. She sensed her mother's on-going frailty. Titrit visited regularly, which helped a lot. Tazrut took all the special herbs that Mayam sent and, just as important, wore her amulet all day and placed it under her mattress at night. Best of all, Musa stayed out of the women's quarters when Titrit was visiting.

Aunt Nouri and Uncle Itzak became such an important part of her family, she barely remembered a time before Itzak returned, when the grown-ups talked about him so much that she named her favorite lizardIzzy. Then there was the day when Baba Musa got so angry that he yelled at everybody, but since Itzak came back, things had been better. Then Beni's grandfather, Samir, came to live with them, and Trixie felt she had a grandfather for the first time, and her family was complete.

Auntie Titrit often took Trixie up to their rooftop terrace to look at the world around them, the houses above and below them, the bay in front of the city, the tall mountains rising behind the white houses and, far away, more mountains across the water. She imagined the lands that lay even farther away, places she heard Itzak, Nouri, and Samir talk about, like Bougie and Nahla, Spain and Oran. She wished she could fly like a gull so that she could see all these wonders, even the scary places like Bougie after the armada arrived. Samir and Itzak knew about war, and she believed they could protect her and her family if the Spanish came to Algiers. Besides, Musa was nicer when his brother was around.

One afternoon in June, Trixie was teasing two-year-old Beni by the fountain, tickling him and running away so that he would chase after her in his little toddler steps, while Tazrut sat in the shade with Auntie Titrit, Nouri, and Nouri's old nanny, Fatima. She looked over at Tazrut, glad to see her so content. Then she saw her mother place her hand on her lower abdomen, grimace slightly, and stop breathing for a moment. Trixie glanced at Titrit. Yes, she had seen it as well. Could this be the beginning of her brother's arrival?

She would have to be patient, Titrit had told her. "Even though she is ruled by the moon, a woman's body does not move with the calm grace of a celestial body," she had said. "The child will not slip as effortlessly from Tazrut's belly as a full moon slides from behind a mountain."

A while later, Trixie again saw Tazrut stop breathing. This time her mother made eye contact with Titrit, who nodded an acknowledgment and went to sit close to Tazrut but did nothing more. The group continued to chat quietly about boring female things. Trixie contained her excitement. Titrit had told her that she could only stay with them if she was calm and well-behaved.

When Nouri had given birth to Beni, Titrit and Tazrut had sent her away before the labor became intense, but Trixie had heard the women talk about it afterwards and felt she had learned a lot. This time she hoped she could stay with Tazrut until her baby brother was born. She would have to be very good and very grown-up.

Trixie discovered that when she distracted her mother by telling amusing stories about her menagerie, the women were happy to let her stay. After several hours, the mood began to change. In the late afternoon, Nouri sent Beni home with Fatima, and Emilia came to ask Tazrut about plans for the evening meal.

Titrit answered for her sister. "I don't think she will be eating solid foods tonight."

"Oh," said Emilia, "Is it starting?"

Titrit nodded and smiled, but Tazrut looked worried.

"I'll send for Halima now and make sure we have everything we'll be needing," Emilia assured her.

Soon afterwards, Titrit suggested that they go into Tazrut's room. Nouri and Trixie went with them.

Now that contractions were stronger, Trixie understood she must help her mother relax. She felt the waves emanating from Tazrut's body, then subsiding, in closer and closer succession. As each wave passed, she laughed with pleasure and told her mother how brave she was, and how happy they would be when they could see her baby brother and hold him in their arms. As evening was turning to night, the Kabyle midwife, Halima, arrived. Soon after, Nouri went home.

For many hours, the little group maintained a happy rhythm--Emilia coming and going on errands, carrying news to and from the others, both in this house and next door; Titrit confident and watchful; Trixie loving and attentive to Tazrut's condition; and Halima gossiping about scandalous events in other people's harems: miscarriages, secret love affairs, dishonest slaves, cruel husbands, she knew about them all.

After midnight, Tazrut was reaching a stage in her labor where she could no longer be diverted by Halima's stories or Trixie's soothing words. Titrit decided it was time for Trixie to go to bed. "Come now, off you go. Halima, Emilia, and I will take care of things from here."

"Please, no," Trixie pleaded. The pace of events had quickened dramatically. She could feel her mother's contractions, wave after wave surging through her body, no longer separated from each other, but jumbled like chaotic surf in a rocky cove.

"Mother will drown in those strong waves," she said, too tired to realize she had spoken from the images in her mind instead of ordering her language the way grown-ups expected.

"Ah, yes, I see," said Titrit. "You are too tired to understand. You are right about the contractions. They are not orderly anymore. It's time to leave us to help her navigate this passage."

"You mean my brother will find his way through the narrow opening of the sea cave?"

"Yes, and your mother will push him to safety."

"Will she be strong enough?"

"If you go to bed and sleep soundly. Then she will know that she doesn't have to take care of you. She can give herself over to the wisdom of her body. Remember, she has done this before, when you were born. She may grunt and moan, but she will be fine, and it is time for you to go to bed."

Trixie could see how hard it was for Tazrut already. She reluctantly followed when Emilia took her by the wrist and pulled her determinedly toward the door and down the corridor to her own room. Despite her plan to stay awake and wait until all was still, then sneak back to her mother's side, she fell into a deep sleep minutes after her head rested on her bedding, and she slept through the rest of the night.

When she first woke up, Trixie vaguely sensed something was different about this day, then quickly knew. Tazrut and baby Faisel! As soon as she remembered the labor, she knew her brother's name and that both he and her mother were in trouble. She ran to their room, but the door was shut against her. When she pounded, Emilia came out to shush her and tell her that she could not come in. She heard screams and moans; something was terribly wrong; the sounds were worse than they had been the night before, not as shrill, but more hopeless. Why wouldn't they let her in? Didn't they know she could help?

Distressed and alone, she sneaked up the narrow steps to the rooftop terrace, a place that often offered her solace. No laundry was flapping in the breeze on this still dawn. She stood on a flat, empty space beneath a cloudless pink and blue dome waiting for the sun to peek over the hills to the east. It already lit the tower of the casbah on the hill above her. Now five, she could easily see over the low wall that rimmed the edge of the terrace. The white houses were stacked like over-sized steps below her, all the way down to the ramparts by the sea. Just beyond the watch towers, by portals called the Sea Gate, she saw the ships in the harbor, protected by several rocky islets, the largest one topped by a single scraggly pine clinging to the crumbling walls of an ancient fort.

While she stood on her hillside terrace, the sun reached her and, soon after, the high rocks on the largest island in the bay. Even at this distance, she could make out a gaggle of feisty sea gulls gathered around its one tree, squabbling over some tidbit on the rocks. She'd like to be one of those gulls, she thought. She'd leave the prize, whatever it was, to the others and take off over the sea.

She imagined that her arms were covered with feathers and that she flapped them in agitation, eager to fly away. She had a strange sensation in her chest, as though her breastplate pushed forward and her shoulders rotated back until her arms rose behind her and almost touched. She stretched her neck forward, then took two hops and spread her wings. Could it be? Wings? Yes, she had wings that she could raise high then push down in a motion that lifted her above the sea. She attempted some stronger flaps; yes, she flew swiftly away from the island and toward the northwest.

Reaching a pleasing height, she settled into slow, shallow strokes that, she realized, were under her control. She felt the air, an active presence beneath her belly, and her legs, tucked up under her tail, which she could spread wide for a glide or gather into a rudder to control the direction of her flight.

At home, they had chased her away from her mother; she had been powerless. Here, she soared above the waves, then swooped down to skim the surface, just for fun, then up again, flying in an ecstasy, with an unfamiliar but glorious body that she could control perfectly. From high above the sea, Algiers seemed no more than a pile of small white boxes on the edge of the water, dwarfed by the hills and, beyond them, the mountains where Grandmother Mayam was said to live.

Turning toward the horizon, she noticed dark objects moving toward her on the water. Masts. Ships. Lots of them. Some were bigger than any she'd ever seen, galleys with more oars than she could count, one layer on top of the other. A few seemed to have no oars at all. Some of the ships had square sails that were slack for lack of wind. And almost all were stinky. She could smell them even this far away. She knew that meant slaves chained to their benches. Not free men, like Uncle Itzak and his men when they set off to fetch Moriscos from Andalusia. She knew these ships didn't belong here, and they were headed toward her mother, who would not be well enough to flee. Was it the same armada that had attacked Bougie?

She should tell Uncle Itzak and Grandfather Samir right away. As soon as she had that thought, she found herself back on the terrace of her father's house. How did she get there? Was it all a dream? Had she never left? Had she just sent her mind along with the bird or had she transformed into a bird for a while? She did not know. But the ships were there, and they were heading toward the city. She knew that much, even if she was only five years old.

She went downstairs to tell Emilia she was going to climb over the terrace wall to find Itzak, but everyone was gathered in Tazrut's room. When Emilia saw her open the door, she grabbed her by the wrist.

"Where have you been, naughty girl? We've been looking everywhere for you."

"Let me go; I have to find Uncle Itzak."

"Don't be ridiculous."

"I was watching the sea and I saw ships heading this way. Uncle Itzak has to know. They have flags with crosses flying from their masts, and cannon mounted in their bows. I have to tell him."

"You crazy girl, stop imagining things. Calm down and come see your brother Faisel while Halima dresses him to present to your father."

"We've got to keep him safe, and Ummi, too." She looked over at Tazrut, who lay pale and motionless on the bed. Titrit was at her side with her hand on her sister's abdomen. The two seemed absorbed in each other; neither looked toward her.

"Ummi, Ummi," she cried. Titrit turned her way, but Tazrut did not seem to hear. "We must get her out of the city," Trixie tried to explain to Emilia. It seemed like a nightmare in which she could see and hear them, but they did not know that she was there.

"What you must do is to calm down," said Emilia. "We can't let you near her in this state." The buxom slave stepped between her and her mother, and Trixie grew more desperate.

"But they're coming, they're coming. We must save Ummi and the baby."

Emilia gripped her by an arm, dragged her into the hall, and closed the door firmly behind them.

"Now shush. Your father will be furious if you bother your brother. He is just falling asleep."

"You're hurting me. Let me go. We must tell Itzak so he can save Ummi from the Christians."

"If you don't stop yelling..." Trixie never heard the rest of the threat, for the embodiment of it stood behind the slave. Her father; Musa.

"What is going on here?" He roared. His voice seemed out of a nightmare worse than any she had ever dreamed. Terrified as she was, she had to calm herself and explain what she had seen.

"Baba, they're coming, they're coming..." He MUST understand her, but it was as though he did not even hear her.

"Emilia, you are in charge of this creature," he said. "Lock her in the storeroom at the end of the hall if you have to, just get her out of my way. I want to see my son."

Trixie could hear him still muttering and complaining as Emilia dragged her, kicking and screaming, down the hall. She got some satisfaction knowing she had landed at least one good kick to Emilia's knee and created some ugly scratches on her arms. She would have tried to do some serious damage by biting her, but it was more important to keep screaming. They had to hear her; they had to listen. But no, Emilia shoved her in the storeroom and turned the key in the lock.

She was alone. She pressed her ear to the door. She could hear heavy breathing on the other side, but then the sound grew fainter as the slave moved away.

"Noooooo," she cried. "Someone, please, believe me."

If only she understood how it had come to this.

14. The Armada Arrives

Titrit had been through a rough night; for most of it, she hadn't been sure whether her sister would survive the child's birth, but now it was over and both Tazrut and baby Faisel were sleeping peacefully. When Emilia came back into the room, she asked, "What was that all about?"

Emilia gestured for her to be quiet. "Can't tell you now. Musa is outside the door and wants to see his son," she whispered. "When the baby is cleaned up and ready to be presented, Halima will take him to the nursery. I'll tell Musa to wait there, and his son will be brought to him."

"But what was going on with Trixie? I've never heard her like that."

"I'll tell you about it after I make sure Musa is out of the way. You stay with Tazrut."

As exhausted as she was, Titrit could see that Emilia was even more distressed. Strands of pale blond hair had slipped out of her braids, and her arms, which were bare almost to her elbows, were unnaturally white and blotched with red.

"What's going on? Where is Trixie? Did you take her to see the baby with her father?"

"I just couldn't let her in, not when you were still waiting for the afterbirth. And then the master came and heard her fuss. He told me to shut her in the storeroom at the end of the hall."

"Is that where she is now?"

"She must be. No one would dare let her out."

"Give me the key, Emilia. As soon as Musa is in the nursery, I will look for Trixie. I will come back as soon as I can."

The sobs and pounding heard as Titrit ran down the hall subsided as she turned the key in the lock. She pulled the door open while Trixie pushed from within.

"I've got to find Itzak," the girl cried, clutching Titrit.

"Itzak; what on earth for? Don't you care about your mother, or your new baby brother?"

"Yes, I've got to save them. The Christians are coming. We have to keep them safe!"

"Now, just calm down. How can you possibly know that the Christians are coming? You must have had a nightmare. Everyone is safe now, though it was a rough night."

"But I saw them! I was on the roof, and there were dozens of them, flying flags I've never seen before. It must have been the Christians, and Itzak should know about it."

"Let us go up now; you'll see it was just your imagination."

As they climbed the steep, narrow stairs, Titrit continued. "We won't find anything except sheets drying in the sun and merchant ships anchored in the bay..."

"No, these weren't merchant ships. There were so many...and each had a cannon on its bow."

As they reached the flat rooftop, Titrit took Trixie's hand and walked with her to the low wall. "You see, there are no ships..."

"Yes, there," the little girl pointed north, past the big island with the scraggly tree, toward the horizon.

"Surely that is only a shadow cast by some clouds."

"There are no clouds this morning, Auntie Titrit. Hurry. Tell Itzak. The Christians are coming."

"True, there are no clouds, but you could not see beyond the horizon."

"If you just stand here and watch, you will see them grow bigger, but then it will be too late. I flew out there. I saw them."

"Flew?"

"Like a gull. I don't know how, I just did. Please believe me," sobbed Trixie.

Titrit had heard stories of such things, but in real life? Not likely. Still, she looked again toward the north. The shadow had grown more distinct. Maybe it was made up of separate elements, each moving on its own, like a flock of starlings seen at a distance. Could it be made up of dozens of ships? Was she only imagining it, or did she see masts, and oars that moved like wings flapping low to touch the water, propelling each vessel on toward Algiers along its own path and with its own rhythm?

"How can this be?" For a moment she was frozen, then shook herself into a place beyond belief or doubt to simply accept what she herself could see.

"You were right. We'd better find Itzak; he's the one who will know what to do."

"You believe me," Trixie sobbed. "Oh, Auntie Titrit," and she dissolved into tears.

"Of course, I believe you. But we can talk about that later. You'd better come along, to tell him what we both can see. Let's go this way — I'll help you over the wall. It would be best to keep quiet about the flying part. It is enough that we can see them coming from the terrace."

Itzak believed Titrit right away when she told him that a Christian armada was approaching. He had been anticipating this for a year, since the Spanish captured first Oran to the west, then Bougie to the east. He often wondered how long it would be until they came to Algiers.

He went with Titrit and Trixie to his terrace. From there, Titrit immediately saw that the ships were significantly closer than before. Those in the vanguard could anchor in the Bay within the hour.

"Stay with the girl," Itzak said urgently. "We have made plans for this. I must find Muhmed Reis and go to the Sea Gate with him. The watch will be sounding the cry any minute. Look after my family. I'll tell Nouri and Fatima to go over to your house and to send Samir to meet me by the Sea Gate."

Concerned as she was about the arrival of the ships, Titrit stooped down and held her young niece at arms' length and stared deeply into her eyes.

"What did you mean when you said you flew?"

"I don't know exactly, Auntie. It was like I was a bird. I just flew out over the sea, and I saw that the ships were headed our way."

"Don't say a word about this to anyone else, Trixie. You may have a gift, but there are dangers that go along with such a power."

"It didn't feel dangerous."

"That may be. We shall have to talk with Mayam. But I have heard that those who transform as you describe can become stuck in the new body, or badly injured, or even killed. I just don't know. This is beyond my experience."

"I don't want to die, Titrit. And I don't want to become a bird. I just want to be Trixie, and to see my mother and my baby brother Faisel."

"Can you promise me you'll say nothing more of this to anyone, and that you will never do it again until you have a teacher who knows about these things?"

"Oh, yes, of course I can promise to say nothing about it. No one believes me anyway. But I don't know how to stop from having it happen again. I didn't TRY to do this. It was easy and didn't feel dangerous at all. I became a little girl again by just thinking it."

"All right, then I won't force you to make a promise you don't think you can keep, but please, Trixie, just try not to do it again. Remember, it could be dangerous."

"Would Musa be angry if he knew?"

"Oh, yes, he would be VERY angry."

"Well, he is dangerous when he is angry, and he is already mad at me. I will try hard to stay out of trouble and be just a regular little girl. It hurts Mother when she sees Musa upset with me."

"Good girl. We have a deal. Now we have to get back to Tazrut."

"Will Musa still be with her?"

"I don't know, dear. I can't promise one way or the other. We will just have to be brave and strong, whatever we find."

"I can wish for an urgent message from Itzak telling him that the armada is on its way, and that he should carry out the plans they had agreed upon."

Titrit stared at the little girl, remembering how Mayam had received a mental message, five months earlier, that Tazrut was pregnant and ill. "Perhaps that would be a good idea, dear," she said seriously. "That's just the right thing to do."

High Spanish galleons, galleys with double rows of oars, carracks, galliots, and giant galleasses, all were converging on Algiers. From Itzak's angle it seemed there was no water between them, just a huge city of wooden constructions heaving on the surface of the sea, jockeying for space, trimming their sails, wielding their oars. Most had a single cannon, larger than any he had ever seen, in their prows.

As he watched, mesmerized, from his spot on the ramparts near the Sea Gate, cries and alarms rang forth from every minaret, rolling out over the walls of the city and echoing along the narrow streets within. Moments later, Itzak's colleague, Muhmed Reis, arrived and assured him that Musa was on his way to the casbah to alert the Baldi council.

"Good," Itzak acknowledged. "The old guard better remember our needs as well as theirs. When an envoy arrives from the fleet, as I'm sure he will, you and I shall lead him to the casbah. Just pray that both sides are reasonable, and we can avoid the worst."

As he spoke, a huge transport ship backed up to the largest of the craggy islands in the bay. The deck swarmed with workers - not soldiers, he noted. This was it. They had decided to erect a fort on the old ruins. No surprise there. Perhaps they could avoid a deadly siege.

He went through a swift calculation. Thanks to the unique location of these undistinguished rocks, even a small garrison could control the entire port. The Spanish had proved this in other bays, where they called the stronghold the Peñón, the Rock. With little expenditure or effort, a handful of Christian soldiers could dominate a city without occupying or destroying it.

He felt a glimmer of hope. If their lives were spared, they could gain time to build an effective resistance through bringing more manpower and weapons to Algiers. The first would beget the second. Young men from Andalusia with a knowledge of firearms and a hatred of Christians, that was what they needed. Many, like Itzak himself and his brother Musa, were eager to escape the harsh restrictions imposed by Ferdinand and Isabella after their conquest of Granada in 1492.

Citizens of Algiers were joining Itzak and Muhmed atop the ramparts in response to the alarms. Samir was among them, pushing his way through the crowd to them. "This sight is too familiar," he sighed as he gazed at the armada. "It looks like last year at Bougie."

"Let us hope they are here to build, not to raze."

"My guess is that they only want to create a strong fort for the King's garrison," responded Samir, "so that we will be in the shadow of their cannons for the rest of our lives, while they move on to other projects. Algiers is a minor port, compared to Oran or Bougie."

"Must we submit?"

"They must have thousands of soldiers on those ships. Even without support from local tribes, they could destroy us. We have only a few thousand poorly armed men with neither training nor leadership.

"We can only survive by biding our time. If you and your fellows keep bringing Moriscos to Algiers, we could build a new society right under their noses. Our people will flourish."

"Well, here they come," said Itzak, pointing to a pinnace being lowered from the largest galley. "Soon we will know what they want from us. I'm going down; are you with me?"

Samir and Muhmed nodded their agreement, and the three pushed their way down to the wharf. Muhmed caught the line when the small craft arrived and secured it to a metal ring near the gate, then helped four elegantly dressed courtiers climb awkwardly over the gunwales. Itzak gave them time to regain their dignity before greeting them in Grenadian Spanish and asking if he could be of service. They responded with contempt which he felt was directed both toward himself as a Moor who had fled their land and toward this run-down little city by the sea.

"As you can see, we are unloading supplies," said the first to disembark, gesturing to the carrack now anchored off the craggy rock in the bay while small, shallow-hulled boats rowed between ship and rock. "We will construct a modern fort out of the ruins. If your Sultan agrees to our terms, we will establish a garrison and leave you in peace. You can do nothing to stop us. We would scatter you like pesky flies whisked aside by a stallion's tail."

"And if we have no sultan," asked Itzak. "Since you chased Sultan Abdelaziz from Bougie last year, we have been a free port with only our Baldi Council of Elders for governance. We pay tribute to none."

"Then take us to the Baldi, but you must know that our King will require a peer to sign a treaty, one who can be held accountable if his subjects don't fulfill their obligations. Abdelaziz fled to the mountains rather than meet with us, and you no doubt have heard what happened to the people who stayed behind."

"I am a mere merchant and know nothing of these things," replied Itzak disingenuously. "I shall show you the way to the casbah. The council should be prepared to receive you."

"If they are nothing but a group of elderly Moors, this will be a problem."

"Your excellency, as you can tell from my accent, I was born in your country but have lived here all of my adult life. Perhaps I can accompany you and serve as advisor and translator. Tell our elders who might be acceptable as our leader. I am sure they will accommodate your suggestions."

As he looked around to say goodbye to his father-in-law, he realized that the old man had disappeared into the gathered crowd. He was not surprised. Samir remained loyal to Sultan Abdelaziz. This envoy represented his sworn enemy, and he did not want the Christians to recognize him as an organizer of local opposition.

"Come, Muhmed, we shall show them the way," said Itzak.

As Itzak expected, the elders of Algiers proclaimed their cordial feelings toward King Ferdinand. Of course, they said, they would be happy to send an annual tribute, if the amount was reasonable and within their means.

"You will provide whatever he requests," the envoy responded, "whether you consider it 'reasonable' or not. Our king wants assurance from your city, but also from all the tribes within two days' ride from here, that they will be at peace with our kingdom.

"Furthermore, we hear that Emir Salem ibn Toumi has an excellent cavalry at his disposal on your Plain of Mettajia. Install him as your emir, and we shall take him back with us to negotiate with our king."

The envoy turned with a flourish, followed by his entourage. On his way out, he gestured for Itzak to accompany him.

Within days, Salem ibn Toumi, the Arab emir from the plains of Mettajia, had been established as the puppet Emir of Algiers. The Spanish envoy suggested that he choose Itzak as a translator who knew the culture as well as the language. Samir was delighted.

"You will be my ears and eyes across the sea," Itzak's father-in-law said when he learned Itzak had been appointed to accompany Emir Salem to Spain. "Listen carefully and learn all that you can in the Spanish court, not only about the Maghreb, but also about currents that suggest trouble in Europe: how does King Ferdinand feel about his son-in-law, Henry VIII of England? Or King Louis XII of France and his claims on Milan?

Or Pope Julius II and his fear of a French invasion? For the present, Algiers is but a backwater concern for these great rulers, but to achieve the status that I imagine for us in the future, we must understand what is happening on both sides of the Mediterranean."

"You mean that you want me to be your spy."

"That is one way to put it. I would prefer that you think of yourself as my 'gatherer of information.' We are both intellectuals. Curiosity is in our blood. And that leads me to another point. I have been hearing rumors about thousands of books in Arabic that are hidden from the Inquisition. So far, they have been spared the fires that Cardinal Ximenes lights with such enthusiasm. Second only to ensuring the safety of my daughter Nouri and her son Beni, I would like to rescue those irreplaceable documents of our culture. They are said to include some of the finest medical, scientific, and literary works ever written in our language. If you could bring them here, you would be the savior of a significant part of the history of our people."

"How could I possibly get permission to bring them back?"

"I can provide you with contacts who will obtain permission for you to move freely about the country. You will need to use all your ingenuity to get them out. I can think of no better instrument of Allah for this task than you, my son. Go with my blessing."

Itzak dreaded telling Nouri about the trip. He thought of her as she had been when he first met her in Bougie, as bold and opinionated as a young boy who joined conversations between Itzak and Samir as their equal. He fell in love with her for that, as much as for her beauty.

She ran up to him as he entered the family quarters. "Thank goodness you are here. Will the new emir agree to the terms of the treaty?"

"Of course," Itzak answered curtly. "That's why he was chosen, after all." He heard himself sounding like Musa and was appalled. He must try harder to stay calm. He had to go on this trip; he was determined, but it was asking a lot from her to let him go for two months when the military situation was so tenuous; how could he even ask it of her?

"It's so hard being a woman in times like these," she said." I wish I could come with you to your meetings and help in some way."

He softened at her earnestness. "I know. You were educated like a man. But now you are a mother. Your job is to keep Beni safe."

"Thank goodness he is too young to understand what is going on. I can see how much harder it is on Trixie. She spends most of her time on the terrace watching the men work on the island. She knows what happened in Bougie and worries that it could happen here."

"We all share that concern. But your father and I both think that we are going to be lucky. The envoy says that if the emir signs the treaty, they will finish the fort and leave a garrison of a few hundred soldiers behind - as long as we pay the tribute they ask."

"Do you think it will go smoothly?"

"I certainly hope so, though there is something I do have to tell you." He took a deep breath. "The emir has asked me to come along as translator and diplomat."

"You didn't say yes, surely..."

"But I did, and Samir thinks it is a good idea."

"What about me? And Beni?"

"Samir will be here with you. And you have your new family, not to mention Fatima. You will never be alone when you have your old nanny with you. There is nothing I would like better than to take you along with me. I could show you my homeland, and we could go together to see the villa that I fled so long ago. But you are needed here, not only for Beni, but also for Fatima and Samir. Both are growing old; they need you to care for them as much as they ever cared for you."

"I should have known when I married you," she cried. "Why did I think a corsair would be be content staying at home with his family? You fled Granada to come here, and you were on an adventure to Bougie when I met you. Of course, you won't turn this down. And I know in my heart that if I were a man, I wouldn't turn it down either. My tears are more of frustration than rage," she sobbed as he embraced her.

"I understand, dearest one. You know this is in the service of our people and addresses issues that are your father's greatest concerns. But just as important for me, I go in search of ghosts."

"Your lost family?"

"Exactly. Musa and I abandoned our parents and our sisters when we left home, and by the time we got back to rescue them, it was too late. I can never redeem myself, but perhaps I can learn something more about what happened to them. I've been to Fez; no one had heard of them there. Perhaps someone in Granada will have learned more over the years."

She grew silent.

"I understand this is hard for you," he added. "I married you for your beauty and your intelligence, but also for your courage. You and Samir together can take care of things here. Since it is destined that we stay in Algiers, let us establish ourselves in every way we can. We must build a better life for our son. I will come back with a treasure trove of books and manuscripts to make up for those burned by the Christians in Oran and Bougie. Algiers represents the future for our people as well as for our family."

15. Treasures from Spain

Grapes had shrivelled into raisins on the drying racks, but Itzak had not yet returned from his trip to Spain. Those who left with him signed the treaty and returned, but he was not back. Nouri said that he had stayed on to collect the books that had been hidden from the Inquisitors and was arranging their delivery to his ship. Trixie was worried. She'd heard stories about the inquisitors whispered among the slaves.

On a day in late November, Trixie finally saw the familiar silhouette of Itzak's ship far out at sea. She rushed down the stairs to share the news with her mother. When she reached the door to Tazrut's room, she stopped to calm herself. It would be dark and silent inside, and her mother might be sleeping. She rapped lightly and heard Tazrut's faint response, so she eased in as quietly as she could.

"Is that you, Trixie?"

"Yes, Ummi. I have some wonderful news," she said as she stepped forward. To her surprise, her mother was sitting on a divan sipping tea. She walked over and sat on a cushion at her feet.

"And what is your news, my dearest?"

"Itzak's ship is arriving; I saw it out near the horizon. They must be planning to sneak their cargo in through the Bab al-Wad."

"Ah, they are very wise, and you are very excited," said Tazrut, stroking her daughter's head.

"Oh, yes. He carries a treasure, thousands of books. Now that Nouri is teaching me the alphabet, I will be able to read all of them by my seventh birthday."

"Well, perhaps not all of them. I am happy that you are learning to read, but…"

"Yes, I know. But don't brag about it, and don't mention it to Baba Musa unless I have to."

"It is good that you understand…"

"Because we don't want him to get angry. I know. He will be proud when Faisel learns to read, but he might not think a girl should. And now, Ummi, when can I go to see Itzak? Nouri and Samir both said that they will let me see the books when they arrive."

"Dear, impatient girl. You must calm down. The ship has not even landed yet, so the books haven't been unloaded, much less carried to Itzak's house and unpacked…"

"Yes, yes, of course, you are right…"

"And you should give Itzak a chance to reunite with his family. If you are excited, just think how Beni must feel. He hasn't seen his father in many months."

'Oh, it's so hard to be reasonable,' thought Trixie, 'but I must try.' Looking down at her hands to conceal her impatience, she said, "When can we go over?"

"As soon as we are invited."

"Then you will come too?"

"Yes, I think I am strong enough now. We shall celebrate Itzak's return and to inspect the books as well."

"If only Titrit were here, everything would be perfect."

"If only, my dear. But we must be grateful for the family that we have near-by."

"Someday I will go to Titrit's village and see her, and my Grandma Mayam too."

"I think you probably will, but not until you are a bit older."

"That will be a wonderful day. Will you come with me?"

"I think not, but I will celebrate your departure but rejoice at your return even more."

Itzak gave careful orders for the delivery of his precious cargo. Eager as he was to rush ahead to greet his wife, father-in-law, and son, he knew this was would be a delicate part of his adventure, requiring diplomacy, tact, and a well-placed bribe, big enough to convince the guards to let him through but not so big that they would become suspicious. They wouldn't bring it all at once.

He was in good luck. He had feared the Spanish might already have placed armed guards at all the gates of the city, but he saw some old friends stationed there, along with a Beni Tatije or two he that he didn't know. They all greeted him warmly and asked what he had done in Spain to keep him so much longer than the others. "Ah, business for my brother, of course. We still have contacts in Granada. I have boxes and boxes on board. A little bit of this, a little bit of that, mostly books. My crew shall be carrying things through for the rest of the day and perhaps into the night. I'll be sending donkeys down for them. Here's for your help in providing protection. I'm leaving Muhmed Reis with them to supervise, for I'm eager to see my family."

The guards smiled, knowing well that he had a beautiful wife, and waved him on his way.

Itzak swelled with pride when he saw Beni, grown so big in just the few months he had been away, and Nouri, as strong and beautiful as ever. If she harbored any resentment about his absence, she didn't show it. All this he owed to the generosity and wisdom of one man, he thought: Samir Mazigh.

After Itzak took care to re-connect with his wife and son, he and Samir found time to be alone in the library. They seated themselves on cushions amid the piles of boxes, happily ignoring the more comfortable seating areas of the house to indulge in the pleasure of sitting among their priceless acquisitions. They ordered Joseph, the Kabyle houseboy, to bring them a special treat, coffee brewed from freshly ground beans Samir had acquired from a Tunisian colleague.

"And now, my son," said Samir, "I know we shall spend months, if not years, sorting and admiring our treasure. First let me tell you about things here in Algiers. Then I will be most eager to hear what you learned on your journey."

"I saw enough of our so-called emir while in Spain with him. My guess is that things are not running too smoothly in Algiers," answered Itzak.

Samir rolled his eyes with comic exaggeration. "It is probably even worse than you imagine. His cronies have forced the old Baldi leaders to leave their posts, but he hasn't appointed anyone to take their places. The water system, for example. And supervision of the dung collectors. His men demand exorbitant bribes and provide no services. They seem to believe that water comes into the city and dung goes out on magic carpets supervised by djinn."

"That is bad news at a time when we need to come together to deal with the Christian threat. How is Musa doing?"

"He complains that his ships have to submit to inspection, but I think he prefers dealing with the Spanish rather than the Arabs, whom he considers to be larcenous fools. Many of your corsair colleagues have gone to Shershell to join Kara Hasan. They grew tired of being harassed by the soldiers who rowed over from the Peñón to enjoy the city; even worse, they hated to have to sneak out at night and drag their ships from hiding among the trees along the beach a mile north of the city. It's bad enough that the Beni Tatije guards let no one through the gates without a search and a hefty bribe, but it's even worse that we can't use our local beaches to build or repair ships without the threat of a bombardment."

"Sounds like I was in luck this afternoon. Most of the guards were old friend, hardly a Beni Tatije among them. Still I gave a good bribe and left Muhmed to deal with the details. Sound like I'll have to stick to legitimate trade in the future and work harder than ever to make it pay."

"Indeed. But we have months in which to plan all that. What did you learn about the larger picture during your time in Spain?"

"Enough to realize that we are but a side story to the events that have the attention of King Ferdinand. He's pursuing his strategy of conquering ports and building presidios here in the Maghreb, but meanwhile, France has moved to take some of his holdings in Italy. With all the new wealth from the Indies, Ferdinand can afford these battles, but they are distracting him from his interest here."

"Meanwhile, your old friend Arouj is complicating things. Ferdinand never knows when a small fleet of galliots out of Halq al-Wad will appear to harass his troop ships or raid his villages anywhere between Tunis and Genoa."

"Everyone in Spain was complaining because Cardinal Ximenes and Pedro Navarro were building forts from Oran to Tripoli while Barbarossa was aiding the French, whether that was his intention or not. It made me wonder why the king didn't go after the pirates instead of investing so much time and effort capturing cities along the coast."

"Arouj is an allusive target," Samir reminded him. "He doesn't follow regular shipping lanes; he lurks behind bluffs waiting to attack passing ships, or he raids an unprotected village just because he knows there are no armed men to defend it. He can easily outrun their large war ships in his light galliots."

"Ferdinand seems to forget that Turkish corsairs are not revenge-motivated Morisco. They are just looking for wealth and power no matter where they find it. The King of Spain means no more or no less to them than the King of France or the Pope in Rome. If Henry VIII sailed down from England, he would mean nothing more to Arouj than the others. If Ferdinand shares Cardinal Ximenes's desire to conduct a crusade throughout the Maghreb, he'd better recognize that the Turks are not Moors or Berbers either one. They have ships and artillery and know how to use them."

"Perhaps that has something to do with Arouj's move from Halq al-Wad to Djerba."

Itzak was surprised. "I hadn't heard that. I knew Djerba was the one place that successfully fought off the Spanish assault, but I did not know that Arouj had moved there."

"From what my agents can tell me, Sultan Muhammad seemed to have mixed feelings about it. He considers Djerba to be his, but he did does not dare alienate the Spanish. They by-passed Halq al-Wad and Tunis on their way collecting ports along the coast. He may have come up with the perfect solution: by sending the Barbarossas to Djerba, he simultaneously gets rid of them at Halq al-Wad and increases the chances the Spain won't win Djerba next time they try for it. But it is also possible that Arouj came up with the idea on his own."

"You mean he wanted a place to rule?"

"Exactly. Unlike our Emir in Algiers, Arouj could never be a puppet of King Ferdinand and was unhappy paying such a large share of his take to Sultan Muhammad V. His only loyalty is to his own men. He might make a credible sultan, in Djerba or elsewhere. I've been told that he received a hero's welcome when he arrived there, and he didn't have anything to do with their victory. It takes a gifted commander to get credit when he has not even been present for a battle."

Part Three: The Spanish Presence, 1512-1516

16. The New Order: 1511-12

After one year, Trixie still found the presence of the Christian soldiers both frightening and fascinating. She had heard that their many cannon could shoot balls far enough to reach into the city or damage ships pulled up on the beach, though she had not seen that rumor proven. She understood that the invasions of Oran and Bougie had been catastrophic for the people who lived in those cities, but for her, little had changed, except for the presence of the fort and its soldiers.

At six-years-old, she was big enough to go on her own to visit Beni next door by climbing over the low wall between the terraces. She was drawn there by the many books and scrolls that Itzak and Samir were still unpacking and cataloging in the library. She remembered the afternoon, right after Itzak had returned with his treasures from Spain the year before, when she had asked Nouri how she could learn to read.

"I can teach you," Nouri had answered. She brought out a large sheet of parchment and wrote out the entire Arabic alphabet and started to teach her the letters that very day. When Trixie got home, she shared the exciting news with her mother. Tazrut swore her to secrecy, telling her that Musa must never know, but then she hugged the girl tightly, called Emilia, and ordered the slave to run to the souk to buy a slate so Trixie could practice her lessons.

From that day on, Trixie had gone next door almost daily. She mastered the alphabet and was making progress with reading easy Arabic passages. Through the winter, she had often asked for permission to help Itzak and Samir unpack the books and scrolls from their great trunks. Beni sometimes tagged along, but he was quickly bored and left. She, on the other hand, loved the hours she spent listening to the men talk of the far-away places the books had come from: Granada, Castile, Toledo, Barcelona; she loved the sound of each of the names, but most especially she loved the sound of "Al Andalus," for her a semi-legendary land that her father Musa and Uncle Itzak had fled before she was born. The King and Queen of Spain followed the advice of a wicked advisor who wore a scarlet cape and hat. He convinced them to pursue any Muslim who would not convert to Christianity, even if they fled across the sea to the Maghreb. It all seemed like an adventure story to her.

She was glad that Algiers had given up without a fight, so they hadn't been slaughtered like the people of Oran or chased into the mountains like the people of Bougie. The man in red, Cardinal Ximenes, would have had all these books that she loved so much burned in the square in front of the mosque, and the mosque itself would have been converted into a church.

As the summer of 1511 progressed, Nouri became heavy with child. She was sometimes too tired to take as much care in preparing exercises as she had before, so Trixie started to teach Beni the alphabet. He wasn't really interested, so she took him out to the kitchen garden, where the path was covered with sand, and used a stick to draw the graceful letters of Arabic script. Beni enjoyed that. Soon he happily held the chalk and made circles and lines on Trixie's slate. He even identified the letters when she wrote them.

After his baby brother, Ali, was born in late August, Beni grew tired of his lessons and said that he wanted to go back to see his mother. Trixie thought he was sad because Nouri seemed to love the new baby more than him; she knew what it was like to have a baby brother.

Alone in Beni's house and not wanting to return home to her own mother and brother, she often went to the library where Itzak and Samir spent their time sorting through their many trunks. They taught her how to unpack and handle the books, which were sometimes fragile, and told her how to put each book on a special shelf to be catalogued. She was careful to be very quiet so that they would not mind her presence. They often seemed to forget she was there, and she was as content as she had ever been. As the year went by, she found she didn't even notice the presence of the Spanish soldiers.

When Samir left on a trip to Nahla only two months after baby Ali was born, Trixie could tell that Itzak missed him. When she stopped by the library, he would chat with her more than before. She was flattered by his attention and fascinated by the stories he told her about his travels. Her favorite was about how he met Nouri and fell in love with her. She didn't have a concept of romance, and she was always amazed at the way people in Beni's house seemed to feel about each other. She realized that Emilia might be that way, underneath, but she had to appear tough. She was a slave, after all.

Itzak told her how he had gone to learn about shipbuilding from Arouj Reis.

"You've met Barbarossa?" She could hardly believe it, as though he was claiming to have met a man from a fairy tale.

"I know him very well, and his brothers, too."

"Emilia says they are the meanest pirates in the world.'"

Itzak laughed. "To tell you the truth, Trixie, I would not want to get in a fight with any of the three, but they are excellent sea men, even Isaac, though he isn't as passionate about ships as Arouj and Khizr. But we can't call them pirates any more. Arouj has been Sultan of Djerba for more than a year now, so they have become respectable citizens of the world, all three."

The day Samir returned, Trixie could overhear the two men talking together as she carefully lifted books from a trunk, looked them over, and placed them on the shelves. She found their voices comforting, even when she didn't pay much attention to what they were saying.

She opened a trunk and discovered that all the books had names like "The World Geography" and "Picture Book of the World." The pages were filled with drawings of strange shapes labeled with the names of places she had heard of, like Al Andalus, Granada, Maghreb, and Algiers, and places she hadn't heard of, like Egypt, the Nile, and China. She wanted to ask the men what they meant, but she saw that they were talking intently with each other and wouldn't want to be interrupted.

"Now that he is Sultan of Djerba, he is bolder than ever," Samir was saying. "He spent the past summer harassing Spanish holdings in Italy. He caused a lot of disruption around Naples..."

That got Trixie's attention. Naples was where Emilia came from. She listened carefully as Samir went on.

"Ships couldn't safely come and go from the harbor because of him. Fishermen couldn't set out in the morning, so the market had no fish to sell, and the people had no fish to eat. The villagers had to keep watchmen on every hilltop to warn farmers if ships were coming. Still, the corsairs often grabbed men in their fields and carried them off to the slave market in Tunis."

Trixie kept quiet. She had heard about such things from Fatima and Emilia, who both said that "Barbarossa" was the Devil himself.

"The brothers are spending this winter expanding their fleet in Djerba," Samir told Itzak.

"What do you hear about how the refugees from Bougie are getting along in Kaala? Are they welcomed by their neighbors?"

"Abdelaziz is gathering allies. Many great warrior tribes, like the Zouave, are backing him. It is rumored that his army may be ready to attack Bougie next summer."

"He is a fool if he tries it. The Spanish have cannon in their fort and musketeers among their troops. Abdelaziz doesn't have any artillery. Furthermore, he would not have a navy to blockade the harbor; he has no ships."

"Ah, but what if Abdelaziz acquires an ally with a fleet?"

"You mean Arouj? You were talking about Abdelaziz getting his help three years ago. He would be a dangerous ally. Remember, I spent time with the man. He is a brilliant strategist but wild at heart. I would not trust him."

"Much has changed. Since becoming Sultan of Djerba, he has increased in wealth and influence. Corsairs are flocking to join him. He has a fleet of a dozen ships plus cannon and muskets, even creating his own gunpowder. With his help, Sultan Abdelaziz could regain control of Bougie and, allied with Tunis, control all the Eastern Maghreb."

"You may be right. Ferdinand left only a small garrison behind. If Abdelaziz had support from the sea and cannon, he might stand a chance."

A strange chill came over Trixie. They were not talking to her at all, and yet she felt that every word was somehow about her. Samir had returned from Nahla with news that threatened the quiet pleasures of this library. She knew in her heart that war would return, not only in Bougie, but also in Algiers and even Oran, and it would be Arouj who would bring it.

17. A Far-Off Battle Hits Home

In the summer of 1512, Titrit was enjoying the late afternoon sun while grinding barley with her mortar and pestle, when Meddur rode up. He tied his pony outside the house and headed inside, gesturing her to follow. She knew something important had happened; she had heard him tell Mayam that he would be gone for two nights, and here he was back on the same day, looking agitated.

"On my way through Bab Azzoun," he said, as soon as he saw Mayam, "I saw a donkey caravan that looked like Samir's. I asked one of the drivers if he was returning from Nahla with Samir Mazigh. He said he was. 'We have been there and back in just a few weeks' time,' he told me. 'Our master did not seem to like what he was learning and ordered us home ahead of schedule, pushing us to exhaustion on the way.'

"When I asked him what it was that upset Samir, he said he wasn't sure that he should talk about what they had heard. It didn't take much of a bribe to get the news."

"And the news was…" Mayam asked sharply.

"That Sultan Abdelaziz has marched on Bougie with a big army collected in the mountains, while Arouj Reis blockaded the port with a fleet of a dozen armed ships."

"Well, tell us," demanded Titrit. "Is it over?"

"I hope what I heard was mistaken," Meddur stalled.

"Just tell us," Mayam declared. "We already know Abdelaziz must have lost, or you wouldn't be so reluctant to speak."

"This is what I heard. That the cannon breached the wall of the fort, and Arouj rushed through the gaping hole, sword raised, waving his men to follow. Suddenly, he collapsed in front of them. The men forgot the battle and thought only of saving their Baba and getting him to a good physician."

Both women were silent, so Meddur continued. "They carried him off to Tunis. The whole fleet abandoned the fight. They say that his arm was blown off, though I don't know if that is true. At any rate, it was over. Abdelaziz and his army fled back to the mountains. The siege ended in disaster."

Mayam sat still when he was done. Titrit and Meddur waited for her to speak.

"Forces are shifting," she said at last. "We have Spaniards occupying ports from the West and, now that Arouj is Sultan of Djerba, Turks encroaching from the East. Not since Dihya Kahina's day have we seen such threats from outsiders. These battles may seem far from Jadizi, but they involve us. We must consider all the tribes in the mountains, from here to Bougie and from Tunis to Djerba, our kinsmen, for we share a common enemy.

"Modern times require wider knowledge the world than in Dihya Kahina's time. I believe my granddaughter Sycorax has been chosen to serve our people in the future. She represents the best of our two strands, those who went to Al Andalus, whom the Christian call Moors, and those who stayed in the Maghreb, we Amazigh, whom they call Berbers. She must be taught the lessons learned on both sides of the sea. Itzak and Samir are teaching her about Algiers and Spain. You and I will prepare her with the wisdom of the Goddess, when it is our turn to take over her training."

Listening to this speech, Titrit heard an echo of her mother's voice from seven years earlier:

> *Your destiny is to watch over your sister and her daughter.*
> *Look upon no man, except for momentary pleasure. Think not of*
> *having a child, unless you are prepared to leave it here with me.*
> *You must watch out for your sister, and if evil befalls Tazrut,*
> *tutor Sycorax in the ways of revenge. His own child shall turn*
> *against him and plague him all his days.*

It seemed her role would be more demanding than she had thought. Trixie might have to take revenge on far more than just her father. Titrit didn't mind doing without a husband; she had already enjoyed several pleasant dalliances with men and seemed to enjoy them more because they would not end in a long and contentious commitment. She could never make a choice like Tazrut's, to submit to the will of another. But she could imagine partnerships like those she had seen between Mayam and her companions. She remembered a petulant pretty-boy who lived with them in her childhood. He presumed that his role as Mayam's lover assured him status among the village elders. When he tried to tell Mayam what she should do, she dismissed him immediately, and when he tried to raise a faction against her, he was driven from Jadizi.

But now Titrit was twenty-seven years old and thinking about having a baby of her own, her role as protector of Tazrut and Sycorax was about to become much more challenging.

"She is so young," said Titrit aloud to her mother. 'And I am getting so old,' she said to herself.

The next day, Titrit went down to Algiers. She spent time with Tazrut and even tried to interest Faisel in conversation, but he ignored her, as usual. Everyone seemed to think things were perfectly normal. She almost wondered if Meddur's information had been mistaken, of if Samir had withheld the news from the women and children. Rather than ask Tazrut about it, she contrived to get Trixie alone by suggesting they go up to the rooftop terrace together.

"Have you something to tell me," Titrit asked as soon as they were alone.

Trixie looked startled at the question but answered earnestly. "Yes. It happened again."

"You transformed into a bird and flew?"

"No, I became a spider and listened to the grown-ups talk about the siege at Bougie. While I felt I was a spider, they all looked like animals too, but not in a scary way. That part was fun."

"What part was not fun?"

"When Samir described the battle, he came to the part where Barbarossa, I mean Arouj, had his arm blown off. I felt it in my own body, as though I had a terrible injury. I remembered what you had told me, and I was afraid I could get stuck, but as you see, I didn't. Still, it was scary. I was afraid to sleep last night. I knew I'd have nightmares."

"Mayam thinks you will someday have a role in these affairs."

"Why me? I'm only a little girl."

"We cannot know why, only that it is your fate. Some day you will come to Jadizi to study with Mayam and me, but for now it is best that you stay here, to learn as much as you can about Spain as well as Algiers and Kabylia. We are lucky that Samir has come into your life. He has a subtle knowledge of all these affairs. He and Itzak will be good teachers for you until it is time for you to come to the mountains and live with us."

Three months after Titrit's visit, Emilia burst into Trixie's room unannounced and declared, "Wait 'till I tell you the story I heard at the souk, Miss Spider."

"I'm sorry I ever told you about that," Trixie retorted. "Now all you do is mock me."

"I'm not mocking you, just teasing," apologized Emilia. "What do you expect after your wild tale about turning into a spider and watching Arouj lose his arm in battle? You are either lying or crazy, and I know you too well to think you are crazy.

Besides, I don't consider it a lie. Just an exaggeration. I've heard you tell too many wild tales to Beni to be surprised. Though I wouldn't have guessed you'd choose a spider; a crow, more likely, because they are known to be spies."

"If I could turn myself into a crow, I'd have followed you to the souk and I'd already know your story, but here I am, just a girl stuck at home in my own body. What have you heard?"

"Well, my friend Enrico…"

"The cobbler?"

"How many Enricos do we know who have a shop in the souk?"

"I thought your friend Enrico was the slave of Mustafa ibn-Ismail."

"He is, but his master lets him earn extra money on his own. I think he counts on him to be his ears and eyes at the souk. Enrico understands many languages and reports everything back to Mustafa."

"Like a crow. What is the amazing story that your friend, this spy for Mustafa, has told you this time?"

"It's about the Barbarossas."

"What can they have done? Surely Arouj isn't back causing trouble already. Last I heard they didn't know if he would live or die."

"His brother Khizr is still well enough to be a problem. In fact, he started it as soon as he left Bougie, before he even got back to Tunis. It would be enough to make Arouj furious, if he isn't too weak to care."

"What happened?"

"Well, when he sailed out of Bougie, Khizr just happened to wander a bit north into the straights of Sicily, and he happened to run across a merchant ship from Genoa. Of course, he couldn't resist capturing it."

"That should make Arouj happy."

"Perhaps, but in this instance, Genoa decided to teach the Barbarossas a lesson. They put together their own armada and sailed off to Halq al-Wad to destroy the Turkish pirates."

"What happened?"

"Khizr had no warning until someone at the fort at the mouth of the gullet saw sails in the distance, but Khizr is a clever man and a quick thinker. He ordered his men to sink all his ships in the Lake of Tunis, which is apparently very shallow and has a muddy bottom."

"Why did he do that? Why not fight on the sea?"

"That sounds like a question Beni would ask. Because he didn't have time. In fact, Enrico said he only got to sink six of the twelve ships before the Genoese arrived at the Customs House. Khizr and his men dropped everything and ran for their lives across the causeway toward Tunis. The Genoese troops landed their men and the chase was on. I don't know how far it was to the gates of the city, but apparently only Khizr and a remnant made it there. He was lucky that they were allowed in. The Genoese didn't want a fight with Sultan Mohammad, so they turned back. They took the six ships they found at anchor plus the one Khizr had captured and headed home."

"No wonder Enrico says Arouj would be angry. Khizr lost the entire fleet plus the captured ship."

"But there is more."

"Khizr slunk off in shame?"

"Not at all. Enrico says that he raised the six ships from the mud, repaired them, loaded them with lumber, and headed for Djerba with all who were left of his men. Now he is using the lumber to build more ships. By the time Arouj is well enough to return to Djerba, the fleet will be as big as before."

"Wait until I tell Beni," said Trixie. "He'll love this story."

"Yes," commented Emilia, "but for once he'll want to play the role of Khizr rather than Arouj."

18. Hasan al-Wazzan From Fez

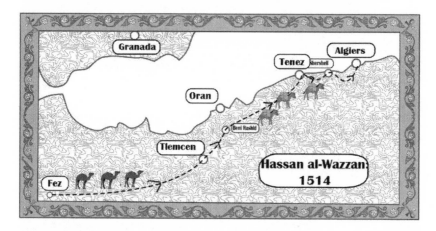

On Trixie's ninth birthday, she woke with a delightful sense of anticipation. She had seen a golden lion coming toward Algiers from the west. In the way of dreams, he continuously changed forms as he traveled along the caravan roads. Usually he was a human dressed like a high-ranking man of the Maghreb riding on a horse beautifully caparisoned in red felt decorated with a green pentagram. The wonderful thing was that at night he became a lion who explored his surroundings. Like a great cat, he prowled the desert around his campsite or the narrow streets of the city quarters near the inns and palaces in which he stayed. Sometimes he turned into a tradesman, or a beggar, or a scholar, a judge, or a holy man. Wherever he found himself among strangers, he engaged with them and learned their ways. If he was camping in the wilderness, he communed with the birds and beasts of the forest or desert. When he had time to himself, he took out his journals and wrote down all that he had seen, from the daily customs of the people to the produce and goods sold in the souk, the quality and abundance of the water, and the fruitfulness of the fields and orchards.

She ran into her mother's room, eager to report her wondrous dream.

"It was so real, Ummi, and he was on his way here, I'm sure."

"I am so glad you have had a happy dream," said Tazrut. "This must be a sign of good things to come."

"Oh, yes, I do think it is a sign. I know there is no real man like this, but just seeing him in my dreams gave me hope. I felt I could see the world through his eyes. I would like to do that. He was a man, but he was also an intelligent beast who could not be misled by the words of others, because he understood truth from their faces and gestures. I wonder if I will recognize him when he gets here."

"Silly girl. Dreams are not fulfilled in that sort of way. But perhaps a special man will come, and you will learn from him."

"I can't wait, Ummi, I can't wait. May I go over and tell Beni about it? He will be really interested."

Trixie thought of her lion dream the first time she saw Hasan al-Wazzan, envoy from the Sultan of Fez, at Itzak's house. She couldn't be sure; this man was young and playful, and his stories were so full of fantastical adventure, she wondered if he, like Emilia, might exaggerate a bit. She listened to him describe the Land of the Blacks, as he called the realm south of the great desert. He'd visited it on a trip by camel caravan to Timbuktu and then on to Cairo. She knew nothing about these exotic places except from a map she had discovered in a trunk from Granada. Hasan claimed to have traveled through the great desert before he was even twenty years old. He said he had been to battlefields with the Sultan of Fez when they went to see the progress of their wars against the Portuguese. And now he, a man who looked barely older than Itzak's houseboy Joseph, was on a mission across all the Moorish cities of North Africa to learn how they were coping with the threat of the Spanish presence along the coast.

Hasan spent his free time with Itzak and Samir in the library reading, sorting, and cataloging the books and manuscripts from Spain. Sometimes, after she finished a lesson with Nouri, she went to watch them unpack the trunks. Her favorite moments came whenever they lifted a large, illuminated book from a pile and placed it on a stand and allowed her to be the one to gently open it and turn the pages to reveal the beauties within. The images were sometimes stiff on the page, but they often seemed more real to her than the objects they represented in the world. Trees bending to follow the margin of the page; gilded fruit hanging from a branch as though waiting to be plucked by an angel; a plump sultan sitting on a cushioned throne surrounded and supported by Arabic lettering that swirled around him. She stared at a rose twining up a margin and reached out to touch the stem, then pulled back her hand, feeling as though a sharp thorn had pricked her finger. Text and image worked together to create in her sensations she had never felt before, beauty so great that it evoked a sense of the union between that which was without and that which was within.

Both Hasan and Samir encouraged Trixie's interest in calligraphy as well as her general eagerness to read and understand things. Samir happily brought out his calligraphic supplies and demonstrated his most elegant interpretations of his favorite blessing, Masha Allah, Glory be to God, for her. Then Hasan shared his own exotic styles for the same blessing. Trixie copied out his inscription and made a miniature scroll for herself to remind her that Allah is present in every wonderful thing.

"Let me bless that for you, so it will protect you from the evil eye," said Hasan al Wazzan in a half-joking tone.

"How can words drawn on a piece of paper protect me," she asked. "I see the amulets and talismans the women cling to, but I think they believe there is magic in words because they don't know how to read."

"That is a sensible response, young lady. You are quite right, as far as you go. But many holy men believe there is more than that, if only we could learn the secret. I lived for some days with a marabout who practiced a discipline involving figures, letters, and numbers. I learned from him that, more than the words, it is the attitude you bring to them that creates power. If you seek the deeper meaning in a passage, you become aware of Allah's presence in those words as in all things. In the same way, holy men finger their beads to calm themselves, but only the best of them are able to be present with the pain of the people who seek their help and thus be true healers."

She looked into his eyes. Yes, it was as she thought. They were golden brown, like those of a great lion. This was the man from her dream, she was now sure.

One day, Itzak was carefully removing books from a trunk that he'd opened for the first time, and Hasan was carefully creating a new variation on Masha Allah. Suddenly Itzak cried out, startling the others and causing Hasan's hand to slip so that the reed pen spread a wide swath of black ink across the page. Samir gasped and Trixie almost wept when she saw the beauty of Hasan's elegant lines ruined. She felt as though the word of God, even the beauty of nature, had been marred by a sacrilege. She looked toward Itzak. He held up a quarto volume with strange lettering on its cover.

"Look what I found when I pulled on a loose corner at the bottom of this trunk. It looks like Hebrew. Samir, what does it say?"

Samir and Hasan answered at the same time.

"Ha Torah," they exclaimed, for both had learned a bit of Hebrew while studying the Kabbalah.

Trixie rushed over, with the two men not far behind. They watched Itzak carefully lift an entire false bottom from the trunk. At least three dozen books were revealed to them, all in Hebrew. They took the volumes one at a time and inspected them carefully.

"I see those same letters on other books," Trixie said.

Itzak laughed. "This is your chance to learn a third alphabet. Hasan, can you teach her how to recognize these letters? Then she can help us with the sorting."

She quickly learned the word "Torah" and followed Samir's instructions by starting a neat pile of books that had those Hebrew letters in its title.

Suddenly there was an urgent knock on the library door.

It was Joseph.

"Samir, you must come immediately. One of your agents has arrived from Bougie. He says that Sultan Abdelaziz has returned to the city and is making preparations for a new siege. They're already bombarding the Spanish forts."

"Where is the agent? Why didn't you bring him here?"

"He was so exhausted that he fell asleep before I could say a word."

"I will awaken him immediately," Samir responded. "He will have time to sleep later. Hasan and Itzak, if you will excuse me," he apologized, "I will let you know everything as soon as I hear my man's report. Meanwhile, continue with your important business here."

"What extraordinary news," Hasan al-Wazzan said to Itzak after Samir had gone. "Are his sources reliable?"

"None more so."

"If it is true, I must go there as quickly as I can. My sultan will want to know all about the siege and how all factions feel about the Spanish presence."

The men seemed to have forgotten Trixie. She hoped for a moment that she would be invited to go along with them. For hours each day, she had been treated like an apprentice, allowed to handle the treasured books and even encouraged to read a new language. Would they just walk away from her now?

The two men decided to go to Samir's rooms to hear the news as soon as possible. She followed them out of the room. 'If they don't see me,' she thought, 'I can listen in on their meeting.' Then Itzak turned to lock the door and noticed her. "Go find Beni and play with him, Sycorax."

She knew what she wanted to do, and it wasn't to play with Beni. Would it be worth the risk of becoming stuck in the form of a spider? No, because she'd never get to Samir's quarters if she was that small. A sea gull would be too conspicuous in the house, but perhaps another kind bird; a crow? Too raucous. A dove. That would be perfect. They'd think it was from one of their own coops.

She had forgotten Titrit's warnings about the dangers of transformation by the time she had run up the stairs to the terrace, where she thought she could inconspicuously turn into a dove and fly past windows until she came to the right one. The men would never think it odd to have a dove perched on the outer sill. She would hear everything.

Nervous and excited, she emerged on the terrace -- and saw Beni leaning over the wall and pointing toward the Peñón with Faisel at his side. Her heart sank. Nouri and Tazrut lounged on carpets and pillows in the shade while Fatima and Emilia played with two-year-old Ali. She couldn't carry out her plan.

Beni was the first to notice her. "Look," he cried. "I was just telling Emilia that the soldiers on the Peñón are waving to us. I can tell that they are shouting something, but they are too far away to hear what it is. Come here, Trixie, and wave back to them."

Trixie went reluctantly. This was not a new game. Emilia had started it. Sometimes she waved a colored scarf at them, and they waved back. She didn't have time for such silliness now, but she seemed to have no choice. Then she had an idea.

"Come on, Beni, let's go down to see Ahmed," she suggested

"Ummi, may we? I'm old enough," Beni insisted

"I'll make sure he doesn't get into trouble," Trixie assured Nouri, "as long as Faisel doesn't have to come along; he's still too stubborn and never does what I say."

Nouri turned to Tazrut, who nodded her permission, then qualified it by saying, "Maybe we should send Emilia or Fatima along with them."

"That's a good idea. All right, you go ahead, but behave yourselves. Even Ahmed has a limit to his patience."

Trixie and Beni went down the stairs while Emilia and Fatima were still bickering over which of them should supervise. The children went directly to the kitchen and, as Trixie had hoped, found Joseph there, obviously in deep conversation with Ahmed.

"What's going on?" Trixie was sure they must know something and hoped they would with share it with her.

"We can only guess from who arrived and how he got here. This man is not a routine messenger from Nahla. He is a special courier all the way from Bougie."

"It's true," added Ahmed. "The man is Mustafa. I've known him since he was a boy. He would do anything for Samir."

"It's obvious that he rode hard to get here, and he was on a horse hired from a hostel along the way. It was about to drop from exhaustion, but he just handed the reins to a stable boy and ran up here. He looked like he hadn't slept for days."

At that moment, Emilia came in through the kitchen door. Seeing Trixie talking with Joseph and Ahmed, she immediately demanded, "What are you up to?"

"Something is going on in Bougie," Trixie answered.

"So that's it." Emilia's manner grew serious. "I'll find out as much as I can, don't you worry. Itzak is sure to tell Nouri. Fatima will overhear their conversation and I'll get her to tell me everything."

Trixie looked at her with a new respect. "You're like Samir," she said. "You gather information. What on earth do you do with all your knowledge? You're only a slave."

"That's just it, I have nothing but my wits and determination to help me survive. The more I know the better I can deal with things that are outside my control."

"Like me," Trixie said. "Children and slaves are alike that way."

She knew she had to resign herself to relying on others.

"Come on," Emilia said to Trixie and Beni, "We have to get to the family quarters. And you two," she said turning to Joseph and Ahmed, "I'll come back later to hear all you know."

That evening, before bed, Emilia slipped quietly into Trixie's room and whispered in her ear.

"We were right," she said. "The agent who galloped in was reporting on new fighting. It's not only Sultan Abdelaziz. Barbarossa came from Djerba to help by blockading the harbor and bringing his cannon to bombard the forts. They think they can get rid of the Spanish garrison this time."

Trixie nodded in response, but inwardly she was surprised. She thought Arouj would have learned his lesson the first time; it wasn't his city, after all.

Emilia put her finger to her lips and looked around like a conspirator before going on. "Not only that, but Hasan al-Wazzan said he would leave for Bougie as soon as he could say his formal goodbyes to Emir Salem, and Itzak said he wanted to go along. Then Samir said he did too."

Trixie gasped. Why would the men travel so far to see a war? She'd seen enough of it in her images of Arouj at the walls of Bougie.

Emilia ignored her and went on. "The men say they are going there to celebrate certain victory, but Nouri is afraid it will turn out like the last time, or worse. 'Cannon balls don't care where they land,' she said. 'The men are like young boys who don't realize they could die.' Then she chased me from the room. I wouldn't be surprised if she talked Itzak and Samir out of going. Neither one can bear to see her cry."

19. The Sultan of Djerba and Jijelli

In the end, Nouri convinced Itzak he should not go off on another long adventure, especially not one that included certain warfare and possible death. Samir, however, could not be dissuaded. "I'm sixty-one years old," he declared. "If Abdelaziz wins, I will celebrate the restoration of my beloved city. If I die at the siege, I will be content, for I will be at home. If I survive but the city is destroyed, I will be miserable, but at least I will have seen Bougie one last time."

Itzak couldn't suppress his frustration. "Here I am, a man in my prime, and I am forced to sit at home while you go off on a great adventure. How can I bear it? I love Bougie as much as you do."

"Never fear, my son. If the walls fall and the Spanish are expelled, you will join me there with our dearest Nouri and the boys. After we have re-taken the city, we will need young families to restore its former glory."

On the day before Samir's departure with Hasan al-Wazzan, all the slaves in the household were busy with last-minute packing. Even Samir's experienced caravan staff was in a flurry as they readied tents and supplies for the trip, which would entail five days of challenging mountainous travel. Samir planned a stop-over in Nahla, where he could rest and catch up on the latest news. He would have a good idea what to expect before he got to Bougie.

"Well, you two," Hasan said to Trixie and Beni on the last night, "I will miss you both."

"You don't have to go," responded Trixie. "Why would you want to visit a war anyway?"

"I know why," chimed in Beni. "Because it's exciting. Please let me come with you. I have asked Abba and Samir, but they said no. Maybe you could convince them."

Hasan laughed. "Sorry, Beni, you're not old enough. Even I didn't start going on long journeys until I was fifteen, and you are only six. Just wait, your turn will come. Remember, war is more than an exciting adventure. I learned that when my best friend died in my arms during a battle between my people and the Portuguese, and we were only observers in our Sultan's entourage. He's the sultan who sent me on this journey to meet all the Muslim rulers of the Maghreb and report how they get along with each other and what they think about outsiders. In other words, war is exactly what my sultan wants to hear about."

"But Fez is far away," Trixie pouted. "Why do you care what is going on in all these other places anyway?"

"We are all connected, Sycorax." When Hasan al-Wazzan called her by her full name, it made her feel very grown-up. She smiled at him, ready to believe everything he said.

"On your terrace you can watch the merchant ships arrive from distant ports. You can even see the soldiers from across the sea standing guard on the ramparts of a fort in your very own bay. When we let visitors in, we have to know whether we can trust them or not."

"That's why we have guards at our gates," said Beni.

"Exactly," answered Hasan. "In Fez the Portuguese pretend to support local leaders, but they are just using them until their power grows enough to take over. I fear that is what the Spanish are doing here in Algiers. They have defeated Oran and Bougie, desecrated the mosques, burned the books, and oppressed the people. At some point citizens must stand up to these outsiders, even at the risk of their lives."

"I'd just let in the good guys and tell my guards to cut off the heads of the bad guys," declared Beni.

"Ah, yes, my boy, but how would you tell them apart? The very wicked know how to disguise themselves and trick you into trusting them. Besides, there is more to it. Every city is made up of people who are both good and bad, but it is about belonging and having everyone do their share.

"Let me tell you a story:

Hasan al-Wazzan's Fable

Once there was a beautiful cormorant who could fly up in the air and swim under the sea. She lived in the land of the birds and often went to visit the land of the fish. She spent most of her time perched on a high rock with her shimmering wings spread wide to warm herself in the sun.

One day the tax collector for the sultan of the birds came to her and said, 'You must pay taxes for the privilege of living among us.'

'But I am not one of you,' she said. 'Are birds able to live under water?' With that, she plunged into the sea and swam, with bubbles streaming behind her, past the small minnows and out into the deeper ocean until she came to the land of the fishes. They recognized her and welcomed her. They did not care that she disappeared in the morning to devour minnows near the shore. When she was among them, she was cordial and charming, until one day the tax collector of the sultan of the fishes came to her and said, 'You must pay taxes for the privilege of living among us.'

'Why should I give you money,' she asked. 'I am not a fish. I can breathe air and fly in the sky.'

She swam to the surface of the sea, spread her wings, and flew away to the land of the birds.

'I am a bird after all,' she said.

"The moral of my tale is that we must all know who we are and pay what is due," Hasan al-Wazzan explained. "The bird wanted the benefits of living among others but preferred not to pay her share. That may seem like a good way to live, but society requires give and take. When she realized she would have to pay taxes wherever she lived, she decided to return to her own kind."

"But people can just leave if they don't like the ruler. Samir didn't like the Spanish who conquered Bougie, so he came to Algiers."

"Ah, yes, but in his heart, he is still with his people in Bougie. Sometimes it is necessary to fight back. For generations, our people in Andalusia fought against the invading Christians, but the time came when they had to leave to survive. Sultan Abdelaziz's followers left to gain strength, but now they feel ready to re-take their city. It isn't that different here. Itzak hates the Spanish in the Peñón. Musa, on the other hand, feels that Emir Salem is looking out for his interests, so he supports the regime. If a more powerful leader comes along, some might still prefer Salem while others might embrace a change."

"Who do you think should be ruler of Algiers?" asked Beni. Trixie heard defiance in his question. She knew that he wanted Hasan to support Itzak and say that it must be someone who would chase away the Spanish.

"That is not for me to say," answered Hasan. "I do not pay taxes here. My job is only to observe how things are done in other places and tell my Sultan what I learn."

"You really have what the bird wanted, belonging to more than one world," Trixie realized. She was thinking of Tazrut, who lived in Algiers but missed Jadizi and could not go there. In her heart Trixie believed her mother would be healthier if she lived among her own people.

"In a sense that's true," said Hasan, referring to her comment about the cormorant in his story. "I am from Fez, but I was born in Granada. Now I am living in Algiers; next week I will be in Bougie. That may not seem as extreme as breathing air or breathing water, but it is a very real difference. I am a faithful Muslim, but I study magic, sorcery, and divination. I speak Arabic, Spanish, Portuguese, and many dialects of both Italian and Berber. I may sometimes feel confused by my allegiances, but if I remain true to my deepest values, I will serve the good of all. That is why other sultans do not charge me taxes. They know I am loyal to another, not just looking out for myself."

"What do you give to them so they will let you stay?" Trixie asked.

"My value is my knowledge of things they cannot know without my help," he answered.

Trixie remembered the man in her dreams, who changed back and forth between his human and lion forms to explore the world around him. She hoped she could be like that one day, learning to transform into the best version of herself for each world through which she passed. But, she realized, for the transformations to be safe, she had to know who she was at her core. If she didn't know what she stood for, she might become stuck in the body of a spider or a gull.

Trixie continued having lessons with Nouri almost every day. More and more, they included discussions of politics and power as well as training in reading and writing. Nouri was the best teacher in every subject, but Trixie missed Samir's gentle eloquence when he talked about geography and society and even war. Itzak tried to take his father-in-law's place, but sometimes became impatient and judgmental when he talked about people he didn't like, which included all Christian armies and most religious leaders, whether Christian, Muslim, or Hebrew.

One night after Grandfather Samir and Hasan al-Wazzan had been gone more than a month, Trixie sat up with a jolt in the night. She had dreamed of a lion who was prowling among the empty buildings and piles of rubble of a defeated city in the fading light at the end of day. The scene was so melancholy that she could almost smell the odor of dust and decay in her sleep.

Later that morning, as Trixie descended the stairs from the terrace on her way to her afternoon lesson with Nouri, Beni came running toward to her. "Grandfather Samir is back," he shouted, not even waiting until he was close to her before sharing the news. "We knew he was on his way, but now he's here!"

"You see," she answered happily, "I told you he was coming."

"You were right. He did stop at Nahla on the way. Bougie was defeated, but he has a lot to tell us. Come on; hurry up."

But the eager children had to wait. Nouri postponed the lesson to give Samir a chance to rest and refresh himself. Itzak sent Joseph next door to share the news with Musa.

The whole family (except Faisel, who was left at home with Emilia) gathered at sunset to hear Samir's report. They had already heard the biggest news: that not even the forces of Abdelaziz and Arouj Reis combined could chase the Christians from Bougie.

Samir described what he had seen, and it was exactly as Trixie had dreamed it. He even reflected the melancholy she had experienced. "The most cultured, rich, and beautiful city in the Maghreb is now barely a shadow of itself," he reported. "It is home to a half-starved population cowering among the ruins; it has fewer people than Algiers now."

"You were fools to ever think African tribesmen could defeat an Iberian army," declared Musa with contempt.

"It didn't seem foolish when we first heard about it," responded Itzak. "All the news suggested it would work."

"You're right, Itzak," said Samir. "That is certainly how it was when we arrived. We had high hopes, but on the second night, Hasan pointed to dark clouds gathering on the horizon. He didn't have to say anything. I could tell the rains were coming. Some of the volunteers were already slipping off to their villages. The tribesmen probably would not have agreed to join the fight if they hadn't already been desperate after two years of drought. They could not risk another missed planting."

"Only fools trust fickle tribes," muttered Musa. "What did you expect?"

"We expected to succeed, as you will remember if you stop to think," responded Samir. "One fort had already fallen and the other was severely damaged. We had enough troops, and Arouj provided both cannon and powder. But it wasn't fated.

"One morning, while I was standing with Hasan al-Wazzan looking down on the Bay of Bougie and the siege under way below, a messenger arrived to report that a watch post to the west had spotted a fleet made up of five large Men-of-War. This was not just the annual replacement of soldiers and supplies for the garrison. Each ship could carry at least a hundred land troops. Soon the number of Christians would more than double. And just then the threatening clouds broke open, and the rain beat heavily on the canopy above us which had been rippling in the sun just minutes before.

"Within the hour, we saw the five ships sailing proudly before the wind, straight into the bay with all the confidence of the conquerors that they were. Hasan and I took our entourage down to Sultan Abdelaziz's camp. The fighters from both armies were already assembled. The sultan stood before them and, with great dignity, described the situation.

"'Go back to your villages and fields,' he told them. 'We can do nothing more here. Save yourselves now to fight another day.'"

"What did Arouj do," Itzak asked.

"He turned away in a rage. I saw Khizr step in front of his brother so that he would not start his own war with Abdelaziz. He was like a wild bull, stamping his feet and snorting. Literally, I saw his nostrils flare. He tore hair from his beard in frustration. The winter season had begun. The volunteers would go home to plant their seeds. They could not let their families starve come spring. It was fated."

"What did Barbarossa do then?" asked Beni. Trixie was surprised to hear him speak up in a family meeting of this importance, but she knew he could not believe that his hero would simply walk away in defeat.

"Ah, Beni, that is a good question. He was too strong a leader to sacrifice himself and all his men for a lost cause; the numbers were not with him. With Khizr's help, he calmed himself, gathered his troops and announced that they would set sail for Jijelli in the morning."

Trixie was most concerned about her own special friend. "What about Hasan al-Wazzan? Where did he go?"

"He found a berth for himself and his closest associates with Arouj. We said goodbye on the beach the next morning. I returned to Nahla for a short stay, then came here to what I am now resigned to accept as my final resting place."

Three months after Samir's return, Itzak received a letter from Hasan al-Wazzan which he read to the others:

I am writing from Tunis, where I am enjoying the court of Sultan Muhammed V, who sends greetings to you and your family. I have received fresh news from Jijelli. As you know, there has been a great drought. I moved on to Tunis rather than place a burden on Arouj to feed me and my entourage.

After I left, Arouj took it upon himself to save the people of Jijelli from starvation. He placed his twelve ships in a line across the straights between Sicily and Sardinia, like floats on a seine net, to catch whatever tried to pass between them. Within two days he had captured three Spanish cargo vessels filled with grain. When he towed these ships behind him into the harbor of Jijelli, the people bowed down and asked him to be their sultan. You will not be surprised to hear that he accepted eagerly.

My dear friends, you should keep your eyes on this man. He is a brilliant strategist and a stern leader, but he knows when to be generous. He has extraordinary energy that might be of use to you in Algiers someday, if the Spanish presence becomes too much of a burden for you.

"I don't think this will be the end of Arouj's battles," said Samir. "He is ambitious, and now that his missing arm has been replaced by one of silver, everyone is even more fascinated with him. But the tribes in Eastern Kabylia are not going to be happy to have him in their midst."

Samir's prediction proved true. The next spring, 1515, on a warm day when Titrit had joined Trixie in Algiers to see how her lessons were going, another letter arrived from Hasan. Samir read it aloud to the others:

I have received news that an army led by Sidi Ahmed al-Khadi, who now lives in the village of Koukou, has joined forces with the skilled fighters from Zouwa and is marching toward

Jijelli to attack Arouj. He is leading troops on both horse and foot. I hear they have great fervor but may be short on artillery.

"Ahmed al-Khadi, I know him well," said Samir, looking up from the letter. "He is from Bougie and fled to Kalaa with Sultan Abdelaziz."

"You should pay attention to this, Trixie," said Titrit. "Could you explain more, Samir? The children need to understand how our people decide when to fight; some day we may have to make such a choice here."

"In my experience, war has as much to do with politics as with battles," answered Samir. "The dynasty of the Hafsids, ruled by Sultan Muhammed V of Tunis, has been weakened not only because Sultan Abdelaziz has lost Bougie to the Spanish, but also because the Ottomans are encroaching on Egypt, just to their east. Sultan Muhammed could send help to Jijelli, but he would be reluctant to encourage Arouj. Al-Khadi is probably gambling on Tunis not taking sides. Now he is leading an army that reflects the changing alliances in the area."

"Koukou and Zouwa have joined against their common enemy," said Itzak. "Al-Khadi may be strong enough to take Jijelli from Arouj."

"Indeed," answered Samir. "Such things are political realities. But in this case, I don't think it will work, even if the Hafsids stay out of it."

"Why not?" Trixie wanted to know. "Won't the people of Jijelli want to ally with neighboring tribes rather than Turks and renegades?"

"Arouj saved Jijelli from starvation; he is their hero. Al-Khadi would be good at raising an army, but I don't think that he can be an effective general. And don't forget, Arouj has artillery. Religious passion can only go so far toward winning a war."

That night, Trixie woke up screaming. She had dreamed she was standing on the walls of a town she'd never seen. A great lion was seated next to her, and a mob roared around them, on the ramparts, in the streets, and outside the gates. Only she and the lion were silent.

An army approached along the road, led by a horseman who carried a severed head on the end of his lance. They were followed by another man, also on horseback, whose left arm glittered in the sun as though made of silver--not his armor, but the arm itself seemed made of silver. Behind him came an army of many hundreds, some on foot, some on horse, armed with swords, bows and arrows, and some with muskets. Behind the troops, teams of camels pulled a half dozen light cannon, and behind them came baggage carts filled with supplies and women, followed by livestock and spare horses.

The gates opened. The man with the silver arm paused at the threshold and turned to face the army. Next to him the bearer of the head raised his lance straight up in the air so that all could see the bloody prize impaled upon its point. He lowered the lance and its gruesome burden, then thrust it high into the air. He repeated the action twice, and each time the crowd inhaled as one when he lowered the lance and exhaled a collective 'hurrah' as he thrust it high again, so loud that even in her dream, Trixie could not hear her own terrified screams.

She awakened to find her mother and Titrit leaning over her with concern. 'What are they doing in this strange city,' she wondered before realizing she was at home in her own bed, and Titrit was spending the night with them in Algiers.

"Shush, darling, shush," Ummi whispered in her ear. "You must be quiet. Don't wake your father."

Titrit echoed Tazrut's words. "Shush, Trixie. You must tell us what is wrong. What have you dreamed?"

To Trixie, the man with the silver arm and the lion seemed as real as the two women leaning over her. They listened carefully to her dream, and she was comforted enough to go back to sleep. The last thing she heard was Titrit saying to Tazrut, "Now I'll go next door to tell Itzak about Trixie's dream."

It made Trixie feel safe, knowing that her Auntie Titrit and her Uncle Itzak were there to protect her.

20. The King is Dead: 1516

In early 1516, a supply ship arrived at the Peñón about midday. Not long afterward, the flag over the fort was lowered to half-mast. Joseph came to Itzak to say that a skiff was rowing in from the fort to the Sea Gate, flying the flag of the garrison commander.

When Itzak and Samir arrived at the ramparts, crowds of excited Algerines already lined the streets and piers and walls, curious to find out what was happening.

As soon as the commander stepped from the skiff onto the dock, the word started to spread. King Ferdinand was dead and Cardinal Ximenez had been declared regent of Aragon, Castile, and Leon. A young prince named Charles would come from Belgium as grandson and heir to Ferdinand and Isabella. The consolidation of the Spanish throne would be complete. All the Iberian Peninsula except that belonging to Portugal would be his.

What would happen now? Would the garrison abandon its post? Would Algiers refuse to recognize the new king's right to collect their tribute?

"I don't see this making much difference for us," Itzak remarked to Samir. "Salem ibn Toumi is still our emir; he and his corrupt Arabs are still exploiting us. We are as powerless now as we were when Ferdinand was alive."

"What if we could persuade Salem to stop paying tribute to Spain and get rid of the garrison?" Samir asked. "We could argue that we signed the agreement with Ferdinand personally. Now that he is dead, it is void."

"I am not sure we are strong enough to expel the Spanish," answered Itzak. "Many of us, including my own brother, approve of the current situation. Salem believes his alliance with Spain protects him from the threat of tribes like the Koukou, who tried to take Jijelli from Arouj. They could turn their ambitions to the west at any time."

"You're right. Salem is no warrior. He enjoys the comforts of his palace in the casbah, but if he believed he could collect the revenues, just as he does now, and have the funds go into his own pocket instead of to Spain, he could feel differently," said Samir. "If we kicked out the Spanish and got the support of the local tribes, he could be the most important ruler between Fez and Tunis."

"You have just said that he is not a warrior," responded Itzak. "He is not brave enough to defy Spain. Remember, it didn't work for Abdelaziz."

"Ah, but what if we convinced him that Sultan Arouj has grown stronger, as Hasan al-Wazzan has been suggesting in his letters?"

"He is not so inflated with his own power as to ignore the danger of inviting an ambitious rival to come here with an army."

"Frankly, I think he may be that vain and inflated," answered Samir. "You know perfectly well that he thinks he's smarter than anyone. If we get the support of the Baldi, we can start flattering him. He knows that Tunis could swallow us whole, but he probably believes that he could control an insignificant upstart like as Arouj."

The next morning, the leaders of the Morisco community went together to meet with the elders of the Baldi. Most of the men on both sides felt that this was the perfect opportunity to change their situation. They disagreed on many details, but all realized that the Iberian Peninsula would be unsettled until a new ruler was in place. They should exploit the fact that regime change was a time of conflict and civil war.

Itzak brought up the idea of inviting Arouj, Sultan of Jijelli and Djerba, to help.

Musa was the first to object. None of the other Moriscos joined him, but many of the Baldi did. Why should they trust a blood-thirsty corsair who grew up in the Ottoman Empire and only looked after his own interests?

Itzak stood to answer their objections. "First, because he is strong. He could have won at Bougie," he said to the assembly.

They responded with skeptical groans.

"He would have won, if only the local volunteers had not been eager to get home to care for their fields after the first rain, and if only a fleet had not arrived from Spain," he insisted.

"'If only, if only.' We can't stake our lives on 'if only.'"

"But look what he has done since. Did he go back to Djerba with his tail between his legs? No. He rowed into Jijelli towing three large ships crammed with grain. What a brilliant move. He saved their lives and doubled the number of fighting men who promised allegiance to him. He is gaining support wherever he goes. Remember Hasan al-Wazzan, envoy from the Sultan of Fez? I have received correspondences from him.

"He writes that Arouj is a brilliant strategist and a stern leader who is loved by his followers, in part because he is careful not to over-tax them." He paused to let this sink in. The heavy taxation imposed by the Spanish was the greatest complaint of the Baldi. "He specifically told me that we here in Algiers might find Arouj useful to us if the Spanish presence becomes too much of a burden. I am for convincing the emir to bring him here with as big an army as he can muster. "

Itzak knew he had convinced enough of the crowd to have a solid faction behind him. They marched together to Salem's palace. If Arouj could free them from the oppressive garrison on the Peñón, then Arouj was the one they wanted.

As predicted, the size of the crowd convinced Salem ibn Toumi that his days were numbered if he did not give in to the demands of the Andalusian immigrants and their allies. With so many Baldi supporting the idea of inviting Sultan Arouj to help them chase out the Spanish, they said, he could become the sultan of the entire region.

Salem was skeptical but agreed to send an emissary to Jijelli to ask the corsair-turned-sultan to do for them what he had not been able to do for Bougie. "And you, Itzak Ibrahim, shall carry the message. You have convinced us to invite him. Now convince him to come to our aid."

Itzak glanced over at his brother. Musa was red in the face and speechless with rage. He wondered if the family could survive this stark difference in their views of what would be best for the future of their city.

One evening, Emilia returned from a weekly visit with her friends in the baths more excited than usual.

"I've just heard a rumor about Itzak's mission to Jijelli," she bragged to Tazrut and Trixie. "They say that Arouj is on his way here now with an army of thousands. Not only that, Khizr is coming by sea carrying even more men, along with artillery and supplies."

"How do you know that?" Tazrut didn't believe the story.

"A new group of Christian slaves has arrived at the Bagnio. Some are from Naples, and they told me."

"You believe helpless slaves?" Tazrut was still skeptical.

"They had been held in Tunis, where there's a glut of slaves on the market. Some of the crew were renegades. When they stopped to take on water and supplies, they heard all about it," replied Emilia.

"It's what I most feared," cried Trixie. "It was bad enough in dreams; he can't come here in person. I won't let him."

"I doubt he'll be asking your permission," replied Emilia sarcastically before Tazrut could silence her.

"There, there." Trixie felt her mother take her in her arms, trying to comfort and distract her. "Musa will keep us all safe. Your dream has no meaning except that you're afraid. We all are."

Part of her wanted to relax against her mother's bosom and sob her fears away, but when she heard her father's name, her body stiffened again. "Trust Musa? He doesn't care a thing about me--or about you either. The only one he cares about is Faisel." Trixie knew it was true as she said it, even though she could see that the words hurt Tazrut.

"Now, Trixie, think about what you are saying."

"Terrible things are going to happen, Ummi. Here in Algiers. We must leave. We can go to Jadizi, where we will be safe. We can take Faisel with us."

"We will be safe here. Arouj Reis is our friend. He will help us get rid of the Spaniards on the Peñón."

"I've seen him. He is a cruel tyrant who can toss a man's head in the air as though it were a plaything. He could be worse than the Spanish."

"What can I say to that, my dear? It was a nightmare, that's all. Arouj is a soldier. It is his job to kill when he must. Even your Uncle Itzak has blood on his hands. Sometimes a man must fight."

"Arouj is worse than that. Tell her, Emilia. Tell her what your people say about him. The slaves know, Ummi. They know what happens to those who are captured by him."

Emilia crossed her arms across her breast and set her jaw firmly but said nothing.

"If you won't tell her, Emilia, I will. They take little boys and cut off their private parts and do things so terrible to little girls that even the slaves won't talk about it."

"How do you know that, Trixie? Surely you are too young..."

"I asked old Fatima what made eunuchs different from other men, and she told me. And that's not all she told me. She's been a slave for a long time and has seen everything. She said that there are some things you never forget, things that happened long ago that she remembers as though they were yesterday. She was taken with her brother. He was made into a eunuch and she was the one who cared for him until he healed. Many of the other boys died."

"But he is not coming here to capture us. He is coming to help us. He is Muslim, as we are. He will join our sultan to make Algiers strong. I have heard that his men love him, and that he gives food to the poor."

Trixie looked solemnly at her mother. "Ummi," she said, "will you be one of those who goes to the gates of the city to greet him? Will you cheer for him no matter how much blood he has on his hands?"

"I will be grateful for his help and hope that someday I will be able to celebrate a victory and acknowledge him as a hero."

"Oh, Ummi. If only I could see things through your eyes."

'Or you could see them through mine,' she thought.

Trixie turned her face to the wall and curled into a fetal position, hoping to empty her mind of all images. She felt her mother crawl in behind her and spoon up against her, but even that didn't help. She remembered what Titrit had said about transforming into a bird or beast: that she might see something she couldn't handle. Now she had learned that the same thing could be true of dreams. She had seen it and she knew that Fatima's words were true. 'Some things you never forget.'

21. Sultan Arouj: 1516

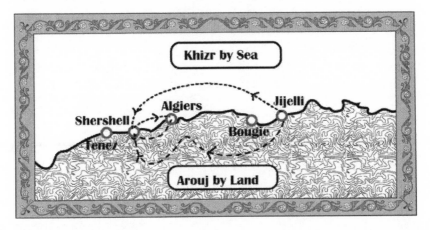

As Itzak rode with the official delegation to welcome Sultan Arouj, he was mounted on the finest stallion he had ever known, better than the ones they'd kept on their land back in Granada. This horse from the stable of Emir Salem was descended from stock brought to the Maghreb by Arab invaders 700 years earlier, lively and intelligent, exquisitely sensitive to the slightest nuance of control and resistant to any rough or insistent pull on the reins.

Just ahead of Itzak rode Emir Salem, whose steed was larger than his own and just as graceful, with a finely chiseled head and slender but powerful limbs. Its equipage was all in red, while the sultan himself wore a caftan embroidered in gold and an elaborate turban of the purest white, conspicuously displaying a large brooch surrounded by draped strings of pearls. He wore boots of bright red leather, embellished with designs in golden sworls. His entourage reflected his colors, though more modestly. Each rider wore a scimitar at his side and a dagger tucked into his waistband, and each horse was dressed out with red yarn plaited into its mane and tassels of red hanging from its halter and reins.

The emir's slaves set up the camp around his elegant pavilion, a tent with exquisite silk hangings lining its inner sides and priceless carpets covering its floor, all carefully arranged to convey the wealth, status, and authority of the Emir of Algiers. Itzak was impressed by the luxurious fabrics and the elegantly uniformed attendants, and even by Salem himself, who was dressed in fine, fresh brocade on his dais, but he did not fail to notice the emir's unease. He continuously shifted on his pile of pillows, then had his favorite page boy, a lad on the brink of puberty, help him get up each time. Once up, he paced nervously to the entrance of the tent, then asked a pair of eunuchs to pull back the embroidered fabric at the entrance into symmetrical drapes. Satisfied with the effect, he settled back on his throne and sent his page boy out to see how he would look to anyone who approached. The answer seemed satisfactory, for Salem was still for a while, but then sent an attendant off to see what he could learn about the approach of the former corsair and his army. When the report was whispered in his ear, he became visibly agitated. Itzak took this as evidence of Arouj's imminent arrival and excused himself to find a good spot for watching the approach of their guests.

When he saw Arouj, he knew Salem had reason to be concerned. The Sultan of Jijelli and Djerba was astride an Arabian stallion even larger and more elegant than Salem's and, worse, he seemed as comfortable on horseback as he would be at sea. He was followed by 800 mounted corsairs and rows and rows of tribal volunteers, stretching as far as Itzak could see. They paraded past his vantage point, a seemingly endless multitude of baggage carts, beasts, slaves and camp followers. This was no rag-tag army, but a well-organized military operation. If there were to be a battle of equipage, Itzak could see that Arouj would have the advantage, certainly in volume and possibly in elegance. The rumors seemed true; in his two years since becoming Sultan of Jijelli, the bold privateer had become one of the wealthiest men in the Maghreb.

Fortunately, Arouj had the good taste not to offend the emir by keeping him waiting. He dismounted, signaled a steward to take charge of the disposition of their accommodations, arranged himself with a select group of attendants, and strode with confidence toward the pavilion. Itzak slipped into the tent and reached the sultan's side before Arouj presented himself to the guards at the entrance. He knew too much about the old corsair's rash and impetuous temperament to be optimistic about this encounter.

When their new ally entered the tent, the assembly emitted a barely audible gasp. Even his terrible reputation had not prepared them for the forceful presence of the man. He was a decade younger than Salem and a good six inches taller. Both probably weighed over 200 pounds, but the corsair carried his bulk in his shoulders, massive chest and powerful legs, while the sultan carried his in his gut. Sitting on his throne with his knees spread wide, he looked like an ornately clothed toad staring vacuously into the distance. 'Perhaps,' thought Itzak, 'he does not seem alert, but is ready at any moment to send forth his lightning-fast tongue to impale the unsuspecting fly.' He knew that if Samir had heard his thoughts, he would have replied with a sardonic, 'Not likely.'

And then there was the silver arm, which Arouj had cultivated into his defining characteristic and greatest strength. Luxurious brocades, silk hangings and elegantly disposed attendants were impressive, but a limb crafted by a master metalworker shining amid the bright red and yellow of his robes was without compare.

'Disaster,' thought Itzak. 'He will never be subservient, and Salem will have to do battle with him and his army rather than merely the garrison of 200 Spaniards on the Peñón."

He should have known not to underestimate Arouj. Ever a master showman, as he entered the pavilion, he adjusted himself subtly and became simply a large man with little more than normal charisma, the epitome of modesty and decorum. Even his wild red beard and muscular form seemed tamed, and he draped his riding cape over his left arm so that the crowd would not be distracted or intimidated by its silver power and beauty. His attendants were as disciplined as he. They bowed toward the emir, then backed into inconspicuous positions far from the dais, near the sides of the tent. As Arouj salaamed deeply to Salem, Itzak felt everyone around him start to breathe again.

The formal greetings and exchange of gifts went well, and the meal was lavish and gracious. After dinner, however, the mood changed. When Salem said they would set off together right after dawn, Arouj replied, "No, I'm afraid you don't understand. I have some business to take care of before I can come to Algiers. I must go to Shershell to negotiate with their sultan, Kara Hasan, for more men and ships to add to our cause. I'll make a forced march, which should bring me there day after tomorrow. I should to arrive in Algiers in about two weeks. Then we shall be well equipped to take care of the Spanish."

Bowing graciously to the emir, he then unexpectedly implored, "Your highness, if you could lend me your Andalusian advisor, Itzak Ibrahim, for a week or two, I would like to have him accompany me to Shershell, to help persuade Kara Hasan to assist us. My brother Khizr is on his way there now, with a fleet of sixteen galliots carrying our artillery and supplies, along with some five hundred first rate fighting men, mostly Turks and renegades. We will fill out our ranks with men from Shershell and join you in Algiers as soon as we can."

Itzak was as stunned as the emir and all his retinue at the audacity of the man. They had been outmaneuvered from the start, and now their camp was entirely encircled by the tents and baggage of the army from Jijelli. Soon, Itzak reflected, Kara Hasan would find himself in a similar situation. His small fleet would be hemmed in by the ships of the master strategist. He could hardly resist the request to attend Arouj, though he worried about Nouri and his two sons. Would Salem be fool enough to trust such a clever general as an ally? But he could not think of any alternative.

Itzak had brought his houseboy, Joseph, with him as a servant. "Ride back swiftly," he told the boy. "I don't want Nouri to worry when the emir returns, and I am not with him. I should be gone about two weeks. Tell her I could not refuse to serve."

They left the encampment before dawn, and the vanguard arrived outside the walls of Shershell in the mid-afternoon of the next day, after marching straight through the night. Itzak himself was among those sent ahead to announce their arrival to the city. He was quickly ushered into the chambers of Sultan Kara Hasan.

Itzak performed all the gracious obsequies due to a sultan from a visitor who had come in peace. He was flattered to discover that Kara Hasan remembered him from their last encounter. "You were looking for your father-in-law, not far west of Bougie, as I recall. Did you find him safe?"

"Indeed. I followed your suggestion and sought him in his ancestral village. Now, praise Allah, he resides in Algiers with me."

"What brings you here?" Kara Hasan was abrupt, even disrespectful. "I recognize some among your retinue from my days in the company of Arouj Reis."

"As you have surmised, I have come here with Arouj himself, who is now Sultan of Jijelli as well as Djerba. He has accepted a request from the Emir of Algiers to help us rid ourselves of the Spanish garrison on our Peñón. He graciously entreats you to meet him in friendship outside the city gates to talk of arrangements that would be to your mutual advantage."

"So, the rascal is still trying to help the locals win back what is properly theirs. He would be better served staying in a home port with his hard-won riches and continuing with what he does best, leading corsairs on successful ventures against the Christians. For an old sea dog, he has a strange yearning for land. I suppose he wants me to cover for him from the sea, in case a fleet from Spain arrives while he's going about his bloody business."

Itzak ignored the sarcastic reference to the debacle in Bougie the year before. "I think you should discuss these details directly with him. He awaits you at his camp outside your gates."

"Oh, does he? Imagine, Baba Arouj waiting for me. Well, we meet as peers. The least I can do is accompany him into my fair city. Most of my people are countrymen of yours from Andalusia, and fine ones at that."

"Yes, I am aware of how many have come here and prospered, and how many you have rescued from affliction. You are a hero of my people." Itzak was sincere as he said this, though he feared the flattery would further entice Kara Hasan into the deadly hands of Baba Arouj. He dared not show any hint of doubt for Kara Hasan's safety, but when he saw him puff up with pride at the praise, he feared the worst.

They rode forth with a hastily organized party made up primarily of colleagues who had fought with Arouj in the old days. They arrived at the camp, which was already efficiently taking shape, and dismounted in front of the handsome pavilion erected for the occasion. It was only slightly less elegant than that of Emir Salem.

Itzak was surprised to see Arouj emerge from his tent and greet Kara Hasan as an old friend and companion-in-arms. They exchanged elaborate and ever-more complimentary salaams as they stood together looking each other over. Kara Hasan did not seem impressed by the silver arm, though he might not realize how little the amputation had hindered Arouj in battle. If the two were to join in physical combat, Itzak would bet on the one-armed man over Kara Hasan, especially if the weapon of choice were to be the scimitar.

At last they got down to business.

"We seek your help in battle," opened Arouj.

"And if I don't feel inclined to leave the safety of my home port," countered Kara Hasan.

"As you see, I have assembled a formidable army."

"Yes, but you seem to be lacking a navy, and I see no artillery among your equipage. Strange for a man of your experience."

"Aha. That is only an appearance. If you will look out to sea from a higher vantage point, you will discover Khizr's fleet sailing toward the setting sun. Soon they will have blockaded your port."

Hasan paled visibly. "Perhaps you make a convincing case for me to join you," he stammered, stalling for time.

"Perhaps," answered Arouj who then, to the amazement of all who had not seen it done before, raised his silver arm until its hand gleamed in the last rays of the setting sun. On that signal, four of Arouj's largest guards stepped forward, seized Kara Hasan and forced him to his knees. Faster than sight, a fifth swung his scimitar so forcefully that its blade struck Hasan's head cleanly from his body in a single blow. The bulk of him fell forward into the dust while his head bounced awkwardly on the ground, took a wobbling roll, and lay still, except for the blinking eyes and gaping mouth, though even these soon grew still. Two dark puddles of blood spread slowly from the severed flesh.

Kara Hasan's followers were shocked and unable to move for a few moments. Startled as he was, Itzak could still appreciate that the execution was a masterful stroke. Kara Hasan's supporters were too stunned to react. When Arouj's men, old familiars from former battles, asked for their weapons, they handed them over without objection. After that, the city belonged to Arouj, who became Sultan of Shershell, Jijelli, and Djerba while significantly increasing the size of both his land troops and his fleet for the assault on the Peñón.

22. The Marabout: 1516

The night that Itzak was leaving Shershell to return to Algiers, Trixie again dreamed of the man with the silver arm. He was riding toward the walls of a fortified city. He drew up at the gate and dismounted with the slow, fluid movements of a dream figure. A man in a bright orange turban and dark red caftan rode out through the gate accompanied by a large troop of followers. The man in the orange turban and his attendants dismounted and bowed deeply, showing great respect for their guests. Arouj (for she knew it was he, even in her dream) seemed to acknowledge him in peace, then signalled the guards next to him to step forward and seize him. They forced him to his knees and cut off his head before his attendants could react. The man never fought or protested. He seemed to accept this as a judgment, as his fate, almost as though he had been waiting for it.

She woke up screaming: "The head! The head!" In her mind's eye, it rolled like a ball across her floor. On each revolution, it winked and smiled at her. "Take it away," she shouted just before she came fully awake. "Help!"

Tazrut was the first to reach her. She climbed into the bed and held her daughter in her arms, but Trixie twisted away, even when her mother tried to sooth her.

"It's only a dream," Tazrut repeated over and over. "Only a dream…"

"Only a dream?" Trixie cried. "It may be a dream, but it's horribly real. Why don't you believe me? It's what he does. People submit to him, then he cuts off their heads. Don't trust him. Don't let him come here."

"Trixie, is this Arouj again?"

"Oh, Ummi, don't you understand? He's bringing death and destruction. He will kill anyone who gets in his way…"

She knew that her mother thought she was hysterical. She must calm down, trust her own truth, and speak carefully. She'd seen what he'd done; more importantly, she'd understood why. He wanted wealth and power. All who stood in his way were simply obstacles, like thorny shrubs to cut while clearing a trail. How could she explain what she knew to Tazrut?

"Ummi, I…" as she looked toward her mother, she sensed movement across the room. Looking in that direction, she saw something almost as frightening as her dream; her father in the doorway, with Emilia following behind.

"No," she screamed. "Don't come near me. You want to kill people who know too much." As she screamed, the panic swallowed her. "Help, Ummi, please help me." She couldn't stop herself, even though she knew it was useless. She was overwhelmed by terror. In that moment, Musa and Arouj were one for her. If she bowed her head to him, he would cut it off. Even as she thought it, she wondered if she really believed it. Part of her knew better, but she feared them both. She must calm down and warn her father of the danger they were in…

She drew in a deep breath and held it, counting slowly, then exhaling, trying to still her beating heart, but when she heard Musa speak, she descended back into that world in which she could not tell the two apart.

"Make her be quiet," Musa ordered. As if inside her dream, Trixie saw him grab Tazrut by her upper arm and pull her roughly away. Emilia came to her, looming so large she could not see her father or her mother, her poor, helpless mother, who was crying in the background. If only she could reach her…

"Don't touch her," she screamed. "Stop him, Emilia, stop him."

"Now, now," Emilia said earnestly. Trixie knew she was trying to help, but she still couldn't stop sobbing. "You know you cannot keep Musa from coming into your room any more than you can prevent Arouj from coming to Algiers," Emilia told her. "The men will do what they will do. You are just a child and have no control. This is how things are."

Trixie heard Emilia's voice become more soothing the longer she spoke, but she also heard what was going on behind her. Eli, the Nubian eunuch, filled the doorway as he entered the room. She struggled to hear the conversation between him and Musa. Then Tazrut was at her side again, still sobbing.

"Shush, Ummi, shush," she crooned as her mother crawled into her bed and clung to her. She was desperate to hear the men more clearly. They were talking about her nightmare, and Musa was learning that something like this had happened before. He called Emilia over to give him the details, then came to her bedside and stood over her, staring down in confusion and, just perhaps, with a bit of fear.

"Emilia says this is not the first time you have had a dream like this."

Trixie could not respond. She turned and buried her head in her mother's bosom.

"Answer me, or I will send your mother away," he shouted. "You might never see her again."

Emilia spoke up for her. "As I told you, more than a year ago, she dreamed of a man with a silver arm who cut off someone's head. Later we learned about the beheading of Ahmed al-Khadi, and some of us wondered if she had had something more than a normal dream."

"The slaves in the marketplace have heard rumors of this," Eli told Musa. "They whisper that she is possessed. How else did she know of al-Khadi's death before the news reached us?"

"Nonsense," answered Musa. "She's always been a troublesome girl. She has learned that her mother will run to her side if she screams. Why would a djinni bother to possess such an insignificant creature?"

"That is how they work, Master. They choose the last person you would suspect. They do their work in secret and sow their seeds in silence."

"What do you know about these things, Eli?"

"I have seen it among my people. I know that as soon as such an evil dream comes, the dreamer must get up and spit three times, on three sides of the bed, and when she lies down again, she must change the side she sleeps on. Spit him out and the djinni will not come back. He will know that he cannot gain possession of this person."

"It sounds like nonsense to me," Musa declared, "but Emilia, see that it is done. Tomorrow I shall go to Sidi Abdullah in his mountain retreat. He will know how to tell real possession from fake. Either she is lying, and he will expose her, or she is possessed, and he will chase the djinni from her."

"Sidi Abdullah is far away, but he is not the only holy man who understands these things," Eli pointed out. "Go to the souk at daybreak and ask for Sidi Yousouf. Only a eunuch can be trusted to touch a woman or girl, and you cannot defeat a stubborn djinni without the laying on of hands. You will find him there, dressed in filthy rags and talking to himself as if mad. He is uncouth, but if she is possessed, he will know what to do."

"You're right; I should take care of this matter without delay. Girl," he said, turning to Sycorax, who was clinging to her mother, "If I hear any more from you, I personally shall whip the djinni out of you. A nightmare does not come from Allah. It comes from evil spirits who seek out the wicked. One has found a comfortable home in you. I have always feared the worst. After the morning prayers, we shall seek the holy man in the souk."

Musa turned and left, with Eli following.

"What should we do," Tazrut asked. Trixie was alert to the answer; she felt her life depended on it.

"I will go to Nouri and bring Fatima here," answered Emilia, taking charge. "The old one will know. You stay with Trixie and help her spit out the genie, as Musa and Eli directed."

"Wait," said Trixie. "I have this." She drew a small sack from under her pillow and remove the miniature scroll she had made when she practiced calligraphy with Hasan al-Wazzan. "It says *Masha Allah*, 'Glory be to God.' If I cling to this, perhaps it will persuade Musa that I am not possessed anymore."

"It may help; focus on it and stay as calm as you can, then do as your mother tells you to spit out the djinni, and we can tell them that you have rid yourself of the it."

By the time Emilia returned with Nouri and Fatima, dawn was breaking.

"I've seen this before," said Fatima in a tremulous voice. "Young girls are well known to be sensitive to forces outside themselves. Your father must know this, so you may still be in danger. If a sidi decides that a person is possessed, he will stop at nothing to get rid of it. Why I remember back in Nahla…"

"Stop," cried Tazrut. She, too, had heard of women who had died when a holy man tried to free them from djinn. "In Jadizi we told such stories about Arabs to frighten little children from abandoning our old ways. Surely these tales are not true."

"Ah, my dear, you have not lived through many wars, or seen many infidelities, if you say that," Fatima said soothingly. "When life gets out of control, someone must be blamed. It is as simple as that. It is always the weak who are chosen. Slaves, women, children. If a man cannot resist the allure of a young boy and rapes him, whose fault is that? Why the boy's, of course. We women agree to cover ourselves so that we cannot be blamed for exciting a man, do we not? Only when you become as old and wrinkled as I will you be free of fear, and they will still find a way to blame you if they need an excuse for their own wicked thoughts."

"Ummi, what shall I do?" Trixie was desperate for her mother's advice. "My other dream came true. We learned that he'd carried al-Khadi's head to Jijelli. What if Arouj really has taken another head?"

She was hoping the older women would comfort her, but instead they grew silent. 'They are frightened because they believe me but think there is nothing they can do about it,' she thought. She realized that they knew things about men--and perhaps about life--they could not explain, and she did not yet understand. There was no comfort in that. She had to take charge herself.

"If we wait, word will come from Shershell, and we shall know whether my dream was true or false. Then maybe they will believe me and not think I'm possessed," she said aloud.

"Not necessarily," Nouri replied. "Many want to welcome Arouj into Algiers. They do not want the people to be afraid of him. Even Itzak and Samir think that it is more important to get rid of the Spaniards at the Peñón than to keep Arouj away. Some even hope to get rid of Emir Salem. Why should an Arab rule our city? Only because he negotiates bad deals with Christians, not because he makes things better for the rest of us."

Tazrut put her hand on her daughter's shoulders and looked at her with a gentle and compassionate expression Trixie had never seen before.

"My dear one," she said, "you carry a heavy burden. I wish it were not so. As a child I saw Mayam struggle with the weight of her knowledge, and I ran away rather than risk opening myself to those forces. But you are stronger than I ever was. It's time for you to go to live with Titrit and Mayam, for only they can help you with these things that come unbidden. You may always be right, but you will not be loved for it, and you will not be believed. Not here, anyway."

She felt the truth of all that had been said. She now lived in fear of the next dream or the next vision. Her flight in the body of a gull and her eavesdropping in the form of a spider no longer felt like exciting adventures. Titrit and the owl were right. Her 'gift' could be dangerous. Even Tazrut said so.

"I must hide before they come back with the exorcist. Then you can send word to Titrit. She will take me to Jadizi in secret." She said it with the confidence of clear knowledge. This was what they must and would do, though the adults did not know it yet.

As they were discussing what would be best, Joseph arrived from next door.

"The kitchen boy just told me that Musa and Eli are on their way from the souk with Sidi Yousouf. The Sidi is ranting in some strange tongue, and a crowd has gathered. The kitchen boy laughed at the sight. He was still laughing when he told me about it. He said Musa was beside himself with frustration. 'I will never allow this creature in my house,' he declared, but Eli told him it was the only way to deal with the situation. 'She's brought me to this,' he cried out. The boy didn't know who he meant, but when he heard Musa say coldly, 'I'll kill that evil child,' he realized it wasn't funny and ran ahead to tell me what they'd said. The last he saw, Musa was beating Eli in the street and saying he would never let the filthy holy man come into his house, he'd take care of it himself."

Trixie looked at the women gathered around her. She knew they couldn't protect her from her father if he burst into the room. He could be worse than the exorcist, because his rage was personal.

Emilia stepped forward. "Joseph, take her over the wall to Itzak's house and hide her in the pantry. Ahmed will know what to do. Meanwhile, Nouri and Fatima, go down to the front door as though you were on your way home. Wait there until Musa arrives. Tell him that the djinni has been driven out and that Sycorax has fallen into a deep sleep. Then go home and send a servant to Jadizi to fetch Titrit. Tazrut and I will place some pillows under the covers so if Musa looks in, he will believe she is still here."

"He'll be happy to have an excuse to get rid of me" said Trixie. "Once I'm out of town, let Samir remind him how troublesome I am, and that I should be sent to Jadizi. He will be glad that someone else says it first, because it's what he really wants, just to be rid of me."

Part Four: Preparing a Kahina,
1516-1518

23. The Trip to Jadizi

Well before dawn, Titrit woke to find Mayam sitting on her bed and touching her gently on the shoulder. "You must get up and go to Algiers right away. Meddur will go with you."

"Trixie?"

"Of course. I don't 'see' it clearly, but I woke from a dream knowing that she's in trouble. Leave as soon as you can," said Mayam.

"Must I? I think I'm strong enough, but I really don't feel ready to be away from baby Mairnia yet."

"Titrit, we talked about this."

"I know, but I didn't really understand what it would be like. How could I know until my baby suckled at my breast..." her voice trailed off as she realized she had no defense; she had promised to set aside her own needs for Trixie's if it was required.

"No woman can. But now we are dealing with something bigger than that. I'll take care of Mairnia. You must fetch Sycorax and bring her here. Her life is in danger. It is time for her to learn the things that only we can teach her."

It was mid-morning when Meddur parted from Titrit at the edge of the casbah. "Be sure to visit Nouri first," he reminded her. "Don't risk confronting Musa until you know what is going on in his house."

"Don't worry, I won't. I will send you word if there is any problem with our plan. If all goes well, we'll be in Jadizi by nightfall."

When Titrit knocked, the door to Itzak's house was opened by Joseph who gasped "Mushah Allah" when he saw her.

"Why do you look so shocked," she asked. "Surely it is not unusual for me to come to this house."

"The rumors must be true. She does have second sight, and you do as well."

"That is what the slaves are saying, is it?"

"My mistress says it as well."

"And I suppose she told you about it directly; you couldn't possibly have heard it while listening at doors or windows."

The boy blushed nervously. "Come in quickly. We are all now part of the plot. We just didn't think you would be here until evening. Nouri sent for you well after dawn."

"Take me to her."

"I suspect someone will already have told her you are here."

Joseph had hardly finished his sentence when Nouri came into the room. "Titrit, Allah be praised," she exclaimed.

"Things must be serious. You are not even surprised that I am here."

"You and my messenger must have passed on the road. I am learning to expect anything from the women of your family. Naturally you and your mother would know to come."

"What has Trixie done that is so dangerous for her?"

"She has had two nightmares that frightened her so much she woke up screaming. Both seem to be about real events, and Musa found out."

"Ah," replied Titrit. "So that is it. What did he do?"

"Eli said that Trixie might be possessed, so they went to fetch Sidi Yousouf. We were afraid he'd perform an exorcism, so we disguised Trixie in a turban and old burnous of Joseph's. Now she is hiding in our stables, waiting for you to take her to Jadizi. Ahmed found a donkey basket big enough for her. She can hide in it until she's out of the city."

"What did Musa say when he discovered she had disappeared?"

"He doesn't know yet. When they got back to the house, he and the sidi made quite a scene. He raged against his ungrateful daughter who forced him to bring such a 'stinking eunuch,' as he put it, into his house. As you can imagine, the sidi did smell of the streets and spoke with a heavy accent from the far side of the desert. Then Yousouf became incoherent and bizarre, apparently because he wanted Musa to buy an olive-wood carving of a sleeping camel that he had under his filthy rags and didn't understand what was said about Trixie's nightmare."

"He was probably drunk," commented Titrit.

"Lucky for us if he was. We were afraid he would want to start the exorcism right away. Then Musa would have discovered that Trixie was gone. That would have been a disaster."

"What is Musa doing now?"

"He's with Samir, who is convincing him to send her to Jadizi, the sooner the better, to protect the entire household."

"Will he agree to that?"

"Trixie said she would send her thoughts out to Musa, to open him to the idea. She said that she sent Mayam a message, too. As soon as I saw that you were here, I knew that things would go as Trixie willed them."

Titrit didn't see Trixie when she entered the stable, so she called her name. The cover of a large reed basket rose up and Trixie peeked out.

Titrit laughed at the sight in spite of the seriousness of the situation.

"Can you travel all the way to Jadizi in there," she asked.

"I won't have to. Look," and with that, she stood up in the basket and revealed that she was dressed in turban and burnous and surrounded by clothes and other soft goods to pad her for the journey. "I'll be comfortable with all these things around me and when we get far enough outside the city, I'll climb out and ride openly on the donkey. Nobody will recognize me."

"Can you breathe when you are in there?"

"Oh, yes. I've been practicing. The basket is loosely woven, and I can easily lift the lid to see what is happening when it's safe. I'll be fine."

When they were out of the Ibrahim's neighborhood, Titrit pulled into an alley and Trixie climbed out. "It will be safer if you ride openly past the gate. The guards will recognize me, and I'll introduce you as Hakeem, a distant cousin, and let them inspect all our packages if they wish, though I don't think they will."

Once outside the Bab Azzoun, Trixie looked about curiously. "I thought there was a Bedouin encampment here."

"You are not the only one who knows that trouble is coming," answer Titrit. "They have moved on."

"Will they come back?"

"If they think it is safe, they will, but their goat-hair walls aren't thick enough to protect them from cannon balls or even scimitars. They would have no protection during a time of war."

They rode in silence up a row of steep coastal hills, then down to a bright plain covered with orange groves. The early summer fruit were the size of Trixie's fist and hung like green, yellow and orange balls from their dark-leaved branches. About halfway across the plain, Titrit turned from the caravan trail into an orchard and gestured Trixie to follow. When they had gone far enough to be concealed from the trail, Trixie got down from her donkey and took off her turban with obvious relief.

"I'll be glad not to wear this for a while," she sighed.

Titrit removed two tribal blankets from a pack and handed one to Trixie. "Here, use this instead of the burnous. The village will be expecting me to come home with a girl, not a boy."

Trixie laughed. "It's all right with me either way. Just as long as I don't have to cover my face behind a veil or hide in a stuffy basket."

They spread their blankets near a creek that wandered through the center of the orchard. After enjoying dates with flat bread and water, Titrit demonstrated the various ways that the blanket could be worn, depending on the need for warmth or protection from the sun. They refilled their water jugs, then resumed their journey.

A second set of hills was so steep the trail rose by means of sharp switchbacks. Trixie could see a river rushing along the bottom of the gorge below and the looming cliffs of a rugged mountain on the other side.

The day had been sunny when they lunched in the orchard, but now they were literally climbing into the clouds. The first long arms of fog snaked from the sea in the north toward the hill, then the donkey carried her upward through white wisps of fog until she was inside the cloud itself, surrounded by tiny water droplets that dampened her hair, her hands, her face, and the outside of her clothes. She was glad to have her new blanket.

Ten minutes later, they rode from the mist into bright sunlight. She had often seen fog roll in from the Mediterranean and engulf Algiers, but she was not prepared for the experience of looking down on clouds from so far above. The world rolled like a soft white sea under the pure, blue dome of the sky. Ahead of her, Titrit, her donkey, the rocky trail, and the mountainside all shimmered in the sudden sun, which cast sharp shadows beneath them. Each cedar, pine, juniper and oak, each bush, shrub and bramble, stood out from its background with exaggerated clarity

"It is like we've traveled through a portal into a different world," Trixie cried.

"It's new to you," Titrit replied. "But you're right. Our mountains are set apart from Algiers. Our ancestors did not come here by choice, but they found a better place than they had left. Perhaps they had a golden age on the coastal plains, but that was centuries ago. Now we do what we can to preserve our ways here above the clouds."

They turned off the caravan trail onto a narrow path that wound along the side of the mountain and climbed gradually up towards a ridge. The houses of Jadizi appeared to be stacked, one on top of the other, about the crest. They came to rocky terraces planted with vegetable gardens and fruit trees, then houses made of mud, surrounded by olive trees and grape arbors. Farther on, stone houses stood closer together and were often two stories high.

The trail became a cobbled street that led them to a modest square. A minaret, barely taller than the houses, watched over the space. Men in baggy pants, belted tunics, and turbans strolled together singly and in pairs. Several women in colorful blouses and dark pantaloons walked purposefully in the direction Titrit and Trixie were taking. Both men and women paused to offer a brief salaam to Titrit as she passed.

A group of children, squatting in the shade of an olive tree playing a tossing game with stones, stopped and stared. When Titrit pulled up her donkey, they stood up and ran toward her, chattering. Trixie had learned enough of their language from her mother to catch what they were saying. They offered to help with the few possessions Trixie had time to pack. They seemed to know who she was and asked eager questions about her. In Algiers, she had never been acknowledged like this in a public place. When she went out with her mother or Emilia, she was just an anonymous child being shuttled from one house to another, and a female child at that.

They pulled up in front of a substantial building whose facade was covered with ivy, and whose additions seemed to have grown out of the hillside.

"Here we are," said Titrit. "Mayam's house."

As Trixie dismounted, an old woman emerged from a barely visible wooden door. This must be the grandmother she had never met. She stood mute, one hand still on her donkey's neck, the other raised spontaneously to her mouth, staring at the old woman, whose face was as shriveled as a dried apple. Its creases were accentuated by the elaborate dark tattoos on her forehead, chin, and both cheeks. The thick coils of her dark hair, streaked with gray, were partly covered by a black scarf trimmed in yellow and white. Her bodice and skirt were both black, with bright, geometric patterns down the front and on every hem. She wore so much jewelry that she jangled as she approached with a firm and determined step that belied her age.

"Don't just stand there gaping," she said. "I have heard your voice, so I know you can talk. You are wise for such a young girl, to call to us in your time of need."

Titrit nudged her. "This is your grandmother Mayam. She welcomes you to our village and to our home. Surely you have something to say…"

> *Trixie managed a simple salaam and stuttered something that the others seemed to accept as appropriate. The reality hit her suddenly. This ugly old woman, striding out the door, unveiled, spoke as though she would teach her granddaughter Sycorax a thing or two, whether she liked it or not. She wasn't meek, like Tazrut, or accommodating, like Emilia. Mayam made no effort to comfort or protect Trixie, but at least she did not treat her with cruel contempt. This world above the clouds operated from rules Trixie did not yet understand.*

Mayam led the way into a cool, spacious room that had doors on three sides. The light stucco walls were decorated with triangles, diamonds and elaborate crosses, painted in dark blue, the same color as the trim around the windows and doors. She recognized the design over the front door as a sign against the evil eye, a stylized hand with a wide, lid-less eye staring from the palm, and one by the hearth that represented the Goddess in geometric patterns.

"And here is the youngest girl of our clan," said Mayam proudly. "Little Mairnia, Titrit's daughter." A blue-eyed infant lay propped up on a pile of pillows near a low settee. She stretched out her pudgy arms and gurgled happily when she saw Titrit, who swept her up into the air and spun her around with delight.

Trixie was startled into speaking. "Titrit's daughter?" She looked at her aunt, as if seeing her for the first time. "I didn't know you had a husband. And he let you come down to Algiers to get me?"

Titrit pulled the infant to her and laughed. "But I don't have a husband, Trixie. Mayam takes care of the little one when I have other business." Both women laughed when they saw the confusion on her face.

"Up here, you will learn about the many ways women and men work together," said Mayam, "but in this one thing, women are clearly superior. We can create new life. No man can do that alone, no matter how much he prays to the Goddess or any god, even Allah. Our Heavenly Goddess oversees the coming into life just as Gazul attends to the going out. But there is time enough for you to learn about these things, including the difference between the man, Meddur, who is Mairnia's social father in the tribe, and that other man, the one who impregnated me but does not have a role in her life in Jadizi. Meanwhile, let's bring in your possessions, and we'll show you where you will be sleeping."

A low bed had been arranged for Trixie in an alcove off the main room. She put her few things there and was given a brief tour of the rest of the building. Then they went back into the big room and settled into a circle on settees and pillows. Titrit had picked up baby Mairnia and begun to nurse her when a vigorous, heavily bearded man in baggy pants of light brown wool, a loose white shirt, with cummerbund and embroidered vest, came in through the front door. For a moment Trixie wondered if this was the father of Titrit's baby, but Mayam introduced him as Meddur, her husband. It seemed that her beautiful aunt had no partner in her bed, but the old crone could boast of one in hers. 'Stranger and stranger,' thought Trixie.

"We have been looking forward to your arrival," he said, greeting Trixie warmly and seeming completely at ease with the scene of the baby suckling at her mother's breast. "I understand you have dreams that have caused some concern in the city."

She didn't know how to answer.

Titrit had a suggestion. "This is a good time for us all to hear your tale. Just describe exactly what happened. We all want to hear it in your own words."

"They are horrible nightmares. It has only happened twice. Each time, I saw Arouj Reis cut off someone's head, and I woke up screaming. The first time, we found out he really had done it, just like in my dream." She didn't tell them about her other experience, when she, in the form of a spider, had witnessed the scene of Arouj on the pile of rubble, his arm shattered and spouting blood, and how she had felt it in her own arm--or left front leg, actually, since she had been a spider. She didn't mention that, or the time she had flown like a gull over the sea. She had told Titrit before and assumed Mayam knew about those transformations. Now they were just talking about the dreams that had caused trouble in Algiers, just the ones Musa knew about.

She felt Mayam's serious gaze. "It is hard for one so young. You have received a strong inheritance from our ancestors. Your mother, Tazrut, fled from all this, but you don't seem to have a choice. It has come to you, even down there and with a Muslim father."

"I don't do anything to cause it," Trixie insisted.

"It is nothing to be ashamed of," Titrit replied. "You are but one in a long line who have been chosen."

"What do you mean," she asked.

"Have you heard of Dihya Kahina," asked Mayam.

"My Aunt Nouri told me about her. She thought I should know the story because it might teach me something about what she calls my 'gift.' But I think of it as more as a curse. Who wants to see horrible things that turn out to be true?"

"Dihya was called al-Kahina, The Priestess, by the Arabs, but she really was a leader in all things, secular and religious. Long ago, she created a confederation of tribes to fight the invaders. She defeated the Arabs so badly they retreated and did not come back for five years. When they returned, they had grown strong enough to destroy her."

Then Trixie remembered what she had heard. "They cut off her head, didn't they, and carried it to their caliph on the end of a lance?" As she said it, the images flooded her: a man on a large brown horse, holding up a bloody head on the end of his lance, and then another image, Arouj, standing before the walls of a city while another man's head bounced across the ground in front of him. "But I didn't see HER head," she said. And yet, she wondered, did Dihya's fate have something to do with her fear? She had been killed in battle and beheaded like one of Arouj's enemies.

"Of course not, Trixie. Dihya died forty-one generations ago, in a time like this, when our way of life was at risk. We think it is possible that the Goddess is preparing the way for a new kahina, a woman who can lead us in battle against the new threat. Now Kabylia is being invaded by Christians from the west and Turkish corsairs from the east. Even our Arab neighbors don't know whom to trust. We may not be able to keep out of the wars, but that does not mean that a new kahina would be certain to suffer the same fate."

Trixie, turning pale, remembered the day she had seen the Spanish fleet come into the Bay of Algiers, and her dream of Sultan Arouj who was now on his way to chase the Spanish from the Peñón. "Why me? Why do I see these things? I don't know anything about war, and I don't want to learn."

"Neither did Dihya, when she was your age. We don't know why the 'sight' has come to you, but we do know that you are descended from her."

"From Dihya? How?"

"Before her final battle, she 'saw' that the Arabs would defeat her and thus conquer all of the tribes who had consolidated around her. She knew that her sons would be executed unless they embraced Allah as creator and supreme being, so she told them to convert. Then she sent her pregnant daughter-in-law, Dhyanaia, to the west with a nomadic tribe. Dihya 'saw' that Dhyanaia would bear a daughter and found a village in the mountains, where she would build a shrine dedicated to the Goddess, so that her ancestors would not be forgotten. Dhyanaia kept alive Dihya's vision of the eternal cycle of birth and death."

"Your dreams and visions are part of the story," said Meddur. "For you, as for Mayam and Titrit, past and future are not clearly separated. We need to learn what you 'see,' so that we can be ready to protect our way of life."

"Our goal is to prepare you to carry on the lineage," said Titrit.

24. Arouj Arrives

Itzak was relieved to see Salem prance forth on his handsome steed to greet Arouj and his army at the Bab al-Wad, the Western Gate of Algiers, when they arrive from Shershell. The emir and his elite guard were dressed in the same red and gold outfits they had worn when they had met Arouj on the Plains of Mettajia two weeks earlier. Citizens of Algiers lined the streets and the ramparts around the gate, waving and cheering the men as though they were already the saviors of the city. Itzak took this to mean that Salem approved of the defeat of Kara Hasan, since it had yielded both troops and ships to aid the assault on the Peñón.

The two leaders, Salem and Arouj, rode as comrades at the head of a grand procession through the gate and up the steep streets to a reception in the palace, an old building in need of repair but elegantly furnished and, most important, the best fortress Algiers had to offer. Itzak saw his brother Musa in the crowd and salaamed to him briefly, but they did not speak. Itzak was eager to get home to his family, so he gave his excuses to Arouj's bodyguard, Mustafa, in case he might be missed, and slipped away.

Itzak was barely home before Musa stormed in after him, ranting and spluttering. "What is this?" He cried. "I'm being told that I have to put up a filthy Turk, a nobody, a pirate, a reis from Arouj's stinking fleet."

"Calm down, brother. What are you talking about?"

"The emir, that Arabian embodiment of gracious hospitality," Musa responded sarcastically, "invited Arouj and even his brothers, Khizr and insignificant Isaac, to be guests in his palace for the duration of their stay in Algiers. Arouj pretended that he could not accept, saying, 'how could I, when my men would be relegated to rough camps on the edge of town?' This forced Salem to extend the same offer to all his men, even the lowest foot-soldiers and scurvy corsairs. We are now commanded to open our doors to the vile Turks, renegades, and tribesmen that Arouj calls his 'army.' They are nothing but filthy pirates and ignorant barbarians. I won't let one of them into my home; I don't want them anywhere near me or my family."

"You forget," replied Itzak, "I was nothing but a 'filthy pirate' during our early years in Algiers, and it was a 'filthy pirate' that brought us to safety. You became a respectable merchant, but we purchased our first ship with money earned by me, risking my life, dumb kid that I was."

"You know what I mean. Arouj claims he needs housing for his men, but this is just a ruse for placing a spy in every household. He knew we could not refuse to offer hospitality, once the subject had been raised."

"After spending the better part of two weeks in Arouj's company," answered Itzak. "I've learned that it is not wise to object to his wishes. The best way forward is to feel flattered if he chooses you to be among those who have the privilege of hosting one of his men. He is generous to those who serve with him and deadly to those who do not. Just pray that you get assigned a relatively civil guest. I will go to Iscander, Arouj's right hand man, and volunteer to host my good friend Hadim Hasan Reis. Perhaps if you are among the first to step forward, and I vouch for you, you will find yourself with a gracious and stimulating visitor."

"But... but... even the Arabs are better than these..."

"My dear brother, I recommend that you go as soon as possible and tell him that you would like to host a distinguished officer. Perhaps Salah Reis. The captains are a cut above other fighting men, both in intelligence and in their relationships with Baba Arouj. You would curry favor just by making the offer."

"Khizr and the fleet are arriving even now. I saw the ships entering the bay as I came here," said Musa. "They ..."

Musa broke off mid-sentence as a great boom resounded through the city. Itzak was jolted, even though he had guessed that the Spanish would fire warning shots from their largest cannon when they saw Khizr's galliots arrive. At last the war had come to them.

"It would be politic," he said to his brother, "to make ourselves conspicuous by going down to welcome them, for they are here to liberate us, are they not? And look what they have accomplished already. Khizr had sixteen ships when he left Jijelli. He arrives in Algiers with twenty-two. That is a nice piece of magic, making ships multiply just by visiting an old friend in a neighboring city. Let's ask Samir to join us. This is the day we have been waiting for."

Musa looked at him with disgust. "I'm going home," he said and stomped out.

Itzak and Samir passed through the Bab Azzoun and walked along the east side of the river to the beach amid the almost constant boom of cannon fire, though the projectiles splashed far from the ships that had been rowed down the beach beyond their range. Emir Salem and Sultan Arouj stood near the water's edge, well out of reach of the cannon fire, surrounded by a crowd of functionaries.

"I'll just stay back here," said Samir. "It's best for me to operate in the shadows. You join the group; we must be well informed."

"I understand," Itzak responded. Then he saw a stout, formidable man in a brightly patterned turban above exceedingly bushy eyebrows approaching the group from his dinghy. "There's Khizr. Won't you even go down to greet him?"

"You can extend my best wishes for now. I have no doubt that we shall have occasion to talk over the coming months."

As Itzak approached the group, he noticed his young friend from Halk al-Wad, Hadim Hasan, now reis of one of Khizr's galliot's, coming toward them from the water's edge. The group consisted of the most important men in Algiers: Emir Salem, Sultan Arouj, and Khizr Reis, plus their closest confidants: Salem's advisor, Hakim; Arouj's right hand man, Iscander; and Khizr's protege, Hasan.

"All we have to do is unload the equipment from the ships, set up the siege, and arrange accommodations for the thousands of men and beasts," said Hasan with a laugh.

"While avoiding cannon fire," Itzak joked back. "No work here for a diplomat like me."

Then Arouj turned to him and said, "Ah, Itzak Ibrahim, just the man we need. Tomorrow morning you will be our envoy to carry an offer of free passage to the Captain of the Garrison."

Itzak had no choice but to bow and express his gratitude for the privilege of serving. "I will report to you at dawn to receive your epistle."

With a confirming nod, Arouj turned away and dispatched Iscander to check on the transfer of artillery to the established locations.

By late afternoon, the job was done. As the last cannon were hauled across the beach, the various captains who had been supervising the job climbed aboard their ships. Slaves shoved them free of the beach, the oars were engaged, and the twenty-two galliots gave the Peñón wide birth as they rowed to the beach a mile northwest of the Bab Al-Wad, where they would be free from the constant harassment of the cannon.

At dawn, Itzak reported to Arouj's headquarters in the palace. The team in charge of billets, which took up most of the space allotted to administration, seemed to have been up all night. Little wonder; they had to find accommodations for Arouj's army of over 1200 men, plus the more than 6000 tribesmen and villagers from Jijelli, Djerba, Shershell and many towns between. Since Algiers had only a scant 4000 households, Salem's generosity as a host was going to challenge the entire community. Would they tolerate this invasion into their homes? If Musa was any indicator, they might not.

When Itzak finished his business, he went down to the beach, where Arouj greeted him effusively. "Here you are again, being sent to ask a commander to trust me enough to come out of his fortress in peace."

Itzak lowered his head modestly. "Perhaps this one has heard the tale of what happened to the last. He might be reluctant to negotiate."

"It matters little to me whether he leaves or stays. We are willing to give them safe passage to Spain, but we are also willing to let them sit on their rock, far from home, no longer able to row across the bay for refreshment and entertainment, while enduring the constant bombardment of our cannon. It is their choice."

"Aren't you afraid of reprisal from Spain?"

"That will come when it will come, whether the garrison stays or goes. They want to keep their little fort, and they want to destroy me. When and how will be in the hands of their untried boy-king, Charles, and Allah, of course. I find our circumstances far more satisfactory than those of the men on the Peñón."

Arouj handed Itzak the message for the captain and dismissed him.

Old Muhmed and his crew were waiting at the Sea Gate. Their small brigantine was the only ship preparing to launch this tense morning. The city and even the water in the bay were still and silent.

As they rowed toward the Peñón, Itzak thought of stories he had heard about messengers who had been received by leaders who did not like the message. In Constantinople, he had heard, their heads were cut off, preserved in cedar pitch, and sent back as the return message. He hoped this tradition was not practiced by mere captains of small garrisons surrounded by formidable foes.

When he landed and was ushered inside the fort, he paid careful attention to the thick walls, the modern, heavy cannon strategically placed to defend the fort from any direction, the well-armed guards at the ready with their muskets and cross bows. He memorized every detail and wondered how his information would affect Arouj's plans.

The Captain received him, attended by a half-dozen, well-armed guards. "I have seen you before, Itzak Ibrahim. I was a captain of the guard when you came with Emir Salem to King Ferdinand's court. You were respected then, and are still respected by me." Itzak bowed graciously in the European manner and mumbled his genuine appreciation, since he took this to mean his head would remain on his shoulders, but when he looked up, he saw that the captain was not done.

"You should know that your pirate captain, Barbarossa, insults us with his message. Does he think we are cowards who can be dissuaded from our duty by either threats or courtesies? We are loyal Spaniards who will follow the orders of our Regent, Cardinal Ximenes, and our young King Charles. We know what happened to your Arouj in Bougie--both times. Tell that upstart Turk it will be even worse for him here."

Arouj stood boldly on the pier, directing the slaves who installed artillery during the brief ceasefire that accompanied the exchange of messages. When he saw Itzak approach, he extended his hand for the reply from the Peñón, read it quickly, then handed it back.

"Take this up to Emir Salem," he said with grim satisfaction. He pointed out the spot where Salem strutted back and forth above the ramparts, watching over the crews near the Sea Gate and pointing out details of the work to his son, Amal, with obvious enthusiasm.

Salem turned pale when he read the reply from the Captain of the garrison but saw the concern on his son's face, so covered his distress. "If they want a fight, we'll give them one," he declared so all could hear, while clapping Amal on the shoulder and drawing him near.

Itzak suspected Arouj knew that his cannon were too feeble to defeat the Peñón. His goal must be to become the most powerful leader in the Maghreb, one city at a time. He would deal with the Spanish later, after he had had time to acquire powerful allies and get rid of rivals, such as Emir Salem

As the weeks went on, the constant barrage from both sides made homes near the Sea Gate uninhabitable. Even citizens living far up the hill were disrupted day and night by the constant noise. Donkeys grew skittish, children couldn't sleep, and irritable men abused their wives and slaves.

Nevertheless, things could have been much worse. Algiers still had full access to all the riches of the region: a steady supply of water, produce and meat from the rich agricultural lands around them, and even occasional goods brought in from caravans traveling east or west. If a trading ship were so inclined, it could still do business with the city by landing outside of the reach of the Spanish cannon and walking the mile or so to town. Merchants from Genoa and Naples still carried on business when they could.

Itzak was satisfied that at last Algiers was challenging the garrison, showing Spain that he and his people would not be intimidated. He was content with his family life and enjoyed sharing a hookah with Samir and his new houseguest, Hadim Hasan, each evening.

The more he learned about the young Reis, the more he admired his brilliance. He knew that Hasan had been captured by Khizr on a raid when only a boy of five or six and had risen through the ranks quickly, but he had not appreciated how much the young man had learned about strategy and naval operations along the way. He started out as just another pretty boy in attendance on Khizr, but when his master saw how quick he was, he cultivated his progress, and now Hasan was commander of a ship, a leader among the finest corsairs in the known world.

"How long do you think this current situation in Algiers can last," Samir asked Hasan one evening as the three men sat around the hookah. "We are supposed to be destroying the fort, but it is clear to everyone that we do not have the fire power to get the job done."

"Only a few weeks more," Hasan replied confidently. "Baba Arouj is already starting to send his volunteers back to their homes."

"Isn't that a dangerous move? What if the Christians decide to attack," asked Itzak?

"Khizr doesn't think they will, and he is far less rash than Arouj. When the brothers agree, they never fail. The garrison will not be foolish enough to attack before their reinforcements arrive, which won't happen until late spring."

"Most Algerines will be happy to see Arouj's rowdy volunteers go," commented Samir. "They consume huge quantities of food and drink, which might be good for grocers and vintners, but raises the prices for the rest of us. They really don't contribute enough to the economy to justify their offensive behavior. Perhaps life can return to normal."

Twenty days after the barrage began, Itzak received a message ordering him to report to Emir Salem. "Alone," the messenger emphasized. "He wants your opinion about the state of affairs, as a leading member of the Morisco community".

After hearing the Emir state his concerns, Itzak agreed with him. "Things seem at a stalemate, but I believe it would be best if we were rid of the Spanish."

"At what cost," asked the Emir. "The citizens used to be appalled at the behavior of the garrison, but the Turks are worse. I hear nothing but complaints. They strut around as though they own the place. Shopkeepers say that they are aggressive and insulting. They treat their hosts like servants. No woman or child is safe. As far as I know, there have been no rapes or assaults inside a home, but as you know, there are many on the streets. Children cannot go outside to play. Women must be accompanied to go to the souk or the baths. We have little freedom from their insults."

"I know little of those things," answered Itzak. "My house guest, Hasan Reis, is as gracious as anyone I've ever known."

"Do you still support their presence? I sense that most of the people are eager for the Turks and their volunteers to leave," Salem said, clearly hoping for advice.

"That is a military decision that I am not competent to address. I know of no way to get rid of the Spaniards without the help of Arouj. If we have not accomplished it by spring, we shall almost certainly need to defend ourselves from a Christian assault. Without the corsairs, we would be at a serious disadvantage. Your Beni Tatije are valiant warriors, but I doubt that they would be sufficient to defend us; a cavalry is of limited use when the enemy comes from the sea."

"You are a diplomat. You were there when I signed the treaty in Spain. Do you think I could re-negotiate?"

"Are you suggesting that I take a trip out to the Peñón to ask the Captain if he thinks he might"

"I am not thinking of him; I am thinking of the Regent in Spain, Cardinal Ximenes, and perhaps of the new king, when he arrives. I'm just wondering about what you think, whether in your opinion such a move would be feasible…"

"Have you discussed this with Arouj Reis?"

"Well, um, I…, he…, um…, I have suggested something of the kind."

"And what does he say?"

"That things are going along just fine. These delays are to be expected. The Peñón was built by Navarro; we can't expect it to fall in a single month. That his men are young and rowdy, but he will speak to them. 'They are good boys, really,' he says."

"I see. Yes, that sounds like Arouj. Has he suggested that any of them should marry Algerine women? That would indicate they are planning to stay here permanently."

"As a matter of fact, he has. His brother Khizr is considering a match. A woman whose family he rescued from Granada some years ago. He is offering an impressive dowry."

"He is a wealthy man," responded Itzak, trying not to reveal any of the complex emotions that he felt. This conversation was giving him a good idea of which way the wind was blowing. The Turks were acting as though they already owned the city because, in fact, they did own it.

"They all are wealthy, it would seem," answered the sultan whimsically. "Well, I appreciate your consultation. If it is Allah's will, we will breach the walls within the week."

25. Trixie's Education Begins

Trixie imagined herself running to Tazrut's room, crawling into bed next to her mother and cuddling, then she realized that the roosters she heard were not her familiar friends, strutting and scratching in the garden outside the kitchen door; the cooing doves were not the favorites who nestled in her hands during long summer evenings on their rooftop terrace. Like everyone else in Jadizi, they were strangers. Tazrut, Faisel, Beni, Nouri, Itzak, Emilia, and Samir were far away.

She had slept in the clothes she'd worn under Joseph's burnous when she left home, so there was little to do but straighten her shirt and pantaloons before joining Titrit in the kitchen.

"What should I do," she asked her aunt. "I've never had to prepare food or clean up after a meal, but I've watched Ahmed in Itzak's kitchen. He has many helpers."

Titrit laughed. "We keep it simple here," she said. "But you do have a lot to learn. We'll start by giving you tasks that help you know where things are. Today we'll send you to fetch water, feed the chickens, collect eggs, make the fire, sweep the floor, and prepare vegetables. The children of the village will show you where to go and how to do the first chore. When you finish breakfast, you can go outside with an amphora and ask the first child you meet to show you where to fill it."

Trixie didn't have to seek children to help her. She was hardly out the door when two or three of them greeted her and asked where she was going. They could see very well that she was carrying an amphora, so she said that she was needed to fill it but wasn't sure how to find the well.

"We can take you to the main well in the town square," said a bold girl, "but we'd rather show you a better place if you have time."

"I would like that," she said. They set out along the road. Soon more children joined the group, following like little lambs. The biggest boy among them, who was named Idir, proudly carried her amphora and led the parade.

They walked to the other side of a wadi on the outskirts of town, a place where the water bubbled out of the hillside, swirled over and around rocks in a shallow creek bed, then cascaded over a ledge into a quiet pool in the ravine. Even at midday, the spot was cooled by the splashing water and the touch of a light breeze.

They showed her how to hold the amphora at a little waterfall and laughed to see how awkward she was with the large jug. They were surprised to discover that she, Mayam's granddaughter, did not know many things that they took for granted, like the names for common objects. When a bright yellow butterfly fluttered in a lazy spiral onto a red blossom, Trixie pointed to it and asked, "What do you call this?"

"It's an 'ibrbilu," laughed a little girl. "Be careful, or you'll scare it away."

"Do you think so?" Trixie moved her finger even closer to it and said, "I think it will come to me." She opened her hand, and it flew over to land on her palm, where it stood peacefully gazing at her, until she gave it a nod, and it fluttered on its way.

"Be still," Trixie said to the children, "and I will call some local spirits."

A dragonfly appeared, as if from nowhere, its iridescent wings vibrating in the air, its needle-thin body glittering, aquamarine and gold, in the sun. Soon a half-dozen shimmering creatures danced above the water and darted in and out among the grasses. In the eyes of the youngsters, each one was a tiny fairy come to delight them. The insects alighted on their heads, shoulders, and fingertips before swooping off to play in the miniature waterfall below the artesian well.

"Like magic," said a little girl, amid the "oohs" and "aahs" of the others.

'Magic,' thought Trixie. 'Could that be what it is?'

The children were her teachers and her friends. They showed her how to watch over the herds of sheep and goats on mountain slopes and to drive flocks of geese from one garden to another to feed on bugs and weeds. She learned how to milk the cows and feed the cattle, donkeys, and mules, and she became intimately acquainted with all the horses and camels of the village. Titrit joked that the chickens were so enamored of her they would stretch out their necks to welcome her blade, accepting her gift of a gentle death. Even the camels cooperated with her the very first time they met her.

The children were always eager to hear about life in Algiers. They squealed in disbelief when she said that the women and children lived in special quarters separate from the men, and that slaves took care of the cooking and all the errands, such as gardening and caring for the chickens and doves.

A curious six-year old was confused. "Then what do you do all day?"

Before she could answer, the biggest boy, Idir, spoke up. "Don't be silly. They rest and play games. Tell us about important things. Tell us about the sea," he demanded. "We've never seen ships or pirates. What about them?"

Trixie envied him his ignorance of these dark things. She made up stories about imaginary 'days of old,' a time before she was born, when Christian pirates had come freely to Algiers and grabbed innocent boys and girls and sold them as slaves in Florence or Venice or Genoa, places far away across the sea that they had never heard of.

"And then came the corsairs, who fight on our side," she said. "They capture Christians and bring them home to be our slaves. They also rescue Muslims from Spain, where the Christians are mean to them. But there are Spanish soldiers on an island in our bay who force our own corsairs to land a mile away and sneak in through a western gate. They have cannon and will shoot if our ships come too close to their fort."

"We'd chase them away if they tried to do that to us," claimed Idir.

She laughed at his innocence and told them about the armor the Spanish soldiers wore, even on their heads, and how strong the island fortress was, so they would know that it wouldn't be that easy to get rid of them.

"If anyone can do it, it will be Arouj Barbarossa, the Turkish corsair with the silver arm. He can cut off people's heads as easily with one arm as other men could with two." Like Emilia, she exaggerated sometimes, but usually in the service of a greater truth.

"Who's scarier," asked Idir, "the Spanish soldiers or the man with the silver arm?"

"I don't know," answered Trixie. "I am afraid of both."

She was sure that Arouj would bombard the Peñón as soon as he arrived, and that the fort would fire their cannon on the city in return. Even if the shots could not reach the Ibrahim home high on the hill, Trixie feared the fighting would distress Tazrut. Arouj would ruin everything. His rough soldiers would replace the Spanish who often came to the city to shop and were friendly with Emilia. They would be confined to the Peñón. She was not so sure that the city would be any safer than before.

"It's time to visit the shrine of the Goddess," Titrit said to Trixie one afternoon after the chores were done.

She followed Titrit over a stone bridge across a wadi to a steep path that snaked up a hill until they arrived at a meadow surrounded by low hills where they had an almost unobstructed view of the sky in all directions.

Trixie had been there before, with sheep who liked to graze nearby. She had stood before the four-foot high stele and studied the familiar image chiseled into its face--a design that she had seen in one form or another all her life. It was painted on the walls in Mayam's house and had been the shape of the amulet given to Tazrut when she was pregnant, to protect her from the evil eye. The basic figure was a simple triangle, but her arms were extended, almost like a welcoming embrace. Above her floated a circle and a crescent, representing the phases of the moon. Trixie had always thought of figures like this as merely decorations, but on this day, she stood with Titrit before the engraving and knew that there was profound meaning to be found here.

"My earliest memory is of this place." Titrit told her. "I was only three or four years old. It was a time of plague, and our baby brother Izil had fallen sick with a fever. Has your mother, Tazrut, told you about his death?"

When Trixie remained silent, Titrit went on. "She could not accept Mayam's impotence. In her mind, the Kahina should have been able to save her own son by appealing to the Goddess. Tazrut felt betrayed by Mayam's impotence and thought her acceptance of her son's fate was a weakness. She did not understand that acceptance can be a place on the way to wisdom."

Trixie felt that the mystery of Tazrut's alienation from her family was being revealed.

"I stood right here," Titrit went on, "a little girl holding my big sister's hand and watching Mayam cradle our baby brother, cold as he was, while our father piled sticks on the stone slab near the stele. Mayam lay little Izil on the carefully prepared bed. Then she stepped back, and our father lit the fire. It is seared in my mind. Izil burned like a little lamb, crackling and dripping what fat he had left, which further fueled the fire."

Trixie felt the horror, even after all these years. What Mayam must have suffered, and yet she did not flinch. She also felt how Tazrut rebelled, and how Titrit watched in stunned silence. Was there meaning in the death and in the cremation? Titrit seemed to think so, but Tazrut had not found it. Pain and confusion perhaps, but not consolation or meaning.

"We waited until the ashes were cool, then Mayam swept them, along with a few tiny bits of bone, into an urn, which we buried here, where the sheep so love to graze. While Mayam was leading the prayers to the Goddess that night, Tazrut leaped up and stood before her screaming, "How can you pray to her? She is evil; she will betray you again."

"Mayam's face turned into a mask of pain as she watched others pull her daughter from the gathering to silence the disruption. Then she lifted her arms to the moon, which hung above us in the night sky, and continued with her prayers. When she was done, she turned to face us, and I saw something beyond resignation, a loving acceptance of loss and even of the anger and hatred she heard in her daughter's voice. I knew that I would never fully understand my mother's strength, that I could never be like her, but I also knew that I would not rebel against her Goddess the way my sister had. It was all beyond my comprehension, but it was the life into which I was born.

"Afterwards, I found Tazrut drawn in on herself, as tight as a ball but silent. She was exhausted from cursing and sobbing but was unrepentant. Then, two months later, our father died as well. She has never forgiven Mayam or the Goddess."

Trixie thought of her mother, once a young child and now such a sad woman, so far from Jadizi and cut off from her tribe. She had escaped Mayam, but she had not found happiness, or wisdom either.

As Trixie evoked the presence of her own mother, the arms of the geometric form on the stone seemed to curve toward her in a welcoming gesture. Her head leaned slightly to the left, as though nodding in acceptance and greeting. Trixie felt enfolded by a benevolent, all-knowing mother, greater than any mortal. For a moment, she felt that all was as it should be. Perhaps Tazrut had left Mayam, and she herself had left Tazrut, as part of a larger scheme. Perhaps one day she would return and protect her own mother from all harm. Who knew what loving acceptance and forgiveness might achieve?

At dusk, Mayam joined them at the shrine. "We will sit here to wait," she said to Trixie. "She will rise soon, before sunset. Pay attention to the time and place in relation to the setting sun. You must learn how the moon progresses from day to day. Sometimes she will rise before dark, sometimes in synchrony with the setting of the sun, and sometimes well after dark. As you probably already know, she will wax a little bit each night for two weeks until full, then wane for two weeks until dark."

"Of course, I've seen the moon rise and set lots of times, almost every day. I'm ready to learn about the meaning of things." Trixie was impatient to learn more. Sitting quietly on a hillside hardly felt like an education.

Her mentor simply smiled and told her she would have to be patient. "The secrets of life cannot be revealed to you until the rhythms of the moon, which influence everything else, are deep inside you," Mayam told her. "To know the moon is to know the Goddess. She has many moods but also predictable patterns. You need to learn both."

They walked home in silence. Titrit prepared mint tea with honey, and Mayam joined them before the hearth on this late summer evening. After they finished drinking, Titrit asked if Trixie had any questions.

"Am I still young enough to be buried among the children, in the embrace of the Divine Mother," she asked, almost wishing that the answer would be 'yes.'

"No, you are already like clay shaped by the potter; you are soft but formed. When you are old enough to have a baby yourself, you will be initiated as an adult, made strong like clay that is fired in the kiln. Then you will be of use to the tribe and gain beauty along with age and accomplishments. When your time is up, you will join the Heavenly Mother in the firmament, high above the petty trials and successes of life, but not as an untested infant."

"What about the other shrines that I have seen around the village? Will I be learning more about them as well?" Trixie asked.

"Of course," said Mayam. "We turn to whichever god or goddess suits our situation. The Mother Goddess is the one most able to embrace all of your feelings and concerns now. Choosing her does not mean that you have turned away from the others."

Trixie went back to the shrine often that spring and summer, as she began to feel the rhythms of the waxing and waning lunar cycle that accompanied the daily changes in its path. The sun played out a steady counterpoint, rising and setting in regular increments to complete its annual pattern. Her consciousness expanded to a new awareness of majestic forces beyond the world that she could touch. She even felt her body changing from the new activity; she felt stronger, and more connected with the world around her.

'Some day,' she thought, 'I will know when the moon is going to rise and when it will set and when it will be invisible. I'll even understand the patterns of the stars that move so slowly across the sky, and the ones that shoot as fast as flaming arrows, and what they all portend.'

Each night that she sat alone beneath the great expanse of sky near the shrine, she felt as though the universe was beginning to open itself to her. This was most true when the moon had set but the sun had not yet come up, and the sky glittered with its myriad of stars, spreading above her both vastly distant and intimately present. She realized she would need as many nights as there were stars in the firmament to really understand the nature of the universe.

26. Trixie's Education Continues

Sitting on a mountain slope looking out over a wide vista and concentrating on four vultures roosting on the wind-twisted limbs of an ancient pine, Trixie felt like one of those hulking birds staring down on a world of mortal struggles, waiting to see who would live and who would die while preparing to deal with the remains of the day. In the weeks since coming to Jadizi, she'd begun to accept that Arouj was an instrument of forces beyond either her scope or even his own, part of a world in which individuals, tribes, and empires ebbed and flowed, clashed against each other or lived in peaceful co-existence, with no more individual control over events than flotsam and jetsam on the waves. By watching how birds soared, Mayam told her, she would begin to see, or at least sense, the invisible forces at work in the world. This knowledge would help her predict the weather, a skill especially valued in mountains, deserts and at sea.

The first rays of the sun reached the tip of the highest branch and gradually spread downward until the tree was fully illuminated. The hunched birds straightened and fanned their black wings, absorbing the warmth. The sunlight moved farther down the mountainside and heated the earth below the tree. One at a time the birds leaned forward on wide-spread wings to catch the warm updraft. Trixie watched them float like dark, wide-spread V's, tilting on the unstable air, leaning from one side to the other to pick up the scent of something dead or dying.

"Watching the birds is easy," she told Titrit. "They are there. I see them, and I can learn things about them most people don't notice. Shouldn't that be enough for an eleven-year-old girl? Why should I be the one cursed to see things far away?"

"As you have noticed," Mayam replied, "the vultures do not struggle against their fate. They harness the power that's available to them. Learn what you can from them. Someday soon we will take you to the coast to study pelicans, gulls, and terns. Each uses the wind to his own advantage in his own way."

Trixie's heart jumped. "Will we be going to Algiers?" She was both excited and terrified at the thought.

"Only when you are ready. We will visit cliffs north of the city, the best place for watching sea birds riding wind and waves."

"Will I see my mother?"

"I doubt that Musa would let your mother come out to see us," answered Titrit.

"But I could go into Algiers as 'Hakeem', and Ummi could come over to Itzak's house to see me."

"It would be risky, and the consequences could be dire. What if Musa discovered you and stopped you from returning to Jadizi?"

Trixie immediately saw what would happen. "I would be locked in a room, and they would bring an exorcist to drive out my evil djinni. I would have even less power than I do now."

"Yes. We cannot teach you to stop 'seeing;' we can only help you to be less afraid. That will not please your father."

"What will happen to Ummi if the Christians come?"

"You know better than anyone how Sultan Arouj is. He will not negotiate for peace. There will be a battle."

"We must go to her right now and bring her here, where she'll be safe. I'll be able to comfort her and make her happy."

"She may be your mother, but remember, she is my sister and Mayam's daughter. We will do all in our power to preserve her life. Your job is to learn what you can and to save your people when it is your turn. That is the way you will help your mother."

"Teach me to control the weather, not just read it. I want to go down there and call up a storm that will blow all the ships away. Then the battle will never happen, and we'll all be safe." For just a moment, as she said that, she thought she heard a far-away voice saying, "Yes, I can help you do that."

But no, it was just her imagination. There was no such offer. To the contrary, Mayam was saying, "you sound like a petulant four-year-old. Understanding may not be the same as controlling, but it is of great value. We learn to predict what will happen through observing subtle signs, and we can make wise choices. There is no guarantee that things will work out the way we want. Musa is a fool, but your mother gave herself to him willingly. You do not have the power to make her happy, though it is true that you are a comfort to her. We must accept certain things, like death or loss of a loved one, because we cannot change them, or even understand them. For now, you must trust your elders."

"Maybe Faisel can protect her."

"He does not have the wisdom or the inclination for that. He's not like you were at his age."

Trixie's heart sank. "You're right. He has always been Musa's darling," she said sadly.

"Don't despair. We still have time. Meanwhile, you must learn about war. We will give you a pony steady enough to carry you into battle and willing to sacrifice her life for you. You will train together."

"If I am to have a pony, can it be the one I've named Hasnai? She's young, but we have a special bond."

"I think it is meant to be. Hasnai is yours. Meddur will train you together."

After his first afternoon working with Trixie and Hasnai, Meddur reported back to Mayam. "There is not much I need to teach either of them. Hasnai already lets Trixie grab her mane and swing up onto her back without objection. Trixie is eager to introduce her to saddle and bridle. They are made for each other."

Trixie found time to ride the hills with Hasnai every evening, no matter how many other chores she might have. She had been given the additional responsibility of weapons training and now spent long sessions with children her own age as well as full-grown men and women. Because it had been many years since the townspeople had fought a battle, many of them were as ignorant of weapons as Trixie. She began with bow and arrow. That was the easiest, for she had unerring aim and a strong arm, though the distance of her arrow's flight was limited.

Her young friend Idir became her enthusiastic opponent in sword play. Meddur carved a pair of wooden swords and showed them the rudiments of the art, then let them parry and whack while he critiqued their encounters. She was taught how to handle the lance as well, and learned all its best uses in warfare, but she found it an awkward weapon, even when she was given one scaled to her size.

When the nights were growing longer, Trixie yearned more than ever to see her mother. "Why don't I ever dream of her," she asked Titrit one evening.

"Do you ever have images from home in your mind?"

"Not clearly. Sometimes I think I hear things, or I have a faint glimmer of a presence. Once I heard a soft voice that sounded like Ummi calling 'Emilia.' Another time I heard a whining that I'm sure was Faisel. I often hear cold words that I can't understand but that sound like Musa."

"He's the one whose presence is blocking you from 'seeing' more," said Mayam. "Your fear of him is like a thick fog surrounding those you love."

"You're right. He wants to be rid of me forever," she said.

"Titrit, bring us the large serving bowl. Fill it halfway, and bring it here, along with a vial of oil."

Titrit brought the bowl of water and poured oil down its edge until it created a shimmering skim on the surface of the water. In the flickering light from the hearth, the reflection of objects in the room seemed to swirl around and take phantom shapes on the oil.

"What do you see?" Mayam asked.

"Light flickering in a skim of oil."

"Keep looking. Is there anything within it?"

"Wait, I see the kitchen of Ahmed, Itzak's cook." Her voice shifted into a deep, sonorous register. "He's talking with a woman, probably Emilia; she often stops by his kitchen on her way home from errands. I'm not seeing clearly; everything is blurry and dream-like. Her back is to me, but I can see him, covered in flour. Even on his nose," she said with an affectionate smile. "Baklava dough is on the table in front of him. I always liked him best when he was making pastry. He wasn't like Musa's cook, who usually chased Beni and me out of his kitchen. He always seemed to have a leg of lamb on the block in front of him and dry blood on his apron..." her voice began to drift away, as though with the fog.

"What are you seeing now," Mayam asked softly.

"It's still Ahmed talking to a woman who may be Emilia."

"Does she answer?"

"I can't tell. She has on her haik. Maybe she's on her way home from the souk. I can't see her...wait. Now he is looking up from his dough at her." Trixie paused in her narration, as though listening intently.

"I can't hear him clearly," she said at last. "He is still looking at her and shaking his head, as though in sorrow. Now he has lowered his head again and is rolling the dough. It is already so thin it might tear, but he doesn't seem to notice."

Trixie was silent for several minutes, then said to the others, "This may be a true scene, but it doesn't have any meaning. Now it's gone."

Mayam waited for Trixie to return fully to the present, then said, "you do have a knack for 'seeing'. It will take practice, but you will learn to use it."

"Why can't I see my mother? She is the one I care about most."

"With time, you may gain more control, though these things are not often what we wish them to be."

Trixie poured the water into a bowl and then added a light layer of oil, as she often did in the morning now. It was a simple procedure; no tricks were involved. She stared at the reflective surface until she saw vague shapes. Only rarely did she see a distinct scene or hear words, like the time she saw Ahmed talking with the woman she thought might be Emilia. Sometimes she was bored, but she continued to sit before the bowl and stare quietly at its slowly swirling surface.

Vague reflections shifted, then coalesced, and a scene appeared, as clear as her visionary dreams. She grew completely still, and everything was preternaturally quiet. Three men stood together next to a steaming pool in a bath house. Two were wrapped in large cotton towels, the third, a huge, muscular man with a sparse beard, was wearing nothing but a loin cloth. His shoulders and arms glistened with sweat. One of the other two had a full, red beard and held his towel around his chest with a stunning silver arm.

Recognizing Arouj, she felt like a mouse watching a snake slither past, frozen with terror even though she was not the prey. She tried to look away but couldn't.

The third man was old and flabby, so fat that his towel could barely encircle his girth. He stepped toward a marble massage table, put aside his covering, and lay face down on the slab.

'No,' she tried to shout, even while knowing they could not hear her. She could only witness, not alter, events.

It played out slowly.

The glistening giant skillfully massaged the fat man, his back, his arms, his thighs, and lulled him into trusting surrender. The man with the red beard picked up a large napkin made of thin, white cotton, from a pile. He quietly placed it in the left hand of the masseur, who tapped the fat man on his shoulder, signaling that it was time for him to roll over. The man responded with some effort, shifting his bulk and raising his head in the process. As he began to turn, the masseur adroitly wrapped the napkin around his neck and held onto one end while Arouj took the other in his strong right hand. Each one swiftly pulled on his end of the napkin as the fat man's eyes popped open in surprise. Reflexively raising his hands to try to stop the tourniquet from tightening, his heavy upper body lost its support, and the noose pulled taut. He flailed, he kicked, his face turned dark red, his eyes protruded, but there was no escape; he could not breathe, and, before Trixie's eyes, he died.

When the scene dissolved, she looked up, cold as a corpse but covered in sweat. What had she seen?

Titrit and Mayam were watching her intently. Titrit touched her on her arm and spoke to her gently, to call her back to awareness of the world around her. "Enough, dear, enough. Tell us what you can."

"It was as clear as my nightmares," she said simply. "Arouj will now be Sultan of Algiers."

27. Regime Change: Fall 1516

Musa sat at his desk staring at his account books. Just when things had been going so well, Arouj had come along to ruin it all. The honey business had exceeded his expectation. The captain of the garrison had been tolerant of merchants carrying on business if they paid their tariffs. He had established relationships with all the agents from major ports who still lived in Algiers.

Some European cities would not allow ships with Christian slaves at the oars to row into their harbors. He discovered that others were less principled. Venice, for example, did not care how ships were powered: by Christians, Muslims, or God's own breath in the sails. He negotiated a deal, and just as the honey was beginning to travel abroad, Arouj arrived and began to bombard the Peñón. All legitimate trade stopped, though illicit activities continued through secrecy and graft.

As Musa was fretting over his books, Eli knocked at his study door. His house guest, Saleh Reis, was asking to see him. Musa had to admit that Saleh was a decent fellow, a cut above expectation, though his opinion of the rest of the corsairs had not been altered by getting to know this one, whom he considered an exception. The others were a scurvy lot, and he hoped they all would move on to other ports as soon as possible, but he told Eli to let Saleh Reis enter.

After the usual salutations, Saleh cleared his throat and said, "I am sorry to bring you this terrible news, but Emir Salem is dead."

Musa fell back into his desk chair in shock. "What has happened?"

"The story is still unclear. He was found in his bath. A messenger from Arouj has just given me the news. He said that all of us who care about the well-being of Algiers should come to the main mosque for mid-day prayers. All the important men of the city will be there, I am sure, so I thought I should invite you to come along. We can leave as soon as you are ready."

Musa's mind was racing. He had been hoping that Arouj would accept failure and return to Jijelli or Djerba, or wherever he chose, just so he got out of Algiers. Now he feared the worst, that Arouj would make a play for power.

He must get in touch with the commander of the garrison; together they could create a coalition to assure a smooth transition to Salem's son, Amal. But Saleh must not guess that this might be his plan.

He found himself stammering to Saleh. "I am not sure I can be ready to go right away. I must put my things in order..."

"I can wait here," said Saleh cordially. "I'm sure it won't take you long to put away your books. It would be unseemly for us to have to rush along the streets. Let us leave in a timely fashion, for this is a day of historic importance for the city."

Meddur and Titrit traveled down the trail to Algiers. Their mission was to discover how much the people of Algiers knew about the scene Trixie had 'witnessed.'

The closer they came to the city, the larger the crowd of people fleeing up toward the mountains and east along the caravan route. When Meddur saw his friends, Misdak and Fareed, among them, he called them aside to find out what they knew.

"The city is in a panic," Fareed told him. "It appears that Salem is dead and Arouj will seize power."

"Do you know any more?" Titrit pressed Meddur's friends for information.

"Mostly rumors," answered Misdak. "But the situation is serious."

Fareed nodded vigorously. "This morning, on our way to the souk, we were almost trampled."

"And would have been, but we jumped into a doorway just in time," Misdak added, taking over the story. "A troop of Arabs galloped up behind us at full speed on the narrow street. Their faces were covered, and none spoke a word, but we recognized the trappings on their horses. They looked like Beni Tatije tribesmen escorting young Amal ibn Salem to escape the city."

"About fifteen minutes later, a band of armed men rode through the streets crying, 'Emir Salem is dead. Arouj is Sultan of Algiers.' People scattered."

"All the stories we heard were the same: that Arouj had gone to the baths to meet the emir and found him on the floor, dead. He flew into a rage and yelled at the guards, 'How could you leave an old man unattended? You are responsible for this as surely as if it had been done by your own hands.' Some say he tried to kill them on the spot, but they convinced him Salem must have died of a heat stroke."

Titrit exchanged glances with Meddur. They had a better idea than anyone could suspect of what had happened.

When they had heard all that their friends had to tell, Titrit and Meddur resumed traveling against the stream of mountain tribesmen, Bedouin, and Beni Tatiji all leaving Algiers.

When Titrit and Meddur reached the Bab Azzoun, they were challenged by guards with Turkish accents, confirming that Arouj was already in charge. People could leave freely but had to be cleared to enter the city. Titrit told them that they had come to see her brother-in-law, Itzak Ibrahim. The name proved to be an effective password, for Itzak was known to be a true friend to Arouj.

They rode their donkeys through silent streets, past shuttered shops, then up towards Itzak's house in the casbah. Titrit quickened her pace. This was not a happy occasion, but she was looking forward to seeing Itzak to report how Trixie was progressing.

Rounding a corner in a narrow street, she was surprised to see a crowd of men climbing toward them on a larger street perpendicular to theirs. Itzak and Samir were among them.

Meddur dismounted and gestured Titrit to stay on Sidi. He held both donkeys by their reins as the crowd passed. When Itzak drew near, he called him by name. He and Samir joined Meddur and Titrit at the entrance to their narrow side street.

"You seem to know what has happened" said Itzak.

"Let's just say that we knew Salem was dead before we left Jadizi," Titrit told him.

"I won't ask any more about that; it is out of my ken," he said quietly, drawing near but not close enough to suggest any impropriety.

"We are on our way from the mosque to Salem's burial. Will you join us?"

"Of course. What more can you tell me?" She, too, spoke softly; neither Samir nor Meddur could hear the question, for they were moving forward with the crowd. She bent her head toward Itzak as he walked beside her donkey, his elbow sometimes grazing her knee.

"I praise Allah for the day that I arranged for Saleh Reis to be placed in my brother's home," Itzak said in response to her question. "If it had not been for that tactful and considerate corsair, things might have gone badly for Musa today.

"Hadim Hasan came to me this morning to tell me that Salem was dead. He strongly suggested that I should be present at the mosque, where Arouj would make an important announcement. Samir and I went next door to get Musa, but Eli told me that he had already left with Saleh Reis. It is good that he was seen with an ally of Arouj."

"Did you see him there?"

"Yes, right next to Saleh. Musa's face was pale, but his brow was dark and contracted, like a tortured man. The imam made no announcement about Salem's death until he came to the blessing for our ruler, when he simply said 'Sultan Arouj' instead of 'Emir Salem.' That was all, but enough for those present to understand exactly what was going on. I saw Musa cover his face with his hands.

"Then Arouj made a speech in which he blamed Salem's bodyguards for leaving him alone at the baths. He almost started a fight right there in the mosque, but Khizr came to his side and calmed him, telling us, 'Forgive him. He loved Salem, who hoped to free you all from the oppressive Spanish presence. Do not fear, if we find that any human hand has been responsible for the emir's death, that man will pay. Now is the time for our thoughts and prayers to be with him whom we have lost. His wives are preparing his body. We shall bury him this afternoon.' Many in the crowd seemed angry, but they were aware of Arouj's armed men standing at every door and said nothing."

A large crowd milled uneasily outside the gate to Salem's palace. Titrit looked around, wondering if Arouj's troops might be stationed on every corner and peering down from every roof.

She could see over the people from her seat on Sisi. When the gates opened, six strong men struggled with their heavy load out through the crowd, which parted to let them pass. The mourning wives followed, and behind them, the children and slaves, though the eldest son, Amal, was conspicuously absent.

The procession went out the small Bab Sidi Ramadan, over a bridge, and up a knoll to the cemetery, where the emir was laid to rest under the watchful eye of Arouj, who announced he would build a shrine to honor Salem as a hero of Algiers. Everyone cheered, but few believed a word spoken by their new sultan. Titrit, Itzak and Samir were relieved Musa was not at the burial. They saw groups forming in the crowd, and it was easy to tell which ones were spreading dangerous rumors against Arouj. They feared Musa could have fallen in with the worst of the potential rabble rousers.

After the service, Meddur parted from the others to see what he could learn from Kabyle acquaintances in the city. Titrit returned with Itzak and Samir to their house, where Nouri joined them in the study.

"Few believe the official story," Itzak told Nouri. "Some men whisper that there were bruises on the emir's neck, and others that Arouj bribed Salem's bodyguards to leave their master, but I have heard no evidence to support either claim, though people understand that Algiers wasn't big enough for two sultans."

"Do you think Arouj actually believes he can get away with such a blatant assassination," Nouri asked.

"He certainly thinks so, and I do too," Itzak replied. "He neutralized us all by placing his own people inside our homes. He has been infiltrating the palace, waiting for his moment which has come. If anyone opposes him, it will be seen, reported, and dealt with."

"That's why I'm worried about Musa," said Titrit. "Is he safe?"

"He contained himself. I have no doubt that it was Saleh's presence that kept him under control. When the service was over, he did not even look at me. He headed back to his house, whether by choice or Saleh's insistence I do not know. He will have to be careful, or he will put our whole family at risk."

Titrit was worried after hearing this. "I must go to my sister," she said. "Nouri, will you come with me?"

"I'd better not. I have Beni and Ali to think of, not to mention their little brother or sister who will arrive in the spring."

"Ah, I am glad to hear some good news among all this confusion. Let me just stop in to say hello to the boys and Fatima before I go next door. I don't have long if I'm to meet Meddur for the ride home."

When she and Nouri reached the family room, they found Faisel playing with Beni and Ali. "Where is your mother," Nouri asked. "Didn't Emilia come with you?"

"No, I came on my own. My baba is in a bad mood and Ummi is no fun. I don't know where Emilia is. I just came over by myself."

"Well, you can come with me; I'm on my way to your house now," said Titrit.

"Do I have to? It's more fun here."

"They'll be worried about you. Come on. We can go over the terrace wall."

"Are you kidding?"

"No, I'm not too old to do that; you'll see. Let's go."

When Musa got home from the mosque, he was angry and frustrated. He even brushed away his adored (and adoring) son Faisel, who came to greet him. "Just leave me alone," he shouted at the boy, then added remorsefully, "I'll come to see you in a little while."

This incident made him even more agitated. He paced his room, his mind bouncing back and forth between his distress that Arouj had made himself sultan after pulling off an obvious assassination, and his shame at treating his son so badly. Faisel would now be more important to him than ever; he was his hope for the future. Unless, of course, he pursued another plan that he had been thinking about. He could take a second wife, marry young Saba, a beautiful girl from Granada who could give him more sons and raise them in his own traditions. Her family seemed receptive; they had not been able to get their wealth safely to Algiers, but they were well connected, both among Moriscos and the Baldi. Yes, he decided, he could start anew once the awful Turks were gone. He needed to forge deeper links with his own people, the newly arrived families from Granada. His only sensible path was to cultivate trade with the Christians, which meant keeping the Beni Tatije as the pro-Spanish rulers in Algiers.

'Surely,' he thought, 'the majority of Algerines must hate Arouj even more than they hate the Spanish. But how can we get rid of them? They have artillery and the Arabs don't.'

"The garrison, of course" he said aloud.

He was sure all the Baldi and many of the Moriscos would rise up if they thought they could win. How could he contact the Captain on the Peñón?

'Emilia,' he thought. 'She will know how to reach them.'

He called Eli. "Tell Emilia to come to me, but don't let anyone else know."

When she arrived, he challenged her, asserting what he had only guessed. "I know you signal the soldiers on the fort. What is your code? It is urgent that I have contact with them, tonight if possible."

It was as he had suspected, and she answered immediately.

"I hang a scarf from the terrace wall. Red means 'no contact, it's too risky.' Yellow means 'meet me near the sea gate.' Blue means 'look for a message.'"

"How do you deliver a written message?"

"I have a friend with a cross bow. He stands on the ramparts near the Sea Gate after dark and shoots a missile that reaches the Peñón. They may have trouble finding it, but the commander makes them seek it out when he sees the blue scarf in the morning; he is always interested in information about the city, now more than ever. In return for my messages, he has promised me he will intercede for me with the Regent in Spain."

"You are a spy for the Spanish." He tried to sound threatening, thinking he could intimidate her into doing his will.

"You might say that, but it sounds to me that, with my help, you might become an active conspirator against your own people, which is worse," she replied.

"You put it bluntly."

"Yes, and I risk my life if I help you. How would you reward me?"

"I'll give you anything you ask," he replied.

"Anything?"

"Your freedom? That would be easy, but you would still be a blond Christian in Algiers, hardly an enviable position. You are better off as my slave."

"I hear you are thinking of taking a second wife..."

He was shocked at the nerve of her. She seemed to be presuming that he should raise her to that position.

"And take her I will. I have no intention of making you a concubine, much less wife."

"We shall see. I have a feeling Saba's family might want to reconsider, now that Arouj is making himself Sultan of Algiers.

You may no longer seem to be such a good match. But I will help you, and we can discuss the terms of payment after the current situation is resolved."

What was she implying? He decided that Emilia was a more formidable figure than he had realized.

Tazrut looked startled to see Titrit and Faisel arrive in her room together. "Why is Faisel with you," she asked.

Titrit realized that Tazrut hadn't known Faisel had gone next door. "I found him playing with Beni and Ali, so thought I should bring him here with me," she answered.

"Wasn't Emilia with you, Faisel?"

"No, I couldn't find her, and Baba was in a bad mood, so I just decided to go over to play with Beni."

"Well, never mind. Run along, I want to talk with your Auntie Titrit."

Faisel pouted and seemed resentful, but he left.

"Thank goodness you have come," Tazrut said. "I've been going mad with worry. What is going on? Emilia is the only one who tells me anything, and she seems to have disappeared."

"Have you heard that Emir Salem is dead?"

"Yes, I know that much. Won't his son, Amal, take over? Musa has been saying that the Spanish would leave us alone as soon as Barbarossa gave up and went away."

Titrit grew pale, hearing her sister refer to Arouj by the disparaging name the Christians used. "Musa must be careful. You may not have heard. Arouj has declared himself Sultan of Algiers. He has spies everywhere. It is dangerous to speak against him, even in private."

"There's nothing I can tell Musa. He doesn't listen to me, especially now."

"What do you mean, 'especially now'?"

Tazrut began to cry. "He wants to take a second wife," she said. "I know I'm worthless, but it is hard to think of a young girl moving in and being favored. Am I just being selfish? I'm not so old yet, am I?"

Titrit embraced her sister. "Don't be silly. He is the selfish one, and he wants to feel important by showing others that he can afford as many wives as he wants. You knew that this was a possibility when you moved to Algiers. But is it definite?"

"I don't know. Emilia thinks so. There's a family that recently arrived from Andalusia with a daughter of fifteen. They are said to be short of cash but with good connections, and she is beautiful."

"You might like having another woman living here. At first it would be hard, but you would be the senior wife, with the loyalty of Emilia and Eli. A young girl could bring comfort to you, now that Trixie is away."

"I had not thought of that. And it would make Musa happy again, like he was when we were first married. Things have been difficult since the bombardments started."

"Does he beat you?"

"Only when I provoke him by saying something foolish, and when he's already upset."

That was not the answer Titrit had hope for. It had been a long time since she had been so worried about her sister.

28. Disaster Averted

*"Wait and see, people of Algiers, our King will send a
fleet to destroy you," cried one soldier.*

*"They will come with war ships and huge cannon,"
called another.*

*"Your so-called sultan will lose his other arm, and his
head along with it."*

"We will wreak revenge like you have never seen before."

*"Save your lives. Overthrow your tyrant. Join with us and
live in peace under the gracious rule of our young king and his
Regent, Cardinal Ximene."*

"Just listen to them," said Itzak as he stood with Samir on the
ramparts near the Sea Gate. The jeers of the Spanish soldiers
drifted across the water from the Peñón as they had every day
that week.

"These shouts will take a toll," commented Samir. "The
Spanish fleet will certainly return some day, and they will
probably have Salem's son Amal with them. If they defeat us,
we'll all be accused of treason. Not a pretty picture."

"I'm afraid my own brother is already on their side. These
mocking threats will inflame him even more."

"As if Musa needed any more reason to be outraged. Since Saba's family decided to marry her to Khizr, he's been in a rage."

"He can't believe he was turned down for someone he considers a filthy Turk. And the marriage is to take place within the week."

"Humiliation does not sit well with him. We shall have to save him from himself, for the sake of the family. I fear for Tazrut."

Musa watched the jeering soldiers from his terrace. Just a few days before, he had despaired; now his confidence was returning. He couldn't make out all the words at that distance, but he smiled at the wild energy of the soldiers. There were only two hundred of them, but they were well-armed and experienced fighters. Arouj had already sent away his volunteer troops, leaving only his own men and some Moriscos. Since Musa had established contact with the Commander of the Peñón, he knew that revenge would be his. The garrison, the Beni Tatije led by Salem's son Amal, and the Baldi who hated the Turks and their renegade corsairs, were plotting together. He had studied the Commander's plan and considered it infallible.

'Wait a few days; they'll learn who's in charge,' he thought. 'Now that Saleh Reis has been given his own home, I can operate freely. And when we succeed, my reward will be a mansion as fine as the one that has been given to Saleh, and Saba will be mine.'

On a fine September day two weeks after Emir Salem's death, Trixie rode Hasnai alongside Titrit and Sidi to a promontory just north of Algiers to study the flight patterns of sea birds. She was wearing her, or rather Joseph's, burnous and turban to be sure that no one would recognize her.

On their way across the plains of Mettajia they thought they saw a large gathering of armed men on horses in the distance, but they couldn't be sure. Perhaps it was just a herd of sheep or camels being taken to better grazing in mountain pastures.

The streets were unusually crowded when they had passed through the Bab Azzoun. Most of the men heading toward the souk drove wagons loaded with goods or led donkeys with over-flowing baskets draped across their backs. The city seemed far more prosperous than either expected in this time of uncertainly.

"I'm not claiming to be a seer," joked Trixie, "but can't you imagine weapons hidden under the straw in those wagons?"

Titrit laughed uncomfortably. "Let's hope not."

They passed out through the Bab al-Wad, across the bridge, and climbed the highest hill, which had steep cliffs facing the bay. From their perch they could see the beach to the north where the corsairs kept their ships safe from the cannons on the Peñón. The activities seemed normal: ships hauled out for repairs and men building new ones. They paid little attention; Trixie focused on a neat line of pelicans which rose and fell in precise relation to the surges of the sea, skimming so close to the surface that their wing tips and their reflection seemed to touch.

As Titrit scanned the wider environment, looking for unusual sights or birds that could teach a new lesson, she noticed unusual activity near the docks on the Peñón. It looked like men were preparing to launch a small fleet of brigantines.

"Something is going on," she said to Trixie. "Look at the fortress, then at the soldiers on the ramparts of the city. Aren't things busier than usual on both sides?"

"I don't know. Maybe. Look over that way, on the north beach. A group of men are walking across the sand toward the corsairs' flee."

"There must be a dozen or more. Do you think they are armed?"

"Not that I can see," answered Titrit. "Whoever they are and whatever arms they are carrying, they will be out-numbered. Look. Corsairs are pouring out of every ship; they must have been expecting these visitors."

"It doesn't look like a fight."

"Something is going on. Itzak will know, and if he's not at home, we can count on Samir. Please, Auntie Titrit. I can pretend to be a boy, so they won't recognize me, even in the casbah. They let us pass out through Bab al-Wad, and the same guards will still be on duty. They'll let us back in. Then maybe I can see Ummi, too."

As they headed down the southeast side of the promontory, they saw an unusual cloud of dust rising faintly on the far side of the city, moving from the mountains down toward the plain.

"Maybe it WAS a cavalry troop we saw earlier," said Titrit. "Let's hurry."

Musa had been pacing back and forth on the rooftop terrace all morning. His day had come at last. He wondered how long it would take for the men to reach the beached fleet, overwhelm the guards, and start the fire. At the sign of smoke, the cavalry would charge down from the hills, the disguised Beni Tatije would seize their concealed weapons, and soldiers would row in from the Peñón to secure the city.

He wished he had chosen a better place to watch the events unfold. He could not see the spot where the corsairs' ships were beached, nor the ramparts by any of the gates of the city, although he had a good view of the fortress on the Peñón. Earlier, he'd seen the small boats readied at the docks, but they had not yet been launched. He felt as though the entire city was holding its breath, waiting for the smoke signal to rise beyond the hill to the northwest of Bab al-Wad.

The wait was agonizing. He was in a cold sweat in the balmy autumnal air, and his stomach cramped like a tight cannon ball in his belly. When the sun reached its zenith, he began to despair and called Eli to him.

"Go to the souk. See if you recognize any Beni Tatije among the vendors. Listen for rumors. See if the usual guards are on duty at the Bab al-Wad."

Eli had a good idea what his master was talking about; not much in the household was secret from him. He walked swiftly down to the souk but saw no signs of concealed weapons or disguised Beni Tatije. He casually fell into conversation with a vendor he knew well and asked how business was going. The man, a Kabyle from a mountain village who had moved with his entire family to the city and made his living selling fruits and vegetables, commented that it had been a strange day.

"We had quite a crowd of vendors; more Arabs than usual. I think they are having to find new ways to make a living now their emir has died. They were easily discouraged. We didn't have enough customers to please them, I suppose, so they packed up and went home early."

Eli muttered sympathetically and moved on to the plaza near the Bab al-Wad. He leaned his bulk against a pillar in the shade of an archway that provided a good vantage point for inconspicuously watching the ramparts. The usual Turkish and renegade guards were on duty, and customs checks seemed to be proceeding normally, thought they were quite busy.

He reported back to his master. All was normal at the souk and at the Bab al-Wad; there was no sign of trouble anywhere he went.

This was the worst possible news for Musa. What now?

It had been such a good plan, and with such excellent allies. Could it have failed? Not through natural means, he was sure. He recognized the signs. It all began when his daughter fled to her refuge in the mountains. Since then he had been cursed. First Arouj came to Algiers. Then Emir Salem was killed. Then Saba had been given to Khizr. Now the best plan for revolt had fizzled. It had to be the result of a malicious intelligence.

"I warned you about this," said Eli. "On the day of Trixie's disappearance, I told you 'When a possessed person spits out a djinni, but there is no holy man to catch it, it can run loose in the household or even throughout the city.' This may just be the beginning, not the end, of your woes."

Musa was distracted from Eli's words by movement on the Peñón. Perhaps the uprising was only delayed, not canceled. Hope sprung up within him, only to be dashed as a bright red flag fluttered on the wall of the fortress.

Red; Emilia had told him, "red means no contact, too risky."

Perhaps she knew more. He rushed across the courtyard to find her.

Titrit was amused by the look on Joseph's face when he opened the door and saw Trixie standing there in his old burnous, her hair concealed within a white turban.

"If I hadn't recognized my own clothing, I would never have guessed it was you," he said. "What are you doing here? Do you know what's going on?"

"No; we came to ask Itzak," answered Trixie. "We saw some strange things."

"The master went out early. Let me take you to Nouri. We know little, but there are rumors. Slaves have seen things. Servants are talking. If anyone knows anything, it will be Samir. He is already with Nouri."

"And who is this," the old man teased; he had recognized her immediately.

"My cousin Hakeem, visiting from my village," responded Joseph with a wink.

"Of course. I recognize his burnous. He bears a remarkable resemblance to someone else I know."

Fatima cackled. "So, you've decided to become a boy full time, have you?"

Trixie blushed. "It's a convenient disguise," she answered. "No one ever questions me. Now that I'm here, please, can I go next door to see my mother?"

"Not now, Trixie. It might be too dangerous," said Nouri. "We don't know how either Itzak or Musa is involved in the things that are going on out there. If this is an uprising, they might not be on the same side."

"Let me go over to see if Tazrut knows anything," Titrit offered. "If it's safe, I'll bring her back with me. If I don't return soon, it means you should stay away." She looked Trixie straight in the eyes. "Do you understand? It is not just a suggestion. This could be a life and death situation."

She was relieved to see Trixie nod in compliance.

Titrit almost bumped into Eli as she rounded the corner at the foot of the stairs from the roof.

"Perhaps this is not a good time for you to visit," he said, insinuating that his master would be displeased.

'Goddess, help me,' she said to herself, knowing that Eli could prevent her from seeing her sister. She must not be intimidated. "Out of my way; you know that it is my duty to protect and aid your mistress, my sister."

To her relief, Eli quickly stepped aside, as though he recognized the presence of a powerful spirit. There would have been trouble if he had called Musa.

Titrit found Tazrut in her room, huddled among pillows on her favorite divan. Emilia sat beside her, looking disheveled but holding a damp compress to her mistress's eyes while softly singing a lullaby in her own language. Even in the dim light of the shaded room Titrit could see that her sister's arm was covered in bruises. She dreaded to see what was behind the compress. She could see dark red spots around the edges that looked like they came from a bloodied nose.

She paused briefly to compose her outrage before announcing her presence, then stepped towards the two women on the divan and spoke gently. "How can I help?"

Hearing her sister's voice, Tazrut began to sob with a hoarse voice that made it clear she had been crying for a long time and had only recently been calmed into silence.

"Just go away," moaned Tazrut. "Leave me alone. No one can help. I have lost my daughter, and now my son...my son..." She couldn't continue.

Titrit looked to Emilia for guidance and explanation.

"The master is in a state. He has taken Faisel from our care, and you see what he has done to your sister. He says that Arouj is an assassin and that the little witch, meaning Trixie, knew it all along. He says the djinni that had possessed her is loose in the city, and it is all Tazrut's fault for giving birth to her and bringing Mayam's curse into his home in the first place."

As Emilia told this tale, Tazrut's sobs rose and fell in a sustained hysteria that wracked her frail body.

"Enough, Emilia. Give her respite. She cannot bear to hear these fantasies spoken again. Let me take charge of her now while you go next door to fetch Nouri. Trixie is with her; she should come along as well."

At the mention of Trixie, Tazrut stopped sobbing and sat up. "Trixie? Here? Don't bring her to this house. We don't know what he'll do. He is in a rage against her. Take her back to Jadizi as fast as you can. She'll be safe there."

When Titrit hesitated, Tazrut insisted. "Go. Go now. Leave Emilia with me and take Trixie to safety as soon as you can."

When Itzak returned from the ramparts near the Bab al-Wad, where he had followed the progress of the aborted coup, Joseph and Titrit rushed up to him.

"Thank goodness you are here," Titrit exclaimed.

He had never seen her look so agitated. "What is going on? Does it have to do with Musa? Have they come for him?"

"What are you talking about," asked Titrit. "We have a lot to tell you. Hurry. We must join Nouri and Samir. Trixie is with them."

"What has he done?"

"Beaten Tazrut and railed against Trixie, calling her a witch, and raving about a djinni loose in the city," answered Titrit. "We think he's gone mad."

"Perhaps, but he must be desperate." Itzak was putting the pieces together in his mind as they entered the family room.

Samir stood up and raised his hand when Itzak and Titrit entered the room. "We must all be calm. Itzak, I presume that you have come to us with news greater than the concerns of this family. Perhaps we should hear what you have to say before we talk about what the rest of us know."

"You are wise as ever, my father. Let us be calm and take things one at a time.

"There was an uprising planned for today, but Arouj has known about it for weeks. He may have evidence against Musa. I'm afraid they'll come for him."

Everyone was silent. It made sense to all of them. Whenever Musa was upset, he blamed Tazrut, and if he had been involved in the plot, its failure would have been as big a disaster as any he'd known since arriving in Algiers.

"Perhaps he is innocent," said Nouri.

"Perhaps, but I doubt it," answered Itzak. "If he did take part in the planning, we may all be in trouble."

"How much do you know," Samir asked.

"It was a coordinated attack between the Peñón and the Beni Tatije, plus a significant number of Baldi and Morisco supporters. I don't know how Arouj found out about it, but he cleverly let the men enter Algiers with their hidden weapons, and he ignored the cavalry who lay in wait two miles from the city, planning to sweep down when they saw smoke signaling the fleet had been set on fire. Several hundred of Arouj's men were hiding in the ships. When the conspirators arrived on the beach, they were greeted politely and told that it was rumored that the Spanish might send soldiers from the garrison to make mischief with the fleet, so they had increased the number of their guards."

"That's what we saw," cried Trixie. "That's why there was no fight."

"Oh, how I wish I could have been there to see the looks on their faces when they realized they had been out-foxed," said Nouri.

"No fight at all? No one died? No one was arrested?" Samir could hardly believe it.

"Nothing. Not a word. Not even a raised voice. The conspirators pretended they were friends who would be shocked at the idea that the Spanish might send soldiers to harm the ships, and they had to slink away."

"What happens now? Will it all blow over?"

"Your guess is as good as anyone's. It is as though it never happened. The Spaniards are snug in their fort, the Arabs have returned to their plains, and the Baldi are back in their comfortable homes."

"But Tazrut has suffered bruises and a bloody nose," said Titrit.

"I hate Musa so," cried Trixie. "I wish he were dead."

The others looked shocked.

"Careful Trixie," cautioned Titrit. "Your anger could do more damage than you realize. He is still your father, and part of the family. If he is accused of treason, all of us will suffer."

"We must hope that no one suspects him."

"If we are to survive this, Musa must do nothing to call attention to his dissatisfaction." Itzak felt all their eyes on him as he spoke. Yes, it was time for him to step up and take charge of the family, as though he were the older brother.

"Titrit and Trixie, Tazrut is right. Your presence will make things more dangerous for her. Is Meddur with you?"

"No, we came alone; we thought we would be leaving well before this, to get home before dark."

"Take Joseph with you. He can spend the night in Jadizi and return tomorrow. Avoid strangers on the road. I will do everything I can to protect Tazrut and get Musa to calm down."

"**H**ow dare she," said Musa when he learned that Titrit had come to see her sister. "Sneaking over the roof as though she's a criminal. I'll show her..."

He was on his way out the door when Eli's soft voice behind him said, "Master..."

"Don't you 'Master' me in my own house," he stammered, realizing he wasn't making any sense even as the words came out. Perhaps he did need to calm down. But it was outrageous. In his own house!

"Sir, your wife is already bleeding and hysterical. Titrit will have returned to Itzak's house by now. Think of the consequences. The others already know what you have done to your wife and may suspect that you have been involved in other things."

"I was within my rights in beating her. I'm taking Faisel from her. I'll not have her pagan ways influencing my only son."

"But the boy is attached to her; he could learn to hate you if you keep him from her. And you may be in great danger if anyone suspects you of misdeeds. There may be a better way," suggested Eli.

Musa paused. Perhaps there was reason to be cautious. "What are you thinking?"

"Call Emilia to you. She may be the key not only to your family problems but also to the future of your dream of Spanish dominion in Algiers. So far you have ruled her with threats. It is time to offer her rewards she can't resist. Otherwise you are at risk of exposure."

'Yes,' he thought. 'If she agreed to convert, I would take her as an official concubine. If she produced a fair-skinned son, I might even marry her.'

29. Strange Offerings to a Cruel God

Trixie took out the bowl and oil and sat between two candles staring at the gently swirling surface. Even though it was well after midnight, she wanted to make sure her mother was safe.

Images began to take shape. Tazrut was asleep in her bed. But where was Faisel? There. The scene shifted; he was asleep in the room attached to hers. And Emilia? As the question entered her mind, the scene gradually shifted again. Another bed. But in a different part of the house. Her father's room. He was in his bed, but not alone. A flowered shift was draped over a chair near-by; Emilia's favorite dressing gown. She had seen enough. She turned away and snuffed out the candles.

The next morning, Trixie shared the news with Titrit. "Emilia has become Musa's lover," she said simply.

After a thoughtful silence, Titrit answered, "Perhaps she has discovered the best way to protect Tazrut and Faisel, as well as herself."

Musa felt very clever and powerful. Why had he never thought of it before? Emilia was his, and he was sure that she admired him. What did he need with a fifteen-year-old virgin like Saba? Here was a real woman who understood just what he needed and did everything he wanted. Fair skinned, blond, buxom, why had he never noticed how voluptuous she was? She would be much more to him than just a link to the garrison. She would prove to be a solace at home and might give him hope that there could be a way to overthrow Arouj.

On the Friday after the aborted uprising, his brother and Samir suggested that they should be seen in public to demonstrate their loyalty to the new regime. They suggested he accompany them to the main mosque for mid-day prayers.

As the three men walked down the steep streets toward the southeast corner of the walled city, they saw friends and acquaintances dressed in their finest brocaded caftans and elaborate turbans, also on their way to the old domed structure with the tall minaret, the main mosque of Algiers.

After the three performed their ablutions at the fountain in the courtyard, Musa entered the main prayer hall with Itzak on his right and Samir on his left. He felt they seemed anxious and protective of him. Should he be worried? Everyone knew he was no fan of Arouj, but they could not suspect that he had coordinated plans with the garrison.

He looked around the vast room with its vaulted ceiling and delicately patterned, latticed windows high up in its walls. So many men filing in, so many men already at prayer, and yet it was muffled, almost still. Perhaps he was just nervous, but the crowd seemed subdued, cowed.

The Imam briefly addressed the congregation from his raised pulpit. That seemed normal, though the old man's voice was not as resonant as usual. When he stepped aside, Sultan Arouj took his place. Musa looked around. Had everyone else expected this? He hadn't.

Then he saw the sultan's guards shut all the gates. Two stood in front of each door. The worshipers were all trapped inside; he, Musa, was trapped with them.

He dared not panic or call attention to himself. Like the others, he knelt in exaggerated stillness and heard the words from on high, words from the sultan, words that passed judgment and demanded retribution. Might this lead to words that would grant pardon or to words of forgiveness? He hoped so. Arouj now held the power of life and death over them all, and over him. Musa did not want to die. He hadn't done anything wrong. It wasn't his fault the garrison and the Beni Tatije had swayed some Baldi to rebel.

He trembled as soldiers passed systematically though the crowd, removing each man's turban and using it to bind his arms and hands behind his back. It felt like a lifetime, watching all the leading citizens humiliated and forced to kneel, helpless and bareheaded, on their prayer rugs. Finally, it was their turn. He, Itzak, and Samir were bound and forced to kneel with all the others.

Then the soldiers passed along the rows of men and pulled certain of them to their feet. One by one, they were led to the main door, where they formed a long line, a procession of prisoners of all ages and descriptions. Who was being chosen? Who would be spared? Was it a lottery, or was there a logic to the choices? With their turbans off, they were strangely vulnerable, as though fully naked before a crowd. Some had scraggly gray hair, others thick black locks cascading down their backs, and still others had no hair at all. What did they have in common? Were they all seen as traitors against Arouj? Would he be selected among them?

A soldier approached and stood behind Musa. He must rise. Itzak and Samir stared but could do nothing to help. He felt limp, but a tug from behind raised him to his feet. His brother looked up at him with compassion and a touch of fear. In that moment, Musa saw the terror in Itzak's eyes and knew that Itzak had not betrayed him; he was afraid that they would come after him, too, for nothing more than being the brother of a traitor.

He was pushed to the end of the line of at least two dozen men. At first, he could not see what was happening, though there were cries, even screams, coming from the courtyard. He saw the man closest to the doorway propelled forward and pushed to his knees. The man's head was separated from his body in a single clean stroke. Musa gasped and lost all volition. One man after another met the same fate, like lambs led to slaughter. After each stroke of the scimitar, one soldier dragged the headless corpse to the side while another lifted the head by the hair and placed it on a pile against the wall. Musa was pushed ever closer to the door until there were only three or four bound men left in line with him, shivering with fear, staring at the bodies that lay like rag dolls tossed carelessly across the paving stones. A trail of blood led from each corpse back to the doorway, and a gruesome pyramid of five, ten, perhaps twenty heads was stacked against the wall. As Musa stood in the doorway with the others behind him, Arouj raised his hand. "Enough," he called out in his booming voice.

Musa swooned to the floor. Though he did not lose consciousness, he lost control of his bowels, making his shame complete.

A guard freed his hands and helped him rise. He felt only gratitude and relief. When asked to hand over his purse, he did so as though he were bestowing a voluntary gift. Arouj seemed a god-like ruler. It was as though the essence of each victim had passed into him and each death had enlarged him. He had achieved the status of a deity in Musa's eyes. Arouj was his angry and vengeful god, and he would do anything to serve this man who had spared him.

30. The Winter of Discontent

Musa's craven devotion to Arouj did not last. In the months following his narrow escaped from death, he slowly recovered. Only the thought that the armada would arrive in the spring gave him hope.

Emilia encouraged him. "When the fleet arrives," she would say, "the Commander of the Garrison will tell them you have been a loyal informant. You will be rewarded for your help."

"But what will happen to my family? The Spanish and the Beni Tatije will know that members of my family have ingratiated themselves to Arouj."

"You will be their protector, and they will be grateful forever."

"Not Tazrut and her horrid girl. And not that old hag in Jadizi; not Mayam."

"Even them. What do they care who rules the city if you are all safe? You will show that you are a natural leader when the Spanish defeat Arouj and his feeble followers. You will stand at the right hand of a new governor and tell him whom to trust and whom to punish. It is the Turks who ruined your life, not the Moriscos or the Baldi. Point out the Barbarossa loyalists to the victors when the battle is over, and you will become a man of power."

Little by little, he started to believe her version of the future. Yes, the Turks were to blame. Itzak had been led astray by them. Even Tazrut and Titrit might be innocent. He could protect them. Then he thought of Saba. With Khizr destroyed along with his brother Arouj, Saba would be free to re-marry. Musa would not stoop to that. She did not deserve to be his wife. He would make her his concubine. He drifted into a fantasy in which Saba and her family were under his control. Sometimes he was condescendingly kind to them and at other times sadistically cruel, but always they were filled with gratitude toward him, their savior.

When the nights grew long and cold, the women of Jadizi spent their evenings in front of the fire, spinning their spring rovings into yarn and weaving the yarn into blankets. During the summer, Trixie had collected herbs, leaves, and even fungi and branches from trees. In the fall, she learned how the collections could be transformed into dyes to create the many-colored yarns for winter projects: yellow, brown, green, and red, dyes in shades that would vary, depending on the color of the natural yarn. She also learned how to make potions and elixirs to be used in healing. She was fast becoming a skilled herbalist and sometimes accompanied Titrit and Mayam when they went to treat sick or injured villagers.

Her favorite activity for winter nights was to weave by the fire. She liked to see how the colorful skeins looked together in a rug and spent long minutes standing before her loom rearranging the yarn and imagining the design that would slowly grow up the vertical length of the warp as she slid her shuttle through the shed and drew the yarn back and forth, row after row. Even though she worked only in stripes, her cloth was lumpy and uneven. She glanced over at Titrit, whose blanket grew so quickly it seemed like magic. But Mayam was the master. Her strong hands twisted the yarn as she worked, until her threads were fine enough to create infinitely detailed patterns on her complex projects, which always drew a fine price from the agents who came to purchase her best work.

'If only it didn't go so slowly,' thought Trixie. She missed the longer days when she and Hasnai could gallop to exhaustion on mountain trails before the light was gone, but then she remembered Titrit's cautioning words, 'Be patient. Each object you create has a life: it is conceived in your mind and gestates as you work on it; only if you are careful will it be born as a thing of use and beauty.'

"**I**'m afraid for Ummi," Trixie said to Titrit one evening while they were preparing vegetables and herbs for their lamb stew.

"Why don't you gaze in the oil? Since Musa's humiliation, you seem to see into their home more clearly than you used to."

"That was true for a while, but it's gone dark again. Please, Auntie Titrit, I must go back to Algiers. I could find a way to see Ummi, and I could resume my studies with Nouri and Samir."

"It seems so dangerous," answered Titrit.

"I can pretend to be Joseph's cousin again; we can call me 'Hakeem.' People will get used to seeing me in the neighborhood. Best of all, I could see my mother."

"If Musa found out ..."

"How would he? I won't go to his house. Ummi can come to see me at Itzak's."

"What about Eli and Faisel? Either of them would tell."

"I can avoid Eli, and I think I might fool Faisel."

"What about Beni?"

"He'd never tell. He loves to pretend, so it would be like an adventure for him."

"I'm almost convinced," said Titrit. "Let's ask Mayam."

To their surprise, Mayam answered, "Yes. It's time. You need to learn more about the events of the world. No one in Algiers except Khizr knows more than Samir. He has informants from Fez to Tunis and even in Spain. For all I know, he hears from Constantinople, Rome, and Venice as well. Go with my blessing and come back to share all that you learn with us. It will help us prepare for the arrival of the armada."

Excited and encouraged, Trixie took out her bowl that very evening. Almost immediately, she saw a familiar scene: Ahmed, in his kitchen, talking with a woman that looked like Emilia. This time she could hear them speaking. The woman seemed to be asking if he knew a remedy for nausea. Her voice sounded like Emilia's, but Ahmed called her "Yasmine," so it could not be the companion of her childhood. But if things went as Mayam had promised, she would soon be in Algiers herself, and she would see both of her old friends again in person. Her mouth watered as she thought of Ahmed's honey-soaked pastries.

In December, Trixie rode to Algiers with Titrit. She kept the hood of her burnous raised and avoided eye contact with people on the streets, but she never felt in danger, even when she entered her old neighborhood. The city was so busy that people thought nothing of an unfamiliar lad riding along the streets of the Casbah.

Arouj had begun construction projects all over the city, but especially around the waterfront and the gates. He was clearly preparing for a siege. Her only risk would be encountering Faisel, but she had a hunch he wouldn't recognize her. In fact, she wasn't sure that she would recognize him either, it had been so long since they had seen each other.

When Joseph opened the door, he gasped. "You risked coming back."

"Joseph, from now on she is your cousin, Hakeem," said Titrit. "She will not change into her own clothes or be known by any other name as long as she is here. You, Samir, and Beni will be in on it. Some of the other servants may guess, but we must think of the children. Ali must know her only as Hakeem."

"Yes, I understand," said Joseph. "Beni will enjoy the excitement. He'll never tell."

"Take 'Hakeem' to the library, and I will go next door to tell Tazrut."

Nouri, Itzak and Samir welcomed 'Hakeem' to the room that she loved so well. "You'll see your mother in just a few more minutes," Nouri assured her. "She has missed you so."

When Tazrut entered, Trixie was surprised at how small she seemed, no bigger than a child. She was dressed in a dun-colored shift with her hair covered in a plain green scarf. The simplicity of her dress made her seem as vulnerable as a young girl.

"Trixie, is that you?" She heard the familiar voice for which she had yearned, but it seemed so hesitant. Only then did she realize she was still dressed as a boy, and that she had grown much taller while she was away. Her mother really wasn't sure who she was.

"Ummi," she said in a voice that was part sigh, part question, and part delight. The moment she had longed for was here at last, yet they could barely recognize each other. Was it possible they had become strangers?

"Yes, Ummi, yes, it's me," she cried with more confidence, pulling the turban from her head and letting her long hair spring free as she stood before her mother as herself, an almost-woman and apprentice herbalist from Jadizi, but still Trixie. At last mother and daughter were in each other's arms, two women of almost the same height. 'She still thinks I'm a frightened little girl who needs protecting,' Trixie realized. 'But she feels so small and frail in my arms; I am the one who must take care of her now.'

Ummi was crying against her shoulder. "Masha Allah, you are safe," she sobbed.

"Of course, I'm safe; you are the one in danger now. Does Emilia still protect you?"

"Emilia doesn't have much time to spend with me anymore," Ummi replied. "We have several new slaves who take care of the household and are with me a lot. Haven't you heard the news? Emilia has converted to Islam and has been formally recognized as Musa's concubine."

Titrit was startled. She started to respond, "After all these years? Surely, he did not just…'" when Trixie cut her off.

"Then my sighting in the oil was true. I thought it was Emilia. She is called Yasmine now, isn't she?"

"Trixie, you'll make a believer out of me," Itzak said, shaking his head. "I've always doubted what others call your 'gift,' but you are certainly right about Emilia's name change. How did you 'know'?"

"I 'saw' a woman standing with Ahmed in his kitchen. I thought perhaps she was Emilia, but I decided it wasn't when I heard Ahmed call her 'Yasmine.'"

"Do you also know that she is carrying your father's child?"

"She didn't look pregnant," Trixie answered.

"No," Itzak laughed in response. "She is still at the stage of feeling sick all the time. That is the only way it 'shows.'"

"If Emilia is pregnant, it is unlikely the baby is Musa's," said Trixie, "though it might be the reason she has seduced him so completely."

"What do you mean by that?" Itzak looked at her sharply.

"Musa has not been her only lover. When I heard she started treating him so well, I wondered if it was because she needed to cover the consequences of her other relationship."

"Trixie, please, don't say such a thing," cried Titrit.

Trixie looked her aunt directly in the eyes and said, "You're the one who says you'll always believe the things I 'see,' or at least try to learn more before you decide if they are true or not. I am saying aloud something that I know to be true about Emilia--I mean Yasmine."

"You're right, Trixie," Titrit apologized. "I was just shocked to hear it spoken. Who is the father?"

"I don't want to say. Emilia has been good to us. I remember how she comforted you, Ummi, more than once, saying, 'it's not just you, Tazrut. He gets angry at others for no reason as well.'" Tazrut nodded to confirm what Trixie was saying.

Itzak stared at Trixie, wanting to know more. "Does he beat Emilia, too?"

"Not often, I don't think," she answered, but turned to her mother. "Ummi, you would know better."

Titrit suddenly interrupted their speculation. "I just realized the implications. We all know that Emilia spent time with soldiers from the garrison. She was always looking for a Christian patron to ransom her."

"Are you implying that Emilia could have helped Musa forge a link with the Peñón," asked Itzak. Trixie saw that he was shocked at the idea. "If she gave Musa information from the garrison, he could easily have conveyed it to the Baldi and, by way of the souk, to the Arabs," said Itzak.

"Her relationship with the soldiers was there for all to see," Samir commented. "At least until Arouj arrive and made it too dangerous for them to come to the city."

"And I tried to save him from his own foolishness," remarked Itzak. "I did not believe that he was central to the plot, even though he was singled out at the mosque."

Nouri spoke up for the first time. "How could she possibly be a liaison? There's no way she can meet with the soldiers now."

Itzak nodded in response. "True, but she might have a way of getting messages to them. We should know better than to underestimate her."

One morning in April, when the only snow left on the mountain lay in deep crevices or under thick trees on northern slopes, Itzak arrived in Jadizi unannounced. Titrit felt a familiar surge of warmth run up her spine and spread to her arms and legs when she saw him. She smiled and looked down like a modest young girl, then boldly picked up her chin and looked as directly at her lover as she would have in greeting any other man — or woman, for that matter. It was often so when she saw Itzak, especially when it was unexpected.

Titrit was pleased to notice that Itzak had eyes only for Mairnia, who was now a toddler. It was a rare treat for her to see them together. "Go ahead," she said to encourage him. "Greet her while we wait for tea. She has grown more cautious since you were last here."

Little Mairnia had been watching the spindle twirl around and around, twisting the rovings into yarn. Now Mayam had set it aside. Mairnia stood with one hand resting on the stool and the other reaching tentatively for the spindle, tempted to pick it up. She looked to her mother for approval. Noticing the bearded man with the colorful turban coming toward her, she grew still and stared, the spindle and yarn forgotten.

Laughing, Titrit picked her up, and Mairnia buried her head in her mother's shoulder. Itzak reached out to take her, but she drew back just slightly. Titrit carried her to the divan, and Itzak sat down next to them. Mairnia eyed him coyly, buried her head in her mother's shoulder again for a moment, then looked back at him and smiled. He returned her smile. By the time the water boiled, Mairnia was standing with her hands on his knee, staring up into his face.

The intimacy between Titrit and Itzak had taken both by surprise. It had started in a blaze of passion, three years earlier, on the night Trixie dreamed of a crowd that cheered at a severed head on the end of a lance, a time before Trixie moved to Jadizi.

Titrit had covered herself in a haik and had gone next door to tell Itzak about Trixie's dream. She thought her best choice was to leave through the Musa's kitchen door onto the alley and around the corner to see if she could get in through Itzak's kitchen. If no one responded to her knock, she planned to go to the front door and rouse the family if necessary. She felt it was time for Itzak to understand the accuracy and depth of Trixie's "gift."

She stepped up to the recessed doorway in the alley and raised her hand to knock. By chance, Itzak was approaching along the alley and saw her in the shadows. He reached out to touch her, realizing she could not see him, but knowing instinctively it was Titrit.

When she felt his hand through her outer garment, that light touch had radiated through her in waves that pulsed from her chest, where it began, outward in all directions until her skin from the top of her head to the soles of her feet, pulsed gently in anticipation of the next touch. He stepped forward. How many times could such a thing have happened on a narrow alley near the Casbah of Algiers? It was like a dream then and still like a dream to her now, and she was sure that, increasingly, their passion was intensified by risk.

In those early days, the danger had been irrelevant to them. Their bodies sought union through their robes and in the dark. They understood each other without speaking. They were bound by their shared need to save their young niece and by their shared vision of a greater future. Was it sordid and furtive? Not to either of them. It was surrender to a passion that was larger than themselves. It was a physical union that sealed their unwritten contract to save Sycorax, who represented the best of the Maghreb, all that Algiers could be in this new world of mercantile and military might. Both knew that if necessary, they would sacrifice their passion in the service of family and, especially, the promise of Sycorax's future.

Titrit had embraced the fate prescribed by Mayam from the start, but she was glad she had fallen into her secret affair with the only man whom she could imagine as the father of her child. She had no interest in quarrels or power struggles, and she knew that with Itzak, that would never become an issue. He was devoted to his beloved Nouri, and Titrit would rather support than undercut that union. In the meantime, she would enjoy their shared secret, even when it was little more than a furtive moment in a dark alley.

After tea, Itzak acknowledged that he had come on business as well as pleasure. "We must be realistic. The fleet could set out from Spain any time now. Arouj and his generals are calling on all their allies.

"To survive, we will need as many tribes as possible. We will ask for volunteers from near and far, but some who fought with us last year may not be free this early in the season or may not be able to arrive on short notice. Your presence could influence the outcome of the battle."

"My people have assembled our weapons," said Mayam. "We have been training rigorously all winter. Jadizi is ready to ride as soon as we get the call. My old bones may ache after a session of weapons practice, but I will be as ready as my younger followers for the real thing, when it comes to pass."

31. The Armada Returns: 1517

Armada season had arrived, making everyone along the coast nervous. The mountain villagers were alert as well, particularly Jadizi. Itzak came to check in each week, to share information and keep the village involved in preparations.

"How are you doing," Mayam asked Trixie one morning when she saw her staring into her bowl of water with its skim of oil.

"I don't see anything I can be sure of, and yet I have a feeling."

"We all do. Perhaps it is time, even without a clear sign. Meddur, alert the village. Send three of your swiftest messengers ahead. Titrit, Trixie, and I are going down to the hill east of the Bab Azzoun. They are sure to come, if not today, one day soon. All villagers willing to fight should be armed and ready."

By the time they got down to the coast, men and women from other villages were already arriving. Little by little, the hills and plains around Algiers swarmed with armed volunteers. The atmosphere reminded Trixie of the camel races on market day when the excited crowd argued about the odds. Here they were arguing about which side they should support, or whether they should participate at all. Spain, Sultan Arouj, or neither? What would be best for them? Traditionally, villagers wanted to see how a battle was going before joining a side. Their reward was whatever they could take as booty from the slain.

Word arrived that men in a watchtower far to the west had spotted the fleet. As soon as she got the news, Mayam sent messengers galloping back up the mountain to alert the village.

"This battle will mean more to us than just the spoils of war," said Mayam to her people and to the leaders from other villages. "Arouj leaves us alone and has a reputation for fairness. Better him than the Spanish who are on a crusade and want to turn us all into Christians."

The sun was directly overhead and the fleet not yet in sight when two men rode toward Mayam from the Bab Azzoun. Trixie recognized Uncle Itzak, accompanied by a young Turk who seemed to be of some distinction, given the trappings of his horse and the size of his turban. They approached and spoke directly to Mayam. Itzak introduced his companion as Hasan Agha, who had been promoted from reis of a single galliot to become one of Khizr's most trusted officers, earning the title of agha.

"What can you tell us about the weather? Will the wind stay calm all day, or will Allah help us? Deliver a strong wind, and you will earn a large purse from our generous Sultan."

"In coin stamped with his own image," answered Mayam. "Arouj seems sure he will win, even against great odds, but you must wait a bit longer for my answer. I must see the ships before I can be sure how the wind will impact them. The fleet is close. I already smell it."

A gentle onshore breeze blew the stench ahead of the armada. First one giant galley with 24 oars on each side lumbered into sight, then another, powered by Muslim slaves chained eight or more to an oar. If the galley sank, they would all die, helplessly dragged to the bottom with the ship. If they stayed afloat, they would be rewarded only with blows from the whips of their overseers.

Next came the carracks, huge supply ships powered largely by sails. There were dozens and dozens, perhaps hundreds, of ships all together. As they came near, the crews adjusted sails and began complex formations, some dropping anchors, some holding in place offshore, with the galleys lining up so their cannon faced the beach to provide cover for the transport ships, which backed onto the sand to deploy their landing gear.

'So different from last time,' Trixie thought. She remembered watching the first ship back up to the Peñón when she was only five years old. It had tied up at an ancient mooring on the rocky islet and unloaded men and supplies to build the fort that still oppressed Algiers. 'This time they will land on the beach and lay siege to the city. They will not negotiate with Arouj as leader. They assume that he killed their chosen emir and will never trust him.'

After long minutes in deep concentration, Mayam turned to Hasan, "You will not need Allah's help if the Spanish are foolish enough to land their troops and supplies on the beach and then anchor their transports offshore. Before the soldiers can deploy their artillery and organize their troops, this breeze will intensify. Their sails will be useless as the wind comes straight toward them, and their oars will be inadequate to pull those deep hulls off the sand."

Itzak laughed aloud. "We may be the best sailors in the Mediterranean, but we will stay on land for this battle. What you are telling us is that going toward shore for unloading will seem easy, but after they withdraw, the wind will grow stronger, and they won't dare return."

"Exactly," responded Mayam. "Choose a time when the maximum number of men have landed, but before they are organized to fight. If you attack at the right moment, I foresee a terrible slaughter. The Spanish will lose control of their ships, troops will be stranded on the beach and the day will be yours."

"Will you and the mountain people join us?"

"If all goes as I have said, when we see your cavalry come out of the gates, I will signal my people forward. Spain shall not place another Arab as emir in the casbah of Algiers if we can help it. But if I am wrong, and you stand no chance, I will not risk the lives of my people for you, though my own daughter is one of you and we are kin."

As Itzak and Hasan left for the city, Mayam stood on a well-placed boulder, flanked on one side by Meddur and on the other by his cousin Juba. She easily commanded the attention of the crowd. "Hear me," she shouted. "It is about to begin. Arouj knows that we are here, and that we will help him overwhelm his enemy if he shows courage. Don't let yourselves get within the range of fire from muskets or cannon. We will mount our horses, our camels and our donkeys and mow down stragglers."

Musa watched from his terrace as the Spanish ships deployed equipment and men onto the beach. 'At last, my time has come,' he gloated. 'Arouj was able to out-smart the Beni Tatije, but he can't defend the city from this great armada.'

The Spanish had come with ten thousand men to destroy their enemies and reward their loyal subjects. Not even an evil djinni could change the course of fate now. The commander of the garrison, whom Musa considered his friend although they had never met, promised that his role in providing information over the months would be handsomely rewarded. Soon he would have free access to the best Christian ports on the Mediterranean. He would be rich and powerful.

Musa called Eli to bring refreshment to him. He would watch the battle unfold from here on the terrace. This would be a day of celebration for him.

Trixie stood with the others and watched the troops disembark. The men looked small and vulnerable, like ants hard at work carrying things and scurrying about. First came horses, already saddled, led by cavalrymen. Next came boxes filled with shovels, lumber, and equipment for building fortified trenches on the beach. Even she could tell that they were digging in for a long siege.

Once empty, the ships maneuvered away from the sandy shore while workmen unpacked the gear and soldiers mounted their nervous horses to form into companies.

As the wind began to pick up, Mayam and Titrit mounted their ponies and checked their spears and knives. All around Trixie, people shifted restlessly, waiting for the signal from Mayam, who sat astride her pony at the crest of the hill, where all could see her.

Trixie felt the familiar sea wind growing stronger on her face, raising her hair in wild coils around her head. She called to the wind in recognition, as to a friend. "Come to me," she shouted silently.

"I am coming," she heard a male voice respond. Startled, she looked around. No one was paying any attention to her; all eyes were on the beach.

'Hurry,' she cried silently, again addressing the wind.

"I am here," he answered.

'Stronger,' she commanded, testing to see if it was as it seemed, that she called to the wind, and it answered her.

"I will blow full force," he cried back, and the wind blew even stronger gusts until the loose ends of men's turbans whipped about and sand stung the faces of the soldiers on the beach.

Each time the men dug a trench or erected a retaining wall, it collapsed. Horses shifted and balked as sand blew in their eyes and stung their flanks; cavalry officers struggled to hold their units together. Amid the confusion, the gates of the Bab Azzoun opened to let heavily armored Turks and Moors ride out from the east side of the city. Unseen from Trixie's position, as many more rode out from the Bab al-Wad on the west, while musketeers surged through the Sea Gate onto the docks and beaches to intercept Christians who might try to flee.

Mayam raised her sword and uttered a cry like none Trixie had ever heard, and she picked up the shout, screaming at the top of her lungs with a voice she had never uttered before, deep and dark as a grown man's. Was it her own voice or that of the wind? She did not know.

Mounted Kabyle and Arab cavalry, led by this distant Daughter of Dihya, Trixie's own grandmother Mayam, swarmed down from the hills to help Arouj and his men attack the invaders. Caught off guard, the Christians were trapped between the converging forces from city and countryside. The wind was now so strong the ships in the bay were unable to hold steady. The cannon on the Peñón and on the galleys were of no use, for they would have slaughtered their own men.

Watching from his rooftop terrace in the wild wind, Musa could not believe what he was seeing. Hundreds of troops stumbled on the edge of the water, fighting for firm footing, battling the wind and falling under the blows of Turks, Moriscos, Arabs, and Kabyle villagers, men and women, who surged toward the shore in waves, cutting down the unprepared Spaniards too confused to organize into companies. Men fell and bled in the trenches, half in and half out of the choppy waves. They fell before the relentless onslaught of the defenders, blinded by sand, struck down by relentless warriors and swallowed by the wind-driven waves. 'This cannot be,' thought Musa.

"Save them," he called aloud.

He knew that their only hope was to be rescued but saw the powerful onshore winds forcing some ships to crash against the cliffs and driving others onto the beach. Even the ships anchored in the bay were not safe. Men slid from side to side on their tossing decks, futilely struggling to grasp ropes or cleats, slamming against bulwarks only to slide back the other way. He stared in amazement as a proud old knight toppled overboard and was pulled down by the weight of his armor. Arms raised high, imploring his god to save him, he sank beneath the waves, his helmet and gauntlets reflecting the sunlight through the water like great, glittering jewels cast to the bottom of the sea. 'His fortune is mine,' thought Musa.

"All is lost," he cried to the fierce wind, which seemed to mock him by blowing even harder.

Trixie stood next to Hasnai on the high hill east of Bab Azzoun looking down on the beach, hearing the cries, watching blow after blow from swords of soldiers and tribesmen falling on men sometimes armed only with shovels. Mayam had ordered her not to join in the fight, though she was armed and prepared to defend herself if threatened. The things she saw were worse than her dreams. Then she heard the voice in her ear.

'Your father,' it said, 'is going mad. Soon he will be running on the beach in a desperate attempt to reach the Peñón. You will find him if, just before sunset, you go around the corner of the great wall where it meets the sea.'

She climbed onto Hasnai and rode down to the beach. Soldiers led roped lines of prisoners toward the bagnio, where they would be held for ransom, sold, or set to work as slaves for the city. She shivered as she remembered Emilia's stories. She knew that Muslims and Christians alike were thoughtlessly cruel to those who were powerless before them.

She saw mountain villagers and citizens from Algiers turning over corpses searching for weapons and valuables and sifting through the sand for digging equipment abandoned in the chaos. She recognized some of them as villagers from Jadizi. Tall but still beardless Idir, the boy who had carried her amphora and became her sparring partner, was among them. Perhaps war seemed less romantic to him now.

The long shadows from the western hills crept across an apocalyptic scene already darkened by rolling clouds. There was no rain, only the strong wind that shifted back and forth between east and northeast and drove sand like sharp needles into her skin. She pulled the hood of her cloak over her head, but snakes of her black hair escaped and lashed against her face.

The lowering tide had exposed some rocks and formed a little beach at the southeast corner of the city walls. A single stunted olive tree gnarled its way from what little soil remained. She rode her pony into its lee, the only shelter she could find, and waited to see whether the wind's promise would be fulfilled.

She saw Musa creep out through the Sea Gate with Eli looming behind him. Both wore ragged cloaks, disguised as scavengers. They scuttled along the dock close to the wall, heading towards her rocky beach. When they drew close, she urged her pony forward. She was near the wall; they had moved lower, onto the sand. She rose in her saddle, high above them, darker even than the tall wall behind her, cloak, hair, and skirts whipping around her.

"You are a man of sin," she cried out in her new voice, emboldened by the wind. This was the curse that had been growing inside her since the day he had stepped on her beloved lizard. "Your own corruption has made you mad, like the wild elements that rage around you. You, my own father, presumed to send me from my mother, and then threatened to take her son from her as well. You do not deserve to live.

"The suffering you will now endure you created for yourself," she continued after a pause. "You could have listened to Itzak and Samir, but instead you sought European ports over local allegiances, and you will pay the price for your folly. Neither Spain nor Algiers will honor you. Instead, you will shrivel away in your lonely room. Only someone more powerful than I can remove this curse. Only then can you find peace. And you, Eli, will still serve him, but only when you recognize his impotence and venality. If you encourage him in his quest for power, you shall share his fate."

Briefly, the sea and a slender strip of sky glowed blood red beneath low clouds. Then the rain began, and all went dark. The two men quaking beneath her on the beach disappeared from her sight.

Trixie slid off Hasnai and, reins in hand, groped her way to the Bab Azzoun. Dropping the reins, she pulled her cloak over her head and huddled in the recess of a small door below the great gate. Hasnai stood by her, shielding her from the storm.

Late that night, Meddur found her, arms wrapped around her knees, shivering and staring blankly straight ahead, her loyal mount standing protectively over her. He tied Hasnai behind his own horse, then picked her up, cradling her in his strong arms, and carried her on his horse up the mountains to Jadizi.

32. The Women Gather: 1517

Just a month after the armada was destroyed, word came to Jadizi that Emilia was pacing restlessly, showing signs that she might be about to begin labor.

Trixie and Titrit left with Mayam's blessing, hoping they could get to Algiers in time to be of help. As they approached the Bab Azzoun, they saw crews of slaves hauling stones toward the city from quarries in the hills. More slaves swarmed newly constructed scaffolding, hard at work reinforcing the walls nearest to the gate. Looking toward the beach, she saw that the wreckage of the ships and other debris from the aborted siege were already gone. One invasion was barely behind them, and another was already anticipated.

The city was like a beehive. Busy workers renewed neglected neighborhoods to provide housing for the hundreds of Moriscos arriving regularly from Spain, while peddlers hawked cloth for turbans, second-hand slippers, and other low-grade wares to ready customers. Street vendors squatted in doorways with wilted onions and over-ripe lemons spread on dirty blankets. Tiny shops brimmed with pots and pans on their crowded shelves, shoes and slippers piled on the cluttered floor, and slippers. shawls, burnous, and haiks hanging on the walls and dangling from the ceilings. The city seemed prosperous and secure.

The winding streets with their irregular steps did not seem as steep to Trixie as before, perhaps because she now spent so much time tending sheep, gathering herbs on mountain slopes and riding her pony daily. She had grown bigger and stronger even in the past month.

Titrit and Trixie approached Musa's house through the back alley, passing along the family corral to the heavy wooden doors that led to the stables. A slave boy answered their knock and they stepped into the dark, cavernous space that smelled of animal sweat and dung. Eli appeared as though from nowhere, and the boy led Hasnai and Sisi to their stalls.

Eli led them in silence to a narrow staircase in the far corner. He would not look at Trixie, though she felt his deference and was sure he knew who she was, despite her burnous. They climbed past cramped rooms Trixie had never seen before, a labyrinth of ill-lit storage areas and low-ceilinged cells where house slaves slept. Here there were no arched doorways leading to garden patios with sparkling fountains and shaded colonnades, no gracious windows to let in light, no colorful carpets spread on ornate mosaic floors, only cold stone and ill-trimmed oil lamps. Then they came to an iron grill, beyond which she glimpsed the rooms that she had known in childhood, bright spaces filled with well-remembered beauty.

As Eli fumbled with the key ring hidden in the folds of his orange cummerbund, a slight figure approached on the other side of the gate.

"Ummi," cried Trixie, delighted to see her mother. Eli unlocked the gate and stepped aside for their greeting. When they unwound from their embrace, he urged them to move on to Yasmine's room. "The master is concerned for the health of his child. He has ordered me to rush you quickly to Yasmine's side. And Sycorax; yes, I know it's you, he must not guess that you are here." Retorts came to her mind. Why should she protect him from a powerless girl like herself? But she let it go. There was more important business at hand.

"She is still in the early stages," said Tazrut, filling Trixie and Titrit in on Yasmine's state. "It will be some time before the baby comes, but she is restless and needs loving support." She picked up her pace, bringing Trixie along with her, their arms still linked as they almost ran forward in their excitement.

Yasmine's room was on the other side of the courtyard from Tazrut's, but almost as large and well-equipped, fit for a favored concubine who might give birth to the master's son. Yasmine was standing when they came in, as though she had been pacing anxiously about the room, just as Trixie had 'seen' her in the oil skim early that morning.

"Titrit, how grateful I am that you are here. And who is this? Can it be? Little Trixie? Clever girl to come in disguise--but isn't it still dangerous for you?"

"Musa does not frighten me anymore. I hope to repay you for all the kindness you showed when he threatened to exorcise the djinni. I was terrified, and I still feel you saved my life. I hope that someday I can repay you."

"You've always been a bold girl. I think your new life suits you." Yasmine paused a moment, as though distracted by a deep ache within, then resumed. "I hear you have become a horsewoman. Some think you will become the kahina and unite the mountain tribes."

Trixie smiled. "That will be as it will be. I cannot see that far ahead. I've brought herbs and salves to help you on your journey to motherhood. We have bundles of sage to purify the room and sweet-smelling oil to rub on your belly and back to help prepare your body for the passage of the baby."

"She has learned much, Yasmine," said Titrit. "She picked the ingredients and prepared the herbs and unguents. The child you so often scolded is already a skilled herbalist and has even witnessed war, but this will be the first birth she has attended, so she still has much to learn."

"It is my first one as well, at least in this role," said Yasmine with a nervous laugh. "I hope I can learn to play my part as well as she already knows hers."

"We'll make tea and be comfortable. Then we'll talk of all the things that you hope for your child and make sure that we are ready to receive the baby," Trixie assured her.

Tazrut went to the door and called Eli to bring tea and fruit sorbet for refreshment, while Trixie changed into female clothing in the Kabyle style that she had brought with her from Jadizi. The women settled themselves on comfortable pillows to talk away the time. No one spoke of the scandals of the city; not yet.

In the early afternoon, Halima bustled in with what seemed to be at least a half-dozen bulging parcels. She seemed smaller and stouter than Trixie remembered, covered in an eccentric, striped blanket and wearing bracelets and anklets that rattled with a soft and pleasing rhythm when she moved.

"Here you are," she said to the gathering, taking charge. "And this young girl is Sycorax, I presume. Yasmine, stay where you are. I will come to you."

Halima placed her bags in a corner and rummaged through them for a while, then stepped towards the lounging women holding a silver chain with a talisman against the evil eye dangling from it. "See what I have here for you and your child." She held up the chain. Yasmine stretched out her hands toward the talisman with an expression of gratitude and relief.

"Will this protect the baby from those who wish me ill?"

"It is your best guarantee. Neither envy nor malice can harm you or him while you wear it," Halima assured Yasmine.

"Him?"

"Well, of course we cannot be sure, but..."

"I can be sure," said Trixie quietly. "I have 'seen' it. He will be a fair-skinned boy."

Yasmine held the talisman tightly and dropped back on her pillows. "Fair-skinned," she repeated. "What will become of that..."

The room was silent, except for the splashing of the fountain in the patio and the song of a warbler who belied the dread felt by the women gathered within.

"Will his eyes be blue?" Yasmine asked, fearing the answer.

"No bluer than mine," answered Trixie. She smiled to see that they were all looking at her as though they had never noticed that her eyes were dark cobalt blue.

Then they all started talking at once, for they realized that blue eyes were not much more common among the soldiers in the garrison than among the citizens of Algiers. Even Musa's were closer to hazel than to black. Eye color was no sure evidence of paternity, though it was true that Musa's skin could not be called 'fair.' If he had been athletic, they might have called him swarthy, but as he avoided the sun and had no color in his cheeks, dusky was the best word for his complexion.

"If his eyes are blue, it will be taken as a blessing," said Halima. "In any case, his father will embrace him, for he will remember the pleasure he had when the boy was made, when he looked deep into your eyes and loved you."

Yasmine relaxed visibly. "Can this be true? Did he ever love me? If so, perhaps my boy will be accepted. I fear he could be sent away before I even get to suckle him."

"He will grow up as a free citizen," said Trixie with confidence. "I cannot clearly see your own fate. Musa's intentions are blocked from my vision, but I sense that your boy will do great service for his city."

They all grew still at the thought. A heroic future predicted for the son of a slave, a boy whose paternity was in doubt. Extraordinary. Trixie did not share all that she knew; she 'saw' the tragic end of this son who was not yet out of the womb, but she chose not to share her dark vision.

"We will deal with our fates, Allah willing," said Halima. "In the meantime, we have much to celebrate. We will spend a cheerful day that may be followed by an arduous night, culminating in the birth of a vigorous, healthy boy. I shall enjoy a cup of tea, then examine my patient more intimately. I can see that your bag of waters has not broken, so I am content that I have arrived in the fullness of time and, Allah willing, that you will give birth by morning."

"We are with you, Yasmine," added Tazrut with obvious emotion. "You will not be alone."

"Ah, Tazrut," Halima responded, "how I remember the day when you gave birth to your Sycorax. You had only Yasmine-- Emilia as she was then--and me. You see, my dear Yasmine, how fortunate you are to have so many friends gathered around you."

Yasmine suddenly doubled up and began to cry as though seized by a strong contraction.

Despite her years, Halima was beside her in a moment. "There, my dear, that was an unexpected one."

"No," sobbed Yasmine, "it was no stronger than the others, but I am overcome." She continued to cry. "Why should you love me? What have I done but bring shame to this house? I have sought only to return to my homeland. I have dallied with the soldiers from the Peñón. I have aided in plots against Sultan Arouj. I am nothing but a miserable wretch who does not deserve to be loved and cared for. Tazrut, you, above all, should despise me and wish me and my child ill. It is you who should look on me with an eye filled with hatred and wish for a tragic fate for my son."

Without speaking, Tazrut came to her and sat on her other side so that Yasmine was cradled between her and Halima. "There, my dear, there. We know how Musa is. You have never had the freedom to choose what you shall do. We cannot hate you for what fate has brought your way. I don't know how I could have survived without you at my side all these years. Until Nouri arrived, you were my only friend in Algiers, and you are the one who helped save Trixie from violence. We have been rivals, but we must get past that if we hope to live through these times of war."

As she spoke, the oud player arrived and, without fuss, began to play quietly in the background. The women dried their eyes and sat quietly together, understanding the deep currents that flowed among them without needing to explain anything. They let themselves be soothed by the soft music and the sweet tea, occasionally getting up to walk about the room with Yasmine, who stopped every few minutes to clutch her lower abdomen before continuing.

From time to time one would comment on the colorful throat of a swallow that landed briefly on a roped honeysuckle branch or another would speak gently of the moon that she had seen hanging like a sickle over the bay the night before. And so, the time passed.

In the mid-afternoon, Nouri entered from next door. The others looked up in surprise, as though awakened from a collective dream. The musician stopped playing to give them a chance to catch up with the newcomer, who had been busy with children and household responsibilities during the hours that the group had been focused only on the progression of Yasmine's contractions.

Yasmine brightened when she saw Nouri and started to rise from her spot on the divan with the help of Tazrut and Halima but gasped before she was halfway up. Trixie could see her belly grow round and hard beneath her shift. Tazrut helped her settle back on the divan while Trixie counted the duration of the contractions on her own pulse, as Titrit had taught her.

"A full minute," she announced when it subsided, sounding pleased and proud.

Halima moved even closer to Yasmine, placing her hand gently on the laboring woman's abdomen, but Yasmine struggled to say something.

"Musa," she began, gasping and trying hard to speak. "If he knew..."

"Tell us," said Titrit, urgently.

Yasmine's only response was a scream. "Look."

Water gushed from beneath her shift and she gripped a pillow, pulling it to her chest. Her abdomen grew so hard and tight she couldn't move until the contraction passed.

"Ah, now that baby means business," said Halima as she moved gently behind Yasmine on the divan and supported her body, massaging her neck and speaking softly in her ear. "Forgive us for talking about nonsense. You are the only thing that matters today. You are at the center of the universe. We care only about you and the boy you are creating. Now, just relax in my arms. Let it be. Soon we will clean you up and give you a fresh shift."

Yasmine responded by relaxing in Halima's arms, but within seconds, her abdomen grew tight as a ball and her face turned pale.

"Help me," she cried, looking around in desperation and struggling to escape her own body.

"Yes, yes, we are here," Halima whispered. Titrit signaled to Trixie to bring a wet compress, then used it to stroke Yasmine's brow, face, and neck. They were all aware of only one thing: Yasmine and her need to relax enough to ride the powerful and irregular waves that seemed to have taken over her womb.

As things calmed down, Trixie was aware that the atmosphere had changed. Earlier, they had talked about all the building going on in the city, but now Yasmine was the only object of their attention. They removed her shift and cleaned her up, massaging her all over with Trixie's soothing unguent. Soon she seemed more relaxed, and Halima encouraged her to get up and walk around. Every minute or two, she paused as though in deep concentration, and leaned with her hands pressed against a wall and her head hanging low between her shoulders. When she sat down, she shifted onto her hip, but obviously could not get comfortable. Sometimes a spontaneous cry or deep sigh came forth from her, but she could never stay still for long. She needed help to rise, and once up, she leaned on Titrit for support, though she rarely took more than a dozen steps at a time. Whenever she rested with her hands against the wall, Halima used Trixie's salve to rub her lower back and her hips until Yasmine grew restless again and moved on across the room.

Evening came. Nouri went back home to be with her children. Tazrut ordered refreshments for the group and took turns relieving first Halima and later Titrit in their attempts to help Yasmine find comfort for at least a few minutes at a time. By midnight, that was no longer possible. Soon Yasmine's cries filled the room.

"Don't touch me," she screamed at Halima. Then she accused Titrit of witchcraft. Even Tazrut became the object of her anger. "Go away," she shouted at her. "Don't you dare look at me." With this she held up her new talisman. "You wish me dead and my son consigned to slavery, but I shall escape your evil eye. Trixie, protect me; you know how, I know you do."

Tazrut looked at her with compassion, then looked away, relying on others to help Yasmine.

"There, there," said Halima. "Let's take a look now. Bring over a lantern. That's it, Trixie. Now see, what is that, do you think?"

"What, what," cried Yasmine. "I am splitting apart. Musa has cursed me. I shall die."

Her screams terrified Trixie, and yet Halima smiled as though it was all perfectly normal. "Now, my dear," she said, "we are going to help you to get on the birthing stool. It is time."

"No, no," cried Yasmine. "This is no baby. I have a demon between my legs, and he is splitting me in half." She used the Christian word, 'demon,' rather than the Arabic 'djinni.'

"Come, my dear, come. Whatever he is, we shall get him out of there, and you will be free of him, to take him in your arms if he proves to be a baby instead of a djinni." Gently but persistently, Halima and Titrit coaxed Yasmine to sit up and shift her bottom from the bed to the stool. Once in the squatting position with her knees spread wide, she seemed more comfortable.

"Now push," Halima urged her. "Doesn't your body want you to push? Go with it. Help him out."

"I can't, I can't. I won't. If Musa sees him, he will kill him, and me too."

"Ah, so that's it. Well, my dear, we'll have time to deal with all that in the morning. Meanwhile, you have a baby who is ready to come out, but you must help us take him from you."

Yasmine stopped her screaming and writhing. "I won't," she said.

Then Trixie spoke. "Yasmine," she said. "Your boy will have blue eyes, and Musa will acknowledge him. He will believe that he is the father."

"He'll know and hate the baby. And the real father, what of him?"

"What of him? Musa may suspect he is a soldier from the Peñón, but there is no way he can prove it. How could you have been with such a man while the Peñón and Algiers were fighting each other? Let the boy be raised as Musa's."

Between pants and screams, Yasmine gasped out the story. "His father is not a soldier from the Peñón; he is a Christian slave. You know him, Trixie."

"Yes," the girl answered. "Enrico, the cobbler."

"But he does not know the baby is his. He loves me and I love him, but we are slaves and our boy…" Her screams gave way to sobs, and her body relaxed enough to let the child's head emerge inch by inch until it was out and, with a bit of help from Halima, the shoulders were delivered as well. The boy slipped free into the midwife's hands.

"He is free! That is more important than anything. If his father knew, he would rather his son be born dead than into slavery."

Yasmine's sobs subsided, though tears continued to run down her face. She leaned forward in the stool, and Halima placed the newborn, wet and sticky, on her bare breast. With his tiny fists tucked under his chin, the little boy looked up and found his mother's eyes.

"He knows me," she said, sobbing again, but now with joy.

"Yes, and you shall be his mother," said Halima. "Whatever comes of it, you shall be his mother."

"You're right. I can do it. I know that I shall protect him always. It is so clear to me now. If Musa ever threatens me or my boy, I have tales I can tell. Arouj would believe me; Khizr would believe me. Musa is a traitor; his sin is greater than mine, and he knows it. He will have to give me anything I ask for."

Trixie felt power flowing from Yasmine. She was like a mother lion. No one would take this child from her. They all assured her that they would never reveal her secret unless it was to save her and her son.

As the eastern sky lightened behind Mount Djurdjura, Yasmine said the boy would be named Ishmael. Then she gave him to Halima to clean up, knowing that these women who had received him from her womb would always care for him as much as for their own sons.

33. The Campaign to the West: 1517-18

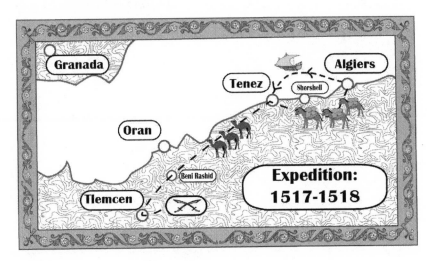

When Trixie and Titrit arrived in July for Trixie's lessons, they were surprised to see the whole family waiting for them. Trixie could tell that Nouri had been crying.

"What's wrong," she asked. "Not Ummi..."

"No," Samir assured her. "Everyone in the family is fine. Beni, take Ali with you to find Fatima. We want to tell Titrit and Trixie what is going on. You can come back to join the lesson later, after Titrit has gone to see Tazrut."

With the boys gone, Samir described the situation bluntly. "The Emir of Tenez has decided that if Spain isn't going to get rid of Sultan Arouj, he will take matters into his own hands. He has raised an army and is headed this way."

"Not more war," gasped Trixie. "Why didn't I see it?"

"Perhaps because it is never going to get here," answered Samir. "Do you remember where Tenez is?"

"To the West, farther away than Shershell. I remember more, too. You told me that for generations they have paid tribute to

Tlemcen, but now they have a ruler named Hamida who has turned Tenez into a more important power in the area, developing strong alliances with both Arab and Berber tribes."

"What a student you are! Your memory is as good as Nouri's was at your age. And what do you predict will happen next, now that we know an army has set out from Tenez for Algiers?"

Trixie was still for a moment. She did not concentrate on the situation but opened herself to the future, as if she was staring into a bowl in the candlelight. After a few moments, she spoke. "Hamida will gather followers along the way, both foot and on horse. Arouj will set out to meet him on the road, as he did when al-Khadi approached Jijelli. Again, the enemy will have no muskets. Arouj will defeat them easily, make peace with the citizens of Tenez, and become their sultan. But this time the leader will escape; Hamida will flee to the mountains."

While Titrit, Nouri, and Itzak stared and her in silence, Samir laughed fondly at the young girl. "You have the wisdom of a seasoned commander, predicting that Arouj will take his army into the field rather than face a siege here at home. No matter how many fighters Hamida picks up along the way, they won't be armed with muskets. Arouj is sure to win, and Itzak will return to us soon."

"That is the plan exactly. We will ride out, defeat their army, go to Tenez to work out an alliance with the people, put an Arouj ally in place, collect a tribute, and ride home."

"If it is so simple, then why is Nouri so distressed about it," Trixie asked. "I think there will be more to it. I think Tlemcen will get involved."

"Now Trixie, you have seen quite enough. The secret to Nouri's tears is not what you think. She is again with child and has become impossibly sentimental. There is nothing more to it than that."

"War is never fair to families," Itzak said in a melancholy voice.

"But do you have to go?" Titrit spoke for herself as much as for Nouri.

"She's wondering what will happen to those who stay behind, if the Spanish attack Algiers before you return," Trixie said, to cover Titrit's outburst. "Nouri and the boys will be vulnerable here in Algiers. They can't count on Musa to protect them, and Samir, wise as he is, is old."

"When the sultan asks, it is a command," answered Itzak. "This is a good time for Arouj to consolidate support with our neighbors to the east. Until the new king arrives in Spain, we are safe from any major military campaigns from them. Khizr will be in charge, and he is as good a military leader and a better diplomat than his brother. More Moriscos arrive every day, and we have the Kabyle allies all around us. Even the Beni Tatije fought on our side against the armada. I think Algiers and all its precious people will be in good hands."

A month later, after two encouraging letters from Itzak, Nouri showed Trixie and Titrit a third letter; this one distressed her. Arouj and his army had defeated Hamida and captured Tenez with minimal difficulty. The Sultan of Algiers allowed only one day of licensed looting and mayhem and made peace with the citizens, assuring that Tenez would be a stout ally of Sultan Arouj.

Then came the bad news:

> We have had a sudden change in plans. Arouj has decided to go to the aid of the dissatisfied people of Tlemcen who want his help to rid them of their sultan.

Trixie looked at Titrit, who had turned pale. This was heavy news for all of them, and a surprise to the others, though not to her.

> He is writing to Fez and Tunis to inform them of his success in Tenez. He hopes they will support him to overthrow the upstart Sultan, Abu Zeyan, in Tlemcen and replace the rightful ruler, Zeyahn's nephew, Abu Hammou, to the throne. I shall write at greater length when I have time.

"Why are they doing this?" Trixie exclaimed. "It is a war they don't have to fight. They defeated the Emir of Tenez; they should come home to protect Algiers."

"My agents tell me that Ximenes, the Regent of Spain, is ill," answered Samir, "and the heir won't arrive for another month. We are safe here for many more months."

Trixie turned to Nouri. "May I hold Itzak's letter," she asked.

"Certainly," Nouri replied, giving her a strange look but handing it to her.

With the letter resting across her palms, Trixie felt Itzak's energy in the vellum and through the writing, penned in his own hand. A familiar sense of 'knowing' rose in her. She sensed that she was seeing into the future, not witnessing something occurring in the moment. She saw a large city, which had to be Tlemcen, and she 'knew' that Arouj was inside its walls.

She began to speak in a voice that seemed to pass through her without first forming words in her mind:

> *"Arouj will fulfill his great ambition. He will add Tlemcen to his conquests and become the most powerful ruler between Fez and Tunis, but he will not live to enjoy the fruits of his labor. His treasures will be strewn across the desert sands, disregarded by the enemy and trod upon by their beasts of burden. His brother and his brother's son will rule hereafter."*

As she became aware of her surroundings, she realized that the others were perfectly still, staring at her. They knew that Khizr's young wife, Saba, was expected to deliver a baby within the month, which made the prophecy seem likely to come true.

"What of Itzak?" Titrit blurted out.

"I've said all I know," Trixie told them. No one doubted the truth of her words, nor did they press her for more.

Approaching the ancient citadel of Al Cala of the Beni Rashid on the way to Tlemcen, Itzak saw thousands of Arab and Berber tribesmen camped on the near-by plains: desert nomads with indigo blue turbans and veiled faces restlessly riding through the grounds on tall, spirited, and well-caparisoned horses; Bedouins squatting by hookahs in front of their camel-hair tents, their families peering out from the dark interiors; Berbers in baggy pantaloons, long sleeved shirts under colorful vests, and carrying scimitars across their backs and daggers in their cummerbunds, riding sturdy ponies well-suited to mountain paths; Arab villagers with hooded burnous and simple white turbans standing in earnest conversation in small groups, their horses hobbled nearby. Itzak's doubts about this venture were swept away when he looked at the gathering. The Sultan of Algiers would have his pick of suitable warriors for the conquest of Tlemcen.

Itzak believed Arouj's plan could work. Tlemcen was as divided now as Algiers had been when Arouj arrived there. Reliable reports indicated that Cardinal Ximenes was too old and sick to organize a large campaign, and the new king was still on his way to Spain. Now was the time to strike.

Arouj and his main force arrived the next day with the ten cannon that had been carried by ship from Algiers to Tenez. They were in high spirits, sharing raucous and amusing tales of confusion caused by Arouj's attempt to employ sails to help the camels pull the cannon-laden carts across the desert. The heat was extreme and there were many accidents along the way, even a few camels lost, but, with extraordinary effort, they reached Al Cala with all their equipment. They were determined to get the cannon across the mountains and deserts to Tlemcen.

Three days later, the army of 3000 (1000 musketeers, hundreds of Moriscos from Algiers, and the 1600 cavalrymen they had picked up in Al Cala) plus hundreds of servants and camp followers and, of course, the cannon, set off for Tlemcen.

Sultan Abu Zeyan had an army three times the size of Arouj's, plus the benefit of a secure fort. Nevertheless, Arouj was confident. He studied the plain south of the city and announced his strategy. "We'll place our cannon in concealed locations near the mouth of this canyon and line up musketeers behind them. The foot soldiers and archers will remain in the rear. When the enemy comes onto the plain, our cavalry will seem to attack; just before they are within range, they will turn and gallop back, as though in fear. The enemy will pursue them into the wide mouth of the canyon, and we will cut them down with our cannon, guns, and cross bows. Yes, it is almost too simple. They have no idea what they are facing."

It happened as Arouj predicted. Here, as on the road to Tenez, the way was strewn with dead and dying soldiers trampled under the hooves of their own retreating cavalry. Those with terrible wounds crawled or limped back toward the city, utterly defeated.

As Arouj stood with his army before the ancient gate of Tlemcen, the huge doors swung wide and a solemn procession of a dozen men emerged on foot. The leader carried a large silver platter upon which rested the bloody head of Sultan Abu Zeyan. They came to a halt in front of Arouj and knelt before him. Arouj gestured to Iscander to receive the gift. Throngs of citizens appeared on the ramparts of the city and poured out the door. The delegation from Tlemcen cried out in unison, "Long Live Sultan Arouj!" The whole army and all the citizens of the city cheered wildly and echoed the cry. It was as Trixie had seen it.

When Trixie arrived for her lessons on a day in late February, she was ushered into Itzak's library. To her surprise, a stranger was there with Samir, Nouri, and Beni. She was quite sure that he had been with Hasan al-Wazzan on his visit two years earlier but could not quite place him.

He was introduced as Rafeeq ibn Mohammad al-Fazi. "I remember you," Trixie blurted out in a rush of pleasant memories. "When you left with Hasan al-Wazzan, you gave me a carved donkey carrying two large baskets woven from dried marsh grass. I still have it. Do you know that you can put tiny packages in the baskets?"

"Then you, Hakeem, must be the little girl we called Trixie in those days. How you've grown."

"I have heard that you were with Hasan al-Wazzan in Bougie. Did you also go with him to Jijelli and then on to Tunis, Cairo, and Constantinople?"

"My, you have been keeping track of our adventures. Yes, I was at his side in all those exotic places."

"But when did you separate, and where is he now," Trixie wanted to know. "Hasan said that Constantinople was the ultimate goal of his mission."

"And it was. Sultan Selim was off conquering the Syrians when we arrived, but various officials housed us well and gave us the run of their prosperous city. Everywhere he went, Hasan emphasized the role of the Sultan Arouj in securing the Maghreb. When it seemed unlikely that the Sultan would be returning to the Capitol, we traveled together to Cairo, on our way back to Fez."

"Cairo," exclaimed Samir. "You might have bumped into Sultan Selim there. I have heard many talks of his conquests in Egypt about the time you must have been passing through."

"That is right. When we arrived in Cairo, Sultan Selim was already there. I learned why he is called 'the Grim.' This was not my first war, but it was the one that turned my beard and hair pure white. The Janissaries strutted through the streets like petty kings, each demanding whatever he wanted from those who did not have the power to say no. I walked past rows of pikes, each topped with a severed head. I saw women brutalized and left to die on the streets. I saw infants taken by an ankle and swung against a wall, then dropped into the gutter. Dogs fed on human flesh; rats thrived in the rubble. All this was at the behest of the Ottoman Sultan Selim, whom they rightly call the Grim."

"May he never choose to lead an army to the Maghreb," muttered Samir.

"He is more interested in expanding north and west into Christian lands than coming here," answered Rafeeq.

"But where is Hasan," asked Trixie.

"He decided to make a pilgrimage to Mecca and Medina before returning to Fez. He sent me ahead with a report to the Sultan of Fez. If he had known Arouj would be Sultan of Tlemcen by the time we got here, he might have decided that Allah could wait. As it is, I am the one who must collect up-to-date news from here and Oran, then visit Tlemcen and ride immediately to report what I learn to our sultan."

"How long will you be here," inquired Nouri.

"Only long enough to refresh my caravan. It is urgent that I get to Arouj and carry a message from him to Fez. We must be allies if we are to prevent the Christians from conquering all of the Maghreb. But never fear, I will pause long enough to collect letters from you to Itzak Ibrahim. They will be safe in my diplomatic packet."

In March, Rafeeq arrived in Tlemcen with personal message for Itzak from his family as well as important information about Oran for Arouj.

Rafeeq's military news was not good. He had learned that a force of 10,000 Christian soldiers had landed in Oran and would march toward Tlemcen within the month. They had artillery that could easily pierce the walls of the ancient city. Arouj had not confronted a force like this since Bougie.

Arouj immediately dictated a letter to the Sultan of Fez and another to the Sultan of Tunis. Itzak took the dictation and added all the rhetorical flourishes proper for classified communication from one sultan to another, and in the best of courtly scripts. No sultan would ignore letters as urgent as these. Arouj, the most powerful sultan in the Central Maghreb needed assistance immediately!

Rafeeq set off the next morning to deliver the message to his Sultan in Fez to the West, and a team of messengers rode off to beg support from faraway Tunis in the East.

Arouj received a return message from Fez sooner than expected. The Sultan wrote that he had assembled an army of 20,000 men and would be setting off for Tlemcen within days. Together they would show Charles, the new boy-King of Spain, that the Maghreb was not his for the taking. With this help, Arouj could win it all—not only defend Tlemcen, but perhaps even drive the Spanish from Oran. His fate and the fate of his followers depended on the timely arrival of the army from Fez.

In May, reports confirmed that the Spanish force was on the march toward Tlemcen. The troops from Fez, however, were nowhere to be seen. Perhaps they had not even left Fez. There was no news from Tunis.

How long could Arouj stay in Tlemcen, hoping that help from Fez would arrive before the Spanish army marching south from Oran? Messengers arrived regularly, reporting the progress of the Spanish, but none came from Fez.

Arouj decided to do the only reasonable thing; he ordered his men to abandon Tlemcen in the dead of night and run for their lives, leaving his volunteers from Al Cala and the people of Tlemcen behind. If the army from Fez arrived before the one from Oran, Arouj's army could turn back and help defend the city. Otherwise, they would keep running for their lives, bringing the treasury with them.

As Itzak fled East from Tlemcen in the dead of night, he remembered that first desperate flight, twenty-three years before, when he was a boy running down the path from his home to escape that other Spanish army. That was a moonlit night, at the beginning of his life adventure. This night was dark and, he feared, would mark the end of his story.

Bad as things seemed now, he had no regrets. As a boy, he had followed Muhmed Reis, the intrepid corsair who led him along the path with courage and determination. He still remembered the scent of blossoms in the night and the touch of a light breeze from the sea promising sweetness at the end of a long and strenuous journey.

'And then there was Musa.' The thought of his brother filled him with regret. He was glad there were no slackers or cowards this time. Sultan Arouj had hand-picked the 1500 corsairs and Moriscos who accompanied him on his campaign: Tenez, then Tlemcen. What a brotherhood! What men!

Many were seasoned corsairs who had fought and celebrated with Arouj for two decades, adventurous men who had been born speaking languages and worshiping gods that reflected their homelands around the Mediterranean, but who now shared Turkish as their common tongue and Islam as their shared religion. Many, like himself, had fled oppression or sought adventure. Others had been carried off against their will, like his dear friend, Hasan Agha, kidnapped and castrated as a boy, then nurtured and educated by an authoritarian but admired captor, in this instance, Khizr. Even now, in Sultan Arouj's absence, Khizr and Hasan protected Algiers. If this current campaign ended as Itzak feared, Khizr would inherit Arouj's realm. Even without Tlemcen it would span the Maghreb from Tenez to Jijelli and include the crown jewel, Algiers. 'We will not lose this land the way we lost Granada.'

Arouj had won against greater odds. Didn't he rise, as though from the dead, to return to besiege Bougie a second time? Hadn't he been rescued from a certain death at the oars of a galley belonging to the Knights of St. John? Wasn't it he, with only a small band of fellows, who captured not one but two papal galleys and single-handedly changed the basic assumptions of naval power in the Mediterranean? From that day in 1505 to the present, the name "Barbarossa" had evoked admiration and fear in all the commercial and political centers of the known world.

This desperate flight would succeed if the enemy failed to learn (or guess) that they had abandoned the city and were already heading home to Algiers.

What would Samir say of the odds that the enemy would not change course to the east and intercept the Algerines on their flight? He'd factor in the youthful enthusiasm of the young Charles, eager to prove himself an aggressive ruler, the angry quest for vengeance from the relatives of the recently displaced Abu Zeyan, and the zeal of the many holy leaders who held power in petty pockets of the Maghreb and wanted to rid themselves of the interloping Turk. Samir would decide that the odds of survival were low, Itzak knew that.

Even while riding for his life, he felt a smile creep across his face. With the addition of Tlemcen, the one-armed pirate from Lesbos became the equal to the Sultan of Tunis in the East and the Sultan of Fez in the West. They had done it! What a tale of glory. Itzak's only regret was that he had to flee without time to send off a last letter to Nouri.

They rode through the dark of the night and into the rising sun. By mid-morning, they reached a steep gorge with a river swollen by the spring thaw in the southern mountains. It could be forded at one spot, but not easily. Once across, they would be safe from their pursuers; if only they could reach it and usher even their stragglers to the other side. He spurred his horse to catch up with the sultan, whose irrepressible energy would be the perfect antidote to his own dark mood.

34. The Initiate: 1518

At dusk, Trixie sat at the shrine of the Goddess as she had all day. The sun had gone down behind the high cliffs three hours earlier, and the gibbous moon, almost completely full, had risen in the east, but the sky was not yet dark. She was hungry, but that did not bother her. The spots on her chin, where she had pricked herself with a needle coated in the black dye from the ancient tribal recipe, still stung slightly, reminding her of her new status. But most of all she was aware of being alone with the Goddess and with the ashes of the children buried in urns around the stele.

She had discovered her first show of menstrual blood the previous day. Now that she had become a woman, she was in a three-day, solitary retreat at the shrine. Two days would be spent alone; on the third day, the women of the village would celebrate her, and on that night, when the moon was at its fullest, they would dedicate her into the service of the Goddess.

Through this first day, she had imagined the voices of those dead children surrounding her, babes who could babble and cry but had not lived long enough to learn to speak. They seemed to call to her as she sat upon the ground that covered them, or when she moved from place to place to experience the nuanced differences between their silent cries. She felt she must acknowledge each one and clasp its insubstantial spirit to her bosom. Did the eternal embrace of the Goddess compensate for the loss of a loving nurse, for never knowing the kiss of an attentive lover, or the joy of a moment of friendship shared over a tasty meal? Could her own attention to their souls comfort them?

She thought not. The only comfort would be for them to be born again to experience those joys in the fullness of a life that lasted long enough to reach self-awareness.

When the sky behind the cliffs had darkened and stars glittered in the firmament, the moon was bright enough to reveal the etching of the Goddess on the stele. Her body was a triangle topped by a horizontal line with vertical tips, indicating raised arms, and a circle denoting her head. Another circle represented the full moon and an inverted sliver of crescent moon hung over it all.

Simple as it was, this primitive figure often seemed to her to come to life, emerging as a robed figure who extended her arms to embrace the initiate kneeling before her. Perhaps the stories were true. Perhaps we did all emerge from her. Perhaps if we died too young, we would return to her earthy embrace. Perhaps, as well, if we survived into maturity, we could ascend into the heavens and join her celestial presence, looking down with compassion on the world below.

Perhaps. But Trixie had seen too much death and destruction to feel certain of such an elevated afterlife. Tempting as it might be to surrender to her embrace, the Goddess was no more present than her own mother, Tazrut. Both were distant and impotent. From what she had seen, it was men who ruled, men who wielded the weapons, men who decided who would live and who would die. Could she really dedicate her life to this deity when she had seen life in the city and knew what war was?

She hardly heard Titrit come, place bread and water under the tree, and slip away. After a while, she went to get her meal, knowing that she must eat to survive these three days in the heat.

She ate slowly, then returned to sit before the stele. In two days, she would speak at her ceremony about the teachings of the Goddess, to share the wisdom that she acquired in silent meditation. But now, even more than any other day during the many months since the destruction of the armada in the Bay of Algiers, she felt only that death had no meaning. Men killed other men. Sometimes they even killed women and children. She had seen that women could kill as well. The Goddess was the giver of life but also an instrument of death. Could she find beauty and hope in that?

These were the cold, lonely images that she contemplated as the almost-full moon rose above her and eventually declined behind the mountain. Finally, she went to sleep.

On her second day at the shrine, Trixie thought of the Christians who had been helpless before the tempestuous winds on the day of the siege. She felt no pride or accomplishment in either her grandmother's wisdom or the legacy of Dihya. She knew that it would be her destiny to ride before the tribes down from the hills to slaughter the enemy when her time came, but she felt more horror than glory in that role. Through the heat of the second day, despair consumed her. By evening, she was so exhausted she did not even hear Titrit place the bread and water under the tree and depart.

She must have dozed off, for when she awoke the sky was dark in the west and the moon was high above her. She thought of her Uncle Itzak, who had left the previous summer to fight the army led by the Emir of Tenez. In his most recent letter, he had written about the rebuilding of Tlemcen, and his excitement at seeing the fulfillment of his dream: a powerful Muslim empire in the middle of the Maghreb, one that could ally with Tunis and Fez to protect all the people who lived along the great stretch of territory from Morocco to Egypt and from the sea in the north to the desert in the south.

The campaign had been a great success. Yet there were still Spanish soldiers on the Peñón, and her mother was still miserable in Algiers, and the Spanish still threatened to get rid of those 'Demon Barbarossas' by sending an army to Tlemcen.

As she struggled to gain the perspective she would need to share at her ceremony in a scant twenty-four hours, Trixie felt more helpless than ever. How would she find meaning in these events? As far as she could tell, the Goddess had little place in the affairs of empires. The men of Jadizi honored her, but men with military and political power turned to Allah for help. Mayam and the other servants of the Goddess were of use to them when they could predict the weather, tell fortunes, heal wounds, or inspire the tribes into battle, but she knew that Arouj considered gunpowder and cannons more reliable than augury or meteorology.

At dawn on her third day, Trixie woke in time to see the sun rise over the distant peak of Mount Djurdjura, framed between two lesser mountains that loomed close by her shrine. The sky brightened. Bit by bit the sun came into view, red at first, then too bright to look at directly. She gazed across the field of the buried children to the valley below, and it seemed that a great panorama appeared before her. She saw two armies, one with thousands of men chasing a much smaller one that might number in the hundreds. She felt her soul pass out of her body — not as though she had become a bird or a spider, for she saw herself still sitting facing east. No, this was her consciousness that went out while the rest of her stayed behind. She swooped as though on a magic carpet toward the phantom figures riding across rugged desert terrain.

At the lead of the smaller army, Arouj rode between two other men. One was Uncle Itzak. The other she took to be Iscander. These three and a small band of officers galloped up the steep slope of a sandy hill near a wadi. Arouj stood up in his stirrups and looked about as though aware of how closely the enemy pursued them.

He gave orders to his men, who galloped down the hill to the baggage carts that were about to ford the wadi. They halted the carts then gestured for them to be overturned. Out poured a great treasure, the riches from the fabled capital of Tlemcen. Gold and silver coins glittered across the trail, while broaches, earrings, bracelets, rings, and jewels sparked in the early morning sun along the river's edge like breadcrumbs to lead hungry birds astray.

Arouj and his companions crossed the ford to catch up with men who had already reached the other side. As they were about to turn toward the east and the distant safety of Algiers, he looked back and saw that his rear guard, made up of foot soldiers and a select corps of cavaliers, were overtaken. They would not make it across the river without more help.

He spoke briefly with Itzak. They appeared to argue. Then, with no time to spare, Itzak turned and galloped away from Arouj, towards the east, followed by a dozen mounted men. The others, in their hundreds, turned westward with their Sultan, to join those they would not leave behind.

The forces of Arouj joined into one, both foot and horse, and climbed the nearby hill to make a stand. The oncoming mounted troops, in their thousands, galloped, shrieking, along the trail, sabers flashing in the sun. Soon a sea of Spanish and Arab horsemen surrounded the hill, outnumbering Arouj's army ten to one.

As the sun rose toward its apex, Trixie sat unmoving as the slaughter climbed higher and higher up the slopes of the hill upon which Arouj and his men fought to the death. Blood flowed into the sand, red as rubies. Intestines spilled forth, briefly coiling like amber, silver, and gold chains before being trampled under horses' hooves.

The men never turned their backs on the enemy but fought face to face, killing and maiming those who kept coming in wave after wave. In the middle of it all was the nemesis who had haunted her dreams, Arouj, swinging his mighty scimitar left and right and using his glittering silver arm as a cudgel, cracking open a skull here, knocking a man from is horse there, always protecting the men near him, always the last man standing in his vicinity. She knew, as they all did, how it would end. This was the death of a hero, like the death of Dihya Kahina, a death in battle.

She was still watching when his turn came. In the end it was an archer who killed him, for none could get within a saber's length of him while he lived. Even as he collapsed to his knees, he struggled to pull the arrow's long shaft from his chest.

When he finally lay still, his foes removed his red cape and laid him out carefully, apart from the others. Then the strongest among them raised his sword and, with one blow, struck his head from his shoulders. The Christian soldiers stood in awed silence as the head with its unmistakable red beard was mounted on the end of a lance.

Now Trixie understood why Itzak had fled before the final battle. Arouj had told him, "You must return to Algiers and tell my brother that he is now Sultan, the new Barbarossa, who shall prove to the Christians that we cannot die. Tell everyone that I encouraged my men to the end. Tell my brother that, if he is lucky, he will die a death as good as mine, and when he does, his infant son shall carry on our line. We will not perish."

Itzak would not have abandoned his fellows unless commanded to do so, and Trixie knew with certainty that Arouj's words had been true. Khizr would become Sultan of Algiers, and his son with Saba would be named Hasan and would come after him.

She watched as the Spanish army fell in line behind the horseman who bore Arouj's head. They turned south, back toward Oran, not east toward Algiers. In this strange way, Arouj led the Christian army away from his people and again saved Algiers from destruction.

The epic of Arouj Barbarossa may have ended, but the rise of Algiers to dominance was just beginning and she, Sycorax, would have a role in establishing its glory. Khizr would be the new Barbarossa. She did not know how she would fulfill her destiny, but she did not doubt that she would do what she must, and Arouj would be the one who had showed her the way. No wonder she had feared him.

Titrit and the recently initiated girls of the village were not surprised to find Trixie unconscious when they arrive in the late afternoon. They revived her slowly, never asking what had happened. Then they bathed her and painted elegant patterns of bright orange henna on her hands and arms and piled her thick, dark hair in two large buns to create an elaborate headdress shaped like a crescent moon, decorated with bright cloth and draped with brass and silver jewelry. Trixie remained passive through all their ministrations. Her mind was a blank. She remembered what she had seen, but she did not know how that vision reflected her role as a woman. She had been taught about the link between female development and the cycles of the moon. Time, like nature, occurred in cycles. Everything that existed was conceived, grew in secret until it was born, was useful for its time, then died. Like Arouj. Was that the key?

When she was fully groomed and dressed, Mayam approached her.

"Here is a talisman that belonged to my mother's mother. It was a gift from a grateful Jewess who stayed in our village after fleeing from Christians who would no longer tolerate her people in Al Andalus. When she left for her Holy Land in the east, she gave us this to protect us from those who would wish us ill."

The pendant was shaped like a hand with a large eye centered on the palm. Its silver was so pure it almost glowed from the last light of the sun.

They feasted, then they danced in their village round, each woman wearing all the bracelets, necklaces, and earrings that she owned, dancing with practiced moves to jangles of their strands of jewelry until they rang not only rhythmically but with a melody of jingles and tings that accompanied the drums and the beat of their feet against the earth. They danced in a communal circle until they entered a syncopated unity. Only then did they break the round and become a snaking line of ecstatic women led by the initiate, Sycorax.

This was Sycorax's moment to devote her life to service of the tribe. They all knew that she would be a leader in her turn, following Mayam and Titrit. One or two village women still remembered the night Mayam had led the dance, and now she was the recognized leader of the village. Many others had danced with Titrit, ushering her into apprenticeship. And now it was Trixie's turn.

Sycorax was aware of it all, the history, the ceremony, the meaning. As she danced, she knew that words had little to do with it. Her new life would be lived at the deepest level she could achieve, for she would be at one with the Goddess, embodying Her whenever the people needed a healer or a leader. She had much more to learn before it became her turn.

In the morning she would tell them what she had seen and what she had learned. She would find a way to take them into this new world, where ships carried people and goods back and forth across the sea and lethal instruments of war could reach even into the mountain strongholds of Kabylia. Her people must unite with those on the plains and on the coast. Only then could Jadizi and Algiers both be safe from the empires that threatened to cross the sea and destroy their way of life.

She dreamed of a new confederacy, one that would combine peoples from urban ports to coastal plains and rugged mountains. She, someday, would become their new Kahina.

Caliban's Epilogue

On nights when the moon was full, mother often reminisced about her initiation. She would build a fire and call forth the many spirits of our isle to dance with her in the same round she had danced that night, when she was a young girl on the brink of becoming a great sorceress. Sometimes her lover, Setebos, would join her there to carouse. When he came, she had no time for me, but when he failed to arrive, she would dance to exhaustion, then recline before the dying embers and tell me about her life in Algiers.

After Arouj died, she told me, she was no longer haunted by nightmares, and her career as a midwife and wise woman grew, both in the mountains and the city. She was consulted for women's problems but was even more renowned for her ability to control the weather, a skill that was of great interest to the new sultan.

Khizr was increasingly called 'Khier ed Din,' the 'Guardian of the Faith,' after he assumed power, and his reputation became greater than Arouj's had ever been. He formed an alliance with the Ottoman Empire so that all the territories under his influence became a province of that empire, and he was its Beylerbey. In this way, he gained the support of the greatest power in the world without giving up any significant influence of his own. He ultimately became the Admiral for the navy of Suleiman the Magnificent. His fleet dominated the Mediterranean Sea throughout the central decades of the century. To Christians, it was as though Barbarossa had never died, but for Muslims, his life became its own legend. He became the most revered (or feared) figure in the Mediterranean world.

When Sycorax was young, both she and Kheir ed Din grew in fame and influence. After the cataclysmic failure of the Spanish siege on Algiers and subsequent ascendance of the Ottoman Empire after 1541, however, my mother's reputation no longer paralleled the arc of Khizr's. When I went to Milan, I learned that no one had ever heard of Sycorax, the Sorceress of Algiers. I tried to describe her powers to a servant in my master's palace, but the man turned pale and said I should not speak of such things, for they might get Prospero in trouble again. He had been expelled from the city because his enemies had claimed that he dabbled in sorcery, and if anyone suspected that he had associations with a 'weather witch' like Sycorax, they might turn against him again.

I have since discovered that there are two kinds of people in the lands that they call 'civilized' (that is, countries that worship 'The One God' and who punish anyone who does not follow their interpretations of their holy books and practices). The first (and most numerous) are the Fools, and the second (typically the most powerful) are the Hypocrites. There is a third group as well, which does not have a name or a dogma. We could call them the 'Wise Ones,' though some call them the 'crazy ones,' the 'witches,' 'alchemists,' 'sorcerers,' or 'demons.' These seekers-into-the-unknown keep their practices secret. As we know from the Inquisition, Fools and Hypocrites may even torture or kill people who present contrary beliefs. That is why I could never speak of what I had seen as a child. William Shakespeare had his character, Prince Hamlet, say, "there are more things in heaven and earth, Horatio, than are dreamt of in your philosophy."[vii] How well I know those words to be true. The Hypocrites control the myths and commandments that can be taught, whether in religion or philosophy, and the Fools believe them. The wise remain silent.

One day, when I was a young man in Milan, I came across a volume in Italian called *A History and Description of Africa and of the notable things therein contained,* written by "A Moor, Baptised as Giovanni Leone but better known as Leo Africanus." You can imagine my excitement. I had high hopes that I would learn what Algiers was really like; I might even read descriptions of people who were my mother's closest relatives and learn why she had been exiled. All I had heard was Ariel's version, and that was biased and spiteful. What would this man, Giovanni Leone, have to say?

It was widely known that the author had been born a Muslim in Granada, raised in Fez, and kidnapped by Christian corsairs near the Island of Djerba in 1516. His captor recognized that his knowledge of Africa would make him of special interest to Pope Leo, so took him to Rome and presented him as a gift. The Pope first become master of the man, then his priest, and finally his sponsor for his conversion to Christianity. The book was written in Italian for Pope Clement, a successor of Pope Leo X, and informed Europeans about the varied geography and complex cultures of North Africa.

One can hardly live in Milan or any other city in Europe without hearing stories of Christians who have been captured by Muslim pirates and carried off to be slaves in Algiers or another port in the Maghreb. Most notable, of course, are those written some decades after Africanus by the Spaniard Cervantes and the Portuguese cleric Haedo, well-educated men who were held as slaves in Algiers for some years. Africanus was unique in my experience, a highly literate Muslim who was carried off to Rome, converted to Christianity, and elevated to the position of advisor to Popes.

I learned that his name was originally "Al-Hasan ibn-Mohammad al-Wezaz al-Fasi." Hasan was his given name; Ibn-Mohammad was a patronymic meaning 'the son of Mohammad;' Al-Fasi simply meant 'from Fez.' Al-Wezaz,' I guessed, could be a transliteration of the Arabic sur-name Wazzan.

Was Giovanni Leone, otherwise known as Leo Africanus, the man my mother had often told me about, the young diplomat from Fez who entered her dreams in the form of a lion? It was quickly clear to me that this must be the case.

As you will remember, Hasan al-Wazzan had been a guest in the home of Itzak Ibrahim, in 1514. When the news arrived that Arouj had joined forces with Sultan Abdelaziz for a second attempt to destroy the Spanish presence in Bougie, Hasan al-

Wazzan and Samir Mazigh went East hoping to witness the victory. Unfortunately, the second siege failed as disastrously as the first. As he writes in his book, Hasan accompanied Arouj from Bougie to Jijelli. Later, he traveled on to Tunis, Cairo, and Constantinople. He then made a pilgrimage to the Holy Land, sending his companion, Rafeeq, on to Algiers and Tlemcen. Hasan was captured on his way back to his sultan and taken to Rome, so he never made it back to Algiers, Tlemcen, or Fez while Arouj was sultan.

In his book, Hasan describes the Maghreb with great objectivity and evocative detail. He often includes the behaviors of holy men, witches, and seers. Hasan consistently debunks charlatans he encountered in Africa, though he studied with some well-known leaders of various sects and became well versed in the Kabbalah. There are indications that he was neither a Fool nor a Hypocrite. Well, perhaps he was a bit of a hypocrite, but in a politic way, as indicated by his conversion to Christianity; it is hard to imagine what would have happened had he refused to accept his master's teachings.

If Hasan al-Wazzan had not been abducted, I believe he would have advised the most powerful sultans of the Maghreb, those of Tunis and Fez, to cultivate relationships with the Barbarossas. He knew that both Arouj and the Ottoman Sultan Selim were brilliant and cruel, but he considered Arouj to be the lesser evil in an era of shifting boundaries and unreliable alliances. He, like Samir Mazigh, would have preferred to see the region stay under the control of its traditional cultures, mixed as they might be. Neither Spanish nor Ottoman control could satisfy the intense tribal feelings so prevalent in the region, nor promote the religious and intellectual diversity of the people.

It is possible that if Hasan had been free to continue his journey West, the future of the Maghreb might have followed a different course, led by an alliance between the sultans of Algiers and Fez. If his ally from Fez had arrived in a timely manner, Arouj would not have fled before the Spanish Army. He could have continued to consolidate power as Sultan of the middle Maghreb. I cannot even dream what would have happened to my mother if events had taken that course. But it was not to be.

Arouj's tragic flaw was his feeling of omnipotence, called hubris by some. He began to believe that everyone except the Christians adored him. Each time he conquered a new city, its warriors and all the surrounding tribes swore allegiance to him, even when he had beheaded their chief. This happened in Jijelli, Shershell, Algiers, and Tenez. When tribesmen by the thousands gathered at Al Cala, vying for the privilege of fighting with him, he left his brother Isaac behind with a mere two hundred men, because he believed all the tribes in the area adored him. He would go to Tlemcen, place his ally on the throne, consolidate his alliance with Fez, and return to Algiers to rule the Central Maghreb from there. He overlooked that local Sidi who did not want to bow to anyone, and who slaughtered Isaac and his men in the dead of night. In other words, the Sidi was a power-hungry upstart, just like Arouj.

When I reflect upon it, I realize that both Sycorax and Prospero were as arrogant and ambitious as Arouj. Both failed to suspect that those closest to them might betray them. Alone on the island, each in turn manipulated supernatural forces to get revenge on their enemies, and each ended by abandoning their practice of magic, forgiving those who had betrayed them, and devoting their lives to truths deeper than the assertion of power over others.

My father, Setebos, was different. Evil as he might have been, he was always bold and glorious, never anxious or sniveling. He was not a kind or gentle being, and rarely very rational, unless he was trying to seduce someone. That's how he whispered into Trixie's ear when she was very young, telling her that he could teach her powers she could never learn from Mayam, who only studied the weather in order to predict it with subtle accuracy. He claimed that his art was far greater. He could strengthen an existing wind and, if inclined, create a tempest out of thin air.

Setebos took his time preparing for the day when Sycorax would be a seasoned sorceress. Little by little, step by step, he convinced her of his superiority. When she became a leader in her community, he proudly counted her among his conquests, until 1541. When Sycorax lost her status in Algiers, she lost her value to Setebos, and he left her to her own devices to face the angry crowds and corrupt courts of Algiers. Similarly, after my mother died, he stopped coming to the island, because he thought me to be of no use to him. He was more calculating than vindictive, but then, he was always the betrayer, never the betrayed.

In a paradoxical way, duplicity and betrayal were Setebos's greatest gifts to Sycorax. In her solitude, she gained wisdom which ultimately led to her spiritual growth. Similarly, Antonio and Sebastian were the instruments of Prospero's salvation by providing him with an opportunity to exercise empathy and manifest forgiveness. Without his time on the island, Prospero would not have gained even the limited degree of compassion that he found in himself when he took responsibility for his former treatment of me and brought me with him to Milan. I had thought he would abandon me to solitude on the island, while leaving behind an abundance of urchins with orders to exercise their torments on me through an infinity of lonely nights.

I'm an old man now. It's been 78 years since Sycorax gave birth to me alone on that isle. For a while I thought I might be immortal, because I believed my father was, but I now know I have been spared that particular curse. I am as hardy as a beast, however, and expect to live a good time more. Long enough, I hope, to tell the rest of my mother's story. I want the world to learn that once there was a sorceress of great power in Algiers, and that she served her people well. I also want everyone to know how she suffered in exile, but also how she adapted to her strange state. She used her talents, both natural and acquired, to make a good life for herself and for me.

With a little bit of luck and a great deal of diligence, someday I will finish telling her tale. Although I did not appreciate it when I was young, there was always a great deal to admire about my mother, Sycorax, the Sorceress of Algiers.

Caliban,
Milan 1615

Trixie's Family Tree

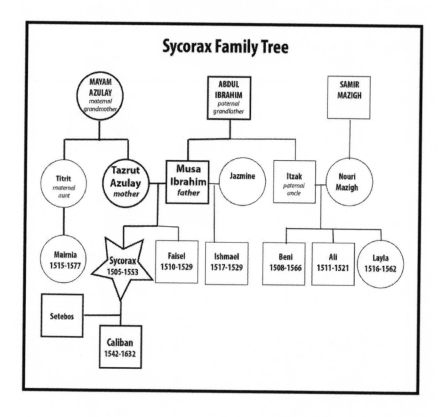

Appendix A: Fictional Characters

Musa Ibrahim's Household in Algiers

Musa Ibrahim: Musa fled Granada with his younger brother Itzak in 1495. He established himself in Algiers as a merchant, providing goods produced in the mountains of Kabylia to European buyers. He married Tazrut Azulay, an Amazighi girl from the Kabylian village of Jadizi, in 1502. He had two children with her, a daughter, Sycorax, born in 1505, and a son, Faisel, born in 1510.

Tazrut Ibrahim: Tazrut, elder daughter of Mayam Azulay, was born in the village of Jadizi in 1484, met Musa Ibrahim when he came to the village to purchase merchandise in 1498 and married him in 1502. She gave birth to her daughter, Sycorax, in 1505 and to her son, Faisel, in 1510.

Sycorax Ibrahim: Sycorax was born to Musa and Tazrut in 1505. She went by the nickname Trixie in the family. When her father thought she had been possessed by a djinni, she fled to her mother's family village of Jadizi and was initiated as a devotee of the Goddess in 1518.

Faisel Ibrahim: Faisel was born to Musa and Tazrut Ibrahim in 1510, on the day that a Spanish Armada came to Algiers.

Ishmael Ibrahim: Ishmael was born to Musa's concubine, Yasmine, in 1517.

Eli the Nubian: Eli was purchased by Musa at the market in Algiers. He became the head slave of the household and Musa's loyal advisor, occasionally protecting others in the household from Musa's rage.

Emilia (later Yasmine): Emilia was a lady's maid from Naples who was captured by the corsair, Itzak Ibrahim, while traveling with her mistress to Spain in 1505. Itzak gave her as a gift to his sister-in-law when Tazrut was pregnant with her first child.

Mayam Azulay's Household in Jadizi

Mayam Azulay: Mayam was the headwoman, or kahina, of the Amazighi village of Jadizi in Kabylia. She gave birth to three children: a daughter Tazrut, born in 1484, a daughter Titrit, born in 1488, and a son Izil, born in 1492, who died in infancy.

Titrit Azulay: Titrit became her mother Mayam's apprentice. She was renowned as an herbalist and a midwife and became an important mentor to her niece, Sycorax. She had one daughter, Mairnia.

Izil Azulay: Izil was Mayam's son who died in infancy and was buried at the shrine of the Goddess in Jadizi.

Meddur Izuri: Meddur was Mayam's lover and a leading elder in the village of Jadizi.

Mairnia Azulay: Mairnia was Titrit's daughter, born in 1516. She had no formally recognized father.

The Itzak Ibrahim Household in Algiers

Itzak Ibrahim. Itzak was Musa Ibrahim's younger brother who fled with him from Granada in 1495. Itzak established himself as a corsair in Algiers, first with his mentor, Muhmed Reis, and then as master of a small fleet. He helped his brother with his shipping business and rescued Moriscos from Granada. Occasionally, he captured European ships and profited from ransom or sale of captives.

Nouri Ibrahim: Nouri was the daughter of Samir Mazigh of Bougie. She was literate in Arabic and Spanish. She met and married Itzak while he was studying shipbuilding in Bougie, married him in 1507 and moved with him to Algiers. She had three children: Beni, Ali, and Layla and was Trixie's first tutor.

Beni Ibrahim: Beni was born to Itzak and Nouri Ibrahim in Algiers in 1508. He and his cousin Sycorax grew up next door to each other and were constant companions in childhood.

Ali Ibrahim: Ali was born in Algiers in 1512.

Layla Ibrahim: Layla was born in Algiers in 1517, while Itzak was away on the campaign to Tenez and Tlemcen.

Samir Mazigh: Samir was a wealthy bookseller and influential political figure in Bougie until the city was captured by the Spanish in 1509. After that, he lived for a while in his ancestral village of Nahla then joined his daughter and son-in-law in Algiers in 1512. He maintained agents who kept him informed of the events and politics of the Maghreb.

Fatima: Fatima was an elderly slave who had been bought at the market in Tunis by Nouri's maternal grandfather in the 1460's. She had been nanny and caregiver to Nouri's mother and moved into the Mazigh household when her mistress married Samir. She had been nanny to Nouri and became nanny to Nouri's three children in Algiers.

Ahmed: Ahmed was the family cook for the Mazighs in Bougie and moved to Algiers with Samir in 1519.

Jacob: Jacob was a kitchen servant in Itzak's household. He was hired out by his impoverished family who lived in a mountain village in Kabylia.

Characters from Shakespeare mentioned in *Trixie*

Antonio: Prospero's brother who usurped the throne of Milan from Prospero with the help of Alonso, King of Naples.

Ariel: An airy spirit who had served Sycorax. She punished him by trapping him inside a tree, where he remained in anguish until Propsero arrived and set him free.

Caliban: A demi-demon, son to Sycorax, Witch of Algiers, and Setebos, a demon/djinni. He was born on an island with no other human than his mother. When she died, he was alone until Prospero arrived with his young daughter, Miranda. They treated him well until he made sexual advances on a maturing Miranda. After that he was treated badly.

Hamlet, Prince of Denmark: Hamlet was the protagonist of one of Shakespeare's best-known tragedies. His soliloquies are often philosophical reflections on the meaning of life (or lack there-of).

Miranda: Prospero's daughter.

Prospero: Duke of Milan who was over-thrown and set adrift on a leaky ship with his daughter and his books. He came ashore on Caliban's island and developed his knowledge of sorcery and magic over the years. He freed Ariel from the tree, made Caliban his slave, and created the tempest that blew his enemies to his shore.

Sebastian: Brother to Alonso, King of Naples and friend of Prospero's treacherous brother Antonio.

Setebos: A djinni who impregnated Sycorax, Witch of Algiers. He was Caliban's father.

Sycorax: The Witch of Algiers who was exiled to a deserted island, gave birth to Caliban, and died before Prospero and Miranda arrived on the island.

Other Fictional Characters

Enrico: An Italian slave in Algiers who had his master's permission to keep a cobbler's shop in the souk. Yasmine's lover.

Fareed: A friend of Meddur who lived in a neighboring village and often traveled to the souk in Algiers with him.

Idir: A boy from Jadizi.

Juba: Meddur's cousin.

Muhmed Reis: A Turkish captain who accompanied Kemal Reis on his 1487 mission sponsored by the Ottoman Sultan, Beyazid II, to aid the Muslim cause in Granada. Muhmed fell ill and remained behind in Algiers when the fleet returned to Constantinople. In 1495, he rescued Musa and Itzak Ibrahim from Granada and became Itzak's mentor in Algiers.

Misdak: A friend of Meddur's from a neighboring village who often traveled to the souk with him.

Mustafa Agha: Arouj Barbarossa's bodyguard who carried him from battle in the siege at Bougie.

Mustafa: A courier in Samir's employ who carried news of Abdelaziz's second attempt to re-occupy Bougie to Algiers.

Sidi Yousouf: A marabout active in and around Algiers who is enlisted by Musa to diagnose and whether or not Sycorax is possessed by a djinni.

Appendix B: Historical Characters

Abdelaziz: Sultan of Bougie who fled to Kalaa after being defeated by the Spanish in 1409. This character is a conflation of Emir Abdelahman, who was probably the leader of Bougie at the time of the siege, with his grandson, Abdelaziz, who became powerful in Kabylia over the following decades.

Ahmed al-Khadi: Leader of a campaign by mountain tribes against Arouj in Jijelli. His head was carried on a lance back to the city.

Abu Hammou: Sultan of Tlemcen displaced by his uncle, Abu Zeyan. He escaped to the Spanish in Oran and marched with the force that expelled Arouj from Tlemcen in 1518.

Abu Zeyan: Sultan of Tlemcen whose head was presented to Arouj before the gates of Tlemcen in 1517.

Al-Hasan ibn Muhammad al-Wazzan al-Fazi, a.k.a. Leo Africanus: Traveler, diplomat, and author, born in Granada, raised in Fez, enlisted into the service of his Sultan, captured by Christian pirates, given to Pope Leo X in Rome, and author of the well-known book, *A History and Description of Africa and of the notable things therein contained*, first published in 1520 and still in print today. He visited Algiers in 1514 and was present at the second siege of Bougie in which Arouj failed to expel the Spanish from their fortresses.

Amal ibn Salem ben Toumi: Son of Salem ibn Toumi, Emir of Algiers (1510 to 1516). Amal fled to Oran when his father was killed in 1516. He went with the Spanish to retake Algiers, which resulted in the failed sieges of that city 1516 and 1519.

Arouj Barbarossa: A Turkish corsair who rose to power in the Maghreb. He was born in Mytilene (Lesbos). His father was a former janissary and his mother was a Christian. He and his next younger brother, Elias, were seamen operating a galliot (whether as privateers or legitimate merchants is unclear). They were attacked by a galley of the Knights of St. Johns. Elias was killed in the battle and Arouj taken captive and forced to work as a galley slave until finally ransomed by his other two brothers. By 1504, he and his youngest brother, Khizr, owned two galliots and were operating out of Tunis. They quickly became successful corsairs and were joined by their surviving brother, Isaac. By 1516 Arouj was Sultan of Djerba, Shershell, Jijelli, Algiers, and Tlemcen. He was killed in battle while fleeing Tlemcen in 1518.

Bayezid II: Ottoman sultan from 1481 to 1512. He sponsored the corsair, Kemel Reis, on a trip to the western Mediterranean to aid Granada, rescue Muslims, and establish an Ottoman presence in the area.

Cardinal Cisneros: see Ximenes Cisneros.

Charles I: King of Spain (1516-1556) who became Charles V of the Holy Roman Emperor (1519-1552. He was crowned in his home country of Flanders and arrived in Spain, ignorant of the language and the culture, in September 1517. Charles sent a well-equipped army to Oran, which marched to Tlemcen and reinstated its the former sultan, Abu Hammou. The Spanish army caught up with Arouj and his men, who had fled, and killed them near a Wadi to the East of Tlemcen.

Dihya al-Kahina: A Seventh Century religious and military leader who formed a coalition of tribes in eastern Kabylia to resist the invasion of Arabs Muslims. The Arabs believed that she was a seer and a diviner. Her army defeated them in battle but, after five years, they returned and defeated her in 703 CE.

Doria, Admiral Andrea: Andrea Doria and Khizr (re-named Kheir ed Din) Barbarossa became the mighty opposites of the Mediterranean Sea through the middle of the Sixteenth Century. During the period covered in this book they met only once, when Genoa sent Doria with a fleet of 12 galleys to Halq al-Wad and destroyed the Barbarossa fleet, causing Khizr to leave Halq al-Wad.

Elias Barbarossa: Brother of Arouj who died when he and Arouj were attack by the Knights of Rhodes.

Ferdinand II of Aragon: King of Castile (1474-1504) as co-regent with his wife, Isabella I and King of Aragon (1479-1516). When Isabella died in 1504, their daughter Joanna inherited the crown of Castile. Ferdinand became King of Naples in 1506 as part of a treaty with France. When Joanna proved unfit to rule, he was officially appointed as Regent of Castile from 1508 until his death in 1516. Ferdinand and Isabella sponsored Christopher Columbus on his voyages to the New World, defeated the last Muslim region in Spain (Granada), and issued the Edict of Expulsion of the Jews. During his reign Ferdinand oversaw the Spanish inquisition and had recurring battles with France over control of Italy.

Hadim Hasan Agha: Khizr's protégé, captured as a boy, castrated, and educated in skills as a seaman. He became a Reis in Khizr's fleet. Khizr (as Kheir ed Din) became Beylerbey of Algiers when it was made a Province of the Ottoman Empire. When Sultan Suleiman made Khizr Adimral of his Navy, Hasan became Regent whenever Kheir ed Din was on campaign.

Hamida: King of Tenez who was defeated by Arouj in the field in 1517. Hamida was later reinstated as ruler in Tenez and became an ally of Algiers under Khier ed Din.

Ibn Khaldoun: A 14th Century Muslim scholar from North Africa sometimes called the father of Sociology.

Isaac Barbarossa: Brother of Arouj and Khizr Barbarossa who was left in charge of the rear guard at the fortress of Al Cala when Arouj took his army to attack Tlemcen. Isaac and all his companions were wiped out by a hostile tribe.

Isabelle I: Queen of Castile and Leon (1474-1504). She and her husband ultimately became co-regents of all the Christian kingdoms on the Iberian Peninsula except Portugal, although their separate kingdoms, particularly Castile and Aragon, continued to maintain their own governing institutions and politics. Both Isabella and Ferdinand were determined to complete the *Reconquista*, the conquest of all the Muslim regions on the Iberian Peninsula, and both were directly involved in the conduct of the war. Isabella was intensely religious and committed to orthodox views reinforced by her confessors, including Cardinal Ximenes Cisneros. She was literate and a patron of the arts. She sponsored the voyages of Christopher Columbus, so when the New World was discovered, it was annexed to the crown of Castile. She had a particular interest in encouraging the spread of Christianity at home and abroad. This included supporting policies related to the conversion of Jews and Arabs, inquisitions into religious orthodoxy, spreading Christianity in the newly discovered lands and conducting a crusade in North Africa.

Kara Hasan: A reis (captain) of a galliot in Arouj's fleet who became Sultan of Shershell until Arouj had him beheaded in 1516.

Kemel Reis: Commander of the expedition to Spain and the Maghreb in the 1490s. His voyage established Turkish corsairs in ports of the Maghreb and increased the practice of raiding Spanish coastal cities and transporting Muslims from Granada and other areas to the Maghreb. In 1503 he captured one of the ships that had sailed to the New world with Christopher Columbus and obtained nautical charts which were taken to Constantinople and ultimately informed the work of Suleiman's cartographer (and nephew of Kemel Reis), Piri Reyes.

Kheir ed Din: Honorific title given to Khizr Barbarossa in gratitude for his service helping Muslims flee from the Iberian Peninsula to the Maghreb. (The phrase translates roughly as "guardian of the faith" and is sometimes spelled "Heyreddin" or "Khayr al-Din.")

Khizr Barbarossa: Arouj Barbarossa's youngest brother. Although his beard was not red, after his older brother was killed and Khizr became Sultan of Algiers, he was often called by his brother's name, Barbarossa. He also acquired the honorific Kheir ed Din or Hayreddin. After Algiers affiliated with the Ottoman Empire, Khizr became its Beylerbay and subsequently served as Admiral of the Ottoman Navy.

Knights of Saint John: Also known as the Knights of Rhodes or the Knights Hospitaller, they were a Catholic military order under charter from the Pope. They resettled in Malta in 1530. Arouj was seized (and his brother Elias killed) by them early in his career.

Korkut: Son of Bayezid II, Sultan of the Ottoman Empire. He sponsored Arouj in his early days of privateering and aspired to becoming sultan himself, but his brother Selim became the new sultan in 1512, the year that Arouj lost his arm at the battle of Bougie. Korkut was executed by his brother in 1513.

Leo X: Pope from 1513 to 1521. He was known for wasteful habits but was also a patron of the arts. He recognized Hasan al-Wazzan's merits and took special interest in the Muslim slave, seeing to his education and sponsoring his conversion. He was concerned about the Ottoman threat to Christian Europe.

Mohammad al-Burtughali: Sultan of Fez for whom Hasan al-Wazzan was envoy in 1515.

Mohammad ibn al-Hasan: Sultan of Tunis during the period that Arouj and his men were staying at Halq al-Wad (the Goleta).

Navarro, Don Pedro: An engineer and captain from Aragon who argued with Carinal Ximenes over how to proceed after Oran was conquered in 1509. He returned to the Barbary Coast in 1510 and conquered Bougie and Tripoli.

Piri Reis: Famous cartographer for Sultan Suleiman and nephew of Kemel Reis.

Salah Reis: A young captain who sailed with Arouj who went on to become one of the most reknowned seamen of the Mediterranean.

Salem ibn Toumi: Emir of Algiers appointed by the Spanish in 1510 and killed by Arouj in 1516.

Selim the Grim: Sultan of the Ottoman Empire (1512-1520). During his reign he increased the size of the Empire through conquests in the Levant and Egypt.

Ximenes Cisneros: Archbishop of Toledo. Cisneros was known for his extreme piety. He encouraged Queen Isabella of Castile to extend the *Reconquista* (defeat of Muslim governments in the Iberian Peninsula) to North Africa. He continued to support this policy when he was made Regent of Castile after Isabella's death in 1504. In 1509, the 73-year-old prelate personally led an expedition to Oran, hoping to initiate a crusade to the interior of Africa but was frustrated by Pedro Navarro of Aragon, whose king, Ferdinand, wished to limit Spanish possessions in the Maghreb to presidios in major port cities.

Glossary

Agha: Title for a high-ranking Ottoman official, such as a commander of the Janissaries. Because of the practice of abducting boys, castrating them, and putting them in service, the term 'Agha' was often used to refer to a eunuch. Thus every eunuch might be called an agha, but not every agha was a eunuch.

Al Cala: The fortress of the Beni Rashis where Arouj assembled volunteers to join his army for the conquest of Tlemcen.

Algerine: A person from the city of Algiers. In the time of this narrative, there was no political entity of 'Algeria' and no social identity embracing "Algerians."

Amazigh: Indigenous (i.e. descended from people who were there before the Arab invasion of the Seventh Century) people of North Africa. Europeans referred to these people as Berbers and the region (now called the Maghreb) as Barbaria. For informative videos about the Amazigh people on *youtube.com*, try the hashtag: #Amazigh.

Armada: The Spanish word for a naval fleet.

Bab al-Wad: The River Gate, on the western side of Algiers

Bab Azzoun: The Gate of Grief, on the southeast side of Algiers

Bagnio: A prison for slaves or captives held for ransoms.

Baldi: The long-time citizens of the city of Algiers as distinct from Bedouin, peasants, or newcomers.

Beni Rashid: A tribe in the mountains north of Tlemcen.

Berber: See *Amazigh.*

Beylerbey: Ottoman title for governor of a Province.

Brigantine: A small vessel with rowing benches, distinct from the modern sailing ship of the same name.

Burnous: A hooded cloak woven in one large rectangle and used as an outer garment.

Carrack: A large sailing ship used for trade or transport.

Casbah: A fortified castle typically providing the residence for the ruler of a walled city.

Corsair: Originally an old French word for pirate or privateer, corsair is used here to remind readers that any given band of pirates can be heroes or villains depending on whom they attack or benefit.

Djinni: Transliteration of the Arabic term for a supernatural being (usually spelled *'genie'* in English) that may be good, like Aladdin's djinni hiding in a lantern until called to serve, or evil, like a demon that possessed a human being, causing disease or insanity. *Djinn* is the plural form of djinni.

Emir: A title for a leader who typically would be subordinate to a sultan.

Galliot: A small, swift galley with oars and sails used by corsairs on the Mediterranean.

Galley: A long, slender ship propelled primarily by oars.

The Goleta: See *Halq al-Wad.*

Haik: An outer wrap consisting of a single large rectangle, usually white, typically worn with a veil.

Halq al-Wad: Known as La Goleta to Europeans, Halq al-wad was the Arabic name for the "gullet" or narrow passage between the sea and the Lake of Tunis. It was well fortified. With the permission of the Sultan of Tunis, the Barbarossas used it as their home base for many years.

Hamsa: A hand-shaped amulet with an eye in the palm used to ward off the evil eye.

Imam: A Moslem religious leader associated with a mosque.

Janissaries: Turkish foot soldiers recruited from outside the Ottoman Empire, often by abduction, and sometimes castrated, raised in strict military discipline by their captors, and put into lifelong service to the state.

Kabbalah: A mystical Jewish tradition that explores the relationship between physical and spiritual levels of existence.

Kabyle: Tribes of the mountainous area east and south of Algiers.

Kahina: An Arabic word for a seer or diviner. This title was given by Muslims who invaded North Africa in the Seventh Century to the Berber priestess/queen named Dihya who created a coalition of tribes to resist them.

Lateen sail: A triangular sail attached to a long spur and rigged to a low mast.

Madrasa: A Muslim religious school for advanced learning.

Maghreb: North Africa from Morocco to Tripoli, including Tunisia and Algeria. Also known as Barbaria, its coastline was called The Barbary Coast.

Marabout: An unorthodox, charismatic religious leader who often wielded political power.

Moor: A Muslim who lived in the Maghreb or the Iberian Peninsula (as well as some islands of the Mediterranean) in the Middle Ages and Early Modern period, typically of Amazigh (Berber), Arab, Spanish, and/or mixed descent.

Morisco: A Muslim who was forced to convert to Christianity. The term was often used to refer to any Muslims who fled from Spain to North Africa.

Pasha: A title of high command in the Ottoman Empire.

Peñón: The Spanish word for "rock," used to denote a rocky island, particularly one off the coast of North Africa on which the Spanish built a fortress, such as the one in the Bay of Algiers.

Pinnace: A light sailing ship often used as a tender.

Presidio: The Spanish term for a fortified base established in an area under their influence.

Reis: A Turkish title for a captain, leader, or commander.

Reconquista: The name Christians gave to their centuries-long campaign to retake the Iberian Peninsula from Muslims.

Renegade: A person who deserts or betrays his or her people, commonly used to refer to a Christian or Jew who became a Muslim.

Roving: Wool that has been carded into a long cord in preparation for spinning into yarn.

Sidi: An honorific used for a marabout or religious leader.

Souk. A marketplace.

Sultan: The Muslim title for the highest-ranking leader.

Zouave: A confederation of Kabyle tribes noted for their military prowess.

Reading List

I read many books and articles while preparing for and writing Trixie. *This is a list of the ones I found most entertaining. They did not always agree with each other, which helped me feel free to follow Shakespeare's example and create a world that felt emotionally true and self-consistent, not necessarily historically accurate.*

Africanus, Leo. *The History and Description of Africa and of the Notable Things Therein Contained.* Three volumes. London: Forgotten Books, 2015. *www.ForgottenBooks.com.*

Bradford, Ernle. *The Sultan's Admiral: Barbarossa – Pirate and Empire-Builder.* Foreword by John Freely. Taurisi Parke Paperbacks, 2014.

Davis, Natalie Zemon. *Trickster Travels: A Sixteenth Century Muslim Between Worlds.* Hill and Wang. New York, 2006.

De Sosa, Antonio. *An Early Modern Dialogue with Islam: Antonio de Sosa's Topography of Algiers (1612).* Edited by Maria Antonia Garces. Translated by Diana de Armas Wilson. Notre Dame, Indiana: University of Notre Dame Press, 2011.

Garces, Maria Antonia. *Cervantes in Algiers: A Captive's Tale.* Nashville: Vandervilt University Press, 2002.

Hess, Andrew C. *The Forgotten Frontier: A History of the Sixteenth Century, Ibero-African Frontier.* Chicago: The University of Chicago Press, 1978.

Lane Poole, Stanley with Lieut J.D. Jerrold Kelley, U.S. Navy. *The Story of the Barbary Corsairs.* London: G.P. Putnam, 1890. [Dodo Press, London, UK www.dodopress.co.uk].

Morgan, J. *A Complete History of Algiers. To which is prefixed, An Epitome of the General History of Barbary, from the earliest Times: Interspersed With many curious Remarks and Passages, not touched on by any Writer whatever, Volume I.* London: Printed for the Author, by J. Bettenham, 1728. [HardPress Publishing, Miami, FL www.hardpress.net].

Wikipedia.org. *Wikipedia was a marvelous resource because it had articles about Algiers, the corsairs, the Maghreb, and the 16th Century from many perspectives. It didn't overcome my handicap of reading French poorly and Arabic not at all, but it did comfort me by presenting articles that contradicted each other and weren't always from and English Language and/or Christian perspectives.*

End Notes

---

[i] All citations for *The Tempest* are to *The Arden Edtion of the Works of William Sahespeare, The Tempest*, edited by Frank Kermodes (London: Methuen & Co.)0, 1964).

[ii] As with so many details, the exact source of Shakespeare's knowledge of these events is controversial among scholars, though all agree that the language of the play echoes descriptions written by men who were aboard a ship that was were blown off course and wrecked on an island in the Caribbean while on its way to the Virginia Colony.

[iii] Thus when J. Morgan [see "Credits"] wrote his history of Algiers almost two centuries later, the story was still current. As he wrote: "Often have I heard *Turks* and *Africans* unbraiding *Europeans* with this disaster; saying scornfully, to such as have seemed to hold their Heads somewhat loftily, "What! Have you forgot the Time, when a *Christian*, at *Algiers*, was scarce worth an Onion?" *A Complete History of Algiers, Volume I* (London, 1718) page 305. I have modernized the passage only by using the modern "s" in place of the eighteenth-century version.

[iv] Caliban is quoting from Shakespeare's play, *I,ii,226-7*.

[v] I do not know whether this is a good or a bad theory about Shakespeare's intention in this line, but since I find it charming, I chose to have Caliban use it, though I'll also point out that Caliban himself says says that his mother brushed "wicked dew" ... with raven's feather from unwholesome fen..." (I,ii, 323-4), so Prospero may also have used commonplace dew in his conjuring.

[vi] Shakespeare's play, *I,ii,364.*

[vii] *Hamlet, Prince of Denmark, I,v,167-8.*

Made in the USA
Columbia, SC
25 September 2020